Surrender

MELANIE MILBURNE
LUCY ELLIS
JOANNE ROCK

MILLS
BOON

First Published in Great Britain 2016
By Mills & Boon, an imprint of HarperCollins*Publishers*
1 London Bridge Street, London, SE1 9GF

HER EXQUISITE SURRENDER © 2016 Harlequin Books S. A.

Surrendering All But Her Heart, Innocent In The Ivory Tower and *Full Surrender* were first published in Great Britain by Harlequin (UK) Limited.

Surrendering All But Her Heart © 2012 Melanie Milburne
Innocent In The Ivory Tower © 2011 Lucy Ellis
Full Surrender © 2012 Joanne Rock

ISBN: 978-0-263-92052-9

05-0216

Printed and bound in Spain
by CPI, Barcelona

SURRENDERING ALL BUT HER HEART

BY
MELANIE MILBURNE

From as soon as **Melanie Milburne** could pick up a pen she knew she wanted to write. It was when she picked up her first Mills & Boon at seventeen that she realised she wanted to write romance. After being distracted for a few years by meeting and marrying her own handsome hero, surgeon husband Steve, and having two boys, plus completing a Masters of Education and becoming a nationally ranked athlete (masters swimming), she decided to write. Five submissions later she sold her first book, and is now a multi-published bestselling, award-winning *USA TODAY* author. In 2008 she won the Australian Readers Association's most popular category/ series romance, and in 2011 she won the prestigious Romance Writers of Australia R*BY award.

Melanie loves to hear from her readers via her website—www.melaniemilburne.com.au—or on Facebook: facebook.com/pages/Melanie-Milburne/351594482609.

CHAPTER ONE

'YOU'LL have to see him.'

Natalie could still hear the desperation and pleading in her mother's tone even as she pressed the call button for the lift leading up to Angelo Bellandini's swish London office. The words had taken up residence in her head. They had kept her awake for the last forty-eight hours. They had accompanied her like oversized baggage on the train all the way from her home in Edinburgh. They had clickety-clacked over the tracks until they had been like a mind-numbing mantra in her head.

'You'll have to see him. You'll have to see him. You'll have to see him.'

Not that she *hadn't* seen him in the last five years. Just about every newspaper and online blog had a photo or information about the playboy heir to the Bellandini fortune. Angelo Bellandini's fast-living lifestyle was the topic of many an online forum. His massive wealth—of which, to his credit, only half was inherited; the other half had been acquired through his own hard work—made him a force to be reckoned with.

And now she *had to reckon with him, on behalf of her wayward younger brother and his foolish actions.*

A prickle of apprehension fluttered like a faceless,

fast-footed creature down the length of her spine as she stepped into the glass and chrome capsule of the lift. Her hand shook slightly as she reached for the correct floor button.

Would Angelo even agree to see her, given the way she had walked out of his life five years ago? Would he hate her as much as he had once loved her? Would the passion and desire that had once burned in his dark brown gaze now be a blaze of hatred instead?

Her insides shifted uneasily as she stepped out of the lift and approached the reception area. Having grown up with comfortable wealth, she should not be feeling so intimidated by the plush and elegant surroundings. But when they had first met Angelo had never revealed to her the extent of his family fortune. To her he had been just a hard-working, handsome Italian guy, studying for a Master's degree in business. He had gone to considerable lengths to conceal his privileged background—but then, who was she to talk?

She had revealed even less about hers.

'I'm afraid Signor Bellandini is unavailable at present,' his receptionist said in a crisp, businesslike tone in response to Natalie's request. 'Would you like to make an appointment for some other time?'

Natalie looked at the model-gorgeous young woman, with her perfectly smooth blonde hair and clear china-blue eyes, and felt her already flagging self-esteem plummet like an anchor to the basement. Even though in the lift she had reapplied lip-gloss and run her fingers through her nondescript flyaway brown hair, it was hardly the same as being professionally groomed. She was aware her clothes looked as if they had been slept in, even though she hadn't slept a wink for the last twenty-four hours, and that her normally peaches and cream complexion was grey with worry. There were damson-coloured shadows under her eyes and her cheeks had a hollow look to them. But then that happened every year at this time, and had done so since she was seven years old.

She straightened her shoulders with iron-strong resolve. She was not going to leave without seeing Angelo, even if she had to wait all day. 'Tell Signor Bellandini I'm only in London for the next twenty-four hours.' She handed her personal business card over the counter, as well as the card of the hotel she had booked for the night. 'I can be contacted on that mobile number or at my hotel.'

The receptionist glanced at the cards and then raised her eyes to Natalie's. *'You're* Natalie Armitage?' she asked. *'The* Natalie Armitage of Natalie Armitage Interiors?'

'Er…yes.'

The receptionist's eyes sparkled with delight. 'I have some of your sheets and towels,' she said. 'I just adored your last spring collection. Because of me, all of my friends now have your stuff. It's so feminine and fresh. So original.'

Natalie smiled politely. 'Thank you.'

The receptionist leaned towards the intercom. 'Signor Bellandini?' she said. 'A Miss Natalie Armitage is here to see you. Would you like me to squeeze her in before your next client or make another appointment for later this afternoon?'

Natalie's heart stalled in that infinitesimal moment before she heard his voice. Would he sound surprised to find she was here in person? Annoyed? Angry?

'No,' he said evenly, his deep baritone and sexy accent like a silky caress on her skin. 'I will see her now.'

The receptionist led the way down an expansive corridor and smiled as she came to a door bearing a brass plaque with Angelo's name on it. 'You're very lucky,' she said in a conspiratorial undertone. 'He doesn't normally see clients without an appointment. Most people have to wait weeks to see him.' Her eyes sparkled again. 'Maybe he wants to slip between your sheets, so to speak?'

Natalie gave a weak smile and stepped through the door the receptionist had opened. Her eyes went straight to where Angelo was seated, behind a mahogany desk that seemed to have a football field of carpet between it and the door that had just clicked shut, like the door of a prison cell, behind her.

Her throat tightened. She tried to unlock it by swallowing, but it still felt as if a puffer fish was lodged halfway down.

He looked as staggeringly gorgeous as ever—maybe even more so. The landscape of his face had barely changed, apart from two deep grooves that bracketed his unsmiling mouth. His raven-black hair was shorter than it had been five years ago, but it still curled lushly against the collar of his light blue business shirt. His face was cleanly shaven, but the dark pinpricks of persistent masculine stubble were clearly visible along his lean cheeks and stubbornly set jaw. His thickly lashed eyes were the same deep, espresso coffee brown, so dark she could not make out his pupils or his mood.

He rose to his feet, but whether it was out of politeness or a desire to intimidate Natalie wasn't quite sure. At six foot four he was impressively, imposingly tall. Even in heels she had to crane her neck to maintain eye contact.

She sent the tip of her tongue out to moisten her

concrete-dry lips. She had to keep her cool. She had spent most of her life keeping her emotions under the strictest control. Now was not the time to show how worried she was about the situation with her brother. Angelo would feed off that and work it to his advantage. All she had to do was pay for the damage Lachlan had caused, then get out of here and never look back.

'Thank you for seeing me at short notice,' she said. 'I understand how busy you are. I won't take up too much of your time.'

Those incredibly dark, inscrutable eyes nailed hers relentlessly as he reached across to press the intercom. 'Fiona, postpone my engagements for the next hour,' he said. 'And hold all my calls. On no account am I to be interrupted.'

'Will do.'

Natalie blinked at him as he straightened. 'Look, there's really no need to interrupt your busy schedule—'

'There is every need,' he said, still holding her gaze with the force of his. 'What your brother did to one of my hotel rooms in Rome is a criminal offence.'

'Yes,' she said, swallowing again. 'I know. But he's been going through a difficult stage just now, and I—'

One of his jet-black brows lifted satirically. 'What "difficult stage" would that be?' he asked. 'Has Daddy taken away his Porsche or cut back his allowance?'

She pressed her lips together, summoning control over emotions that were threatening to spill over. How dared Angelo mock what her brother had to deal with? Lachlan was a ticking time bomb. It was up to her to stop him from self-destructing. She hadn't been able to save her baby brother all those years ago, but she would move heaven and earth to get it right this time with Lachlan.

'He's just a kid,' she began. 'He's only just left school and—'

'He's eighteen,' Angelo said through tight, angry lips. 'He's old enough to vote and in my opinion old enough to face up to the consequences of his actions. He and his drunken friends have caused over a hundred thousand pounds' worth of damage to one of my most prestigious hotels.'

Natalie's stomach nosedived. *Was he exaggerating?* The way her mother had described it had made her think it hadn't been much more than the cost of a carpet-clean and the replacement of a few furnishings—perhaps a repaint on one of the walls.

What had Lachlan been thinking? What on earth had made him go on such a crazy rampage?

'I'm prepared to reimburse you for the damage, but before I hand over any money I'd like to see the damage for myself,' she said, with a jut of her chin.

His dark eyes challenged hers. 'So you're prepared to foot the bill personally, are you?'

She eyeballed him back, even though her stomach was churning at the menacing look in his eyes. 'Within reason.'

His top lip curled. 'You have no clue about what you're letting yourself in for,' he said. 'Do you have any idea what your brother gets up to when he's out night-clubbing with his friends?'

Natalie was all too aware, and for the last few months it had been keeping her awake at night. She knew why Lachlan was behaving the way he was, but there was little she could do to stop him. Lachlan had been the replacement child after Liam had died—the lost son re-incarnated. Since birth he had been forced to live not his own life but Liam's. All the hopes and dreams their parents had envisaged for Liam had been transferred to Lachlan, and lately he had started to buckle under the pressure. She was terrified that one day soon he would go, or be pushed too far.

She already had one death on her hands. She could not bear to have another.

'How do you know Lachlan is responsible for the damage?' she asked. 'How do you know it wasn't one of his friends?'

Angelo looked at her with dagger-sharp eyes. 'The room was booked in his name,' he said. 'It was his credit card that was presented at check-in. He is legally responsible, even if he didn't so much as knock a cushion out of place.'

Natalie suspected her brother had done a whole lot more than rearrange a few sofa cushions. She had more than once witnessed him in the aftermath of one of his drinking binges. Lachlan wasn't a sleepy drunk or a happy, loquacious one. A few too many drinks unleashed a rage inside him that was as terrifying as it was sudden. And yet a few hours later he would have no memory of the things he had said and done.

So far he had managed to escape prosecution, but only because their rich and influential father had pulled in some favours with the authorities.

But that was here in Britain.

Right now Lachlan was at the mercy of the Italian authorities—which was why she had come to London to appeal to Angelo on his behalf. Of all the hotels in Rome, why had he stayed at one of Angelo Bellandini's?

Natalie opened her bag and took out her cheque-book with a sigh of resignation. 'All right,' she said, hunting for a pen. 'I'll take your word for it and pay for the damage.'

Angelo barked out a sardonic laugh. 'You think after you scrawl your signature across that cheque I'll simply overlook this?' he asked.

She quickly disguised another swallow. 'You want more than one hundred thousand pounds?' she asked, in a voice that sounded too high—squeaky, almost.

He looked at her, his eyes meshing with hers in a lockdown that made the silence throb with palpable tension. She felt it moving up her spine, vertebrae by vertebrae. She felt it on her skin, in the ghosting of goose bumps fluttering along her flesh. She felt it— shockingly—between her thighs, as if he had reached down and stroked her there with one of his long, clever fingers.

He didn't say a word. He didn't need to. She could read the subtext of that dark, mocking gaze. He didn't give a toss about the money. It wasn't money he wanted. He had more than enough of his own.

Natalie knew exactly what he wanted. She had known it the minute she had stepped into his office and locked gazes with him.

He wanted her.

'Take it or leave it,' she said, and slammed the cheque on the desk between them.

He picked up the cheque and slowly and deliberately tore it into pieces, then let them fall like confetti on the desk, all the while holding her gaze with the implacable and glittering force of his. 'As soon as you walk out of here I'll notify the authorities in Rome to press charges,' he said. 'Your brother will go to prison. I'll make sure of it.'

Natalie's heart banged against the wall of her chest like a pendulum slammed by a prize-fighter's punch. How long would her brother last in a foreign prison?

He would be housed amongst murderers and thieves and rapists. It could be *years* before a magistrate heard his case. He was just a kid. Yes, he had done wrong, but it wasn't his fault—not really. He needed help, not imprisonment.

'Why are you doing this?' she asked.

His mouth lifted in a half-smile, his eyes taunting hers with merciless intent. 'You can't guess, *mia piccola*?'

She drew in a painfully tight breath. 'Isn't this taking revenge a little too far? What happened between us *is* between us. It has nothing to do with my brother. It has nothing to do with anyone but us.' *With me*, she added silently. *It's always been to do with me.*

His eyes glinted dangerously and his smile completely vanished until his lips were just a thin line of contempt. 'Why did you do it?' he asked. 'Why did you leave me for a man you picked up in a bar like a trashy little two-bit hooker?'

Natalie couldn't hold his gaze. It wasn't a lie she was particularly proud of. But back then it had been the only way she could see of getting him to let her go. He had fallen in love with her. He had mentioned marriage and babies. He had already bought an engagement ring. She had come across it while putting his socks away. It had glinted at her with its diamond eye, taunting her, reminding her of all she wanted but could never have.

She had panicked.

'I wasn't in love with you.' That was at least the truth…sort of. She had taught herself not to love. Not to feel. Not to be at the mercy of emotions that could not be controlled.

If you loved you lost.

If you cared you got hurt.

If you opened your heart someone would rip it out of your chest when you least expected it.

The physical side of things…well, that had been different. She had let herself lose control. Not that she'd really had a choice. Angelo had seen to that. Her body had been under the mastery of his from the first time he had kissed her. She might have locked down her emotions, but her physical response to him still echoed in her body like the haunting melody of a tune she couldn't forget no matter how hard she tried.

'So it was just sex?' he said.

Natalie forced herself to meet his gaze, and then wished she hadn't when she saw the black hatred glittering there. 'I was only twenty-one,' she said, looking away again. 'I didn't know what I wanted back then.'

'Do you know now?'

She caught the inside of her mouth with her teeth. 'I know what I don't want,' she said.

'Which is?'

She met his gaze again. 'Can we get to the point?' she asked. 'I've come here to pay for the damage my brother allegedly caused. If you won't accept my money, then what will you accept?'

It was a dangerous question to be asking. She knew it as soon as she voiced it. It hung in the ensuing silence, mocking her, taunting her for her supposed immunity.

She had *never* been immune.

It had all been an act—a clever ploy to keep him from guessing how much she'd wanted to be free to love him. But the clanging chains of her past had kept her anchored in silence. She couldn't love him or anyone.

Angelo's diamond-hard gaze tethered hers. 'Why don't you sit down and we can discuss it?' he said, gesturing to a chair near to where she was standing.

Natalie sank into the chair with relief. Her legs were so shaky the ligaments in her legs felt as if they had been severed like the strings of a puppet. Her heart was pounding and her skin was hot and clammy in spite of the air conditioning. She watched as he went back to the other side of his desk and sat down. For someone so tall he moved with an elegant, loose-limbed grace. His figure was rangy and lean, rather than excessively gym-pumped, although there was nothing wrong with the shape of his biceps. She could see the firm outline of them beneath his crisp ice-blue shirt. The colour was a perfect foil for his olive-toned skin. In the past she had only ever seen him in casual clothes, or wearing nothing at all.

In designer business clothes he looked every inch the successful hotel and property tycoon—untouchable, remote, in control. Her hands and mouth had traced every slope and plane and contour of his body. She could still remember how salty his skin tasted against her tongue. She still remembered the scent of him, the musk and citrus blend that had clung to her skin for hours after their making love. She remembered the thrusting possession of his body, how his masterful touch had unlocked her tightly controlled responses like a maestro with a difficult instrument that no one else could play.

She gave herself a mental slap and sat up straighter in the chair. Crossing her legs and arms, she fixed her gaze on Angelo's with a steely composure she was nowhere near feeling.

He leaned back in his own chair, with his fingers steepled against his chin, his dark gaze trained with unnervingly sharp focus on hers. 'I've heard anybody who is anybody is sleeping between your sheets,' he said.

She returned his look with chilly hauteur. 'I don't suppose *you* are doing so.'

His lips gave a tiny twitch of amusement, his dark eyes smouldering as they continued to hold hers. 'Not yet,' he said.

Natalie's insides flickered with the memory of long-ago desire. She'd fought valiantly to suppress it, but from the moment she had stepped into his office she had been aware of her body and its unruly response to him. He had always had that power over her. Just a look, an idle touch, a simple word and she would melt.

She couldn't afford to give in to past longings. She had to be strong in order to get through this. Lachlan's future depended on her. If this latest misdemeanour of his got out in the tabloids his life would be ruined. He was hoping to go to Harvard after this gap year. A criminal record would ruin everything for him.

Their father would crucify him.

He would crucify them both.

Natalie blamed herself. Why hadn't she realised how disenfranchised Lachlan was? Had she somehow given him some clue to her past history with Angelo? Had her lack of an active love-life made him suspect Angelo was the cause? How had he put two and two together? It wasn't as if she had ever been one to wear her heart on her sleeve. She had been busy building up her business. She had not missed dating. She'd had one or two encounters that had left her cold. She had more or less decided she wasn't cut out for an intimate relationship. The passion she had experienced with Angelo had come at a huge price, and it wasn't one she was keen to pay again.

She was better off alone.

'I understand how incredibly annoyed you are at

what my brother has supposedly done,' she said. 'But I must beg you not to proceed with criminal charges.'

His dark brow lifted again. 'Let me get this straight,' he said. 'You're *begging* me?'

Natalie momentarily compressed her lips in an attempt to control her spiralling emotions. How like him to taunt her. He would milk this situation for all it was worth and she would have to go along with it. He knew it. She knew it. He wanted her pride. It would be his ultimate trophy.

'I'm asking for leniency.'

'You're grovelling.'

She straightened her shoulders again. 'I'm asking you to drop all charges,' she said. 'I'll cover the damages—even double, if you insist. You won't be out of pocket.'

His gaze still measured hers unwaveringly. 'You want this to go away before it gets out in the press, don't you?' he said.

Natalie hoped her expression wasn't giving away any sign of her inner panic. She had always prided herself on disguising her feelings. Years of dealing with her father's erratic mood swings had made her a master at concealing her fear in case it was exploited. From childhood her ice-cold exterior had belied the inner turmoil of her emotions. It was her shield, her armour—her carapace of protection.

But Angelo had a keen, intelligent gaze. Even before she had left him she had felt he was starting to sum up her character in a way she found incredibly unsettling.

'Of course I want to keep this out of the press,' she said. 'But then, don't you? What will people think of your hotel security if a guest can do the sort of damage you say my brother did? Your hotels aim for the top end of the market. What does that say about the type of clientele your hotel attracts?'

A muscle flickered like a pulse at the side of his mouth. 'I have reason to believe your brother specifically targeted my hotel,' he said.

She felt her stomach lurch. 'What makes you think that?'

He opened a drawer to the left of him and took out a sheet of paper and handed it to her across the desk. She took it with a hand that wasn't quite steady. It was a faxed copy of a note addressed to Angelo, written in her brother's writing. It said: *This is for my sister.*

Natalie gulped and handed back the paper. 'I don't know what to say… I have never said anything to Lachlan about…about us. He was only thirteen when we were together. He was at boarding school when we shared that flat in Notting Hill. He never even met you.'

Nor had any of her family. She hadn't wanted Angelo to be exposed to her father's outrageous bigotry and her mother's sickening subservience.

'You must have said something to him,' Angelo said. 'Why else would he write that?'

Natalie chewed at her lip. She had said nothing to anyone other than that her short, intense and passionate affair with Angelo was over because she wanted to concentrate on her career. Not even her closest girlfriend, Isabel Astonberry, knew how much her break-up with Angelo had affected her. She had told everyone she was suffering from anxiety. Even her doctor had believed her. It had explained the rapid weight loss and agitation and sleepless nights. She had almost convinced *herself* it was true. She had even taken the pills the doctor had prescribed, but they hadn't done much more than throw a thick blanket over her senses, numbing her until she felt like a zombie.

Eventually she had climbed out of the abyss of misery and got on with her life. Hard work had been her remedy. It still was. Her interior design business had taken off soon after she had qualified. Her online sales were expanding exponentially, and she had plans to set up some outlets in Europe. She employed staff who managed the business end of things while she got on with what she loved best—the designing of her linen and soft furnishings range.

And she had done it all by herself. She hadn't used her father's wealth and status to recruit clients. Just like Angelo, she had been adamant that she would not rely on family wealth and privilege, but do it all on her own talent and hard work.

'Natalie?' Angelo's deep voice jolted her out of her reverie. 'Why do you think your brother addressed that note to me?'

She averted her gaze as she tucked a strand of hair behind her ear. 'I don't know.'

'He must have known it would cause immense trouble for you,' he said.

Natalie looked up at him again, her heart leaping to her throat. 'A hundred thousand pounds is a lot of money, but it's not a lot to pay for someone's freedom,' she said.

He gave an enigmatic half-smile. 'Ah, yes, but whose freedom are we talking about?'

A ripple of panic moved through her as she held his unreadable gaze. 'Can we quit it with the game-playing?' she said. 'Why don't you come straight out and say what you've planned in terms of retribution?'

His dark eyes hardened like black ice. 'I think you

know what I want,' he said. 'It's the same thing I wanted five years ago.'

She drew in a sharp little breath. 'You can't possibly want an affair with someone you hate. That's so… so cold-blooded.'

He gave a disaffected smile. 'Who said anything about an affair?'

She felt a fine layer of sweat break out above her top lip. She felt clammy and light-headed. Her legs trembled even though she had clamped them together to hide it. She unclenched her hands and put one to her throat, where her heart seemed to have lodged itself like a pigeon trapped in a narrow pipe.

'You're joking, of course,' she said, in a voice that was hoarse to the point of barely being audible.

Those dark, inscrutable eyes held hers captive, making every nerve in her body acutely aware of his sensual power over her. Erotic memories of their past relationship simmered in the silence. Every passionate encounter, from their first kiss to their blistering bloodletting last, hovered in the tense atmosphere. She felt the incendiary heat and fire of his touch just by looking at him. It was all she could do to stay still and rigidly composed in her chair.

'I want a wife,' he said, as if stating his desire for something as prosaic as a cup of tea or coffee.

Natalie hoisted her chin. 'Then I suggest you go about the usual way of acquiring one,' she said.

'I tried that and it didn't work,' he returned. 'I thought I'd try this way instead.'

She threw him a scathing look. 'Blackmail, you mean?'

He gave an indifferent shrug of one of his broad shoulders. 'Your brother will likely spend up to four years waiting for a hearing,' he said. 'The legal system in Italy is expensive and time consuming. I don't need to tell you he is unlikely to escape conviction. I have enough proof to put him away for a decade.'

Natalie shot to her feet, her control slipping like a stiletto on a slick of oil. 'You bastard!' she said. 'You're only doing this to get at me. Why don't you admit it? You only want revenge because I am the first woman who has ever left you. That's what this is about, isn't it? Your damned pride got bruised, so now you're after revenge.'

His jaw locked down like a clamp, his lips barely moving as he commanded, 'Sit down.'

She glared at him with undiluted hatred. 'Go to hell.'

He placed his hands on the desk and slowly got to his feet. Somehow it was far more threatening than if he had shoved his chair back with aggressive force. His expression was thunderous, but when he spoke it was with icy calm.

'We will marry as soon as I can get a licence. If you do not agree, then your brother will face the consequences of his actions. Do you have anything to say?'

She said it in unladylike coarseness. The crude words rang in the air, but rather than make her feel powerful they made her feel ashamed. He had made her lose control and she hated him for it.

Angelo's top lip slanted in a mocking smile. 'I am not averse to the odd moment of self-pleasuring, as you so charmingly suggest, but I would much rather share the experience with a partner. And, to be quite frank, no one does it better than you.'

She snatched up her bag and clutched it against her body so tightly she felt the gold pen inside jab her in the stomach. 'I hope you die and rot in hell,' she said.

'I hope you get some horrible, excruciatingly painful pestilent disease and suffer tortuous agony for the rest of your days.'

He continued to stare her down with irritatingly cool calm. 'I love you too, Tatty,' he said.

Natalie felt completely and utterly ambushed by the use of his pet name for her. It was like a body-blow to hear it after all these years. Her chest gave an aching spasm. Her anger dissolved like an aspirin in a glass of water. Her fighting spirit collapsed like a warrior stung by a poison dart. Tears sprang at the back of her eyes. She could feel them burning and knew if she didn't get out of there right now he would see them.

She spun around and groped blindly for the door, somehow getting it open and stumbling through it, leaving it open behind her like a mouth in the middle of an unfinished sentence.

She didn't bother with the lift.

She didn't even glance at the receptionist on her way to the fire escape.

She bolted down the stairs as if the devil and all his maniacal minions were on her heels.

CHAPTER TWO

NATALIE got back to her hotel and leant against the closed door of her suite with her chest still heaving like a pair of bellows. The ringing of her phone made her jump, and she almost dropped it when she tried to press the answer button with fingers that felt like cotton wool.

'H-hello?'

'Natalie, it's me…Lachlan.'

She pushed herself away from the door and scraped a hand through her sticky hair as she paced the floor in agitation. 'I've been trying to call you for the last twenty-four hours!' she said. 'Where are you? What's going on? Why did you do it? For God's sake, Lachlan, are you out of your mind?'

'I'm sorry,' he said. 'Look, I'm only allowed one call. I'll have to make it quick.'

Natalie scrunched her eyes closed, not wanting to picture the ghastly cell he would be locked in, with vicious-looking prison guards watching his every move. 'Tell me what to do,' she said, opening her eyes again to look at the view of the River Thames and the London Eye. 'Tell me what you need. I'll get there as soon as I can.'

'Just do what Angelo tells you to do,' Lachlan said. 'He's got it all under control. He can make this go away.'

She swung away from the window. *'Are you nuts?'* she said.

He released a sigh. 'He'll do the right thing by you, Nat,' he said. 'Just do whatever he says.'

She started pacing again—faster this time. 'He wants to marry me,' she said. 'Did he happen to mention that little detail to you?'

'You could do a whole lot worse.'

Her mouth dropped open. 'Lachlan, you're surely not serious? He *hates* me.'

'He's my only chance,' he said. 'I know I've stuffed up. I don't want to go to prison. Angelo's given me a choice. I have to take it.'

She gave a disgusted snort. 'He's given *me* a choice, not you,' she said. 'My freedom in exchange for yours.'

'It doesn't have to be for ever,' he said. 'You can divorce him after a few months. He can't force you to stay with him indefinitely.'

Natalie seriously wondered about that. Rich, powerful men were particularly adept at getting and keeping what they wanted. Look at their father, for instance. He had kept their mother chained to his side in spite of years of his infidelities and emotional cruelty. She could not bear to end up in the same situation as her mother. A trophy wife, a pretty adornment, a plaything that could be picked up and put down at will. With no power of her own other than a beauty that would one day fade, leaving her with nothing but diamonds, designer clothes and drink to compensate for her loneliness.

'Why did you do it?' she asked. 'Why his hotel?'

'Remember the last time we caught up?' Lachlan said. Natalie remembered all too well. It had been a weekend in Paris a couple of months ago, when she had been attending a fabric show. Lachlan had been at a friend's eighteenth birthday party just outside of the city. He had been ignominiously tossed out of his friend's parents' château after disgracing himself after a heavy night of drinking.

'Yes,' she said in stern reproach. 'It took me weeks to get the smell of alcohol and vomit out of my coat.'

'Yeah, well, I saw that gossip magazine open on the passenger seat,' he said. 'There was an article about Angelo and his latest lover. That twenty-one-year-old heiress from Texas?'

She tried to ignore the dagger of jealousy that spiked her when she recalled the article, and the stunningly gorgeous young woman who had been draped on Angelo's arm at some highbrow function.

'So,' she said. 'What of it? It wasn't the first time he'd squired some brainless little big-boobed bimbo to an event.'

'No,' Lachlan said. 'But it was the first time I'd seen you visibly upset by it.'

'I wasn't upset,' she countered quickly. 'I was disgusted.'

'Same difference.'

Natalie blew out a breath and started pacing again. 'So you took it upon yourself to get back at him by trashing one of the most luxurious hotel rooms in the whole of Europe just because you thought I was a little peeved?'

'I know, I know, I know,' Lachlan said. 'It sounds so stupid now. I'm not sure why I did it. I guess I was just angry that he seemed to have it all together and you didn't.'

Natalie frowned. 'What do you mean?' she said. 'I'm

running a successful business all by myself. I'm paying for my own home. I'm happy with my life.'

'Are you, Nat?' he asked. 'Are you really?'

The silence was condemning.

'You work ridiculous hours,' Lachlan went on. 'You never take holidays.'

'I hate flying, that's why.'

'You could do a desensitising programme for that,' he said.

'I don't have time.'

'It's because of what happened to Liam, isn't it?' Lachlan said. 'You haven't been on a plane since he drowned in Spain all those years ago.'

Natalie felt the claws of guilt clutch her by the throat. She still remembered the tiny white coffin with her baby brother's body in it being loaded on the tarmac. She had seen it from her window seat. She had sat there staring at it, with an empty, aching, hollow feeling in her chest.

It had been her fault he had been found floating face-down in that pool.

'I have to go,' Lachlan said. 'I'm being transferred.'

Her attention snapped back to Lachlan's dire situation. 'Transferred where?' she asked.

'Just do what Angelo says, please?' he said. 'Nat, I need you to do what he wants. He's promised to keep this out of the press. I have to accept his help. My life is over if I don't. Please?'

Natalie pinched the bridge of her nose until her eyes smarted with bitter angry tears. The cage of her conscience came down with a snap.

She was trapped.

* * *

Angelo was finalising some details on a project in Malaysia when his receptionist announced he had a visitor. 'It's Natalie Armitage,' Fiona said.

He leaned back in his chair and smiled a victor's smile. He had waited a long time for this opportunity. He wanted her to beg, to plead and to grovel. It was payback time for the misery she had put him through by walking out on him so heartlessly.

'Tell her to wait,' he said. 'I have half an hour of paperwork to get through that can't be put off.'

There was a quick muffled exchange of words and Fiona came back on the intercom. 'Miss Armitage said she's not going to wait. She said if you don't see her now she is going to get back on the train to Edinburgh and you'll never see her again.'

Angelo slowly drummed his fingers on the desk. He was used to Natalie's obstinacy. She was a stubborn, headstrong little thing. Her independence had been one of the first things he had admired about her, and yet in the end it had been the thing that had frustrated him the most. She'd absolutely refused to bend to his will. She'd stood up to him as no one else had ever dared.

He was used to people doing as he said. From a very young age he had given orders and people had obeyed them. It was part of the territory. Coming from enormous wealth, you had power. You had privilege and people respected that.

But not his little Tatty.

He leaned forward and pressed the button. 'Tell her I'll see her in fifteen minutes.'

He had not even sat back in his chair when the door slammed open and Natalie came storming in. Her brown hair with its natural highlights was in disarray about her flushed-with-fury face. Her hands were clenched into combative fists by her sides, and her slate-blue eyes were flashing like the heart of a gas flame. He could see the outline of her beautiful breasts as they rose and fell beneath her top.

His groin tightened and jammed with lust.

'You…you *bastard*!' she said.

Angelo rocked back in his chair. *'Cara,'* he said. 'I'm absolutely delighted to see you, too. How long has it been? Four hours?'

She glowered at him. 'Where have you taken him?'

He elevated one brow. 'Where have I taken whom?'

Her eyes narrowed to needle-thin slits. 'My brother,' she said. 'I can't contact him. He's not answering his phone any more. How do I know you're doing the right thing by him?'

'Your brother is in good hands,' he said. 'That is as long as you do what is required.'

Her eyes blazed with venomous hatred. 'How can I trust you to uphold your side of the bargain?' she asked.

'You can trust me, Natalie.'

She made a scoffing sound. 'I'd rather take my chances with a death adder.'

Angelo smiled a thin-lipped smile. 'I'm afraid a death adder is not going to hold any sway with an Italian magistrate,' he said. 'I can get your brother out of harm's way with the scrawl of my signature.' He picked up a pen for effect. 'What's it going to be?'

He saw her eyes go to his pen. He saw the way her jaw locked as she clenched her teeth. Her saw the way her slim throat rose and fell. He saw the battle on her face as her will locked horns with his. He felt the energy of her anger like a high-voltage current in the air.

'You can't force me to sleep with you,' she bit out.

'You might be able to force me to wear your stupid ring, but you can't force me to do anything else.'

'You will be my wife in every sense of the word,' he said. 'In public and in private. Otherwise the deal is off.'

Her jaw worked some more. He could even hear her teeth grinding together. Her eyes were like twin blasts from a roaring furnace.

'I didn't think you could ever go so low as this,' she said. 'You can have anyone you want. You have women queuing up to be with you. Why on earth do you want an unwilling wife? Is this some sort of sick obsession? What can you possibly hope to achieve out of this?'

Angelo slowly swung his ergonomic chair from side to side as he surveyed her outraged features. 'I quite fancy the idea of taming you,' he said. 'You're like a beautiful wild brumby that bucks and kicks and bites because it doesn't want anyone to get too close.'

Her cheeks flushed a fiery red and her eyes kept on shooting sparks of ire at him. 'So you thought you'd slip a lasso around my neck and whip me into submission, did you?' she said, with a curl of her bee-stung top lip. 'Good luck with that.'

Angelo smiled a lazy smile. 'You know me, Tatty. I just love a challenge—and the bigger the better.'

Her brows shot together in a furious frown. 'Don't call me that.'

'Why not?' he said. 'I always used to call you that.'

She stalked to the other side of the room, her arms across her body in a keep-away-from-me pose. 'I don't want you to call me that now,' she said, her gaze determinedly averted from his.

'I will call you what I damn well want,' he said, feeling his anger and frustration rising. 'Look at me.'

She gave her head a toss and kept her eyes fixed on the painting on the wall. 'Go to hell.'

Angelo got to his feet and walked over to where she was standing. He put a hand on her shoulder, but she spun around and slapped at his hand as if it was a nasty insect.

'Don't you *dare* touch me,' she snarled at him, like a wildcat.

He felt the fizzing of his fingers where his hand had briefly come into contact with her slim shoulder. The sensation travelled all the way to his groin. He looked at her mouth—that gorgeous, full-lipped mouth that had kissed him with such passion and fire in the past. He had felt those soft lips around him, drawing the essence from him until he had been legless with ecstasy. She had lit fires of need over his whole body with her hot little tongue. Her fingers had danced over every inch of his flesh, caressing and stroking him, branding him with the memory of her touch.

Ever since she had left him he had waited for this moment—for a chance to prove to her how much she wanted him in spite of her protestations. His rage at being cut from her life had festered inside him. It had soured every other relationship since. He could not seem to find what he was looking for with anyone else. He had gone from relationship to relationship, some lasting only a date or two, none of them lasting more than a month. Lately he had even started to wonder if he had imagined how perfectly physically in tune he had been with her. But seeing her again, being in the same room as her, sensing her reaction to him and his to her, proved to him it wasn't his imagination.

She wouldn't be the one who walked out on him without notice this time around. She would stay with him until he decided he'd had enough. It might take a month or two, maybe even up to a year, but he would not give her the chance to rip his heart open again. He would not allow her that close again. He had been a passionate fool five years ago. From the moment he had met her he had fallen—and fallen hard. He had envisaged their future together, how they would build on the empire of his grandparents and parents, how they would be the next generation of Bellandinis.

But then she had ripped the rug from under his feet by betraying him.

She might hate him for what he was doing, but right now he didn't give a damn. He wanted her and he was going to have her. She would come to him willingly. He would make sure of that. There would be no forcing, no coercing. Behind that ice-maiden façade was a fiercely passionate young woman. He had unleashed that passion five years ago and he would do so again.

'In time you will be begging for my touch, *cara*,' he said. 'Just like you did in the past.'

Her expression shot more daggers at him. 'Can't you see how much I hate you?' she said.

'I can see passion, not hate,' he said. 'That is promising, *si*?'

She let out a breath and put more distance between them, her look guarded and defensive. 'How soon do you expect to get this ridiculous plan of yours off the ground?' she asked.

'We will marry at the end of next week,' he said. 'There's no point dilly-dallying.'

'*Next week?*' she asked, eyes widening. 'Why so soon?'

Angelo held her gaze. 'I know how your mind works, Natalie. I'm not leaving anything up to chance. The sooner we are married, the sooner your brother gets out of trouble.'

'Can I see him?'

'No.'

She frowned. 'Why not?'

'He's not allowed visitors,' Angelo said.

'But that's ridiculous!' she said. 'Of course he's allowed visitors. It's a basic human right.'

'Not where he is currently staying,' he said. 'You'll see him soon enough. In the meantime, I think it's time I met the rest of your family—don't you agree?'

Something shifted behind her gaze. 'Why do you want to meet my family?' she said. 'Anyway, apart from Lachlan there is only my parents.'

'Most married couples meet their respective families,' Angelo said. 'My parents will want to meet you. And my grandparents and uncles and aunts and cousins.'

She gave him a worried look. 'They're not all coming to the ceremony, are they?'

'But of course,' he said. 'We will fly to Rome on Tuesday. The wedding will be on Saturday, at my grandparents' villa, in the private chapel that was built especially for their wedding day sixty years ago.'

Her eyes looked like a startled fawn's. 'F-fly?'

'Si, cara,' he said dryly. 'On an aeroplane. You know—those big things that take off at the airport and take you where you want to go? I have a private one—a Lear jet that my family use to get around.'

Her mouth flattened obstinately. 'I'm not flying.'

Angelo frowned. 'What do you mean, you're not flying?'

She shifted her gaze, her arms tightening across her body. 'I'm *not* flying.'

It took Angelo a moment or two to figure it out. It shocked him that he hadn't picked it up before. It all made sense now that he thought about it.

'That's why you caught the train down from Edinburgh yesterday,' he said. 'That's why, when I suggested five years ago that we take that cut-price trip to Malta, you said you couldn't afford it and refused to let me pay for you. We had a huge fight over it. You wouldn't speak to me for days. It wasn't about your independence, was it? You're frightened of flying.'

She turned her back on him and stood looking out of his office window, the set of her spine as rigid as a plank. 'Go on,' she said. 'Call me a nut job. You wouldn't be the first.'

Angelo released a long breath. 'Natalie... Why didn't you tell me?'

She still stood looking out of the window with her back to him. *'Hi, my name's Natalie Armitage and I'm terrified of flying.* Yeah, that would have really got your notice that night in the bar.'

'What got my notice in that bar was your incredible eyes,' he said. 'And the fact that you stood up to that creep who was trying it on with you.'

He saw the slight softening of her spine and shoulders, as if the memory of that night had touched something deep inside her, unravelling one of the tight cords of resolve she had knotted in place. 'You didn't have to rescue me like some big macho caveman,' she said after a short pause. 'I could've taken care of it myself.'

'I was brought up to respect and protect women,' Angelo said. 'That guy was a drunken fool. I enjoyed hauling him out to the street. He was lucky I didn't rearrange his teeth for him. God knows I was tempted.'

She turned and looked at him, her expression still

intractable. 'I don't want to fly, Angelo,' she said. 'It's easy enough to drive. It'll only take a couple of days. I'll make my own way there if you can't spare the time.'

Angelo studied her dark blue gaze. He saw the usual obstinacy glittering there, but behind that was a flicker of fear—like a stagehand peeping out from behind the curtains to check on the audience. It made him wonder if he had truly known her five years ago. He had thought he had her all figured out, but this was a facet to her personality he had never even suspected. He had always prided himself on his perspicuity, on his ability to read people and situations. But he could see now that reading Natalie was like reading a complex multi-layered book.

'I'll be with you the whole time,' he said. 'I won't let anything happen to you.'

'That's hardly reassuring,' she said with a cynical look, 'considering this whole marriage thing you've set up is a plot for revenge.'

'My intention is not for you to suffer,' he said.

Her chin came up and her eyes flashed again. 'Oh, really?'

Angelo drew in a breath and released it forcefully as he went back behind his desk. He gripped the back of his chair as he faced her. 'Why must you search for nefarious motives in everything I do or say?'

She gave a little scoffing laugh. 'Pardon me for being a little suspicious, but you're surely not going to tell me you still care about me after all this time?'

Angelo's fingers dug deeper into the leather of his chair until his knuckles whitened. He didn't love her. He *refused* to love her. She had betrayed him. He was not going to forgive and forget that in a hurry. But he would *have* her. That was different. That had nothing to do with emotions.

He deliberately relaxed his grasp and sat down. 'We have unfinished business,' he said. 'I knew that the minute you walked in that door yesterday.'

'You're imagining things,' she said.

He put up one brow. 'Am I?'

She held his gaze for a beat, before she lowered it to focus on the glass paperweight on his desk. 'How long do you think this marriage will last?' she asked.

'It can last as long as we want it to,' Angelo said.

Her gaze met his again. 'Don't you mean as long as *you* want it to?' she asked.

He gave a little up and down movement of his right shoulder. 'You ended things the last time,' he said. 'Isn't it fair that I be the one to do so this time around?'

Her mouth tightened. 'I ended things because it was time to move on,' she said. 'We were fighting all the time. It wasn't a love match. It was a battlefield.'

'Oh, come *on*,' Angelo said. 'What are you talking about, Natalie? All couples fight. It's part and parcel of being in a relationship. There are always little power struggles. It's what makes life interesting.'

'That might have been the way you were brought up, but it certainly wasn't the way I was,' she said.

He studied her expression again, noting all the little nuances of her face: the way she chewed at the inside of her mouth but tried to hide it, the way her eyes flickered away from his but then kept tracking back, as if they were being pulled by a magnetic force, and the way her finely boned jaw tightened when she was feeling cornered.

'How *were* you brought up to resolve conflict?' he asked.

She reached for her bag and got to her feet. 'Look, I have a train to catch,' she said. 'I have a hundred and one things to see to.'

'Why didn't you drive down from Edinburgh?' he asked. 'You haven't suddenly developed a fear of driving too, have you?'

Her eyes hardened resentfully. 'No,' she said. 'I like travelling by train. I can read or sketch or listen to music. I find driving requires too much concentration—especially in a city as crowded as London. Besides, it's better for the environment. I want to reduce my carbon footprint.'

Angelo rose to his feet and joined her at the door, placing his hand on the doorknob to stop her escaping. 'I'll need you to sign some papers in the next day or two.'

Her chin came up. The hard glitter was back in her gaze. 'A prenuptial agreement?'

He glanced at her mouth. He ached to feel it move under the pressure of his. He could feel the surge of his blood filling him with urgent, ferocious need.

'Yes,' he said, meeting her gaze again. 'Do you have a problem with that?'

'No,' she said, eyeballing him right back. 'I'll have one of my own drawn up. I'm not letting you take away everything I've worked so hard for.'

He smiled and tapped her gently on the end of her nose. 'Touché,' he said.

She blinked at him, looking flustered and disorientated. 'I—I have to go,' she said, and made a grab for the doorknob.

Angelo captured her hand within his. Her small, delicate fingers were dwarfed by the thickness and length and strength of his. He watched her eyes widen as he slowly brought her hand up to his mouth. He stopped before making contact with his lips, just a hair's breadth from touching. He watched as her throat rose and fell. He felt the jerky little gust of her cinnamon-scented breath. He saw her glance at his mouth, saw too the quick nervous dart of her tongue as she swept it out over her lips.

'I'll be in touch,' he said, dropping her hand and opening the door for her. *'Ciao.'*

She brushed past him in the doorway and without a single word of farewell she left.

CHAPTER THREE

'CONGRATULATIONS,' said Linda, Natalie's assistant, the following morning when she arrived at work.

'Pardon?'

Linda held up a newspaper. 'Talk about keeping your cards close to your chest,' she said. 'I didn't even know you were dating anyone.'

'I'm…' Natalie took the paper and quickly scanned it. There was a short paragraph about Angelo and her and their upcoming nuptials. Angelo was quoted as saying he was thrilled they were back together and how much he was looking forward to being married next week.

'Is it true or is it a prank?' Linda asked.

Natalie put the paper down on the counter. 'It's true,' she said, chewing at her bottom lip.

'Pardon me if I'm overstepping the mark here, but you don't look too happy about it,' Linda said.

Natalie forced a smile to her face. 'Sorry, it's just been such a pain…er…keeping it quiet until now,' she said, improvising as she went. 'We didn't want anyone to speculate about us getting back together until we were sure it was what we both wanted.'

'Gosh, how romantic!' Linda said. 'A secret relationship.'

'Not so secret now,' Natalie said a little ruefully as

her stomach tied itself in knots. How was she going to cope with the constant press attention? They would swarm about her like bees. Angelo was used to being chased by the paparazzi. He was used to cameras flashing in his face and articles being written that were neither true nor false but somewhere in between.

She liked her privacy. She guarded it fiercely. Now she would be thrust into the public arena not for her designs and her talent but for whom she was sleeping with.

Her stomach gave another little shuffle. Not that she would be actually sleeping with Angelo. She was determined not to give in to that particular temptation. Her body might still have some sort of programmed response to him, but that didn't mean she had to give in to it.

She could be strong.

She *would* be strong.

And determined.

He wouldn't find her so easy to seduce this time around. She had been young and relatively inexperienced five years ago. She was older and wiser now. She hadn't fallen in love with him before and she wasn't about to fall in love with him now. He would be glad to call an end to their marriage before a month or two. She couldn't see him tolerating her intransigence for very long. He was used to getting his own way. He wanted a submissive, I'll-do-anything-to-please-you wife.

There wasn't a bone in Natalie's body that would bend to any man's will, and certainly not to Angelo Bellandini's.

'These came for you while you were at the lawyer's,' Linda said when Natalie came back to the studio a couple of hours later.

Natalie looked at the massive bunch of blood-red roses elegantly wrapped and ribboned, their intoxicating clove-like perfume filling the air.

'Aren't you going to read the card?' Linda asked.

'Er…yes,' Natalie said unpinning the envelope from the cellophane and tissue wrap. She took the card out and read: *See you tonight, Angelo.*

'From Angelo?' Linda asked.

'Yes,' Natalie said, frowning.

'What's wrong?'

'Nothing.'

'You're frowning.'

She quickly relaxed her features. 'I've got a few things to see to in my office at home. Do you mind holding the fort here for the rest of the day?'

'Not at all,' Linda said. 'I guess you'll have to leave me in charge when you go on your honeymoon, right?'

Natalie gave her a tight on-off smile as she grabbed her bag and put the strap over her shoulder. 'I don't think I'll be away very long,' she said.

'Aren't you going to take the roses with you?' Linda asked.

Natalie turned back and scooped them up off the counter. 'Good idea,' she said, and left.

Angelo looked at the three-storey house in a leafy street in the well-to-do Edinburgh suburb of Morningside. It had a gracious elegance about it that reminded him of Natalie immediately. Even the garden seemed to reflect parts of her personality. The neatly clipped hedges and the meticulous attention to detail in plants and their colour and placement bore witness to a young woman who liked order and control.

He smiled to himself as he thought how annoyed she

would be at the way things were now *out* of her control. He had the upper hand and he was going to keep it. He would enjoy watching her squirm. He had five years of bitterness to avenge. Five years of hating her, five years of wanting her, five years of being tortured by memories of her body in his arms.

Five years of trying to replace her.

He put his finger to the highly polished brass doorbell. A chime-like sound rang out, and within a few seconds he heard the click-clack of her heels as she came to answer its summons. He could tell she was angry. He braced himself for the blast.

'How dare you release something to the press without checking with me first?' she said as her opening gambit.

'Hello, *cara*,' he said. 'I'm fine, thank you. And you?'

She glowered at him as she all but slammed the door once he had stepped over its threshold. 'You had no right to say anything to anyone,' she said. 'I was followed home by paparazzi. I had cameras going off in my face as soon as I left my studio. I almost got my teeth knocked out by one of their microphones.'

'Sorry about that,' he said. 'I'm so used to it I hardly notice it any more. Do you want me to get you a bodyguard? I should've thought of it earlier.'

She rolled her eyes. 'Of course I don't want a bloody bodyguard!' she said. 'I just want this to go away. I want *all* of this to go away.'

'It's not going to go away, Natalie,' he said. 'I'm not going to go away.'

She continued to glare at him. 'Why are you here?'

'I'm here to take you out to dinner.'

'What if I'm not hungry?'

'Then you can sit and watch me eat,' he said. 'Won't that be fun?'

'You are totally sick—do you know that?' she said.

'Did you like the roses?'

She turned away from him and began stalking down the wide corridor. 'I hate hothouse flowers,' she said. 'They have no scent.'

'I didn't buy you hothouse flowers,' he said. 'I had those roses shipped in from a private gardener.'

She gave a dismissive grunt and pushed open a door leading to a large formal sitting room. Again the attention to detail was stunning. Beautifully co-ordinated colours and luxurious fabrics, plush sofas and crystal chandeliers. Timeless antiques cleverly teamed with modern pieces—old-world charm and modern chic that somehow worked together brilliantly.

'Do you want a drink?' she asked uncharitably.

'What are you having?'

She threw him a speaking glance. 'I was thinking along the lines of cyanide,' she said.

He laughed. 'Not quite to my taste, *mia piccola*,' he said. 'Can I have a soda and lime?'

She went to a bar fridge that was hidden behind an art deco cabinet. He heard the rattle of ice cubes and the fizz of the soda water and then the plop of a slice of lime. She fixed her own glass of white wine before she turned and passed his drink to him with a combative look on her face.

'I hope it chokes you,' she said.

He lifted the glass against hers in a salute and said, 'To a long and happy marriage.'

Her gaze wrestled with his. 'I'm not drinking to that.'

'What will you drink to?'

She clanged her glass against his. 'To freedom,' she said, and took a sip.

Angelo watched her as she moved across the room,

her body movements stiff and unfriendly. She took an-other couple of sips of her drink, grimacing distastefully as if she wasn't used to drinking alcohol. 'I drove past your studio on the way here,' he said. 'Very impressive.'

She gave him a quick off-hand glance over her shoulder. 'Thank you.'

'I have a project for you, if you're interested,' he said.

She turned and looked at him fully. 'What sort of project?'

'A big one,' he said. 'It's worth a lot of money. Good exposure for you, too. It will bring you contacts from all over Europe.'

She stood very still before him, barely moving a muscle apart from the little hammer beat of tension at the base of her throat. 'Go on,' she said, with that same look of wariness in her gaze.

'I have a holiday villa in Sorrento, on the Amalfi Coast,' he said. 'I bought another property nearby for a song a few months back. I'm turning it into a luxury hotel. I'm just about done with the structural repairs. Now it's time for the interior makeover. I thought it would be a good project for you to take on once we are married.'

'Why do you want me to do it?' she asked.

'You're good at what you do,' he said.

Her mouth thinned in cynicism. 'And you want a carrot to dangle in front of me in case I happen to find a last-minute escape route?'

'You won't find an escape route,' he said. 'If you're a good girl I might even consider using your linen exclusively in all of my hotels. But only if you behave yourself.'

The look she gave him glittered with hatred. 'You've

certainly got blackmail down to a science,' she said. 'I didn't realise you were this ruthless five years ago.'

'I wasn't,' he said, taking another leisurely sip of his drink.

She tightened her mouth. 'I'll have to think about it,' she said. 'I have a lot of work on just now.'

'How capable is your assistant?' Angelo asked.

'Very capable,' she said. 'I'm thinking of promoting her. I need someone to handle the international end of things.'

'It must be quite limiting, not being able to do the travelling yourself,' he said.

She lifted a shoulder in a dismissive manner. 'I manage.'

Angelo picked up a small photo frame from an intricately carved drum table next to where he was standing. 'Is this Lachlan as a toddler?' he asked.

Her deep blue gaze flickered with something as she glanced at the photo. 'No,' she said. 'It's not.'

Angelo put the frame back on the table and, pushing back his sleeve, glanced at his watch. 'We should get going,' he said. 'I've booked the restaurant for eight.'

'I told you I'm not having dinner with you,' she said.

'And I told you to behave yourself,' he tossed back. 'You will join me for dinner and you will look happy about it. I don't care how you act in private, but in public you will at all times act like a young woman who is deeply in love. If you put even one toe of one foot out of line your brother will pay the price.'

She glared at him, her whole body bristling with anger. 'I've never been in love before, so how am I going to pull that act off with any authenticity?' she asked.

Angelo gave her a steely look. 'Make it up as you

go along,' he said, and put his glass down with a dull thud next to the photo frame. 'I'll be waiting outside in the car.'

Natalie waited until he had left the room before she picked up his glass. She mopped up the circle of condensation left on the leather top of the table with the heel of her hand and then wiped her hand against her churning stomach.

Her eyes went to the photo of Liam. He was standing on the beach with a bucket and spade in his dimpled hands, his cherubic face smiling for the camera. It had been taken just hours before he died. She remembered how excited he had been about the shells he had found. She remembered the sandcastle they had built together. She remembered how they had come back to the pool with their parents to rinse off. She remembered how her mother had gone inside for a rest and her father had left her with Liam while he made an important phone call...

She gently straightened the photo frame with fingers that were not quite steady. And then, with a sigh that burned like a serrated knife inside her chest, she went to get ready for dinner.

The restaurant Angelo had booked was a popular one that attracted the rich and the famous. Natalie had been a couple of times before, but no one had taken much notice of her. This time everyone looked and pointed as she came into the restaurant under Angelo's escort. A couple of people even took photos with their phones.

She tried to ignore the feel of his hand at her back. It was barely touching her but it felt like a brand. She could feel the tensile strength of him in that feather-light touch. It was a heady reminder of the sensual power he had over her.

Still had over her.

The *maître d'* led them to a table and then bustled off to fetch drinks after he had handed them both menus.

She buried her head in the menu even though she had no appetite. The words were just a blur in front of her. She blinked and tried to focus. A week ago she wouldn't have dreamed it possible for her to be sitting with Angelo in a restaurant. Ever since their break-up she had kept her distance both physically and mentally. But now she was back in his world and she wasn't sure how she was going to get out of it. How long would their marriage last, given the irreconcilable differences between them? He had loved her once, but he certainly wasn't motivated by love now. Revenge was his goal.

It had taken five years for the planets to align in his favour, but Lachlan had provided the perfect set-up for him to make her pay for leaving him. A man as proud and powerful as he was would not be satisfied until he had settled the score. How long would he insist on her staying with him? He surely wouldn't tie himself indefinitely to a loveless marriage. He was an only child. He was thirty-three years old—almost thirty-four. He would want children in the not too distant future. He would hardly want *her* to be the mother of his heirs. He would want someone biddable and obedient. Someone who would grace his many homes with poise and grace. Someone who wouldn't argue with him or question his opinions. Someone who would love him without reservation.

'Are you still a strict vegetarian?' Angelo asked.

Natalie looked at him over the top of the menu. 'I

occasionally eat chicken and fish,' she confessed a little sheepishly.

His dark brows lifted. 'You were so passionate back then.'

She lowered her gaze to the menu again. 'Yes, well, I was young and full of ideals back then. I've realised since that life is not so black and white.'

'What else have you changed your mind about?' he asked.

She put the menu to one side. 'I haven't changed that much,' she said.

'Meaning you still don't want children?'

Natalie felt the all too familiar pain seize her. She thought of Isabel's little newborn daughter Imogen, of how it had felt to hold her in her arms just a couple of weeks ago—the soft sweet smell, the tiny little starfish hands that had gripped hers so firmly. It had brought guilt down on her like a guillotine.

'No,' she said. 'I haven't changed my mind about that.'

'So you're still the high-powered career girl?' he said.

She picked up her glass and raised it in a salute. 'That's me.'

His dark brown eyes kept holding hers. 'What about when you're older?' he asked. 'You're young now, but what about when your biological clock starts to ramp up its ticking?'

'Not every woman is cut out to be a mother,' she said. 'I'm not good with kids. I think I must have missed out on the maternal gene.'

'I don't believe that,' he said. 'I accept that there are some women who genuinely don't want to have children, but you're a born nurturer. Look at the way you're prepared to put your neck on the line for your brother.'

She gave a careless shrug. 'I hate the thought of ruining my figure,' she said. 'I don't want stretch marks or sagging boobs.'

He made a sound at the back of his throat. 'For God's sake, Natalie, surely you're not that shallow?'

She met his gaze levelly. 'No, but I'm convinced some of your recent lovers have been.'

He gave her a glinting smile. 'So you've been keeping track of me over the years, have you, *cara*?' he asked.

'Not at all,' she said, looking away again. 'It is of no interest to me whatsoever who you sleep with. I have no hold over you. We dated. We broke up. That's it as far as I'm concerned.'

'We didn't just date,' he said. 'We lived together for five and a half months.'

Natalie picked up her drink, just for something to do with her hands. 'I only moved in with you because my flatmate's boyfriend moved in with us and made me feel I was in the way,' she said. 'Anyway, five months is not a long time compared to some relationships.'

'It was a long time for me.'

'Only because you've been playing musical beds since you were a teenager,' she said.

'Now who's talking?' he asked, with a diamond-hard glitter in his gaze as it clashed with hers.

Natalie wasn't ashamed of her past, but she wasn't proud of it either. While not exactly a constant bed-hopper, like some of her peers, she had occasionally used sex as a way to bolster her self-esteem. But the physical sensations had meant nothing to her until she had met Angelo. Not that she had ever told him. While she had been totally open with him physically, emotionally she had always held him slightly distant. She wondered if that was why he had found her so attractive. He was used to women falling head over heels in love with him and telling him so right from the start.

But she had not.

'Careful, Angelo,' she said. 'Your double standards are showing.'

His jaw tensed as he held her look. 'How long did you date the guy you replaced me with?' he asked.

'Not long,' she said.

'How long?'

'Is this really necessary?' she asked.

'I want to know.'

'We went out for a couple of weeks,' she said.

'Who broke it off?'

Natalie found his intent look unsettling. 'I did,' she said.

'So who have you dated since?'

'No one you would know,' she said. 'I try to keep my private life out of the papers.'

'Well done, you,' he said. 'I try to, but it's amazing how people find out stuff.'

'How do you stand it?' she asked.

He gave a little shrug. 'I'm used to it,' he said. 'My family's wealth has always kept us in the spotlight. The only time it cooled off a bit was when I came to study in London. I enjoyed being anonymous—not that it lasted long.'

'You lied to me.'

'I didn't lie to you,' he said. 'I just didn't tell you I came from such a wealthy family. It was important for me to make it on my own. I didn't want my father's name opening any doors for me.'

'You've certainly made a name for yourself in your own right,' Natalie said. 'You have twice the wealth of your father, or so I've heard.'

'For someone who says they have no interest in what I do or who I see, you certainly know a lot about me,' he said with a sardonic smile.

She ignored his comment and picked up her glass again, took a sip. 'What have you told your family about me?' she asked.

'A version of the truth,' he said.

Natalie's eyes came back to his. 'The truth about you hating me and wanting revenge?' she asked with an arch look.

His dark brown eyes gleamed. 'I could hardly tell my parents I hate you, now, could I?'

'What *did* you tell them?'

His eyes kept on holding hers. 'I told them I had never stopped loving you,' he said.

She moistened her lips. 'And they…believed you?'

'They seemed to,' he said. 'Although the real test will be when they see us together. My mother, in particular, is a hard person to fool. You'll have to be on your toes with her.'

Natalie felt her insides quake at the thought of interacting with his parents and other members of his family. How would she do it? How would she play the role of a happy bride without revealing the truth of how things were between them? How long before someone guessed? How long before it was splashed all over the newspapers?

'Why do we have to get married?' she asked. 'Why couldn't we just have an…an affair?'

Those unfathomable brown eyes measured hers. 'Is that what you want?' he asked. 'An affair?'

She ran her tongue over her lips again. 'No more than I want to marry you. I was just making a point,' she said. 'It seems a bit over the top to go to all the trouble of getting married when ultimately we know it's going to end in divorce.'

'You seem very sure it will end in divorce,' he said.

Natalie's heart fluttered like fast moving wings against her breastbone. 'You can't want to be tied to me indefinitely?'

His eyes moved over her leisurely. 'Who knows? You might like being married to me,' he said. 'There will be numerous benefits to wearing my ring and bearing my name.'

She sat up like a puppet suddenly jerked backwards. 'I don't want your name,' she said. 'I'm perfectly happy with my own.'

A steely glint came into his eyes. 'You will take my name,' he said. 'And you will be proud of it.'

She glowered at him, her whole body trembling with anger. 'I will *not* change my name.'

Angelo's eyes warred with hers. 'You will do what I tell you to do,' he said, his voice low but no less forceful.

Natalie stood up so abruptly her chair knocked against the one behind it. Every eye turned to look at her but she was beyond caring. She tossed her napkin down on the table and scooped her purse up with the other.

'Find yourself another wife,' she said, and stormed out.

A camera went off in her face as soon as she stepped outside the restaurant.

'Miss Armitage?' A journalist pushed a microphone close. 'Can we have an exclusive on your current relationship with Angelo Bellandini?'

Natalie tried to avoid the reporter, but another member of the paparazzi cut her off as she tried to escape.

'We notice you're not wearing an engagement ring,' he said. 'Does that mean the wedding's off?'

'I…'

Angelo's arm came around her protectively and he gently led her away from the throng. 'Please give my fiancée some space,' he said.

'Mr Bellandini, do you have a comment to make on your engagement to Miss Armitage?' the first journalist asked.

Angelo's arm tightened around her waist a fraction. 'The wedding is going ahead as planned,' he said. 'I have an engagement ring already picked out for Natalie. I am giving it to her tonight when we get home. Now, please leave us to celebrate our engagement in privacy.'

Natalie was ushered to Angelo's car without further intrusion from the press. She sat back in her seat, her fingers white-knuckled around her purse.

'Don't *ever* do that again,' Angelo said as he fired the engine.

She threw him a cutting glance. 'I am not going to be ordered around by you.'

His hands gripped the steering wheel as tightly as she was clutching her purse. His knuckles looked as if they were going to burst through the skin.

'I will not tolerate you flouncing out on me like a spoilt child,' he said through gritted teeth. 'Do you have no sense of propriety? You do realise that little scene will be all over the papers tomorrow? What were you thinking?'

Natalie gave her head a toss. 'I'm not going to be bullied into changing my name.'

'Fine,' he said. 'It's obviously a sore point with you.

I'm prepared to compromise. I should've realised how important it was to you. It's your trademark.' He paused for a beat. 'I'm sorry.'

She slowly loosened her grip on her purse. 'Are the press always that intrusive?' she asked.

He let out a breath in a sigh. 'I hardly notice it any more,' he said. 'But, yes, they are. It won't last for ever. They'll lose interest once we're married.'

Natalie frowned as she looked at him. 'I hope people don't think I'm marrying you for your money.'

His lips lifted in the slightest of smiles. 'No, *cara*, they'll think it's my body you are after.'

She turned away to stare at the passing scenery, her lower body flickering with a pulse she had thought long ago quelled. 'I'm not going to sleep with you, Angelo,' she said.

'Are you saying that to convince me or yourself?' he asked.

Natalie couldn't have answered either way, so she changed the subject. 'Have you really got an engagement ring?' she asked.

'I have.'

'Do you not think I might have liked to choose it for myself?'

He threw her an exasperated look. 'In my family it's traditional for the man to choose the engagement ring,' he said.

She toyed with the catch on her purse for a moment or two. 'It's not the same one you bought five years ago, is it?' she asked.

'No,' he said.

She sneaked a glance at him but his expression was inscrutable. 'Did you give it to someone else?' she asked. 'As a present or something?'

He brought the car to a standstill outside her house before he answered. 'I donated it to a charity for their silent auction,' he said. 'There's some lucky girl out there now wearing a ring that cost more than most people's houses.'

Natalie chewed at the inside of her mouth. 'I never asked you to spend that amount of money on me.'

His swung his gaze to hers. 'No, you didn't, did you?' he said. 'But then it wasn't money you wanted from me, was it?'

She couldn't hold his look. 'I've seen what money can do to people,' she said. 'It changes them, and not always for the good.'

She felt his gaze studying her for endless seconds. 'What have you told your parents about us?' he asked.

She pressed her lips together. 'Not much.'

'How much?'

She looked at him again. 'It was my mother's idea for me to come and see you,' she said. 'I only did it for her sake.'

'And Lachlan's, presumably?'

Her eyes fell away from his. 'Yes...'

The silence stretched interminably.

'Are you going to ask me in?' he asked.

She gave him a pert look. 'Are you going to come in even if I don't?'

He brushed an idle finger down the curve of her cheek, his eyes focussed on her mouth, his lips curved upwards in a half-smile. 'If you don't want me then all you have to do is say so.'

I do want you.

The words were like drumbeats inside her head.

I want you. I want you. I want you.

She locked out that traitorous voice and pasted an

indifferent look on her face. 'Are you staying in town overnight?' she asked.

'No,' he said. 'I was hoping you'd offer me a bed for the night.'

Natalie felt her heart give a hard, sharp kick. 'I don't think that's such a good idea.'

'Why not?'

'Because… Because…'

'The press will think it odd if I don't stay with you,' he said, before she could think of an excuse. 'I'm not sure if you've noticed, but a car followed us back here. It's parked behind the red car.'

She checked in the side mirror. There was a man sitting behind the wheel with a camera's telephoto lens trained in their direction. Panic gripped her by the throat. Was this how it was going to be? Would she be hounded like a terrified fox with nowhere to hide?

Angelo opened his door and came around to where she was sitting, frozen in dread.

'He'll move on once we're inside,' he said. 'Just try to act naturally.'

Natalie got out of the car and allowed him to take her hand. She felt the strong grip of his fingers as they curled around hers. It was the same feeling she'd had when he had put his arm around her waist earlier.

She felt protected.

'Give me your keys,' he said.

She handed them over. 'It's the big brass one,' she said.

He unlocked the door and held it open for her to pass through. 'How long have you lived here?' he asked as he closed the door.

'Three and a half years.'

'Why Scotland? I thought you said you grew up in Gloucestershire?'

'My mother is a Scot,' she said. 'She grew up in the seaside village of Crail in Fife. I spent a lot of holidays there with my grandparents when I was young.'

'You didn't tell me that before.'

She gave a shrug as she placed her purse on the hall table. 'It didn't seem important.'

'What else didn't you tell me that didn't seem important?'

Natalie turned away from his probing look. 'Do you want a drink or something?'

He stalled her by placing a hand on her arm. 'Tatty?'

She looked down at his hand. How dark and masculine it looked against her paler skin. It dredged up memories she didn't want to resurface. She felt the rumble of them like tectonic plates rubbing against each other. An earthquake of sensation threatened to spill out like lava. She felt the heat of it bubbling like a furnace inside her.

'I asked you not to call me that,' she said.

His hand moved along her arm in a gentle caress. 'I don't always do what I'm told,' he said. 'I like bending the rules to suit me.'

Natalie tried to pull away but his fingers subtly tightened. She met his gaze—so dark and mesmerising—so in control. He knew he had her where he wanted her. She was at his mercy. Lachlan's freedom and future depended on her. Angelo knew she would not do anything to jeopardise it. Her little temper tantrum back at the restaurant had achieved nothing. He would always come after her and remind her of what was at stake.

'Why are you doing this?' she asked. 'You must know how it's going to end.'

His hooded gaze drifted to her mouth. 'I don't care how it ends,' he said. 'This is about the here and now.'

She looked at his mouth. Oh, how she wanted to feel those firm lips move against hers! She remembered the heat; she remembered the blistering passion that burned like a taper all over her flesh. She remembered the sexy thrust of his tongue as it came in search of hers.

Her breath caught in her throat as she felt the breeze of his breath skate over her lips. He lowered his mouth to just above hers. She swept her tongue over her lips, wanting him, aching for him to make the first move.

'Go on,' he said, in a low, husky, spine-melting tone. 'I know you want to.'

Natalie's stomach shifted like a speeding skater suddenly facing a sheet of broken ice. Could he read her so well even after all this time? She fought for composure, for self-control, for anything.

'You're mistaken,' she said coolly. 'I don't want any such thing.'

He brushed a finger over her tingling bottom lip. 'Liar.'

It took all of her resolve and then some to step back, but somehow she did it. She moved to the other side of the room, barricading herself behind one of the sofas set in the middle of the room. 'I think you should leave,' she said.

'Why?' he asked. 'Because you don't trust yourself around me?'

She sent him an arctic look. 'I'm not going to be a slave to your desires.'

'Is that what you think you'll be?' he asked. 'What about your own desires? You have them. You can deny them all you like but they're still there. I can feel it when I touch you.'

'What we had five years ago is gone,' Natalie said. 'You can't make it come back just to suit you.'

'It never went away,' he said. 'You wanted it to, but it didn't. You were scared of the next step, weren't you? You were scared of the commitment of marriage. You're still scared. What I'd like to know is why.'

'Get out.'

'I'm not going until I give you this.' He took a jeweller's box from inside his jacket pocket. But rather than come over to her he simply set it down on the coffee table. It reminded her of a gauntlet being laid down between two opponents.

'I'll have a car sent to collect you on Tuesday,' he said. 'Pack enough clothes for a week. We'll be expected to go on a honeymoon. If you e-mail me a list of the people you wish to invite to the ceremony I'll have my secretary deal with it.'

'What do you want me to wear?' she asked. 'Sackcloth and ashes?'

'You can wear what you like,' he said. 'It makes no difference to me. But do keep in mind that there will be photographers everywhere.'

'Do you really expect me to pack up my life here and follow you about the globe like some lovesick little fool?' she asked.

'We will divide our time between your place and mine,' he said. 'I'm based in London, but I plan to spend a bit of time in Sorrento until the development is near completion. I'm prepared to be flexible. I understand you have a business to run.'

She gave him a petulant look. 'What if I don't want you to share my house?'

'Get used to it, Natalie. I will share your house and a whole lot more before the ink is dry on our marriage certificate.' He went to the door. 'I'll see you on Tuesday.'

Natalie didn't touch the jeweller's box until he had left. She stood looking at it for a long time before she picked it up and opened it. Inside was an art deco design triple diamond ring. It was stunningly beautiful. She took it out of its velvet home and slipped it on her finger. She couldn't have chosen better herself. It was neither too loose nor too tight—a perfect ring for an imperfect relationship.

She wondered how long it would be before she would be giving it back.

CHAPTER FOUR

NATALIE was in a state of high anxiety by the time Tuesday came around.

She hadn't eaten for three days. She had barely slept. She had been dry retching at the thought of getting on a plane to Italy.

Angelo had called her each day, but she hadn't revealed anything of what she was going through. He had assured her Lachlan was out of harm's way. Her parents had called too, and expressed their satisfaction with the way things had turned out. Her father was greatly relieved that the family name hadn't been sullied by Lachlan's antics. Angelo had miraculously made the nasty little episode disappear, for which Adrian Armitage was immensely grateful. He'd made no mention of Natalie's role in fixing things. She had expected no less from him, given he had never shown an interest in her welfare, but she was particularly annoyed with her mother, who hadn't even asked her how she felt about marrying Angelo. But then Isla had married Natalie's father for money and prestige. Love hadn't come into it at all.

She felt annoyed too at having to lie to her friends— in particular Isabel. But strangely enough Isabel had accepted the news of her marriage with barely a blink of an eye. Her friend had said how she had always thought Natalie had unresolved feelings for Angelo since she hadn't dated all that seriously since. She thought Natalie's aversion to marriage and commitment had stemmed from her break up with Angelo. Natalie hadn't had the heart to put Isabel straight. As close as she was to her, she had never told Isabel about the circumstances surrounding Liam's death.

Natalie heard a car pull up outside her house. Her stomach did another somersault and a clammy sweat broke out over her brow. She walked to the door on legs that felt like wet cotton wool. It wasn't a uniformed driver standing there but Angelo himself.

'I…I just have to get my bag…' she said, brushing a loose strand of sticky hair back behind her ear.

Angelo narrowed his gaze. 'Are you all right?'

'I'm fine,' she said, averting her eyes.

He put a hand on her shoulder and turned her to look at him. 'You're deathly pale,' he said. 'Are you ill?'

Natalie swallowed the gnarly knot of panic in her throat. 'I have some pills to take.' She rummaged in her bag for the anxiety medication her doctor had prescribed. 'I won't be a minute.'

She went to the kitchen for a glass of water and Angelo followed her. He took the packet of pills from her and read the label. 'Do you really need to take these?' he asked.

'Give them to me,' she said, reaching for them. 'I should've taken them an hour ago.'

He frowned as he handed them to her. 'Do you take them regularly?'

She shook her head as she swallowed a couple of pills. 'No,' she said. 'Only in an emergency.'

He was still frowning as he led her out to the car. 'When did you develop your fear of flying?' he asked.

'Ages ago,' she said.

'What caused it?' he asked. 'Rough turbulence or a mid-air incident?'

She shrugged. 'Can't remember.'

His dark gaze searched hers. 'When was the last time you flew?'

'Can we get going?' she asked. 'I don't want to fall asleep in the car. You'll have to carry me on board.'

Angelo glanced at Natalie every now and again as he drove to the airport. She was not quite so pale now the medication had settled her nerves, but she still looked fragile. Her cheeks looked hollow, as if she had recently lost weight, and her eyes were shadowed.

Her concern over her brother was well founded. He had struck a deal with Lachlan, but already Lachlan was pushing against the boundaries Angelo had set in place. The staff at a very expensive private rehab clinic had called him three times in the last week to inform him about Lachlan's erratic and at times uncontrollable behaviour. He had organised a therapist to have extra sessions with him, but so far there had been no miraculous breakthrough. It seemed Lachlan Armitage was a very angry young man, hell-bent on self-destruction.

Speaking with Natalie's father had made Angelo realise how frustrating it must be to have a child who, no matter how much you loved and provided for him, refused to co-operate. Adrian Armitage had hinted at similar trouble with Natalie. Apparently her stubborn streak had caused many a scene in the Armitage household over the years. In spite of all of her father's efforts to get close to her she had wilfully defied him whenever she could. Angelo wondered if it was a cultural thing. He had been brought up strictly, but fairly. His parents had commanded respect, but they had more than earned it with their dedication and love for him. He hoped to do the same for his own children one day.

He turned off the engine once he had parked and gently touched Natalie on the shoulder. 'Hey, sleepy-head,' he said. 'Time to get going.'

She blinked and sat up straighter. 'Oh… Right…'

He put an arm around her waist as he led her on board his private jet a short time later. She was agitated and edgy, but he managed to get her to take a seat and put the belt on.

'Can I have a drink?' she asked.

'Sure,' he said. 'What would you like?'

'White wine,' she said.

'Are you sure it's a good idea to combine alcohol with those pills?' he asked.

She gave him a surly look. 'I'm not a child.'

'No, but you're under my protection,' he said. 'I don't want you getting ill, or losing consciousness or something.'

She started chewing her nails as the pilot pulled back. Angelo took her hand away from her mouth and covered it with his. 'You'll be fine, *cara*,' he said. 'You were in far more danger driving to the airport than you ever will be in the air.'

She shifted restively, her eyes darting about like a spooked thoroughbred's. 'I want to get off,' she said. 'Please—can you tell the pilot to stop? I want to get off.'

Angelo put his arm around her and brought her close against him. 'Shh, *mia piccola*,' he soothed. 'Concentrate on your breathing. In and out. In and out. That's right. Nice and slow.'

She squeezed her eyes shut and lowered her head to his chest. He stroked the silk of her hair, talking to her in the same calm voice. It took a lot longer than he expected but finally she relaxed against him. She slept for most of the journey and only woke up just as they were coming to land in Rome.

'There,' he said. 'You did it. That wasn't so bad, was it?'

She nodded vaguely and brushed the hair back off her face. 'Have I got time to use the bathroom?'

'Sure,' he said. 'Do you want me to come with you?'

Her cheeks pooled with colour. 'No, thank you.'

He gave her a mocking smile. 'Maybe next time, *si*?'

The press had obviously been given a tip-off somewhere between their arrival at the airport and Angelo's family villa in Rome. Natalie watched in dismay as photographers surged towards Angelo's chauffeur-driven car.

'Don't worry,' he said as he helped her out of the car. 'I'll handle their questions.'

Within a few moments Angelo had managed to satisfy the press's interest and sent them on their way.

An older man opened the front door of the villa and greeted Angelo. 'Your parents are in the salon, Signor Bellandini.'

'*Grazie*, Pasquale,' he said. 'Natalie, this is Pasquale. He has been working for my family for many years.'

'I'm very pleased to meet you,' Natalie said.

'Welcome,' Pasquale said. 'It is very nice to see Signor Bellandini happy at last.'

'Come,' Angelo said, guiding her with a hand resting in the curve of her back. 'My parents will be keen to meet you.'

If they were so keen, why hadn't they been at the

door to greet her instead of the elderly servant? Natalie thought bitterly to herself. But clearly there was a different protocol in the upper classes of Italian society. And Sandro and Francesca Bellandini were nothing if not from the very top shelf of the upper class.

Natalie could see where Angelo got his height and looks from as soon as she set eyes on his father. While an inch or two shorter than his son, Sandro had the same dark brown eyes and lean, rangy build. His hair was still thick and curly but it was liberally streaked with grey, giving him a distinguished air that was as compelling as it was intimidating.

Francesca, on the other hand, was petite, and her demeanour outwardly demure, but her keen hazel eyes missed nothing. Natalie felt them move over her in one quick assessing glance, noting her hair and make-up, the style and make of her clothes, the texture of her skin and the state of her figure.

'This is Natalie, my fiancée,' Angelo said. 'Natalie—my parents, Sandro and Francesca.'

'Welcome to the family.' Francesca was the first to speak. 'Angelo has told us so much about you. I am sorry we didn't meet you five years ago. We would've told him he was a fool for letting you go—*si*, Sandro?'

'*Si,*' Sandro said, taking her hand once his wife had relinquished it. 'You are very welcome indeed.'

Angelo's arm came back around her waist. 'I'll see that Natalie is settled in upstairs before we join you for a celebratory drink.'

'Maria has made up the Venetian room for you both,' Francesca said. 'I didn't see the point in separating you. You've been apart too long, no?'

Natalie glanced at Angelo, but he was smiling at his

mother. 'That was very thoughtful of you, *Mamma*,' he said.

Natalie had to wait until they were upstairs and alone before she could vent her spleen. 'I bet you did that deliberately,' she said.

'Did what?'

'Don't play the guileless innocent with me,' she flashed back. 'You knew your mother would put us in the same room, didn't you?'

'On the contrary. I thought she would go old-fashioned on me and put us at opposite ends of the villa,' he said. 'I told you she's incredibly insightful. She must have sensed how hot you are for me.'

Natalie glared at him. 'I'm not sharing that bed with you.'

'Fine,' he said unbuttoning his shirt. 'I'll let you have the floor.'

She frowned at him. 'What are you doing?'

He pulled his shirt out of the waistband of his trousers. 'I'm getting changed.'

Her eyes went the flat plane of his abdomen. He looked amazing—so masculine, so taut, so magnificently fit and tanned and virile. She swung away and went to look out of the windows overlooking the gardens.

'Why did you let your parents think it was you who ended our affair five years ago?' she asked.

'I didn't want you to get off to a bad start with them,' he said. 'I'm their only child. Parents can be funny about things like that.'

Natalie turned around. He was only wearing black underwear now. The fabric clung to him lovingly. Her insides clenched with greedy fistfuls of desire. She had kissed and tasted every inch of his body. She had taken him in her mouth, ruthlessly tasting him until he had collapsed with release. She had felt him move deep within her. She had felt his essence spill inside her. She had been as brazen as she could be with him and yet still he had always been a step ahead of her. He had pushed her to the limit time and time again. Her flesh shivered in memory of his touch. Her spine tingled and her belly fluttered. She drew in a breath as she saw his gaze run over her. Was he too thinking of the red-hot passion they had shared?

'I don't expect you to take the blame,' she said. 'I'm not ashamed of breaking off our relationship. I was too young to get married.'

'That won't cut it with my mother, I'm afraid,' he said. 'She was barely sixteen when she fell in love with my father. She has never looked at another man since.'

'Is your father faithful to her?'

He frowned. 'What makes you ask that?'

Natalie lifted a shoulder up and down. 'They've been together a long time. It's not uncommon for a man to stray.'

'My father takes his marriage vows seriously,' he said. 'He is exactly like my grandfather in that.'

'And what about you, Angelo?' she asked. 'Will you follow in their honourable footsteps, or will you have your little bits on the side if I don't come up trumps?'

He came over to where she was standing. Stopped just in front of her. So close she could feel her body swaying towards him like a compass searching for magnetic north. She fought against the desire to close the minuscule distance. She stood arrow-straight, stiff to the point of discomfort. Her heart was racing; the hammer blows were making her giddy, her breathing shallow and uneven.

Her resolve, God help her, was crumbling.

Angelo slipped a warm hand behind her head at the nape of her neck setting off a shower of sensation beneath the surface of her sensitive skin.

'Why do you fight with yourself so much?' he asked.

Natalie pressed her lips together. 'I'm fighting you, not myself.'

His fingers moved through her hair in a spine-tingling caress. 'We both want the same thing, *cara*,' he said. 'Connection, intimacy, satisfaction.'

She could feel her resolve slipping even further out of her control. Why did he have to look so damned gorgeous? Why did he have to have such melting brown eyes? Why did he have to have such amazing hands that made her flesh tingle with sensation? Why did he have to have such a tempting mouth?

For God's sake, why didn't he throw her backwards caveman-style on the bed and ravish her?

In the end it was impossible to tell who had closed the distance between their bodies. Suddenly she felt the hard ridge of his erection pressing against her belly. It was like putting a match to a decade of dried-out tinder. She felt the flames erupt beneath her flesh. They licked along every nerve pathway, from the top of her scalp to her toes.

Her mouth met his in a combative duel that had no hint of romance or tenderness about it. It was all about lust—primal, ravenous lust—that was suddenly let loose after being restrained for far too long. She felt the scorch of his lips as they ground against hers. And then his tongue thrust boldly through the seam of her lips, making her insides flip over in delight. Her tongue tangled with his, fighting for supremacy, but he wouldn't give in. She felt the scrape of her teeth against his; she even tasted blood but couldn't be sure whose it was. She fed off his mouth greedily, rapaciously, and little whimpers of pleasure sounded deep in her throat as he varied the speed and pressure.

He crushed her to him, one of his hands ruthlessly tugging her top undone so he could access her breast. She felt her achingly tight nipple rubbing against his palm. A wave of longing besieged her. She felt it flickering like a pulse between her thighs. She felt the honeyed moistness of her body preparing for his possession. She rubbed up against him intimately, the feminine heart of her on fire, aching, pulsing, contracting with a need so great it was overwhelming.

He kept kissing her relentlessly, his tongue diving for hers, conquering it with each and every sensual stroke. Her lips felt swollen but she didn't care. She kissed him back with just as much passion, nipping at him with her teeth in between stroking him with her tongue. He tasted just as she remembered him: minty and fresh and devastatingly, irresistibly male.

He tore his mouth from hers to suckle on her breast, his tongue swirling around her areola and over her nipple until her back arched in pleasure. She knew it would take very little to send her up into the stratosphere. She could feel the tremors at her core, the tension building and building, until she was close to begging him to satisfy that delicious, torturous ache.

He brought his mouth back to hers—a slower kiss this time. He took his time exploring her mouth, his tongue teasing hers rather than subduing it. She melted like honey in a hothouse. Her arms went around his neck. Her hands delved into the thick denseness of his hair. Her throbbing pelvis was flush against the hardness of his.

He raised his mouth from hers, his breathing heavy, his eyes dark and heavy-lidded and smouldering with desire. 'Tell me you want me,' he commanded.

Natalie was jolted out of his sensual spell with a resurgence of her pride. 'I don't want you,' she lied.

He gave a deep and very masculine-sounding mocking laugh. 'I could prove that for the lie that it is just by slipping my hand between your legs.'

She tried to back away but he held her fast. 'Get your hands off me,' she said through gritted teeth.

He slowly slid his hands down the length of her arms, his fingers encircling her wrists like handcuffs. 'You will come to me, *cara*, just like you did in the past,' he said. 'I know you too well.'

She held his gaze defiantly. 'You don't know me at all,' she said. 'You might know your way around my body, but you know nothing of my heart.'

'That's because you won't let anyone in, will you?' he said. 'You push everyone away when they get too close. Your father told me how difficult you are.'

Natalie's mouth dropped open in outrage. 'You discussed *me* with my father?'

His hands fell away from her wrists, his expression masked. 'We had a couple of conversations, yes,' he said.

'About what?'

'I asked for your hand in marriage.'

She gave a derisive laugh. 'That was rather draconian of you, wasn't it? And also hypocritical—because you wouldn't have let the little matter of my father's permission stand in the way of what you wanted, now, would you?'

'I thought it was the right thing to do,' he said. 'I

would've liked to meet him face to face but he was abroad on business.'

Natalie could just imagine the 'business' her father was working on. His latest project was five-foot-ten with bottle-blonde hair and breasts you could serve a dinner party off.

'I'm sure he didn't hesitate in handing me over to your care,' she said. 'I'm surprised he didn't offer to pay you for the privilege.'

His gaze remained steady on hers, dark and penetrating but giving nothing away. 'We also discussed Lachlan's situation.'

'I take it he didn't offer to postpone his *business* in order to be by Lachlan's side and sort things out?'

'I told him to stay away,' he said. 'Sometimes parents can get in the way when it comes to situations like this. Your father has done all he can for your brother. It's time to step back and let others take charge.'

'Which you just couldn't wait to do, because it gave you the perfect foothold to force me back into your life,' she said, shooting him a resentful glare.

Those piercing brown eyes refused to let hers go. 'You came to me, Natalie, not the other way around.'

A thought slipped into her mind like the thin curl of smoke beneath a door. 'My father was the one who contacted you, wasn't he?' she said, her eyes narrowed in suspicion. 'I only came to you because my mother begged me to. I would never have come to you otherwise. *He* put her up to it.'

'Your father expressed his concern for you when we spoke,' he said. 'It seems it's not only your brother with an attitude problem.'

Natalie stalked to the other side of the bedroom, her arms around her body so tightly she felt her ribs creak in protest. Her anger was boiling like a cauldron inside her. She wanted to explode. She wanted to hit out at him, at the world, at the cruel injustice of life. The thought of Angelo discussing her with her father was repugnant to her. She hated thinking of how that conversation would have played out.

Her father would have painted her as a wilful and defiant child with no self-discipline. He would have laid it on thickly, relaying anecdote after anecdote about how she had disobeyed him and made life difficult for him almost from the day she had been born. He would not have told of how he had wanted a son first, and how she had ruined his plans by being born a girl. He would not have told of his part in provoking her, goading her into black moods and tempers until he finally broke her spirit. He would not have told of how his philosophy of parenting was 'might is right', how tyranny took precedence over tolerance, ridicule and shame over support and guidance. He would not have told of how he had used harsh physical discipline when gentle corrective words would have achieved a much better outcome.

No, he would have portrayed himself as a long-suffering devoted father who was at his wits' end over his wayward offspring.

He would not have mentioned Liam.

Liam's death was a topic *no one* mentioned. It was as if he had never existed. None of his toys or clothes were at the family mansion. Her father had forced her mother to remove them as soon as Lachlan had been born. The photos of Liam's infancy and toddlerhood were in an album in a cupboard that was securely locked and never opened. Natalie's only photo of her baby brother was the one she had found in the days after his funeral, when everyone had been distraught and distracted. She had kept it hidden until she had bought her house in Edinburgh.

But for all her father's efforts to erase the tragedy of Liam's short life his ghost still haunted them all. Every time Natalie visited her parents—which was rare these days—she felt his presence. She saw his face in Lachlan's. She heard him in her sleep. Every year she had night terrors as the anniversary of his death came close.

With an enormous effort she garnered her self-control, and once she was sure she had her emotions securely locked and bolted down she slowly turned and faced Angelo. 'I'm sure you found that conversation very enlightening,' she said.

His expression was hard to read. 'Your father cares for you very deeply,' he said. 'Like all parents, he and your mother only want the best for you.'

Natalie kept her mouth straight, even though she longed to curl her lip. 'My father obviously thinks you're the best for me,' she said. 'And as for my mother—well, she wouldn't dream of contradicting him. So it's happy families all round, isn't it?'

He studied her for a heartbeat, his eyes holding hers in a searching, probing manner. 'I'm going to have a shower,' he said. 'My parents will have gone to a great deal of trouble over dinner. Please honour them by dressing and behaving appropriately.'

'Contrary to what my father probably told you, I *do* actually know how to behave in company,' she said to his back as he went towards the *en suite* bathroom.

He turned around and meshed his gaze with hers. 'I'm on your side, *cara*,' he said, with unexpected gentleness.

Her eyes stung with the sudden onset of tears. She

blinked and got them back where they belonged: concealed, blocked, and stoically, strenuously denied. She gave a toss of her head and walked back to the window overlooking the gardens. But she didn't let out her breath until she heard the click of the bathroom door indicating Angelo had gone.

Angelo was putting on some cufflinks when he heard Natalie come out of the dressing room. He turned and looked at her, his breath catching in his chest at the sight of her dressed in a classic knee length black dress and patent leather four-inch heels. Her hair was pulled back in an elegant knot at the back of her head, giving her a regal air. She was wearing diamond and pearl droplet earrings and a matching necklace. Her make-up was subtle, but it highlighted the dark blue of her eyes and the creamy texture of her skin and model-like cheekbones. Her perfume drifted towards him—a bewitching blend of the wintry bloom of lily of the valley and the hot summer fragrance of honeysuckle. A perfect summation of her complex character: ice-maiden and sultry siren.

How could someone so beautiful on the outside be capable of the things her father had said about her? It was worrying him—niggling at him like a toothache. The more time he spent with her, the more he found new aspects to her character that intrigued him.

Yes, she was wilful and defiant. Yes, she had a streak of independence. Yes, she could be incredibly stubborn.

But she clearly loved her brother and was prepared to go to extraordinary lengths to help him. How did that fit in with Adrian Armitage's assessment of her as totally selfish and self-serving?

'You look like you just stepped off a New York City catwalk,' he said.

She lifted a slim shoulder dismissively. 'This dress is three seasons old,' she said. 'I bought it on sale for a fraction of the cost.'

'I like your hair like that.'

'It needs cutting,' she said, touching a hand to one of her earrings. 'This is a good way to hide the split ends.'

'Why don't you like compliments?' he asked. 'You always deflect them. You used to do that five years ago. I thought it was because you were young back then, but you're still doing it.'

She stopped fiddling with her earring to look at him, her chin coming up. 'Compliment me all you like,' she said. 'I can handle it.'

'You're beautiful.'

'Thank you.'

'And extremely intelligent.'

She gave a little mock bow. 'Thank you.'

'And you have the most amazing body,' he said.

High on her cheekbones twin pools of delicate rose appeared, and her eyes moved out of reach of his. 'I haven't been to the gym in months.'

'You're meant to say thank you—not make excuses,' he pointed out.

She brought her gaze back. 'Thank you.'

'You're the most intriguing person I know.'

A mask fell over her face like a curtain dropping over a stage. 'You need to get out a little more, Angelo,' she said.

'You have secrets in your eyes.'

She stilled as if every cell in her body had been snap frozen. But then, just as quickly she relaxed her pose.

'We all have our secrets,' she said lightly. 'I wonder what some of yours are?'

'Who gave you that jewellery?' he asked.

She put a hand to her throat, where her necklace rested. 'I bought it for myself,' she said.

'Do you still have the locket I gave you from that street fair we went to?'

She dropped her hand from her neck and reached for her purse. 'Your parents will be wondering what's keeping us,' she said.

'My parents will think we've been catching up on lost time.'

Her cheeks fired again. 'I hope they don't expect me to speak Italian, because I'm hopeless at it.'

'They won't expect you to do anything you're not comfortable with,' he said. 'They're keen to welcome you as the daughter they never had.'

'I hope I live up to their lofty expectations,' she said, frowning a little. 'But then, I guess no one is ever going to be good enough for the parents of an only child.'

'I'm sure they will grow to love you if you show them who you really are,' he said.

'Yeah, like *that's* going to work,' she said, and picked up her wrap and wound it round her shoulders.

Angelo frowned. 'Why do you say that?'

'No one really gets to be who they truly are on the inside, do they?' she said. 'We all fall into line because of cultural conditioning and family expectation. None of us can say what we really want to say or do what we really want to do. We're hemmed in by parameters imposed on us by other people and the society we live in.'

'What would you do or say if those parameters weren't there?' he asked.

She gave one of her dismissive shrugs. 'What would be the point?' she asked. 'No one listens anyway.'

'I'm listening,' he said.

Her eyes fell away from his. 'We shouldn't keep your parents waiting.'

He brought her chin up with his finger and thumb. 'Don't shut me out, *cara*,' he said. 'For God's sake, talk to me. I'm tired of this don't-come-too-close-to-me game you keep playing.'

Her expression flickered with a host of emotions. He saw them pass through her eyes like a burgeoning tide. They rippled over her forehead and tightened her jaw, but she spoke none of them out loud.

'You won't let me in, will you?' he said.

'There's nothing *in* there.'

'I don't believe that,' he said. 'I know you try and pretend otherwise, but you have a soft heart and you won't let anyone get near it. Why? Why are you so determined to deny yourself human connection and intimacy?'

She stepped out of his hold and gave him a hardened look. 'Didn't my father tell you?' she said. 'I'm a lost cause. I'm beyond redemption. I have a streak of self-ishness and self-preservation that overrides everything else. I care for no one but myself.'

'If that is so then why have you agreed to sacrifice yourself for your brother's sake?' he asked.

There was a hint of movement at her slim throat, as if she had tried to disguise a swallow. 'Lachlan isn't like me,' she said. 'He's sensitive and vulnerable. He doesn't know how to take care of himself yet, but he will. He just needs more time.'

'You're paying a very high price for his learning curve.'

She met his gaze levelly. 'I've paid higher.'

Angelo tried to break her gaze down with the laser force of his but she was indomitable. It was like trying to melt a wall of steel with a child's birthday cake candle. 'I won't give up on you, Natalie,' he said. 'I don't care how long it takes. I will not give up until I see what's written on your heart.'

'Good luck with that,' she said airily, and sashayed to the door. She stopped and addressed him over her shoulder. 'Are you coming or not?'

CHAPTER FIVE

NATALIE was handed a glass of champagne as soon as she entered the salon on Angelo's arm.

'This is such a happy occasion for us,' Francesca said. 'We were starting to wonder if Angelo would ever settle down, weren't we, Sandro?'

Angelo's father gave a benign smile as he raised his glass. 'Indeed,' he said. 'But we always knew he would only ever marry for love. It is a Bellandini tradition, after all.'

'Isn't it also twenty-first century tradition to do so?' Natalie asked.

'Well, yes, of course,' Francesca said. 'But that's not to say that certain families don't occasionally or-chestrate meetings between their young ones to hurry things along. Parents often have a feel for these things.'

'I'm not sure parents should get involved in their chil-dren's lives to that extent,' Natalie said. 'Surely once someone is an adult they should be left to decide what and who is right for them?'

Sandro's dark brown eyes glinted as he addressed his son. 'I can see you have chosen a wife with spirit, Angelo,' he said. 'Life is so much more exciting with a woman who has a mind of her own.'

Francesca gave Sandro a playful tap on the arm.

'You've done nothing but complain for the last thirty-six years about *my* spirit.'

Sandro took her hand and kissed it gallantly. 'I adore your spirit, *tesoro mio*,' he said. 'I worship it.'

Natalie couldn't help comparing her parents' relationship to Angelo's parents'. Her parents spoke to each other on a need basis. She couldn't remember the last time they had touched. They certainly didn't look at each other with love shining from their eyes. They could barely be in the same room together.

'*Papa, Mamma,*' Angelo said. 'You're embarrassing Natalie.'

Francesca came over and looped an arm through one of Natalie's. 'Angelo tells me you are a very talented interior designer,' she said. 'I am ashamed that I hadn't seen your soft furnishings range until I searched for it online. I cannot believe what I have been missing. Do you not have an Italian outlet?'

'I've limited my outlets to the UK up until now,' Natalie said.

'But why?' Francesca said. 'Your designs are wonderful.'

'I'm not fond of travelling,' Natalie said. 'I know I should probably do more in terms of networking in Europe...'

'Never mind,' Francesca said, patting her arm reassuringly. 'Angelo will see to it. He is very good at business. You will soon be a household name and I will be immensely proud of you. I will tell everyone you are my lovely daughter-in-law and I will not speak to them ever again unless they buy all of your linen and use all of your treatments in their homes, *si*?'

Natalie thought of her father's dismissal of her latest range as 'too girly' and 'too Parisian'. She felt more affirmed after five minutes with Angelo's mother than she had in a lifetime with her father.

'I'll get my assistant to send you a catalogue,' she said. 'If you want a hand with anything I'd be happy to help.'

'Oh, would you?' Francesca's eyes danced with excitement. 'I've been dying to redecorate the guest rooms. I would *love* your help. It will be a bonding experience, *si*?'

'I'd like that,' Natalie said.

Francesca smiled. 'I have been so nervous about us meeting,' she said. 'But I am happy now. You are perfect for Angelo. You love him very much, no?'

'I... I...'

Francesca squeezed Natalie's forearm. 'I understand,' she said. 'You don't like wearing your heart on your sleeve, *si*? But I can see what you feel for him. I don't need you to say it out loud. You are not the sort of girl who would marry for anything but for love.'

Angelo came over and put an arm around Natalie's waist. 'So you approve, *Mamma*?' he said.

'But of course,' his mother said. 'She is an angel. We will get on famously.'

Dinner was a lively, convivial affair—again very different from meals taken at Natalie's family home. At the Armitage mansion no one spoke unless Adrian Armitage gave permission. It was a pattern from childhood that neither Natalie nor Lachlan had been courageous enough to challenge.

But in the Bellandini household, magnificent and imposing as it was, everyone was encouraged to contribute to the conversation. Natalie didn't say much. She listened and watched as Angelo interacted with his parents. They debated volubly about politics and religion and the state of the economy, but no one got angry or upset, or slammed their fist down on the table. It was like watching a very exciting tennis match. The ball of conversation was hit back and forth, but nothing but good sportsmanship was on show.

After the coffee cups were cleared Angelo placed a gentle hand on the nape of Natalie's neck. 'You will excuse us, *Mamma* and *Papa*?' he said. 'Natalie is exhausted.'

'But of course,' Francesca said.

Sandro got to his feet and joined his wife in kissing Natalie on both cheeks. 'Sleep well, Natalie,' he said. 'It is a very great privilege to welcome you to our family.'

Natalie struggled to keep her overwhelmed emotions back behind the screen she had erected. 'You're very kind…'

Angelo kept his hand at her back all the way upstairs. 'You didn't eat much at dinner,' he said. 'Are you still feeling unwell?'

'No,' she said. 'I'm not a big eater.'

'You're very thin,' he said. 'You seem to have lost even more weight since the day you came to my office.'

She kept her gaze averted as she trudged up the stairs. 'I always lose weight in the summer.'

He held the door of their suite open for her. 'My parents adore you.'

She gave him a vestige of a smile. 'They're lovely people. You're very lucky.'

Angelo closed the door and watched as she removed the clip holding her hair in place. Glossy brunette tresses flowed over her shoulders. He wanted to run his fingers through them, to bury his head in their fragrant mass.

'You can have the bed,' he said. 'I'll sleep in one of the other rooms.'

'Won't your parents think it rather odd if you sleep somewhere else?' she asked, frowning slightly.

'I'll think of some excuse.'

'I'm sure we can manage to share a bed for a night or two,' she said, looking away. 'It's not as if we're out-of-control, hormonally driven teenagers or anything.'

Angelo felt exactly like an out-of-control, hormonally driven teenager, but he thought it best not to say so. He wasn't sure he would be able to sleep a wink with her lying beside him, but he was going to give it a damn good try.

'You use the bathroom first,' he said. 'I have a couple of e-mails to send.'

She gave a vague nod and disappeared into the *en-suite* bathroom.

When he finally came back into the bedroom Natalie was soundly asleep. She barely took up any room in the king-sized bed. He stood looking at her for a long time, wondering where he had gone wrong with her. Had he expected too much too soon? She had only been twenty-one. It was young for the commitment of marriage, but he had been so certain she was the one for him he hadn't stopped to consider she might say no. It had been perhaps a little arrogant of him, but he had never factored in the possibility that she would leave him. All his life he had been given everything he wanted. It was part and parcel of being an only child born to extremely wealthy parents. He had never experienced disappointment or betrayal.

He had her now where he wanted her, but he wasn't happy and neither was she. She was a caged bird. She would not stay confined for long. She would do her duty to save her brother's hide but she would not stay with him indefinitely.

He slipped between the sheets a few minutes later and lay listening to the sound of her soft breathing. He ached to pull her into his arms but he was determined she would come to him of her own volition. He closed his eyes and willed himself to relax.

He was not far off sleep when he felt Natalie stiffen like a board beside him. The bed jolted with the movement of her body as she started to thrash about as if she were possessed by an inner demon. He had never seen her jerk or throw herself about in such a way. He was concerned she was going to hurt herself.

'No!' she cried. 'No! No! No! *Noooo*!'

Angelo reached for her, restraining her flailing arms and legs with the shelter of his body half covering hers. 'Shh, *cara*,' he said softly. 'It's just a bad dream. Shh.'

Her eyes opened wide and she gulped over a sob as she covered her face with her hands. 'Oh, God,' she said. 'I couldn't find him. I couldn't find him.'

He brushed the hair back off her forehead. 'Who couldn't you find, *mia piccola*?' he asked.

She shook her head from side to side, her face still shielded by her hands. 'It was my fault,' she said, the words sounding as if they were scraped out of her throat. 'It was *my* fault.'

He frowned and pulled her hands down from her face. 'What was your fault?'

She blinked and focussed on his face. 'I… I…' She swallowed. 'I—I'm sorry…'

She started to cry, her face crumpling like a sheet of paper snatched up by someone's hand. Big crystal tears popped from her eyes and flowed down her face. He had never seen her cry. He had seen her furiously angry and he had seen her happy, and just about everything in between, but he had never seen her in tears.

'Hey,' he said, blotting each tear as it fell with the pad of his finger. 'It's just a dream, Tatty. It's not real. It's just a horrible nightmare.'

She cried all the harder, great choking sobs that made his own chest feel sore.

'I'm sorry,' she kept saying like a mantra. 'I'm sorry. I'm sorry. I'm sorry.'

'Shh,' he said again. 'There's nothing to be sorry about.' He stroked her face and her hair. 'There…let it go, *cara*. That's my girl. Let it all go.'

Her sobs gradually subsided to hiccups and she finally nestled against his chest and fell into an exhausted sleep. Angelo kept on stroking her hair as the clock worked its way around to dawn.

He could not have slept a wink if he tried.

Natalie opened her eyes and found Angelo's dark, thoughtful gaze trained on her. She had some vague memory of what had passed during the night but it was like looking at something through a cloudy, opaque film.

'I hope I didn't keep you awake,' she said. 'I'm not a very good sleeper.'

'You're certainly very restless,' he said. 'I don't remember you being like that when we were together.'

She focussed her gaze on the white cotton sheet that was pulled up to her chest. 'I sleep much better in the winter.'

'I can see why you choose to live in Scotland.'

She felt a reluctant smile tug at her mouth. 'Maybe I should move to Antarctica or the North Pole.'

'Maybe you should talk to someone about your dreams.'

She got off the bed and snatched up a bathrobe to cover her nightwear. 'Maybe you should mind your own business,' she said, tying the waist strap with unnecessary force.

He got off the bed and came to stand where she was standing. 'Don't push me away, Natalie,' he said. 'Can't you see I'm trying to help you?'

She glared at him, her anger straining like an unbroken horse on a string bridle. 'Back off. I don't need your help. I was perfectly fine until you came along and stuffed everything up. You with your stupid plans for revenge. Who are *you* to sort out my life? You don't know a thing about my life. You just think you can manipulate things to suit you. Go ahead. See if I care.'

She flung herself away, huddling into herself like a porcupine faced with a predator. But her prickly spines felt as if they were pointing the wrong way. She felt every savage poke of them into her sensitive soul.

'Why are you being so antagonistic?' he asked. 'What's happened to make you like this?'

Natalie squeezed her eyes shut as she fought for control. 'I don't need you to psychoanalyse me, Angelo. I don't need you to fix me. I was fine until you barged back into my life.'

'You're not fine,' he said. 'You're far from fine. I want to help you.'

She kept her back turned on him. 'You don't need me to complicate your life. You can have anyone. You don't need me.'

'I do need you,' he said. 'And you need me.'

She felt as if he had reached inside her chest and grasped her heart in his hand and squashed it. She wasn't the right person for him. She could never be the right person for him. Why couldn't he see it? Did she have to spell it out for him?

'You deserve someone who can love you,' she said. 'I'm not capable of that.'

'I don't know what's happened in your life to make you think that, but it's not true,' he said. 'You do care, Natalie. You care about everything, but you keep your feelings locked away where no one can see them.'

She pinched the bridge of her nose until her eyes watered. 'I've stuffed up so many lives.' She sucked in a breath and released it raggedly. 'I've tried to be a good person but sometimes it's just not enough.'

'You *are* a good person,' he said. 'Why are you so damned hard on yourself?'

Natalie felt the anguish of her soul assail her all over again. She had carried this burdensome yoke since she was seven years old. Instead of getting lighter it had become heavier. It had dug down deep into the shoulders of her guilt. She had no hope of shrugging it off. It was like a big, ugly track mark on her soul.

It was with her for life. It was her penance, her punishment.

'When I was a little girl I thought the world was a magical place,' she said. 'I thought if I just wished for something hard enough it would happen.'

'That's the magic of childhood,' he said. 'Every child thinks that.'

'I truly believed if I wanted something badly enough it would come to me,' she said. 'Where did I get that from? Life isn't like that. It's never been like that. It's not like some Hollywood script where everything turns out right in the end. It's pain and sadness and grief at what could have been but wasn't. It's one long journey of relentless suffering.'

'Why do you find life so difficult?' he asked. 'You come from a good family. You have wealth and a roof over your head, food on the table. What is there to be so miserable about? So many people are much worse off.'

She rolled her eyes and headed for the bathroom. 'I don't expect you to understand.'

'Make me understand.'

She turned and looked at him. His dark eyes were so concerned and serious. How could she bear to see him look at her in horror and disgust if she told him the truth? She let out a long sigh and pushed against the door with her hand. 'I'm going to have a shower,' she said. 'I'll see you downstairs.'

Angelo was having coffee in the breakfast room when Natalie came in. She looked cool and composed. There was no sign of the distress he had witnessed during the dark hours of the night and first thing this morning. Her ice maiden persona was back in place.

He rose from the table as she came in and held out a chair for her. 'My mother has organised a shopping morning for you,' he said. 'She'll be with you shortly. She's just seeing to some last-minute things with the housekeeper.'

'But I don't need anything,' she said, frowning as she sat down.

'Aren't you forgetting something?' he asked. 'We're getting married on Saturday.'

Her eyes fell away from his as she placed a napkin over her lap. 'I wasn't planning on going to any trouble over a dress,' she said. 'I have a cream suit that will do.'

'It's not just your wedding, *cara*,' he said. 'It's mine

too. My family and yours are looking forward to celebrating with us. It won't be the same if you turn up in a dress you could wear any old time. I want you to look like a bride.'

A spark of defiance lit her slate-blue gaze as it clashed with his. 'I don't want to look like a meringue,' she said. 'And don't expect me to wear a veil, because I won't.'

Angelo clamped his teeth together to rein in his temper. Was she being deliberately obstructive just to needle him for forcing her hand? He regretted showing his tender side to her last night. She was obviously going to manipulate him to get her own way. Hadn't her father warned him? She was clever at getting what she wanted. She would go to extraordinary lengths to do so.
But then, so would he.

She had met her match in him and he would not let her forget it. 'You will wear what I say you will wear,' he said, nailing her with his gaze. 'Do you understand?'

Her eyes flashed like fire. 'Does it make you feel big and macho and tough to force me to do what you want?' she asked. 'Does it make you feel big and powerful and invincible?'

It made him feel terrible inside, but he wasn't going to tell her that. 'I want our wedding day to be a day to remember,' he said with forced calm. 'I will not have you spoiling it by childish displays of temper or passive aggressive actions that will upset other people who are near and dear to me. You are a mature adult. I expect you to act like one.'

She gave him a livid glare. 'Will that be all, master?' she asked.

He pushed back from the table and tossed his napkin

to one side. 'I'll see you at the chapel on Saturday,' he said. 'I have business to see to until then.'

Her expression lost some of its intractability. 'You mean you're leaving me here…alone?'

'My parents will be here.'

Her throat rose and fell over the tiniest of swallows. 'This is rather sudden, isn't it?' she said. 'You said nothing to me about having to go away on business. I thought you were going to be glued to my side in case I did a last-minute runner.'

Angelo leaned his hands on the table and looked her square in the eyes. 'Don't even think about it, Natalie,' he said through tight lips. 'You put one foot out of place and I'll come down like a ton of bricks on your brother. He will never go to Harvard. He will never go to any university. It will be years before he sees the light of day again. Do I make myself clear?'

She blinked at him, her eyes as wide as big blue saucers. 'Perfectly,' she said in a hollow voice.

He held her pinned there with his gaze for a couple of chugging heartbeats before he straightened and adjusted his tie. 'Try and stay out of trouble,' he said. 'I'll call you later. *Ciao.*'

CHAPTER SIX

THE private chapel at Angelo's grandparents' villa forty-five minutes outside of Rome was full to overflowing when Natalie arrived in the limousine with her father. The last few days had passed in a blur of activity as wedding preparations had been made. She had gone with the flow of things—not wanting to upset Angelo's parents, who had gone out of their way to make her feel welcome.

She had talked to Angelo on the phone each day, but he had seemed distant and uncommunicative and the calls hadn't lasted more than a minute or two at most. There had been no sign of the gentle and caring man she had glimpsed the other night. She wondered if he was having second thoughts about marrying her now he had an inkling of how seriously screwed up she really was.

Her parents had flown over the day before, and her father had immediately stepped into his public role of devoted father. Her mother was her usual decorative self, dressed in diamonds and designer clothes with a hint of brandy on her breath that no amount of mints could disguise.

Her father helped Natalie out of the car outside the chapel. 'You've done well for yourself,' he said. 'I thought you'd end up with some tradesman from the suburbs. Angelo Bellandini is quite a catch. It's a pity he's Italian, but his money more than makes up for that. I didn't know you had it in you to land such a big fish.'

She gave him an embittered look. 'I suppose I really should thank you, shouldn't I? After all, you're the one who reeled him in for me.'

Her father's eyes became cold and hard and his voice lowered to a harsh, dressing-down rasp. 'What else was I to do, you stupid little cow?' he asked. 'Your brother's future depended on getting on the right side of Bellandini. I'm just relieved he wanted to take you on again. Quite frankly, I don't know why he can be bothered. You're not exactly ideal wife material. You've got too much attitude. You've been like that since the day you were born.'

Natalie ground her teeth as she walked to the chapel along a gravelled pathway on her father's arm. She had learned long ago not to answer back. The words would be locked inside her burning throat just like every other word she had suppressed in the past.

They ate at her insides like bitter, poisonous acid.

Angelo blinked when he saw Natalie come into the chapel. His heart did a funny little jump in his chest as he saw her move down the aisle. She was wearing a gorgeous crystal-encrusted ivory wedding gown that skimmed her slim curves. It had a small train that floated behind her, making her appear almost ethereal, and she was wearing a short gossamer veil with a princess tiara that didn't quite disguise the chalk-white paleness of her face. She looked at him as she walked towards him, but he wasn't sure she was actually seeing him. She had a faraway look in her eyes—a haunted look that made him feel guilty for having engineered things the way he had.

He took both of her hands in his as she drew close. They were ice-cold. 'You look beautiful,' he said.

She moved her lips but there was no way he could call it a smile.

'Your mother chose the dress,' she said.

'I like the veil.'

'It keeps the flies off.'

He smiled and gave her hands a little squeeze as the priest moved forward to address the congregation. He felt her fingers tremble against his, and for the briefest moment she clung to him, as if looking for support. But then her fingers became still and lifeless in the cage of his hands.

'Dearly beloved,' the priest began.

'…and now you may kiss the bride.'

Natalie held her breath as Angelo slowly raised her veil. She blinked away an unexpected tear. She had been determined not to be moved by the simple service, but somehow the words had struck a chord deep inside her. The promises had reminded her of all she secretly longed for: lifelong love, being cherished, protected, honoured, worshipped…accepted.

Angelo's mouth came down and gently pressed against hers in a kiss that contained a hint of reverence—or maybe that was just wishful thinking on her part. Halfway through the service she had started wishing it was for real. That he really did love her. That he really did want to spend the rest of his life with her in spite of her 'attitude problem'.

The thought of her father's hateful words made her pull out of the kiss. If Angelo was annoyed at her breaking away he showed no sign of it on his face. He simply looped her arm through his and led her out of the chapel to greet their guests.

The reception was held in the lush, fragrant gardens at his elderly grandparents's spectacular villa, under a beautifully decorated marquee. The champagne flowed and scrumptious food was served, but very little made it past Natalie's lips. She watched as her father charmed everyone with his smooth urbanity. She watched in dread as her mother downed glass after glass of champagne and talked too long and too loudly.

'Your mother looks like she's having a good time,' Angelo remarked as he came back to her side after talking with his grandfather.

Natalie chewed at her lip as she saw her mother doing a tango with one of Angelo's uncles. 'Deep down she's really very shy, but she tries to compensate by drinking,' she said. 'I wish she wouldn't. She doesn't know when to stop.'

He took her by the elbow and led her to a wistaria-covered terrace away from the noise and music of the reception. Bees buzzed in the scented arras above them. 'You look exhausted,' he said. 'Has it all been too much for you?'

'I never thought smiling could be so tiring,' she said with a wry grimace.

'I should imagine it would be when you're not used to doing it.'

She looked away from his all-seeing gaze. He had a way of looking at her that made her feel as if he sensed her deep unhappiness. He'd used to tease her about taking life so seriously. She had tried—she had really tried—to enjoy life, but hardly a day passed without her thinking of all the days her baby brother had missed out on because of her.

'I like your grandparents,' she said, stepping on tip-toe to smell a purple bloom of wistaria. 'They're so devoted to each other even after all this time.'

'Are yours still alive?' he asked. 'You didn't put them on the list so I assumed they'd passed on.'

'They're still alive.'

'Why didn't you invite them?'

'We're not really a close family,' she said, thinking of all the stiff and awkward don't-mention-what-happened-in-Spain visits she had endured over the years.

Everything had changed after Liam had died.

She had lost not just her younger brother but also her entire family. One by one they had pulled back from her. There had been no more seaside holidays with Granny and Grandad. After a couple of years the beautiful handmade birthday presents had stopped, and then a year or two later the birthday cards had gone too.

A small silence passed.

'I'm sorry I couldn't arrange for Lachlan to be here,' he said. 'It's against regulations.'

She looked up at him, shielding her eyes against the bright sun with one of her hands. 'Where is he?'

'He's in a private clinic in Portugal,' he said. 'He'll be there for a month at the minimum.'

Natalie felt a surge of relief so overwhelming it almost took her breath away. She dropped her hand from her eyes and opened and closed her mouth, not able to speak for a full thirty seconds. She had been so terrified he would self-destruct before he got the help he so desperately needed. She had suggested a clinic a couple of times, but he had never listened to her. She had felt so impotent, so helpless watching him destroy his life so recklessly.

'I don't know how to thank you…I've been so terribly worried about him.'

'He has a long way to go,' he said. 'He wants help, but he sabotages it when it's given to him.'

'I know…' she said on a sigh. 'He has issues with self-esteem. Deep down he hates himself. It doesn't matter what he does, or what he achieves, he never feels good enough.'

'For your parents?'

She shifted her gaze. 'For my father, mostly…'

'The father-son relationship can be a tricky one,' he said. 'I had my own issues with my father. That's one of the reasons I came to London.'

Natalie walked with him towards a fountain that was surrounded by sun-warmed cobblestones. She could feel the heat coming up through her thinly soled high-heeled shoes. The fine misty spray of the fountain delicately pricked her face and arms like a refreshing atomiser.

'You've obviously sorted those issues out,' she said. 'Your father adores you, and you clearly adore and respect him.'

'He's a good man,' he said. 'I'm probably more like him that I'm prepared to admit.'

She looked at the water splashing over the marble dolphins in the fountain and wondered what Angelo would think if she told him what *her* father was really like. Would he believe her?

Probably not, she thought with a plummeting of her spirits. Her father had got in first and swung the jury. He had done it all her life—telling everyone how incredibly difficult she was, how headstrong and wilful, how cold and ungrateful. The one time she had dared to tell a family friend about her father's treatment of her it had backfired spectacularly. The knock-on effect on her mother had made Natalie suffer far more than any physical or verbal punishment her father could dish out.

It had silenced her ever since.

'I guess we should get back to the guests,' she said.

'It will soon be time to leave,' he said, and began walking back with her to the marquee. 'I'd like us to get to Sorrento before midnight.'

Natalie's stomach quivered at the thought of spending a few days alone with him at his villa. Would he expect her to sleep with him? How long would she be able to say no? She was aching for him, and had been since she had walked into his office that day. Her body tingled when she was with him. It was tingling now just from walking beside him. Every now and again her bare arm would brush against his jacket sleeve. Even through the barrier of the expensive fabric she could feel the electric energy of his body. It shot sharp arrows of awareness through her skin and straight to her core. She wanted him as she had always wanted him.

Feverishly, wantonly, urgently.

She was the moth and he was the flame that could destroy her, and yet she just couldn't help herself. But giving herself to him physically was one thing. Opening herself to him emotionally was another. If she showed him everything that was stored away inside her what would she do if he then abandoned her?

How would she ever be able to put herself back together again?

Natalie could barely recall the journey to Sorrento in the chauffeur-driven car. She had fallen asleep before they had travelled even a couple of kilometres. She had woken just after midnight as the car drew to a halt, to find her head cradled in Angelo's lap, his fingers idly stroking her hair.

'We're here,' he said.

She sat up and pushed back her loosened hair. 'I think I dribbled on your trousers,' she said, grimacing in embarrassment. 'Sorry.'

He gave her a lazy smile. 'No problem,' he said. 'I enjoyed watching you.'

The villa was perched high on a clifftop, overlooking the ocean. It had spectacular views over the port of Sorrento and the colourful villages hugging the coastline. With terraced gardens and a ground area twice the size of its neighbours, the villa offered a level of privacy that was priceless. Lights twinkled from boats on the wrinkled dark blue blanket of the sea below. The balmy summer air contained the sweet, sharp scent of lemon blossom from the surrounding lemon groves, and the light breeze carried with it the faint clanging sound of the rigging on a yacht far below.

Angelo left the driver to deal with their luggage as he led Natalie inside. 'My hotel development is much larger than this place,' he said. 'I'll take you there tomorrow or the next day.'

Natalie looked around at the vaulted ceilings and the panoramic arched windows, the antique parquet and the original terracotta floors. 'This is lovely,' she said. 'Have you had it long?'

'I bought it a couple of years ago,' he said. 'I like the privacy here. It's about the only place I can lock myself away from the press.'

'I suppose it's where you bring all your lovers to seduce them out of the spotlight?' she said before she could check herself.

He studied her as he pulled free his loosened tie. 'You sound jealous.'

'Why would I be jealous?' she asked. 'I don't have any hold over you. And you don't have any hold over me.'

He picked up her left hand and held it in front of her face. 'Aren't you forgetting something?' he asked. 'We're married now. We have a hold over each other.'

Natalie tried to get out of his grasp but his fingers tightened around hers. 'What possible hold do I have over you?' she asked. 'You forced me to marry you. I didn't have a choice. Five years ago I made the decision to walk out of your life and never see you again. I wanted to be left alone to get on with my life. But no; you had to fix things so I'd be at your mercy and under your control.'

'Stop it, Natalie,' he said. 'You're tired. I'm tired. This is not the time to discuss this.'

She tugged some more until she finally managed to break free. She stood before him, her chest heaving, her heart pounding and her self-control in tatters.

'Don't tell me to stop it!' she said. '*What* hold do I have over you? You hold all the cards. I know what you're up to, Angelo. I know how men like you think. You'll hoodwink me into falling in love with you and then you'll pull the rug from under my feet when I least expect it. But it won't work because I won't do it. I won't fall in love with you. I *won't*.'

He stood looking down at her with implacable calm. 'Do you feel better now you've got all of that off your chest?' he asked.

Goaded beyond all forbearance, she put her chin up and flashed him a challenging glare. 'Why don't you come and collect what you've bought and paid for right here and now?' she said. 'Come on, Angelo. I'm your little puppet now. Why don't you come and pull on my strings?'

A muscle flickered in his jaw as his dark-as-night gaze slowly moved over her body, from her head to her feet and back again. She felt it peel her ivory gown away. She felt it scorch through her bra and knickers. She felt it burn her flesh. She felt it light an inferno between her legs.

But then a mask slipped over his features. 'I'll see you in the morning,' he said. 'I hope you sleep well. *Buonanotte*.' He inclined his head in a brief nod and then turned and left.

Natalie listened to the echo of his footsteps on the terracotta floor fading into the distance until there was nothing left but the sound of her own erratic breathing...

The bedroom she'd chosen to sleep in was on the third floor of the villa. She woke after a fitful sleep to bright morning sunshine streaming in through the arched windows. She peeled back the covers and went and looked out at a view over terraced gardens. There was a sparkling blue swimming pool situated on one of the terraces, surrounded by lush green shrubbery. She could see Angelo's lean, tanned figure carving through the water, lap after lap, deftly turning at each end like an Olympic swimmer.

She moved away from the window before he caught her spying on him and headed to the shower.

When she came downstairs breakfast had been laid out on a wrought-iron table in a sunny courtyard that was draped on three sides in scarlet bougainvillaea. The fragrant smell of freshly brewed coffee lured her to the table, and she poured a cup and took it to the edge of the courtyard to look at the view over the port of Sorrento.

She turned around when she heard the sound of Angelo's tread on the flagstones as he came from inside the villa. He was dressed in taupe chinos and a white casual shirt that was rolled up past his wrists, revealing strong, masculine forearms. His hair was still damp; the grooves of his comb were still visible in the thick dark strands. He looked gorgeously fresh and vitally, potently alive.

'I thought you might've joined me for a swim,' he said.

'I'm not much of a swimmer,' she said, shifting her gaze. 'I prefer dry land sports.'

He pulled out a chair for her at the table. 'Do you want something hot for breakfast?' he asked. 'I can make you an omelette or something.'

Natalie looked at him in surprise. 'Don't you have a twenty-four-hour housekeeper at your beck and call here?'

'I have someone who comes in a couple of times a week,' he said. 'I prefer my time here to be without dozens of people fussing around me.'

'Oh, the trials and tribulations of having millions and squillions of dollars,' she said dryly as she sat down.

He looked at her with a half-smile playing about his mouth. 'You grew up with plenty of wealth yourself,' he said. 'Your father is a very successful investor. He was telling me about some of the ways he's survived the financial crisis. He's a very clever man.'

She reached for a strawberry from the colourful fruit plate on the table. 'He's very good at lots of things,' she said, taking a tiny nibble.

He watched her with those dark, intelligent eyes of his. 'You don't like him very much, do you?' he asked.

'What makes you say that?' she asked, taking another little bite of the strawberry.

'I was watching you at the reception yesterday,' he said. 'You tensed every time he came near you. You never smiled at him. Not even once.'

She gave a shrug and reached for another strawberry, focussing on picking off the stem rather than meeting his gaze. 'We have what you might call a strained relationship,' she said. 'But then he told you how difficult I was when you had that cosy little chat together, didn't he?'

'That really upset you, didn't it?'

'Of course it upset me,' she said, shooting him a hard little glare. 'He's good at swinging the jury. He oozes with charm. No one would ever question his opinion. He's the perfect husband, the perfect father. He doesn't show in public what he's like in private. You don't know him, Angelo. You don't know what he's capable of. He'll smile at your face while he has a knife in your back and you'll never guess it. You don't *know* him.'

The silence that fell made Natalie feel horribly exposed. She couldn't believe that she had said as much as she had said. It was as if a torrent had been let loose. The words had come tumbling out like a flood. A dirty, secret flood that she had kept hidden for as long as she could remember. Her words stained the air. The contamination of the truth even seemed to still the sweet sound of the tweeting birds in the shrubbery nearby.

'Are you frightened of him, *cara*?' Angelo asked with a frown.

'Not any more,' she said, giving her head a little toss

as she reached for a blueberry this time. 'I've taught myself not to let him have that power over me.'

'Has he hurt you in some way in the past?'

'What are you going to do, Angelo?' she asked with a woeful attempt at scorn. 'Punch him on the nose? Rearrange his teeth for him? Give him a black eye?'

His gaze became very dark and very hard. 'If anyone dares to lay so much as a finger on you I will do much more than that,' he said grimly.

A piece of her emotional armour peeled off like the sloughing of skin. It petrified her to think of how easily it had fallen away. Was this his plan of action? To conquer by stealth? To ambush her by making her feel safe and secure?

To protect her?

'You know, for such a modern and sophisticated man, deep down you're amazingly old-fashioned,' she said.

He reached for her hand. 'You have no need to be frightened of anyone any more, *cara,*' he said. 'You're under my protection now, and you will be while you're wearing that ring on your finger.'

Natalie looked at her hand in the shelter of his. The sparkling new wedding band and the exquisite engagement ring bound her to him symbolically, but the real bond she was starting to feel with him was so much deeper and more lasting than that.

And it secretly terrified her.

She pulled her hand out of his and took one of the rolls out of a basket. 'So, what's the plan?' she asked in a light and breezy tone. 'How are we going to spend this non-honeymoon of ours?'

His eyes continued to hold hers in a smouldering tether that made the base of her spine feel hot and tingly. 'How long do you think you'll be able to keep up this ridiculous pretence of not wanting me?' he asked.

She gave a false-sounding little laugh. 'You had your chance last night and you blew it.'

His eyes smouldered some more. 'I was very tempted to call your bluff last night.'

Hot, moist heat swirled between her legs as she thought of how dangerous and reckless her little taunt had actually been. Was that why she had issued it? Did some subconscious part of her want him to take charge and seduce her?

'Why didn't you?' she asked with a little lift of her brow.

'I don't like being manipulated,' he said. 'You wanted me to take the responsibility away from you. You don't like the fact that you still want me. You've taught yourself not to want or need anyone. It bugs the hell out of you that I stir you up the way I do, doesn't it?'

Natalie tried to push her emotions back where they belonged, but it was like trying to refold a map. She pushed back from the table with a screech of the wrought-iron chair-legs against the flagstones. 'I don't have to listen to this,' she said, slamming her napkin on the table.

'That's right,' he said mockingly. 'Run away. That's what you usually do, isn't it? You can't face the truth of what you feel, so you bolt like a scared rabbit.'

She glowered at him in fury, her fists clenched, her spine rigid. 'I am *not* a coward.'

He came to where she was standing, looking down at her with those penetrating eyes of his. She wanted to run, but had to force herself to stand still in order to discredit his summation of her character.

'How long do you think you can keep running?' he

asked. 'Hasn't anyone ever told you that your feelings go with you? You can't leave them behind. They follow you wherever you go.'

'I don't feel anything for you,' she said through barely moving lips.

He gave a deep chuckle of laughter. 'Sure you don't, Tatty.'

She clenched her teeth. 'Stop calling me that.'

'How are you going to stop me?' he asked with a goading smile.

She stepped right up to him and fisted a hand in the front of his shirt. 'Stop it, damn you,' she said, trying to push him backwards. But it was like a moth trying to move a mattress.

His dark gaze mocked her. 'Is that really the best you can do?'

She raised her other hand to slap him, but he caught it mid-air. 'Ah-ah-ah,' he chided. 'That's not allowed. We can play dirty, but not *that* dirty.'

Natalie felt the stirring of his erection against her, and her body responded with a massive tidal wave of lust. The erotic pulse of his blood thundering against her belly unleashed a deranged demon of desire inside her. She lunged at him, pulling his head down by grabbing a handful of his hair so she could smash her mouth against his. He allowed her a few hot seconds before he took charge of the kiss and pushed through her lips with the sexy thrust of his tongue, claiming her interior moistness, mimicking the intimate possession of hard, swollen male inside soft, yielding female.

She tried to take back control but he refused to relinquish it. He commandeered her mouth with masterful expertise, making her whole body sing with delight. One of his hands drove through her hair to angle her head for better access as he deepened the kiss. His other hand found her breast and cupped it roughly, possessively. Her flesh swelled and prickled in need, her nipples becoming hardened points that ached for the hot wet swirl and tug of his tongue. She moved against him, wanting more, wanting it all.

Wanting it *now*.

Her hands dug into his taut buttocks as she pulled him closer. He was monumentally aroused. She felt the rock-hard length of him and ached to feel him moving inside her. Her inner body secretly prepared itself. She felt the dewy moisture gathering between her thighs. She felt the tapping pulse of her blood as her feminine core swelled with longing. She didn't think she had ever wanted him so badly. She was feverish with it.

Her heart raced with excitement as he scooped her up and carried her indoors. But he didn't take her anywhere near a bedroom. He didn't even bother undressing her. He roughly lifted her sundress, bunching it up around her waist, and backed her towards the nearest wall, his mouth still clamped down on hers. He didn't waste time removing her knickers, either. He simply shoved them to one side as he claimed her slick, hot moistness with one of his fingers.

She gasped against his mouth and he made a very male sound at the back of his throat—a primal sound of deep satisfaction that made all the tight ligaments in her spine loosen. He tortured her with his touch. Those clever fingers got to work and had her shaking with need within moments. She clung to him desperately, her fingernails digging into his back and shoulders as he made her shatter into a million pieces. She sagged against him when the first storm was over. She knew there would be more. There always was with Angelo.

He was never satisfied until he had completely undone her physically.

She reached for the zip on his trousers and went in search of him. Her fingers wrapped around his pulsing steely length. He felt hot and hard and heavy with need. She blotted her thumb over the bead of moisture at his tip and a sharp dart of need speared her. He wanted her as badly as she wanted him. Hadn't it always been this way between them? Their coupling had always been a frenzied attack on the senses. Always fireworks and explosions. Always a mind-blowing madness that refused to be tamed.

He pulled her hand away and quickly applied a condom before pressing her back against the wall, thrusting into her so hard and so fast the breath was knocked right out of her. His mouth swallowed her startled gasp as he rocked against her with heart-stopping urgency.

The pressure built and built inside her again. The sensations ricocheted through her like a round of rubber bullets. It had been *so* long! *This* was what she had craved from him. The silky glide of his hard body, those powerful strokes and bold thrusts that made her shiver from head to foot. Her body was so in tune with his. Everything felt so right, so perfect. Her orgasm came speeding towards her, tightening all her sensitive nerve-endings and tugging at her insides, teasing as it lured her towards the edge of oblivion. She cried out as it carried her away on a rollercoaster that dipped and dropped vertiginously.

She was still convulsing when he came. She felt him tense, and then he groaned out loud as he shuddered and quaked with pleasure, his breathing heavy against her neck where he had pressed his face in that last crazy dash to the finish.

It was a moment or two before he stepped away from her. His expression was impossible to read as he did up his zip and tucked his shirt back into his trousers. Natalie felt a pang for the past—for a time when he would smile at her in a smouldering way, his arms holding her in the aftermath as if he never wanted to let her go.

She quickly suppressed that longing, however. She pushed her dress down and her chin up. 'Was that playing dirty enough for you?' she asked.

His dark, unreadable eyes held hers. 'For now.'

She felt a delicious little aftershock of pleasure ripple through her as his gaze went to her mouth. Was he thinking of how she'd used to pleasure him with it? He had done the same to her; so many times she had lost count. There had been few boundaries when it had come to sex. She had learned how to enjoy her body with him, how not to feel ashamed of its needs and urges. He had opened up a wild, sensual world to her that she had not visited since.

She moved away from the wall, wincing slightly as her tender muscles protested.

His expression immediately clouded with concern. 'Did I hurt you?'

'I'm fine.'

He put a hand around her wrist, his fingers overlapping her slender bones, his thumb stroking along the sensitive skin. 'I'm sorry,' he said. 'I shouldn't have taken things so fast. I should've taken my time with you, prepared you more.'

She gave him a nonchalant shrug and pulled out of his hold. 'Save the romantic gestures for someone you didn't have to pay for.'

A hard glitter came into his eyes. 'Is this really how

you want our relationship to run?' he asked. 'As a point-scoring exercise where we do nothing but attack each other?'

'If you're unhappy with how our relationship runs then you have only yourself to blame,' she said. 'You were the one who insisted on marriage. I told you I'm not cut out for it.'

'I wanted to give you the honour of making you my wife,' he said bitterly. 'But clearly you're much more comfortable with the role of a whore.' He took out his wallet and peeled off a handful of notes. Stepping up to her, he stuffed them down the cleavage of her dress. 'That should just about cover it.'

Natalie took the notes out and tore them into pieces, threw them at his feet. 'You'll need far more than *that* to get me to sleep with you again.'

'You're assuming, of course, that I would want to,' he said. And, giving her a scathing look, he turned and left.

CHAPTER SEVEN

NATALIE spent most of the day in her room. She heard Angelo moving about the villa but she refused to interact with him. She was determined to avoid him for as long as she could. Hunger was a minor inconvenience. Her stomach growled as the clock moved around but still she remained resolute.

It was close to eight in the evening when she heard the sound of footsteps outside her door, and then a light tap as Angelo spoke. 'Natalie?'

'Go away.'

'Open the door.'

She tightened her arms across her body, where she was sitting cross-legged on the bed. 'I said go away.'

'If you don't unlock this door I swear to God I'll break it down with my bare hands,' he said in a gritty tone.

Natalie weighed up her options and decided it was better not to call his bluff this time. She got off the bed, padded over to the door, turned the key and opened the door. 'Yes?' she said with a haughty air.

The lines that bracketed his mouth looked deeper and his eyes, though currently glittering with anger, looked tired. 'Can we talk?' he asked.

She stepped away from the door and moved to the

other side of the room, folding her arms across her middle. She didn't trust herself not to touch him. Her body had switched on like a high-wattage lightbulb as soon as he had stepped over the threshold. She could feel the slow burn of her desire for him moving through her. Her insides flickered with the memory of his possession. It was a funny sensation, like suddenly stepping on an uneven surface and feeling that rapid stomach-dropping free fall before restoring balance.

'Are you all right?' he asked.

She sent him a chilly look. 'Fine, thank you.'

He drew in a long breath and then released it. 'What happened this morning…I want to apologise. What I said to you was unforgivable.'

'You're right,' she said, shooting him another deadly glare. 'And, just for the record, I don't forgive you.'

He pushed a hand through his hair. Judging from the disordered state of it, it wasn't the first time that day he had done so. 'I also want to apologise for being so rough with you.' He swallowed tightly and frowned. 'I thought… I don't know what I thought. Maybe I didn't think. I just wanted you.' His eyes darkened as they held hers. 'I have never wanted anyone like I want you.'

Natalie's resolve began to melt with each pulsing second his eyes stayed meshed with hers. She felt the heat of longing pass between them like a secret code. It was there in his dark as night eyes. It was there in the sculptured contours of his mouth. It was there in the tall frame of his body, pulling her like a powerful magnet towards him. She felt the tug of need in her body; she felt it in her breasts, where they twitched and tingled behind her bra. And, God help her, she felt it rattle the steel cage around her heart.

'Apology accepted,' she said.

He came to her and gently cupped her right cheek in his hand, his eyes searching hers. 'Can we start again?' he asked.

She gave a little frown. 'Start from where?'

His mouth curved upwards. 'Hi, my name is Angelo Bellandini and I'm a hotel and property developer. I'm an only child of wealthy Italian parents. I help to run my father's arm of the business while working on my own.'

She gave a resigned sigh. 'Hi, my name is Natalie Armitage and I'm an interior designer, with an expanding sideline in bedlinen and soft furnishings.' She chewed at her lip for a moment and added, 'And I have a fear of flying…'

His thumb stroked her cheek. 'How old were you when you first got scared?'

'I was…seven…'

'What happened?'

She slipped out of his hold and averted her gaze. 'I'd rather not talk about it with a virtual stranger.'

'I'm not a stranger,' he said. 'I'm your husband.'

'Not by my choice,' she muttered.

'Don't do this, Natalie.'

'Don't do what?' she asked, glaring at him. 'Tell it how it is? You blackmailed me back into your life. Now you want me to open up to you as if we're suddenly inseparable soul mates. I'm not good at being open with people. I've never been good at it. I'm private and closed. It must be my Scottish heritage. We're not outwardly passionate like you Italians. You'll just have to accept that's who I am.'

The touch of his hands on her shoulders made every cell of her skin flicker and dance in response.

'You're much more passionate than you give yourself credit for,' he said. 'I've got the scratch marks on my back to prove it.'

Natalie felt that passion stirring within her. His body was calling out to hers in a silent language that was as old as time itself. It spoke to her flesh, making it tauten and tingle all over in anticipation. She wished she had the strength or indeed the willpower to step back from his magnetic heat, but her body was on autopilot. She pressed closer, that delicious ache of need starting deep in her core.

His mouth came down towards hers as hers came up, and they met in an explosion of sensation that made the flesh on her body shudder in delight. He flooded her senses with his taste—mint and male, heat and primal purpose. His tongue darted and dived around hers, subjecting it to a teasing tango that made her spine shiver and shake like a string of bottle caps rattling against each other. Heat pooled between her legs as he moved against her, the thickened length of him exciting her unbearably. She rubbed against him wantonly, desperate for the earth-shattering release that he alone could give her.

He pulled back slightly, his breathing heavy. 'Too fast.'

'Not fast enough,' she said and, pulling his head down, covered his mouth with her greedy one.

His hands worked on her clothes with deliberate attention to detail. She squirmed and writhed as he kissed every spot of flesh as he gradually exposed it. She tugged his shirt out of his trousers and with more haste than precision got him out of the rest of his clothes. She ran her hands over him reverentially. He was so strong and so lean, his muscles tightly corded, his skin satin smooth all but for the sprinkling of masculine hair that went from his chest in an arrow to his swollen groin. She stroked him with her hand, loving the feel of his reaction to her touch. She heard him snatch in a breath, his eyes glittering as she gave him a sultry look from beneath her lashes.

'If you're going to do what I think you're about to do then this show is going to be over before it gets started,' he warned.

She gave him a devil-may-care look and shimmied down in front of him. 'Then I'll just have to wait until the encore, won't I?'

'Dio mio,' he groaned in ecstasy as she took him into her mouth.

She used her tongue and the moistness of her saliva to take him to the brink. She would have pushed him over, but he stopped her by placing his hands on either side of her head.

'Enough,' he growled, and hauled her to her feet.

He carried her to the bed, laying her down and covering her, with his weight supported by his arms to avoid crushing her. His mouth took hers in a searing kiss as his hand caressed her breasts and that aching secret dark place between her thighs.

It was her turn to suck in a breath when he moved down her body to stroke her with his lips and tongue. She felt the fizzing of her nerves as he brought her closer and closer. Her release started far away, and then gathered speed and stampeded through her flesh. She lost herself in a whirlpool of sensation that made her feel weightless and boneless.

She opened her eyes to find him looking at her as he stroked a lazy finger down between her breasts. 'Do you want to finish me off with your hand?' he asked.

She gave him a little frown. 'Don't you want to come inside me?'

'I don't want to hurt you,' he said, gently circling one of her nipples. 'You might still be sore.'

She stroked her hand down his lean stubbly jaw. 'I want you inside me,' she said. 'I want *you*.'

His eyes held hers in a sensual lock that made her belly quiver. 'I'll take it easy,' he said. 'Tell me to stop if it hurts.'

'It's not as if I'm a virgin, Angelo,' she said, with a brittle little laugh to cover her unexpected emotional response to his tenderness. 'I can handle everything you dish out.'

His eyes smouldered as they held hers. 'Don't say you weren't warned,' he said, and covered her mouth with his.

Angelo lay on his side and watched Natalie sleep. From time to time he would pick up a silky strand of her hair and twirl it around one of his fingers.

She didn't stir.

Her stubborn refusal to open her heart to him was like a thorn in his flesh. It was as if she would do anything to stop him thinking she cared about him. He thought back to their break-up, to how she had announced without warning that she was leaving. Her bags had been packed when he'd come home from a three-day workshop in Wales. She had told him she had slept with someone she had met at the local pub. He had stood there in dumbstruck silence, wondering if she was joking.

Their relationship had been volatile at times, but he hadn't really thought she was serious about walking out on him. She had threatened to many times, but he had always thought it was just her letting off steam. He had planned to ask her to marry him that very night. He had wanted to wait until he got back from the workshop so she would have had time to think about how much she had missed him. But then she had shown him a photo on her phone, of her with a man, sitting at the bar, smiling over their drinks. The anger he had felt at seeing the evidence of her betrayal had been like a hot red dust storm in front of his eyes. She had stood there, looking at him with a what-are-you-going-to-do-about-it-look and he had snapped.

He wasn't proud of the words he had flailed her with. He was even more ashamed that he'd pushed her up against the wall like a cheap hooker and given her a bruising parting kiss that had left both of them bleeding.

He shuffled through his thoughts as he looked at her lying next to him like a sleeping angel.

She had *wanted* him to believe she had betrayed him. *But why?*

Hadn't he shown her how much he had loved her? He had said it enough times and shown it in a thousand different ways. She had never taken him seriously. Funny that, since she took life so seriously herself. She rarely smiled unless it was a self-effacing one. He couldn't remember ever hearing her laugh other than one of those totally fake cackles that grated on his nerves because he knew them for the tawdry imitation they were.

Why had she been so desperate to get him out of her life?

He was still frowning when she opened her eyes and stretched like a cat. 'What time is it?' she asked.

'You didn't do it, did you?' he asked.

A puzzled flicker passed through her gaze. 'Do what?'

'You didn't sleep with that guy from the bar.'

She made a business of sitting upright and covering herself with a portion of the sheet. 'I went home with him,' she said after a moment.

'But you didn't sleep with him,' he said. 'You wanted me to think you had. You wanted me to believe that because you knew me well enough to know I would never have let you go for anything less.'

A tiny muscle began tapping in her cheek and her eyes took on a defensive sheen. 'I wasn't ready for commitment. You were pressuring me to settle down. I didn't want to lose my freedom. I didn't want to lose my identity and become some nameless rich man's husband just like my mother.'

'You're nothing like your mother, *cara*,' he said. 'You're too strong and feisty for that.'

She got off the bed and wrapped herself in a silky wrap. 'I don't always feel strong,' she said. 'Sometimes I feel…' Her teeth sank into her bottom lip.

'What do you feel?'

She turned to the dressing table and picked up a brush, started pulling it through her hair. 'I feel hungry,' she said. She put the brush down and swung around to face him. 'What does a girl have to do around here to get a meal?'

Angelo knew it wasn't wise to push her. He had to be patient with her. She was feeling vulnerable and had retreated back to her default position. It was her way of protecting herself.

He only wished he had known that five years ago.

Natalie sat across from Angelo in a restaurant in Sorrento an hour later. He had given her the choice of eating in or out and she had chosen to go out. It wasn't that she particularly wanted to mingle with other people; it was more that she wanted to keep her head when around him. She couldn't do that so well when she was alone with him.

The passion they had shared had stirred up old longings that made her feel uneasy. She was fine with having sex with him—more than fine, truth be told. It was just she knew he would want more from her.

He had always wanted more than she was prepared to give.

How long before he would ask her to think about staying with him indefinitely? Then he would start talking about babies.

His mother had already dropped a few broad hints when she had helped her choose her wedding dress. Natalie's stomach knotted at the thought of being responsible for a tiny infant. She could just imagine how her parents would react if she were to tell them she was having a baby. Her mother would reach for the nearest bottle and drain it dry. Her father wouldn't say a word. He would simply raise his eyebrows and a truckload of guilt would land on her like a concrete slab.

Angelo reached across the table and touched her lightly on the back of her hand. 'Hello, over there,' he said with a soft smile.

Natalie gave him a rueful smile in return. 'Sorry… I'm hardly scintillating company, am I?'

'I don't expect you to be the life of the party all the time, *cara*,' he said. 'It's enough that you're here.'

She looked at his fingers entwined with hers. She had missed his touch so much in the years that had passed. She had missed the way his skin felt against hers, the way he felt under the caress of her hands. She had lain awake at night with her body crying out for his lovemaking. Her body had felt so empty. So lifeless without the sensual energy he shot through it like an electric charge.

'What are you thinking?' he asked, stroking the underside of her wrist with the broad pad of his thumb.

She met his chocolate-brown gaze and felt her insides flex and contract with lust. 'Do you want dessert?' she asked.

'Depends on what it is,' he said with a sexy glint.

She could barely sit still in her chair for the rocket blast of longing that swept through her. 'I'm not in the mood for anything sweet,' she said.

'What *are* you in the mood for?' Still that same sexy glitter was lighting his eyes from behind.

'Nothing that takes too much time to prepare.'

'I can be a fast order chef when the need arises,' he said. 'Tell me what you want and I'll deliver it as fast as humanly possible.'

Natalie shivered as he came behind her to pull out her chair for her. The fine hairs on the back of her neck stood up as his warm wine-scented breath coasted past her ear. She leaned back against him, just for a brief moment, to see if he was aroused.

He was.

She smiled to herself and walked out of the restaurant with him, her body already quaking in anticipation.

Angelo had barely opened the door of the villa when she slammed him up against the wall as if she was about to frisk him.

'Hey, was it something I said?' he asked.

Her dark blue gaze sizzled as it held his. 'You promised me dessert,' she said. 'It's time to serve me.'

The entire length of his backbone shuddered as she

ran her hand over his erection. 'Who's doing the cooking here?' he asked.

She gave him a wicked look and brazenly unzipped him. 'I want an appetiser,' she said.

It was all he could do to stand there upright as she sank to her knees in front of him. He braced himself by standing with his feet slightly apart. When she was in this mood there was no stopping her. He was just happy to be taken along for the ride.

And what a ride it was.

Fireworks went off in his head. He couldn't have held back if he had tried. She ruthlessly teased and caressed him until he was barely able to stand upright. His skin went up in a layer of goosebumps and his heart raced like a fat retiree at a fun run.

She stood up and gave him a wanton smile that had a hint of challenge to it. 'Top that,' she said.

'I can do that,' he said, and swept her up in his arms.

He took her to the master suite. He dropped her in the middle of the mattress and then pulled her by one ankle until she was right between his spread thighs. He leaned over her, breathing in her scent, his mouth coming down to claim her in a sensual feast that had her shuddering in seconds. She bucked and arched and screamed, and even batted at him with her fists, but he wouldn't let her go until he was satisfied that he had drawn every last shuddering gasp out of her.

She lay back and flung a hand over her eyes, her chest rising and falling. 'OK, you win,' she said breathlessly.

'It was pretty damn close,' he said, coming to lie next to her. He trailed a finger down the length of her satin-smooth arm. 'Maybe we should have a re-match some time soon, just to make sure?'

She rolled her head to look at him. 'Give me ten minutes.'

'Five.'

'You're insatiable.'

'Only with you.'

A tiny frown puckered her brow and she turned her head back to look at the ceiling. 'Have there been many?' she asked after a pause.

'Does it matter?'

She gave a careless shrug, but the tight set of her expression contradicted it. 'Not really.'

'I was never in love with anyone, if that's what you're asking.'

'I'm not.'

He sent his fingertip over the silky smooth cup of her shoulder. 'Is it so hard to admit you care for me?' he said.

She shoved his hand away and got off the bed. 'I *knew* you would do this,' she said in agitation.

'What did I do?'

She turned and speared him with her gaze. 'I don't love you,' she said. 'Is there something about those words you don't understand? I don't love you. I *like* you. I like you a lot. You're a nice person. I've never met a more decent person. But I'm not in love with you.'

Frustration made Angelo's voice grate. 'You don't *want* to love anyone, that's why. You do care, Tatty. You care so much it scares the hell out of you.'

She clenched her fists by her sides. 'I can't give you what you want,' she said.

'I want you.'

'You want more,' she said. 'You've said it from the beginning. You want a family. You want children. I can't give you them.'

'Are you infertile?'

She rolled her eyes heavenwards and turned away. 'I knew you wouldn't understand.'

He came over to her and took her by the upper arms. 'Then make me understand,' he said.

She pressed her lips together, as if she was trying to stop an outburst of unchecked speech from escaping.

He gave her arms a gentle squeeze. 'Talk to me, Tatty.'

Her eyes watered and she blinked a couple of times to push the tears back. 'What sort of mother would I be?' she asked.

'You'd be a wonderful mother.'

'I'd be a total nutcase,' she said, pulling away from him. 'I'd probably be one of those helicopter parents everyone talks about. I would never be able to relax. So much can happen to a child. There's so much danger out there: illness, accidents, sick predators on the streets and online. It's all too much to even think about.'

'Most parents manage to bring up their children without anything horrible happening to them,' he said. 'It's easy to look at what's reported in the press and think that the danger is widespread and unavoidable, but you're disregarding all the positive parenting experiences that are out there.'

'I just don't want to go there,' she said. 'You can't make me. No one can make me. You can't force me to get pregnant.'

'I sure hope you're on the pill, then, because I haven't always used protection.'

'Did you do that deliberately?' she asked with a hardened look.

'No, of course not,' he said. 'You were on the pill in

the past…I just assumed… OK, maybe I shouldn't have. I'm clear, if that's what's worrying you.'

'Yes, well, so am I,' she said. 'It's not like I've been out there much just lately.'

'Have you been "out there" at all?'

She tried to look casual about it, but he saw her nibble at the inside of her mouth. 'A couple of times,' she said.

'What happened?'

She gave him a withering look. 'I'm not going to discuss my sex life with you.'

'Did you have sex?'

She looked away. 'It wasn't great sex,' she said. 'More of a token effort, really. I don't even remember the guy's name.'

'What were you trying to prove?'

She looked at him sharply. 'What do you mean by that?'

'I've noticed you have a habit of using sex when you want to avoid intimacy.'

She pulled her chin back in derision. 'That's ridiculous,' she said. 'What sort of pop psychology is that? Isn't sex all about intimacy?'

'Physical, maybe, but not emotional,' he said. 'Emotional intimacy takes it to a whole different level.'

'That's way too deep for me,' she said, with an airy toss of her head. 'I like sex. I like the rush of it. I don't need anything else.'

'You don't want anything else because you're running away from who you really are,' he said.

'I'm sure you're a great big world expert on emotional intimacy,' she said with a scathing curl of her lip. 'You've had five different lovers in the last year.'

'So you *have* been counting.'

She stalked to the other side of the room. 'The Texan heiress was way too young for you,' she said. 'She looked like she was barely out of the schoolroom.'

'I didn't sleep with her.'

She gave a scoffing laugh. 'No, I can imagine you didn't. You would've kept her up way past her bedtime with your silver-tongued charm.'

Angelo ground his teeth in search of patience. 'I'm not going to wait for ever for you, Natalie,' he said. 'I have an empire that needs an heir. I've felt the pressure of that since I was twenty-one years old. If you can't commit to that, then I'll have to find someone else who will.'

She gave him a stony look. 'That's why you forced me into this farce of a marriage, isn't it?' she asked. 'It isn't just about revenge or nostalgic past feelings. It's a convenient way to get what you want. My brother played right into your hands.'

'This has nothing to do with your brother,' he said. 'This is between us. It's always been between us.'

Her slate-blue eyes were hard and cynical. 'Tell me something, Angelo,' she said. 'Would you have done it? Would you really have sent my brother to prison?'

He returned her look with ruthless determination. 'You're still the only person standing between your brother and years behind bars,' he said. 'Don't ever forget that, Natalie. His future is in your hands.'

She put up her chin, her eyes flashing their blue fire of defiance at him. 'I could call your bluff on that.'

He nailed her with his gaze. 'You do that, sweetheart,' he said. 'And see how far it gets you.'

CHAPTER EIGHT

NATALIE walked out in the moonlit gardens when sleep became impossible. She had tossed and fretted for the past couple of hours, but there was no way she could close her eyes without images of the past flickering through her brain like old film footage.

Tomorrow was the anniversary of her baby brother's death.

The hours leading up to it were always mental torture. Was that why she had practically thrown herself at Angelo, in an attempt to block it from her mind? She hadn't seen him since he had stalked out on her after delivering his spine-chilling threat.

She wanted to test him.

She wanted to see if he really was as ruthless as he claimed to be but it was too risky. Lachlan would have to pay the price.

She couldn't do it.

He had a future—the future that had been taken from Liam. Lachlan didn't just have his own life to live; he had that of his baby brother, too. No wonder he was buckling under the pressure. Who could ever live up to such a thing? Lachlan was his own person. He had his own goals and aspirations. But for years he had suppressed them in order to keep their parents happy. He had no interest in the family business. Natalie could see that, but their father could not or would not. Their mother couldn't see further than the label on the next bottle of liquor.

She gave a thorny sigh and turned to look at the shimmering surface of the pool that had appeared as if by magic in front of her. She generally avoided swimming pools.

Too many memories.

Even the smell of chlorine was enough to set the nerves in her stomach into a prickling panic. Before Liam's death she had loved the water. She had spent many a happy hour in the pool at Armitage Manor, practising what she had learned with Granny and Grandad at the beach at Crail. But after Liam had died the pool had been bulldozed and made into a tennis court.

She had never once picked up a tennis racket.

She looked at the moonlit water; a tiny breeze teased the surface. It was like a crinkled bolt of silver silk.

Had she come out here in a subconscious attempt to find some peace at last? Would she ever find peace? Forgiveness? Redemption?

A footfall behind her had her spinning around so quickly she almost fell into the water behind her.

'Couldn't you at least have said something before sneaking up on me like that?' she asked clutching at her thumping chest as Angelo stepped into the circle of light from one of the garden lamps.

'Can't sleep?' he asked.

She rubbed at her arms even though it was still warm. 'It's not all that late,' she said.

'It's three a.m.'

She frowned. 'Is it?'

'I've been watching you for the last hour.'

She narrowed her gaze. 'Don't you mean spying?'

'I was worried about you.'

She raised a brow mockingly. 'What?' she asked. 'You thought I might do something drastic rather than face the prospect of being tied to you for the rest of my life?'

'I was concerned you might go for a swim.'

Her eyebrow arched even higher. 'Do I have to ask your permission?'

'No, of course not,' he said, frowning. 'I was just worried you mightn't realise the danger of swimming alone late at night.'

A hysterical bubble of laughter almost choked her. 'Yeah, right—like I don't already know that,' she said with bitter irony.

His frown gave him a dark and forbidding look. 'You said you weren't a strong swimmer. I thought I should be with you if you fancied a dip to cool off.'

Natalie hid behind the smokescreen of her sarcasm. 'What were you going to do if I got into trouble?' she asked. 'Give me mouth to mouth?'

The atmosphere changed as if someone had flicked a switch.

His eyes smouldered as they tussled with hers. 'What a good idea,' he said, grasping her by the arms and bringing her roughly against him, covering her mouth with his.

His mouth tasted of brandy and hot male frustration. He was angry with her, but she could cope much better with his anger than his tenderness. He disarmed her with his concern and understanding.

She wanted him mad at her.

She wanted him wild with her.

She could handle that. She could pull against his

push. She could survive the onslaught of his sensual touch if she could compartmentalise it as a simple battle of wills, not as a strategic war against her very soul.

His lips ground against hers as his hands gripped her upper arms, his fingers biting into her flesh. She relished the discomfort. She was in the mood for pain. She kissed him back, with her teeth and her tongue taking turns. She felt him flinch as her teeth drew blood, and he punished her by driving his tongue all the harder against hers until she finally submitted.

She let him have his way for a few breathless seconds before she tried a counter-attack. She took his lower lip between her teeth and held on.

He spun her around, so her back was facing the pool, and with no more warning than the sound of his feet moving against the flagstones he tangled his legs with hers so she lost her footing. She opened her mouth on a startled gasp, fell backwards and disappeared under the water, taking him with her.

She came up coughing and spluttering; panic was like a madman inside her chest, fighting its way out any way it could. She felt the sickening hammer blows of her heart. She felt the acrid sting of chlorine in her eyes. She was choking against the water she had swallowed. It burned the back of her throat like acid.

'You...*you bastard*!' she screamed at him like a virago.

He pushed the wet hair out of his eyes and laughed. 'You asked for it.'

She came at him then. Hands in fists and teeth bared, she fell upon him, not caring if she drew blood or worse. She called him every foul name she could think of, the words pouring out of her like a vitriolic flood.

He simply held her aloft, and none of her blows and

kicks came to anything but impotent splashes against and below the water.

Suddenly it was all too much.

The fight went out of her. She felt the dismantling of her spirit like starch being rinsed out of a piece of fabric. She went as limp as a rag doll.

'Do you give up?' he asked, with a victorious glint in his dark eyes.

'I give up…'

His brows moved together and his smile faded. 'What's wrong?' he asked.

'Nothing,' she said tonelessly. 'Can I get out now? I—I'm getting cold.'

'Sure,' he said, releasing her, his gaze watchful.

Natalie waded to the edge of the pool. She didn't bother searching for the steps. She gripped the side and hauled herself out in an ungainly fashion. She stood well back from the side and wrung her hair out like a rope, and pushed it back over her shoulder. It wasn't cold, but she was shivering as if she had been immersed for hours in the Black Sea.

Angelo elevated himself out of the pool with a lot more athletic grace than she had. He came and stood in front of her, his hand capturing her juddering chin so he could hold her gaze. 'You didn't hurt yourself, did you?' he asked.

She flashed him a resentful look. 'It would be your fault if I had.'

'I would never have pushed you in if I didn't think it was safe,' he said. 'The water is deepest this end.'

She wrenched her chin out of his grasp and rubbed at it furiously. 'What if it had been the other end?' she asked. 'I could've been knocked out or even killed.'

'I would never deliberately hurt you, *cara*.'

'Not physically, maybe,' she said, throwing him a speaking glance.

A little smiled pulled up the corners of his mouth. 'So you're feeling a little threatened emotionally?' he asked.

She glowered at him. 'Not at all.'

His smile tilted further. 'It's the sex, *cara*,' he said. 'Did you know that the oxytocin released at orgasm is known as the bonding hormone? It makes people fall in love.'

She gave him a disparaging look. 'If that's true then why haven't you been in love with anyone since we were together? It's not as if you haven't been having loads and loads of sex.'

His eyes held hers in a toe-curling lock. 'Ah, but there is sex and there is *sex*.' His gaze flicked to her mouth, pausing there for a heartbeat before coming back to make love with her eyes.

Natalie felt her hips and spine soften. She felt the stirring of her pulse, the tap-tap-tap of her blood as it coursed through her veins. It sent a primal message to the innermost heart of her femininity, making it contract tightly with need.

'But you're not in love with me,' she said, testing him. 'You just want revenge.'

He stroked a light, teasing fingertip down the length of her bare arm, right to the back of her hand, before he captured her fingers in his and brought her close to his body. She felt the shock of touching him thigh to thigh like a stun gun. It sent a wave of craving through her that almost knocked her off her feet.

'I love what you do to me,' he said. 'I love how you make me feel.'

She could barely think with his erection pressing

so enticingly against her. Her body seeped with need. She felt the humid dew of it between her thighs. She looked up in time to see his mouth come down. She closed her eyes and gave herself up to his devastatingly sensual kiss.

His lips moved with hot urgency against hers, drawing from her a response that was just as fiery. Her tongue met his and duelled with it, danced with it, mated with it. Shivers of reaction washed over her body. She pressed herself closer, wanting that thrill of the flesh to block out the pain of the past.

But suddenly he put her from him. 'No,' he said. 'I'm not falling for that again.'

Natalie looked at him in confusion. 'You don't want to…?'

He gave her a wry look. 'Of course I want to,' he said. 'But I'm not going to until you tell me why you were out here, wandering about like a sleepwalker.'

Her gaze slipped out of the range of his. 'I wasn't doing any such thing.'

He pushed her chin up with a finger and thumb. 'Yes, you were,' he said, his gaze determined as it pinned hers. 'And I want to know why.'

Natalie felt her stomach churning and her shivering turned to shuddering. 'I told you. I often have trouble sleeping,' she said.

His eyes continued to delve into hers. 'What plays on your mind so much that you can't settle?'

She licked her dry lips. 'Nothing.'

His brow lifted sceptically. 'I want the truth, Natalie. You owe me that, don't you think?'

'I owe you nothing,' she said, with a flash of her gaze.

His eyes tussled with hers. 'If you won't tell me then

I'll have to find someone who will,' he said. 'And I have a feeling it won't take too much digging.'

Natalie swallowed in panic. If he went looking for answers it might stir up a press fest. She could just imagine the way the papers would run with it. She would have to relive every heartbreaking moment of that fateful trip. Her mother would be devastated to have her terrible loss splashed all over the headlines. Her father had managed to keep things quiet all those years ago, but it would be fair game now, in today's tell-all climate.

And then there was Lachlan to consider.

How would he feel to have the world know he was nothing but a replacement child? That he had only been conceived to fill the shoes of the lost Armitage son and heir?

She ran her tongue over her lips, fighting for time, for strength, for courage. 'I…I made a terrible mistake…a few years back…' She bit down on her lip, not sure if she could go on.

'Tell me about it, Natalie.'

Oh, dear God, *could* she tell him? How could she bear his shock and horror? Those tender looks he had been giving her lately would disappear. How she had missed those looks! He was the only person in the world who looked at her like that.

'Tatty?'

It was the way he said his pet name for her. It was her undoing. How could one simple word dismantle all her defences like a row of dominoes pushed by a fingertip? It was as if he had the key to her heart.

He had always had it.

He hadn't realised it the first time around, but now it was like the childhood game of hot and cold. He was getting warmer and warmer with every moment he spent with her.

Natalie slowly brought her gaze up to look at him head-on. *This is it,* she thought with a sinkhole of despair opening up inside her. *This is the last time you will ever see him look at you like that. Remember it. Treasure it.*

'I killed my brother.'

A confused frown pulled at his forehead. 'Your brother is fine, Natalie. He's safe and sound in rehab.'

'Not that brother,' she said. 'My baby brother, Liam. He drowned while we were holidaying in Spain…he was three years old.'

His frown was so deeply entrenched on his brow it looked as if it would become permanent. 'How could that have been your fault?' he asked.

'I was supposed to be watching him,' she said hollowly. 'My mother had gone inside to lie down. My father was there with us by the pool, but then he said he had to make a really important business call. He was only gone five minutes. I was supposed to be watching Liam. I'd done it before. I was always looking out for him. But that day… I don't know what happened. I think something or other distracted me for a moment. A bird, a flower, a butterfly—I don't know what. When my father came back…' She gave an agonised swallow as the memories came flooding back. 'It was too late…'

'Dear God! Why didn't you tell me this five years ago?' he asked. 'You never mentioned a thing about having lost a brother. Why on earth didn't you say something?'

'It's not something anyone in my family talks about. My father strictly forbade it. He thought it upset my mother too much. It was so long ago even the press have forgotten about it. Lachlan was the replacement child. As soon as he was born every photo, every bit of clothing or any toys that were Liam's were destroyed or given away. It was as if he had never existed.'

Angelo took her by the upper arms, his hold firm—almost painfully so. 'You were not to blame for Liam's death,' he said. 'You were a baby yourself. Your parents were wrong to lay that guilt on you.'

She looked into his dark brown eyes and saw comfort and understanding, not blame and condemnation. It made her eyes water uncontrollably. The tears came up from a well deep inside her. There was nothing she could do to hold them back. They bubbled up and spilled over in a gushing torrent. She hurtled forward into the wall of his chest, sobbing brokenly as his arms came around her and held her close.

'I tried to find him as soon as I noticed he wasn't beside me,' she said. 'It was barely a few seconds before I realised he was gone. I looked and looked around the gardens by the pool, but I didn't see him. He was at the bottom of the pool. I didn't see him. I didn't *see* him…'

'My poor little Tatty,' he soothed against her hair, rocking her gently with the shelter of his frame. 'You were not to blame, *cara*. You were not to blame.'

Natalie cried until she was totally spent. She told him other things as she hiccupped her way through another round of sobs. She told him of how she had seen Liam's tiny coffin being loaded on the plane. How the plane had hit some turbulence and how terrified she had been that his tiny body would be lost for ever. How she had sat in that wretched shuddering seat and wished she had been the one to drown. How her father had not said a word to her the whole way home. How her mother had sat in a blank state, drinking every drink the flight crew handed her.

She didn't know how much time passed before she eased back out of his hold and looked up at him through reddened and sore eyes. 'I must look a frightful mess,' she said.

He looked down at her with one of his warm and tender looks. 'I think you look beautiful.'

She felt a fresh wave of tears spouting like a fountain. 'You see?' she said as she brushed the back of her hand across her eyes. 'This is why I *never* cry. It's too damn hard to stop.'

He brushed the damp hair off her face, his gaze still meltingly soft. 'You can cry all you want or need to, *mia piccola*,' he said. 'There's nothing wrong with showing emotion. It's a safety valve, *si*? It's not good to suppress it for too long.'

She gave him a rueful look. 'You always were far better at letting it all hang out than me,' she said. 'It used to scare me a bit…how incredibly passionate you were.'

He stroked her hair back from her face. 'I seem to remember plenty of passion on your part too,' he said.

'Yes…well, you do seem to bring that out in me,' she said.

His hands slid down to hers, his fingers warm and protective as they wrapped around hers. 'I think it's high time you were tucked up in bed, don't you?'

Natalie shivered as his gaze communicated his desire for her. 'You want to…?'

He scooped her up in his arms. 'I want to,' he said, and carried her indoors.

Angelo lay awake once Natalie had finally dozed off. It had taken a while. In the quiet period after they had made love she had told him how today was the actual anniversary of her baby brother's death. It certainly explained her recent agitation and restlessness. He thought of her horrible nightmare the other night, how she had thrashed and turned and how worried he had been.

It all made sense now.

He still could not fathom why her parents had done such a heartless thing as to blame *her* for the tragic death of their little son. How could they have possibly expected a child of seven to be responsible enough to take care of a small child? It was unthinkably cruel to make her shoulder the blame. Why had they done it? What possible good did they think it would do to burden her with what was essentially their responsibility?

And where had the resort staff been?

Why hadn't Adrian Armitage aimed his guilt-trip on them instead of his little daughter?

His gut churned with the anguish of what she must have faced. Why had she not told him before now? It hurt him to think she had kept that dark secret from him. He had loved her so passionately. He would have given her the world and yet she had not let him into her heart.

Until now.

But she hadn't told him because she had trusted him. He had *forced* it out of her.

He picked up her left hand and rolled the pad of his thumb over the rings he had made her wear.

He had sought revenge, but it wasn't as sweet as he had thought. He hadn't had all the facts on the table. How differently would he have acted if he had known?

His insides clenched with guilt. He had railroaded her into marriage, not stopping to think of the reasons why she had balked at it in the first place. He had not taken the time to understand her, to find the truth about why she was so prickly and defensive. He had not made enough of an effort to get to know her beyond the physical. He had allowed his lust for her to colour everything else.

He had listened to those barefaced lies from her father. Listened and believed them. How could he ever make it up to her? How could he show her there was a way through this if only she trusted and leaned on him?

Or was it already too late to turn things around?

Angelo brought in a tray with coffee and rolls the next morning and set it down beside her. She opened her eyes and sat up, pushing her hair out of her face. 'I don't expect you to wait on me,' she said.

'It's no bother,' he said. 'I was up anyway.'

She took the cup of coffee he had poured for her. 'Thanks,' she said after a little pause.

'You're welcome.'

'I meant about last night,' she said, biting her lip.

Angelo sat on the edge of the bed near her thighs and took one of her hands in his. 'Would you have eventually told me, do you think?'

She lifted one shoulder up and down. 'Maybe—' She twisted her mouth. 'Probably not.'

'I've been thinking about your parents,' he said. 'I'd like to meet with them to talk through this.'

She pulled her hand out of his. 'No.'

'Natalie, this can't go on—'

'No.' Her slate blue eyes collided with his. 'I don't want you to try and fix things. You can't fix this.'

'Look, I understand this is a painful thing for all of you, but it's not fair that you've been carrying this guilt for so long,' he said. 'Your parents need to face up to their part in it.'

She put her coffee cup down with a splash of the liquid over the sides and slid out of the bed. She roughly wrapped herself in a robe and then turned and glared at him. 'If you approach my parents I will *never* forgive you,' she said. 'My mother has enough to deal with. It will destroy her if this is dragged up again. She's barely holding on as it is. And if this gets out in the press it will jeopardise Lachlan's recovery for sure.'

'I'm concerned about you—not your mother or brother,' he said.

'If you're truly concerned about me then you'll do what I ask.'

Angelo frowned. 'Why are you so determined to take the rap for something that was clearly not your fault?'

'It *was* my fault,' she said. 'I was supposed to be watching him.'

'You were a *child*, Natalie,' he said. 'A child of seven should not be left in charge of a toddler—especially around water. How would you have got him out even if you had seen him in time?'

Her features gave a spasm of pain. 'I would have jumped in and helped him.'

'And very likely drowned as well,' he said. 'You were too young to do anything.'

'I could've thrown him something to hold on to until help came,' she said, her eyes glittering with unshed tears.

'*Cara*,' he said, taking a step towards her.

'No,' she said, holding him off with her hands held up like twin stop signs. 'Don't come near me.'

He ignored her and put his hands on her shoulders. She began to push against his chest but somehow as he

pulled her closer and she gripped his shirt instead. He
brought his head down to hers, taking his time to give
her time to escape if she wanted to.

'Don't fight me, *mia piccola*,' he said. 'I'm not your
enemy.'

'I'm not fighting you,' she said, her gaze locked on
his mouth. 'I'm fighting myself.'

He brushed her mouth with his thumb. 'That's what
I thought.'

She gave him a rueful look. 'I can't seem to help
myself.'

'You know something?' he said. 'Nor can I.' And
then he covered her mouth with his.

CHAPTER NINE

A FEW days later Natalie was wandering around the renovation site of Angelo's hotel development, taking copious notes and snapping photographs as she went along. It was a spectacular development—a wonderful and decadent mix between a boutique hotel and a luxury health spa. Gold and polished marble adorned every surface. Tall arched windows looked out over the sea, or lemon groves and steep hills beyond framed the view. She couldn't believe he was giving her the work. It was a dream job. It would stretch her creatively, but it would springboard her to the heights of interior design.

'Are you nearly done?' Angelo asked as he joined her, after speaking to one of his foremen.

'Are you kidding?' she said. 'I've barely started. This place is amazing. I have so many ideas my head is buzzing.'

He put a gentle hand on the nape of her neck, making an instant shiver course down her spine. 'I don't want you to work too hard,' he said. 'We're supposed to be on honeymoon, remember?'

How could she forget? Her body was still humming with the aftershocks of his passionate possession first thing that morning.

Over the last few days Angelo had been incredibly

tender with her. She was finding it harder and harder to keep her emotions in check. He was unravelling her bit by bit, taking down her defences with every kiss and caress. The same blistering passion was there, but with it was a new element that took their lovemaking to a different level—one she had not experienced with him before. She wasn't ready to admit she loved him. Not even to herself. She knew she admired and respected him. She liked being with him and enjoyed being challenged by his quick intellect and razor-sharp wit.

But as for being in love…well, what was the point of even going there? She could not stay with him for ever. He had already told her what he wanted. He would not choose her over his desire for heirs.

'You have a one-track mind, Angelo,' she said in mock reproach.

He smiled a lazy smile and pressed a kiss to her bare shoulder. 'Are you going to deny you weren't just thinking about what we got up to this morning?' he asked.

Her belly shifted like a drawer pulled out too quickly as she thought of how he had made her scream with pleasure. 'Stop it,' she said in an undertone. 'The workmen will hear you.'

'So what if they do?' he said, nibbling on her earlobe. 'I am a man in love with his wife. Am I not allowed to tell the world?'

Natalie stiffened and pulled away. 'I think I'm just about done here,' she said. 'I can come back another time.'

'What's wrong?'

'Nothing.'

'You're shutting me out,' he said. 'I can see it in your face. It's like a drawbridge suddenly comes up.'

'You're imagining it,' she said, closing her notebook with a little snap.

'I won't let you do this, Tatty,' he said. 'I won't let you pull away. That's not how this relationship is going to work.'

She sent him a crystal-hard little glare. 'How *is* this relationship going to work, Angelo?' she asked. 'You want what I can't give you.'

'Only because you're determined to keep on punishing yourself,' he said. 'You want the same things I want. I know you do. Do you think I don't know you by now? I saw the way you looked at that mother and baby when we had coffee in that café yesterday.'

Natalie gave one of her *faux* laughs. 'I was looking at that mother in pity,' she said. 'Did you hear how loudly that brat was crying? It was disturbing everyone.'

'I saw your eyes,' he said. 'I saw the longing.'

She turned and began to stalk away. 'I don't have to listen to this.'

'There we go,' he said, with cutting sarcasm. 'And right on schedule too. Your stock standard phrase makes yet another appearance. I'm sick to death of hearing it.'

She turned back and looked at him. 'Then why don't you send me on my way so you don't have to listen to it any more?' she asked.

His eyes wrestled with hers, dark and glittering with frustration and anger. 'You'd like that, wouldn't you?' he said. 'You'd like to be let off the emotional hook. But I'm not going to do it. You will be with me until the day I say you can finally go.'

'I'm going back to the villa,' she said with a veiled look. 'That is if that's all right with you?'

He sucked in a harsh breath and brushed past her. 'Do what you like,' he said, and left.

* * *

When Natalie came downstairs at the villa a couple of hours later Angelo was on the phone. He signalled for her to wait for him to finish. He was speaking to someone in rapid-fire Italian, his full-bodied accent reminding her all over again of how much she had always loved his voice. It was so rich and deep, so sexy and masculine it made the skin on her arms and legs tingle.

'Sorry about that,' he said, pocketing his phone. 'I have a development in Malaysia that is proving a little troublesome. The staff member I sent over is unable to fix it. I have to go over and sort it out.'

She set her features stubbornly, mentally preparing for another battle of wills. 'I hope you're not expecting me to come with you,' she said. 'I have my own business interests to see to. I can't be on holiday for ever.'

His expression was hard to read. 'I have made arrangements for you to travel back to Edinburgh this evening,' he said. 'I will fly to Kuala Lumpur first thing tomorrow morning.'

The air dropped out of her self-righteous sails. She stood there feeling strangely abandoned, cast adrift and frightened. 'I see…'

'I'll fly to London with you,' he said. 'I'm afraid I haven't got time to do the Edinburgh leg, but one of my staff will go with you instead.'

'I don't need you to hold my hand,' she said with a hoist of her chin.

His dark brown eyes held hers in that knowing way of his. 'You'd better pack your things,' he said. 'We have to leave in an hour.'

The journey to London was surprisingly not as bad as Natalie had been expecting. Her anger at Angelo was enough of a distraction to keep her from dwelling on her fear. He hardly said a word on the flight. Once he had made sure she was comfortable he had buried his head in some paperwork and architectural plans and barely taken a break for coffee or a bite to eat.

Once they landed he introduced her to his staff member, and with a brief kiss to her mouth was gone.

Natalie watched him stride away as if he had just dumped a particularly annoying parcel at the post office and couldn't wait to get on with his day.

'This way, *Signora* Bellandini,' Riccardo said, leading the way to the gate for her flight to Edinburgh.

'It's Ms Armitage,' she insisted.

Riccardo looked puzzled. 'But you are married to *Signor* Bellandini now, *si*?'

'Yes, but that doesn't mean I no longer cease to exist,' she said and, hitching her bag over her shoulder, marched towards the gate.

Natalie was at her studio a couple of days later, leafing through the paper while she had a kick-start coffee before she opened the doors to her clients. Her eyes zeroed in on a photograph in the international gossip section. It was of Angelo, with his hand on the back of a young raven-haired woman as he led her into a plush hotel in Kuala Lumpur. The caption read: *'Honeymoon Over for Italian Tycoon?'*

A dagger of pain plunged through her, leaving her cold and sick and shaking. Nausea bubbled up in her throat—a ghastly tide of bile that refused to go back down. She stumbled to the bathroom at the rear of the office and hunched over the basin, retching until it was all gone. She clung to the basin with white-knuckled hands, clammy sweat breaking over her brow.

'Are you all right?' Linda's concerned voice sounded outside the door.

'I—I'm fine,' Natalie said hoarsely. 'Just a bit of an upset tummy.'

When she came out of the bathroom Linda was holding the newspaper. 'You know the press makes half of this stuff up to sell papers, don't you?' she said, with a worried look that belied her pragmatic claim.

'Of course,' Natalie said, wishing in this case it were true. How stupid had she been to think Angelo was starting to care about her? He had been playing her like a fool from day one. Reeling her in bit by bit, getting her to pour her darkest secrets out to him and then, when she was at her most vulnerable, swooping in and chopping her off at the knees with his cold-hearted perfidy.

Was this how her mother felt every time her father found a new mistress? How did she stand it? The emotional brutality of it was crucifying.

How could Angelo do this to her? Did he want revenge so much? Didn't the last week mean a thing to him? Had it all been nothing but a ruse to get her to let her guard down? How could he be so cold and calculating?

Easily.

He had never forgiven her for walking out on him. Her rejection of him had simmered for five years, burning and roiling deep inside him like lava building and bubbling up in a long-dormant volcano. He had waited patiently until the time was ripe to strike.

It hurt to think how easily she had been duped. How had she allowed him to do that to her? What had happened to her determination to keep her heart untouched?

Her heart felt as if it had been pummelled, bludgeoned. Destroyed.

'Do you know who the woman is?' Linda asked.

'No,' Natalie said tightly. 'And I don't care.'

'Maybe she's his assistant,' Linda offered.

Assisting him with what? Natalie thought as jealousy stung her with its deadly venom. Her mind filled with images of him in that wretched hotel with his beautiful 'assistant'. Their limbs entangled in a big bed, his body splayed over hers, giving the raven-haired beauty the pleasure it had so recently given *her*.

'Are you all right?' Linda asked again.

'Excuse me…' Natalie raced back to the bathroom.

When Natalie got home after work she wasn't feeling much better. Her head was pounding and her stomach felt as if it had been scraped raw with a grater.

She hadn't heard from Angelo—not that she expected him to contact her. No doubt he would be too busy with his gorgeous little dark-haired assistant. Her stomach pitched again and she put a hand on it to settle it, tears suddenly prickling at the backs of her eyes.

Her phone rang from inside her bag and she fished it out. Checking the caller ID, she pressed the answer button. 'How nice of you to call me, my darling husband,' she said with saccharine-sweet politeness. 'Are you sure you've got the time?'

'You saw the picture.'

Her hand tightened around the phone. 'The *whole world* saw the picture,' she said. 'Who is she? Is she your mistress?'

'Don't be ridiculous, Tatty.'

'Don't you *dare* call me that!' she shouted at him. 'You heartless bastard. How could you do this to me?'

'*Cara.*' His voice gentled. 'Calm down and let me explain.'

'Go on, then,' she challenged him. 'I bet you've already thought up a very credible excuse for why you had your hand on that woman's back as you led her into your hotel for a bit of rest and recreation. And I bet there was more recreation than rest.'

'You're jealous.'

'I am *not* jealous,' she said. 'I just don't like being made a fool of publically. You could have at least warned me this was how you were going to play things. I should've known you would have a double standard. One rule for me, a separate one for you. Men like you disgust me.'

'Her name is Paola Galanti and she's a liaison officer with my Malaysian construction team,' he said. 'She is having some difficulty dealing with a very male-dominated work environment.'

'Oh, so big tough Angelo had to come to her rescue?' Natalie put in scathingly. 'Another damsel in distress to rescue and seduce.'

'Will you stop it, for God's sake?' he said. 'Paola is engaged to a friend of mine. I have never been involved with her.'

'Why didn't you tell me your staff member was female when you told me you had to fly over there?' she asked.

'Because her gender has nothing to do with her position on my staff.'

'You still could have told me, rather than let me find out like that in the press,' she said, still bristling with resentment.

'Thus speaks the woman who didn't tell me a thing about her past until I dragged it out of her.'

Natalie flinched at his bitter tone. She bit her lip and

wondered if she was overreacting. Could she trust him? Could she trust anyone?

Could she trust herself?

'Fine,' she said. 'So now we're even.'

She heard him release a heavy sigh. 'Life is not a competition, Natalie.'

'When are you coming back?' she asked, after a tiny tense silence.

'I'm not sure,' he said, sighing again. 'I have a few meetings to get through. There's a hold-up with some materials for the hotel I'm building. It's all turning out to be one big headache.'

She suddenly thought of him all the way over there, in a steamy hot climate, dealing with language barriers and a host of other difficulties on the top of a decent dose of jet lag. How on earth did he do it? He ran not only his own company but a big proportion of his father's as well. So many people to deal with, so many expectations, so much responsibility.

'You sound tired,' she said.

'You sound like a loving wife.'

She stiffened. 'I can assure you I am nothing of the sort.'

'Missing me, *cara*?'

'Hardly.'

'Liar.'

'OK, I miss the sex,' she said, knowing it would needle him. Let him think that was all she cared about.

'I miss it too,' he said, in a low deep tone that sent a rolling firework of sensation down her spine. 'I can't wait to get home to show you how much.'

She felt the clutch of her inner muscles as if they were already twanging in anticipation. She tried to keep her voice steady, but it quavered just a fraction in spite of her efforts. 'I guess I'll have to be patient until then, won't I?'

'I bought you something today,' he said. 'It should arrive tomorrow.'

'You don't have to buy me presents,' she said, thinking of all the gold and diamonds her father had given her mother over the years—presumably to keep his guilt in check. 'I can buy my own jewellery.'

'It's not jewellery,' he said.

'What is it, then?'

'You'll have to wait and see.'

'Flowers? Chocolates?'

'No, not flowers or chocolates,' he said. 'What time will you be at home? I'm not sure the studio is the right place to have it delivered to.'

Natalie felt curiosity building in spite of her determination not to be out-manoeuvred by him. 'I'm working from home all day tomorrow,' she said. 'I have some design work to do on my next collection. I usually do that at home because I get interrupted too much at the studio.'

'Good,' he said. 'I'll make sure it arrives early.'

'Will you at least give me a clue?'

'I have to go,' he said. 'I'll call you tomorrow evening. *Ciao.*'

She didn't even get a chance to reply as he had already ended the call.

The doorbell rang at nine-fifteen. Natalie answered its summons to find a courier standing there, with a small pet carrier in one hand and a clipboard with paperwork in the other.

'Ms Armitage?' he said with a beaming smile. 'I have a special delivery for you. Could you sign here, please?' He handed her the clipboard with a pen on a string attached.

She took the pen and clipboard after a moment's hesitation. She scribbled her signature and then handed it back. 'What is it?' she asked, eyeing the carrier with a combination of delight and dread.

'It's a puppy,' the courier said, handing the carrier over. 'Enjoy.'

Natalie shut the door once he had left. The pet carrier was rocking as the little body inside wriggled and yelped in glee.

'I swear to God I'm going to kill you, Angelo Bellandini,' she said as she put it down on the floor.

She caught sight of a pair of eyes as shiny as dark brown marbles looking at her through the holes in the carrier and her heart instantly melted. Her fingers fumbled over the latch in her haste to get it open.

'Oh, you darling little thing!' she gushed as a furry black ball hurtled towards her, yapping excitedly, its tiny curly tail going nineteen to the dozen. She scooped the puppy up and it immediately went about licking her face with endearing enthusiasm. 'Stop!' she said, giggling as her cheek got a swipe of a raspy tongue. 'Stop, *stop*, you mad little thing. What on earth am I going to do with you?'

The puppy gave a little yap and looked at her quizzically with its head on one side, its button eyes shining with love and adoration.

Natalie felt a rush of nurturing instinct so strong it almost knocked her backwards. She cuddled the little puppy close against her chest and instantly, irrevocably, fell head over heels in love.

* * *

Angelo checked the time difference before he called. He'd had a pig of a day. His meetings hadn't gone the way he would have liked. He was finding it hard to focus on the task at hand. All he could think about was how much he missed Natalie.

Business had never seemed so tedious. He wasn't sure how it had happened, but in the last week or so making money had become secondary to making her happy. He wanted to see her smile. He wanted to hear her laugh. He wanted to see her enjoy life. God knew she hadn't enjoyed it before now. He wanted to change that for her, but she was so damned determined to punish herself. He still hadn't given up on the idea of confronting her parents. How could she ever be truly free from guilt unless they accepted their part in the tragic death of their son?

He pressed her number on his phone, but after a number of rings it went through to voicemail. He frowned as he put the phone down on his desk. Disappointment weighed him down like fatigue from a fever. His whole day had revolved around this moment and now she hadn't picked up.

He was halfway through a mind-numbing report on one of his father's speculative investments when his phone started jumping around his desk. He reached out and picked it up, smiling when he saw it was Natalie calling him back.

'How's the baby?' he asked.

'She peed on the rug in my sitting room,' she said, 'and on the one in my bedroom, and on the absolutely priceless one in the hall. She would've done worse on the one in the study, but I caught her just in time.'

'Oh, dear,' he said. 'I guess she'll get the hang of things eventually.'

'She's chewed a pair of designer shoes and my sunglasses,' she said. 'Oh, and did I mention the holes in the garden? She's been relocating my peonies.'

Angelo leaned back against his leather chair. 'Sounds like you've had a busy day.'

'She's mischievous and disobedient,' she said. 'Right at this very minute she is chewing the cables on my computer. Hey—stop that, Molly. *Bad* girl. Mummy is cross with you. No, don't look at me like that.' Natalie gave a little tinkling bell laugh—a sound he had never heard her make before. 'I *am* cross. I really am.'

He smiled as he heard an answering yap. 'You called her Molly?'

'Yes,' she said wryly. 'Somehow Fido or Rover doesn't quite suit her.'

'But of course,' he said. 'She comes from a pedigree as long as your arm. Both her father and mother were Best in Show.'

There was a little silence.

'Why a puppy?' she asked.

'I'm away a lot,' he said. 'I thought the company would be nice.'

'I have a career,' she said. 'I have a business to run. I haven't got the time to train a puppy. I've never had a dog before. I have no idea what to do. What if something happens to her?'

'Nothing will happen to her, Tatty,' he said. 'Not while you're taking care of her.'

'What about work?' she asked. 'I can't leave her alone all day.'

'So take her with you,' he said. 'It's your studio. You're the boss. You can do what you like.'

Another silence.

'When will you be back?' she asked.

'I'm not sure,' he said. 'Things aren't working out the way I want over here.'

'How is your assistant?'

'Tucked up in bed with her fiancé,' he said. 'I flew him out to be with her.'

'That was thoughtful of you.'

'Practical rather than thoughtful,' he said. 'She was missing him and he was missing her.'

A longer silence this time.

'Angelo?'

'Yes, *cara*?'

'Thank you for not buying me jewellery.'

'You're the only woman I know who would say that,' Angelo said. 'I thought diamonds were supposed to be a girl's best friend?'

'Not this girl.'

'You're going to have to let me buy you some eventually,' he said. 'I don't want people to think I'm too tight to spoil my beautiful wife with lavish gifts.'

'Being generous with money and gifts is not a sign of a happy relationship,' she said. 'My mother is dripping in diamonds and she's absolutely miserable.'

'Why doesn't she leave your father if she's so unhappy?'

'Because he's rich and successful and she can't bear the thought of going back to being a nobody,' she said. 'She's a trophy wife. She's not his soul mate and he isn't hers. By marrying him she gave up her name and her identity. She's an effigy of who she used to be.'

Angelo was starting to see where Natalie's stubborn streak of independence stemmed from. She was terrified of ending up like her mother—bound to a man who had all the power and all the influence. No wonder she had run at the first hint of marriage from him. No wonder she had fought him tooth and nail when he'd blackmailed her back into his life. He had unknowingly sabotaged his own happiness and hers by forcing her to marry him.

'It doesn't have to be that way between us, Tatty,' he said. 'Relationships are not inherited. We create them ourselves.'

'You created this one, not me,' she said. 'I'm just the meat in the sandwich, remember?'

'Even if Lachlan hadn't provided me with the opportunity to get you back in my life I truly believe I would have found some other way,' he said. 'I'd been thinking of it for months.'

'Why?'

'I think you know why.'

There was another little beat of silence.

'I have to go,' she said. 'Molly is running off with a pen. I don't want ink to get on the rug. Bye.'

Angelo put his phone down and let out a long sigh. His relationship with Natalie was a two steps forward three steps back affair that left both of them frustrated. Was it to late to turn things around? What did he have to do to prove to her he wanted this to work?

Would he have to let her go in order to have her return to him on her own terms?

CHAPTER TEN

A COUPLE of days later Natalie heard the deep throaty rumble of a sports car pulling up outside her house. She didn't have to check through the front window to see if it was Angelo. It wasn't the hairs standing up on the back of her neck that proved her instincts true but the little black ball of fluff that was jumping about, yapping in frenzied excitement at the front door.

She couldn't help smiling as she scooped Molly up in her arms and opened the door. 'Yes, I know,' she said. 'It's Daddy.'

Angelo reached for the puppy and was immediately subjected to a hearty welcome. He held the wriggling body aloft. 'I think she just peed on me,' he said, grimacing.

Natalie giggled. 'What do you expect?' she said. 'She's excited to see you.'

His dark eyes glinted as they met hers. 'And what about you, *cara*?' he asked. 'Are you excited to see me too?'

She felt her body tingle as his gaze read every nuance of her expression. She had no hope of hiding her longing from him. She didn't even bother trying. 'Do you want me to lick your face to prove it?' she asked.

'I can think of other places that would suit me much better,' he said.

An earthquake of need rumbled through her lower body. 'What about Molly?' she asked as he moved towards her.

'What *about* Molly?' he said as he released her hair from the knot she had tied on the back of her head.

'Don't you think she's a little young to be watching us…you know…doing it?'

'Good point,' he said, and scooped the puppy up in one hand. 'Where does she sleep?'

She chewed her lip. 'Um…'

He narrowed his eyes in mock reproach. 'You're not serious?'

'What was I supposed to do?' she asked. 'She cried for ages until I took her to bed with me. I felt sorry for her. She was missing her mum.'

He smiled indulgently and flicked her cheek with a gentle finger. 'Softie.'

'I told you I'd be a hopeless mum,' she said. 'I'd end up spoiling the kid rotten.'

'I think you'd make a terrific mother.'

She frowned and took the puppy from him. 'I'll put her in her carrier in the laundry…'

'Tatty?'

She stilled at the door. 'Don't do this, Angelo.'

'You can't keep avoiding the subject,' he said. 'It's an issue that's important to me.'

She turned around and glared at him. 'I know what you're doing,' she said. 'You thought by giving me a puppy to take care of it would magically fix things, didn't you? But I told you before. You can't fix this. You can't fix *me*. You can't fix the past.'

'How long are you going to keep punishing yourself?' he asked.

'I'm not punishing myself,' she said. 'I'm being realistic. I don't think I can handle being a parent. What if I turn out like my father? Having kids changes people. Some people can't handle it. They lose patience. They resent the loss of freedom and take it out on their kids.'

'You're nothing like your father,' he said. 'I find it hard to believe you are even related to him. He's nothing but an arrogant, selfish jerk. He doesn't deserve to have a daughter as beautiful and gentle and loving as you.'

Natalie felt a warm feeling inside her chest like bread dough expanding. She tried to push it down but it kept rising again.

She wanted to believe him.

She wanted it desperately. She wanted a future with him. She wanted to have his baby—more than one baby—*a family*. But the past still haunted her. Would there ever be a time when it wouldn't?

'I need more time…' she said, stroking the puppy's head as she cradled it against her. 'I'm not ready to make a decision like that just yet.'

He put his hands on her shoulders, his dark chocolate eyes meshing with hers. 'We'll talk about it some other time,' he said. 'In the meantime, I think Molly is just about asleep. It would be a shame not to make the most of the opportunity, *si*?'

She trembled with longing as he gently took the puppy from her and led her upstairs into a world of sensuality she was fast becoming addicted to.

How would she ever be able to survive without it?

Natalie was in the garden with Molly the following afternoon when Angelo came out to her.

'Look, Angelo,' she said excitedly. 'Molly has learned to shake hands. Watch. Shake, Molly. See? Isn't she clever?'

'Very.'

She swung her gaze to his but he was frowning. 'What's wrong?' she asked.

He paused for a moment as if searching for the right words. 'Your mother has been taken ill. She's in hospital. Your father just called.'

Natalie felt the hammer blow of her heart against her chest wall. 'Is she all right?'

'She has an acute case of pancreatitis,' he said. 'She's in intensive care.'

'I—I need to go to her.'

'I've already got my private jet on call at the airport,' he said. 'Don't waste time packing. I'll buy what you need when we get there.'

'But what about Molly?' she asked.

'We'll take her with us,' he said. 'I'll have one of my staff take care of her once we get there.'

The intensive care unit was full of desperately ill people, but none of them looked as bad as her mother—or so Natalie thought when she first laid eyes on her, hooked up to machines and wires.

'Oh, Mum,' she said, taking her mother's limp hand in hers. Tears blinded her vision and her chest ached as if someone seriously overweight was sitting on it.

'I've informed Lachlan,' Angelo said at her shoulder. 'I've sent a plane to collect him.'

She pressed her lips to her mother's cold limp hand. 'I'm sorry, Mum,' she said. 'I'm so sorry.'

Adrian Armitage came back in, after taking a call on his mobile out in the corridor. 'And so you should be,' he said with a contemptuous look. 'This is *your* fault. She wouldn't have taken up drinking if it hadn't been for you.'

Angelo stood between Natalie and her father. 'I think you'd better leave,' he said, in a voice that brooked no resistance.

Adrian gave him a disparaging look. 'She's got her claws into you well and good, hasn't she?' he said. 'I warned you about her. She's manipulative and sneaky. You're a damn fool for falling for it.'

'If you don't leave of your own free will then I will *make* you leave,' Angelo said, in the same cool and calm but unmistakably indomitable tone.

'She killed my son,' Adrian said. 'Did she tell you that? She was jealous of him, that's why. She knew I wanted a son more than a daughter. She killed him.'

'Natalie did not kill your son,' Angelo said. 'She was not responsible for Liam's death. She was just a child. She should never have been given the responsibility of watching over him. That was *your* job. I will not have you blame her for your own inadequacies as a parent.'

Natalie watched as her father's face became puce. 'You *dare* to question my ability as a parent?' he roared. 'That girl is a rebel. She's unmanageable. She won't give an inch. She's black to the heart.'

'That girl is *my wife*,' Angelo said with steely emphasis. 'Now, get out of here before I do something you will regret more than I ever will.'

'Mr Armitage?' One of the doctors had appeared. 'I think it's best if you leave. Come this way, please.'

Angelo's concerned gaze came to Natalie's. 'Are you all right, *cara*?' he asked, touching her cheek with a gentle finger.

'I've always known he hated me,' she said on a

ragged sigh. 'It's true what he said...I overheard him blasting my mother about it when I was about five or so. He wanted a son first. That's why I always felt I wasn't good enough. It didn't matter how hard I tried or how well behaved I was or how well I did at school, I could never be the son he wanted. And then when Liam died... well, that was the end of any hope of ever pleasing him.'

'Some people should never be parents,' he said with a furious look. 'I can't believe how pathetic your father is. He's a coward—a bully and a coward. I don't want you to ever be alone with him. Do you understand?'

Natalie felt another piece of her armour fall away. 'I understand.'

His fierce expression relaxed into tenderness as he cupped her cheek. 'I'm sorry I didn't know what your childhood was like, and even more sorry that you didn't feel you could tell me,' he said. 'The clues were all there but I just didn't see them.'

'I once told a family friend about my father's treatment of me,' she said in a quiet voice. 'It got back to my father. My mother...' She swallowed tightly over the memory. 'My mother drank really badly after that.' She looked back at her mother and gave another sigh. 'I don't want to lose her. I know she's not perfect, but I don't want to lose her.'

He put his hand over hers and squeezed it tightly. 'Then I'll move heaven and earth to make sure you don't.'

Natalie looked physically shattered by the time Angelo escorted her out of the hospital. Her mother showed some signs of improvement, but it was still too early to tell if the severe bout of pancreatitis would settle. The

doctors had told them her mother would not live much
longer unless she gave up drinking.

He put his arm around Natalie's waist as he led her
out to the car he had organised. 'Lachlan should be
here in the morning,' he said. 'In the meantime I think
you should try and get as much rest as you can. You
look exhausted.'

'I don't know how to thank you for everything you've
done,' she said. 'You've been…amazing.'

He put an arm around her shoulders and drew her
into his body. 'Isn't it about time someone stood up for
you?' he said.

'Funny that it's you.'

'Why is that?' he asked.

She gave a little shrug. 'I just thought you'd be the
last person to take my side.'

He pressed a kiss to the top of her head. 'Then you
don't know me all that well, do you?'

Angelo took her to his house in Mayfair. It was an
immaculately presented four-storey mansion, with beautiful gardens in front as well as behind. Wealth and
status oozed from every corner of the building, both
inside and out.

Natalie looked around even though she was almost
dead on her feet. 'This is certainly a long way from that
run down flat we shared in Notting Hill,' she said, once
she had inspected every nook and cranny.

'I liked that flat.'

She gave him a wistful smile. 'Yes, I did too.'

'Come here.'

She came and stood in the circle of his arms. 'You'd
better not tell my twenty-one-year old self about this,'
she said. 'She would be furious with me for obeying
your command as if I had no mind of my own.'

He smiled as he gathered her close. 'I won't tell her if you won't.'

She nestled up against him, loving the warmth and comfort and shelter of his body. She felt like a little beat-up dinghy that had finally found safe harbour during a tempestuous storm.

If only she could stay here for ever.

Over the next few days Natalie's mother improved enough to be moved to the private clinic Angelo had organised. Many years of heavy drinking had caused some serious liver damage. It would be a long road to recovery and, while her mother seemed ready to take the first tentative steps, Natalie wasn't keen to put any money on her succeeding. She had seen her mother's attempts to become sober too many times to be confident that this time would be any different.

Lachlan was another story. He seemed determined to get well, and had asked Angelo to send him back to Portugal once he was sure their mother was out of danger. He had started to talk to counsellors about his childhood; about the impossible burden it was to be the replacement child. Natalie could only hope this would be the turning point he needed to get his life back on track.

She hadn't seen her father since Angelo had spoken to him at the hospital. She suspected he was worried about running into Angelo again. It seemed pathetically cowardly to stop visiting his wife just to protect himself, but then, she wouldn't be able to bear to watch him pretending to be a loving, concerned husband when she had personally witnessed all his hateful behaviour over the years that told another story.

On the afternoon when Angelo took Lachlan to the

airport Natalie sat with her mother in the sun room at the clinic. She had brought Molly along, hoping it would lift her mother's spirits, but Isla barely gave the puppy a glance.

'I wonder when your father's coming in?' she asked, checking her watch for the tenth time. 'He hasn't been to see me since I came here.'

Natalie felt frustrated that her mother couldn't or wouldn't see that her father was only concerned about himself. 'Mum, why do you put up with him?' she asked.

'What are you talking about?' Isla said. 'What do you mean?'

'He treats you like rubbish,' Natalie said. 'He's always treated you like rubbish.'

'I know you don't understand, but I'm happy enough with my lot,' her mother said. 'He's a good provider. I don't ever have to worry about working. I have the sort of lifestyle other people only dream of having.'

'Mum, you could divorce him and still be well provided for,' Natalie said. 'You don't have to put up with his bullying.'

'He wasn't always difficult,' Isla said. 'It was better in the early days. It was a dream come true when he asked me to marry him after I found out I was pregnant. We were both so certain you were going to be a boy. I even bought all blue clothes. I was happy to have a daughter, but your father took it very hard. He got better after Liam was born. But then...'

Natalie's eyes watered and her throat went tight. It was always the same. The same wretched anguish, the same crushing guilt. Would there ever be a time when she would be able to move on without it?

'I'm sorry...'

Isla checked her watch again. 'Do you think you could call the nurse for me?' she said. 'I want to go home. I'm sick of being here.'

'Mum, how can you think of leaving?' Natalie asked. 'You're supposed to stay on the program for at least a month.'

Her mother reached past Natalie to press the buzzer for the nurse. 'I belong at home with your father,' she said with an intractable look. 'I don't belong here.'

Angelo pulled up just as Natalie came out of the clinic. She had a deep frown on her forehead and her gait was jerky, as if she was terribly upset and trying her best to hide it. It amazed him how easily he could read her now. It was as if a curtain had come up in his brain. He could sense her mood from the way she carried herself. The very times she needed support she pushed him away. She got all prickly and defensive. He could see her doing it now.

He got out of the car and held open the door for her. 'What's wrong?' he asked, taking the wriggling puppy from her.

'Nothing.'

'Hey,' he said, capturing her chin and making her look at him. 'What's going on?'

Her eyes looked watery, as if she was about to cry. 'I really don't want to talk about it,' she said.

'Tatty, we *have* to talk about things,' he said. 'Especially things that upset us. It's what well-functioning couples do. I don't want any more secrets between us.'

'My mother is going to check herself out,' she said in a defeated tone. 'I can't stop her. I can't fix this. I can't fix her. I can't fix *any* of this.'

He brushed the hair back from her face. 'It's not your mess to fix.'

'I can't believe she thinks more of her position in society than her well-being,' she said. 'She doesn't love my father. She loves what he can give her. How can she live like that?'

'Some people want different things in life,' he said. 'You have to accept that. It doesn't mean you're going to be like that. You have the choice to do things differently.'

She was silent as he helped her in the car. She sat with Molly on her lap, her hands gently stroking her ears, her expression still puckered by a little frown.

'I'm sorry my family's dramas have taken up so much of your time,' she said after a long pause.

'It's not a problem,' Angelo said. 'What about your work? Is there anything I can do to help?'

'No, I've got everything under control,' she said. 'Linda is working on a few things for me. She's really excited about the Sorrento project. I e-mailed her the photos.'

'I know you'll do an amazing job,' he said. 'And my mother is excited about you helping her with the villa at home. It's her birthday next weekend. My father is bringing her to London to go to the theatre. They'd like to have a little celebration with us. You don't have to do anything. I'll get my housekeeper Rosa to prepare everything.'

She gave him a little smile that faded almost as soon as it appeared. 'I'll look forward to it.'

Angelo's parents arrived at his Mayfair house on Friday evening. Natalie had made up a collection of her linens for his mother as a present, but it was Molly that most interested Francesca.

They had barely come through the door when she scooped Molly out of Natalie's arms. 'Come to Nonna,' she said with a beaming smile. 'You will be good training for me, *si*? I can't wait to be a grandmother. I've already bought a new cot for Angelo's old nursery. It will be the first room you can help me redecorate, Natalie. I am so looking forward to it.'

Natalie felt her heart jerk in alarm. She glanced at Angelo, but he was smiling as if nothing was wrong. She felt the walls closing in on her. She felt claustrophobic. Panic rose inside her. She felt it spreading, making her head tight and her stomach churn.

'Got to keep the Bellandini line going,' Sandro said, with a teasing glint in his eye.

'Give us time,' Angelo said with an amused laugh. 'We've barely come off our honeymoon.'

'What if I don't want a baby?' Natalie said.

It was as if she had suddenly announced she had a bomb ticking inside her handbag. Sandro and Francesca stared at her with wide eyes and even wider mouths.

Francesca was the first to speak. 'But surely you can't be serious?'

Natalie tried to ignore Angelo's dark gaze. 'I'm not sure I want children.'

Francesca's face collapsed in dismay. 'But we've longed for grandchildren for years and years,' she said. 'I was only able to have one baby. I would have loved to have four or five. How can you not want to give Angelo a son?'

'Or a daughter,' Sandro said.

Angelo put his arm around Natalie's waist. 'This is a discussion Natalie and I should be having on our own.'

her backwards to the bed. He laid her down and began to rid himself of his clothes, all the while watching her with that slightly hooded I'm-about-to-make-love-to-you gaze of his.

'Aren't you going to take off your clothes?' he asked.

She gave him a sultry look. 'I don't know,' she said. 'Should I?'

'You'd better, if you still want them to be in one piece.'

A hot tingling sensation erupted between her thighs. 'This dress cost me a lot of money,' she said. 'I happen to love this dress.'

His eyes glittered as he came towards her. 'I love that dress too. But I think you look much better without it.'

Natalie shivered as he spun her around on the bed and released the zip at the back of her dress in one swift movement. Her bra and knickers were next, along with her shoes.

She tried to turn around but he laid a flat hand on her shoulder. 'Stay where you are,' he said.

She felt that delicious shiver again as his erection brushed against her bottom. It felt hard and very determined. She gave a little gasp as he entered her in a slick hard thrust that made every hair on her head tremble at the roots. He set a fast pace but she kept up with him. Each rocking movement of his hips, each stabbing thrust, sent another wave of pleasure through her. All her nerves were jumping in excitement. She felt the pressure building to a crescendo. Even the arches of her feet were tensed in preparation. Her orgasm was fast and furious. It rippled through her, making her shudder in ecstasy. He emptied himself with a powerful surge that sent another wave of pleasure through her.

But he wasn't finished with her yet.

He turned her and came down over her, his weight supported on one hand as he used the other to caress her intimately. She threw back her head and writhed in exquisite pleasure as he brought her to the brink before backing off again.

'Please,' she gasped as he ruthlessly continued the sweet torture.

'What do you want?' he asked.

'I want *you*.'

'How much?'

'Too much,' she gasped again.

'That makes two of us,' he said, and took her to paradise again.

Natalie stood beside Angelo as they farewelled his parents the following morning. Francesca and Santo each hugged her in turn, and on the surface they were as warm as ever, but she could tell they were struggling to accept the possibility that they would never hold a grandchild of their own in their arms.

Angelo took her hand as the driver pulled away from the kerb. 'I know what you're thinking.'

'They hate me.'

'They don't hate you.'

'I would hate me if I was them,' she said, pulling out of his hold and walking back inside.

'Tatty.'

She swung around to look at him once he had closed the front door. 'This is how it's going to be for the next however many years. Do you realise that, Angelo?' she asked. 'They're going to look at me with that crestfallen look, as if I've ruined both their lives.'

'You have not ruined anyone's life,' he said, blowing out a breath. 'They'll get used to it eventually.'

She felt a tight ache in her chest at how much he was giving up for her. She hadn't even told him she loved him. She wanted to, but it as if the words were trapped behind the wall of her guilt. She had bricked those three little words away and now she couldn't find them amongst the rubble of what used to be her heart.

'But will *you* get used to it?' she asked. 'What about in a couple of years? Five or ten? What about when all your friends have got kids? What if you hold someone else's baby in your arms and start to hate me?'

His expression tightened. 'I think we should shelve this topic until some other time.'

'Why is that?' she asked. 'Because I've touched on a nerve? Go on. Admit it. I've got you thinking about how it's going to be, haven't I?'

A muscle flickered at the corner of his mouth. 'You really are spoiling for a fight, aren't you?'

'I'm just trying to make sure you've looked at this from every angle.'

'You're the one who hasn't looked at this properly,' he bit back. 'Even now you're still punishing yourself for your brother's death, when it's obvious it's no one's fault but your parents'. They're totally inadequate, and always have been, and yet you continue to take the blame. You *have* to let it go, Tatty. You can't bring Liam back. You owe it to him to live a full life. I am sure if things were the other way around you would never have expected him to sacrifice his own happiness.'

She chewed at her lip. There was sense in what he was saying. She hadn't really thought about what Liam would have done if things were the other way around.

Angelo took her hand again and brought it up to his chest. 'Think about it, *cara*,' he said gently. 'What would Liam want you to do?'

Natalie thought of a newborn baby just like Isabel's. The sweet smell, the soft downy hair, the perfect little limbs and dimpled hands. She thought of a little baby that looked just like Angelo, with jet-black hair and chocolate-brown eyes. She thought of watching him or her grow up, each and every milestone celebrated with love and happiness. She thought of how the bond of a child would strengthen what Angelo already felt for her. Just having Molly had brought them closer. He was just as devoted to the little puppy as she was…

She suddenly frowned and glanced around her. 'Where's Molly?'

'She was here a minute ago,' Angelo said.

Natalie pushed past him. 'Molly?' She ran through the house, up and down the stairs, calling the puppy's name. There was no sign of her anywhere—just some of her toys: one of Angelo's old trainers and a squeaky plastic bone. She tried not to panic. She did all the self-talk she could think of on the hop.

Puppies were mischievous little things.

Perhaps Molly had found something new to chew and was keeping it to herself in a quiet corner.

Or maybe she was asleep somewhere and hadn't heard her name being called.

Puppies were either fully on or fully off.

Natalie came bolting back down the stairs just as Angelo was coming back through the front door. 'Have you found her?'

'She's not out on the street,' he said. 'I thought she might have slipped out when we were saying goodbye to my parents.'

'I can't find her.'

The words were a horrifying echo from the past. The gender had changed, but they brought up the very same gut wrenching panic. It roiled in her stomach like a butter churn going too fast. She felt her skin break out in a clammy sweat. Her heart hammered inside the scaffold of her ribs.

'I can't find her. I can't find her.'

'She's probably with Rosa in the kitchen,' Angelo said.

'I've already searched the kitchen,' she said. 'Rosa hasn't seen her.'

He reached for her arm to settle her. 'Tatty, for God's sake—stop worrying.'

Natalie wrenched her arm out of reach. Her heart felt as if it was going to burst through the wall of her chest. She could hardly breathe for the rising tide of despair and guilt.

It was her fault.

She couldn't even be trusted with a puppy. How on earth would she ever cope with a little baby?

'Tatty, calm down and—'

'Don't tell me to calm down!' she cried as she rushed out to the garden. Her lungs were almost bursting as she dashed along the flagstones to the lap pool in the garden.

The smell of chlorine sent her back in time.

She wasn't in the middle of London as a twenty-six-year-old. She was seven years old and she was in Spain and her little brother was missing. People were running about and shouting. Her father was shouting the loudest.

'Where is he? You were supposed to be watching him. *Where is he?*'

Her legs felt as if they were going to buckle beneath her. She couldn't speak for the thudding of her heart. Her skin was dripping in sweat. She could feel it tracking a pathway between her shoulderblades.

She ran along the edge of the pool, searching, searching, but there was no sign of a little body. There was nothing but a stray leaf floating on the surface.

She clutched at her head with both hands, trying to quell the sickening pounding of panic that had taken up residence inside. She was going to be sick. She felt the bubble of bile rise in her throat and only strength of will kept it down.

She had to find Liam. She had to find Liam. She had to find Liam.

'I've found her.'

Natalie's hands fell away from her head as Angelo appeared, carrying Molly in his arms. He was smiling as if her world hadn't completely shattered all over again.

'Here she is,' he said, holding her out to her.

She pushed the puppy away. 'No, take her away,' she said. 'I don't want her.'

Angelo frowned. '*Cara*, she's fine. She was in the wine cellar. Rosa must have accidentally locked her in when she put some new bottles down there a few minutes ago.'

Natalie tried to get her breathing back under control but she was still stuck in the past. All she could think of was her brother's limp little body being lifted from the pool. She could still hear the sound of water dripping from his shorts, from the T-shirt with the yellow lion on the front. She could hear it landing on the concrete.

She could still feel the accusing glare of the sun. It seemed to shine down on her like a scorching spotlight.

Your fault. Your fault. Your fault.

'Tatty?'

She looked at Angelo and suddenly it was all too

much. She had to get away. She could *not* do this. She could not be here.

'I have to leave,' she said. 'I can't do this any more.'

'Don't do this to me a second time, Tatty.'

'I have to do it,' she said tears welling in her eyes. 'I don't belong in your life. I can't give you what you want. I just can't.'

'We can work through this,' he said.

'*I* can't work through this!' She shouted the words at him as she teetered on the edge of hysteria. 'I can *never* work through this.'

'Yes, you can,' he said. 'We'll do it together.'

She shook her head at him. 'It's over, Angelo.'

His mouth pulled tight. 'You're running away.'

'I'm not running away,' she said. 'I'm taking control of my life. You forced me to come back to you. I didn't have a choice.'

His jaw locked. 'I can still send Lachlan to jail.'

She looked at him, with the puppy snuggled protectively against his chest. 'You're not going to do that,' she said. 'You were never going to do that. I *know* you, Angelo.'

'If you know me so well then you'll know if you walk out now I will never take you back,' he said through tight lips.

She felt the ache of losing him for ever settle like a weight inside her chest. It pulled on every organ painfully, torturously. 'I'm not coming back,' she said.

'Go, then,' he said, his expression closing like a fist.

It was the hardest thing she had ever done to turn and walk away from him. She put one foot in front of the other and willed herself to walk forward while everything in her protested.

Don't go. He loves you. He loves you no matter what.

This is the only chance you'll have at happiness. How can you walk away from it?

She allowed herself one last look as she walked out through the front door a few minutes later, bag packed, flight to Edinburgh booked. He was standing with Molly, who was struggling to break free from his arms and go to her. He had an unreadable expression on his face, but she could see the hint of moisture in his eyes.

She walked out of the door and closed it with a soft little click that broke her heart.

CHAPTER ELEVEN

'I HEAR Angelo's got a new lady-friend,' Linda said about a month later as she leafed through one of the gossip magazines during lunch.

Natalie felt a dagger of pain stab her, but she affected an uninterested expression as she put her untouched sushi in the little fridge. 'Good for him.'

'She looks pretty young,' Linda said. 'And she kind of looks like you. She looks devoted to the puppy. Here—have a look.'

Natalie pushed the magazine aside. 'I have work to do, and so do you.'

Linda pouted. 'Yeah, well, we'd have a lot more work to do if you hadn't quit on Angelo's Sorrento deal. Why would you let personal stuff get in the way of gazillions of pounds?'

Natalie gritted her teeth. 'I need to move on with my life.'

'Seems to me you can't really do that until you put the past behind you,' Linda said. She waited a beat before adding, 'Lachlan told me.'

Natalie frowned. 'You were speaking to Lachlan?'

'He calls me now and again to see how you're doing,' she said. 'He kind of told me about…everything. You know—about your little brother and all.'

'He had no right to talk to you about me.'

'He's worried about you,' Linda said. 'It sounds like he's got his stuff pretty much sorted. He thinks it's time you put your ghosts to rest, so to speak.'

'I've got my stuff sorted.'

'Yeah, so why are you so miserably unhappy?' Linda asked. 'You mope around with no energy. You don't eat. You look like you don't sleep.'

'I'm fine,' Natalie said, willing herself to believe it.

'Why don't you take a few days off?' Linda suggested. 'I've got things under control here. Kick back and have a think about things.'

'I have nothing to think about.'

Linda lifted one neat eyebrow. 'Are you sure about that?'

Natalie blew out a breath and finally came to a decision. She had been mulling it over for days. It would be Liam's birthday in a couple of days. She could at least put some flowers on his grave while she was there.

'I need to visit my parents,' she said. 'I won't be away long—just a day or two.'

'Take all the time you need,' Linda said, closing the magazine.

Her mother was the only one home when Natalie arrived.

'You could've called to warn me,' Isla said as Natalie entered the sitting room where her mother was holding a gin and tonic.

'I didn't think kids had to warn their parents when they were dropping by for a visit,' Natalie said.

'I hear Angelo's got himself a new lover.' Isla twirled her swizzle stick.

'I don't believe he's got a new lover,' Natalie said. 'He's not like Dad. He wouldn't betray me like that.'

'You left him.'

'I know…'

'Why on earth did you walk out on him?' Isla asked. 'He's as rich as Croesus and as handsome as the devil.'

'I can't give him what he wants,' Natalie said. 'I don't think I can have a child after what happened to Liam.'

There was an awkward little silence.

'It wasn't your fault,' Isla said on a little sigh. 'I've never blamed you—not really. I know it might've looked like it at times, but I was scared of what your father would do if I contradicted him. He can be quite nasty, as you well know. It wasn't your fault that Liam drowned. If anyone was to blame it was your father.'

Natalie stared at her mother. 'Why do you say that?'

'Because I had a headache when we came back from the beach and went inside to lie down,' she said. 'He said he'd watch you and Liam out by the pool.'

Natalie frowned. 'But he asked *me* to watch Liam. I remember him saying it. He said he had to make a really important call.'

Her mother gave her a worldly look. 'Do you really think it was *that* important?' she asked.

Natalie's stomach churned as realisation dawned. 'He was calling *his mistress*?'

Her mother nodded. 'One of the many he had on the side.'

'Why did you put up with it?' Natalie asked, choking back bitter tears. 'Why did you let him do that to you?'

'I told you why,' Isla said. 'I was scared of what he would do. I had nowhere else to go. There was nowhere else I wanted to go.'

'But you could've got help,' Natalie said. 'You

could've found a shelter or something. There are places for women to go when they're scared.'

'I don't expect *you* to understand,' Isla said. 'I know you want more from your life, with your fancy career and all, but I'm happy with my life. I have money and security. I would have lost all of that if I'd turned up to a shelter with a couple of kids in tow.'

Natalie stared at her mother as if she had never seen her before. Could her mother *really* be that shallow? Had she really sold her soul for diamonds?

'You don't even *like* him,' she said. 'How can you bear to live with him if you don't like him, much less love him?'

Isla raised one of her thin brows cynically. 'Are you telling me you're in *love* with your billionaire husband?' she asked. 'Come on, Natalie, what you really love is his money and what he can give you. It's what all women love. You're no different.'

'I love *everything* about Angelo,' Natalie said. 'I love his kindness. I love that he still loves me, even after I ran out on him. I love his smile. I love his eyes. I love his hands. I love every bit of him. I even love his family. They're not shallow and selfish like mine. They watch out for each other and take care of each other. They stay together because they want to be together, not just for the sake of appearances. I love him. Do you hear me? *I love him.*'

'You're a fool, Natalie,' her mother said. 'He'll break your heart. Men like him always do. They reel you in with their charm and then leave you high and dry.'

'I don't care if he breaks my heart,' Natalie said. 'It will be worth it just to have him for as long as he wants me.'

If he takes me back, she thought in anguish. *Did he really mean it when he said he never would?*

'And how long will that be?' Isla asked. 'You're beautiful now, but what about when your looks fade and you put on a few pounds and have a few more wrinkles than you'd like? What then, Natalie? Is he going to love you then?'

There was a sound at the door, and Natalie spun round to see her father saunter in.

'You have a hide to show your face here,' he said. 'Do you know what day it is?'

Natalie drew herself up to her full height. 'I do, actually,' she said. 'And I'm on my way to the cemetery now, to pay my respects to Liam. But when I leave I am *not* going to take the yoke of guilt with me. That's your burden, not mine. Liam would want me to move on with my life. He would have wanted me to be happy.'

'You killed him,' her father spat viciously, bits of spittle forming at the corners of his mouth. '*You* killed him.'

'I did *not* kill him,' Natalie said. 'I was too young to be left in charge of him. That was your duty of care—but you were too busy lining up another secret assignation with one of your mistresses.'

Her father's face reddened. 'Get out!' He thrust a finger towards the door. 'Get out before I throw you out.'

Natalie stared him down, feeling powerful for the first time in her life. 'You haven't got the guts to throw me out,' she said. 'You're a pathetic coward who has spent years hiding his guilt behind his innocent daughter. I'm not carrying it any more. I pity you and Mum. You've wasted your lives. You don't know the meaning of the word love.'

'I do love you, Natalie,' her mother said, sloshing her

drink as Natalie headed out through the door. 'I have always loved you. Even when you were born a girl instead of a boy I loved you.'

Natalie looked at her with a despairing look. 'Then where the hell have you been all my life?' she asked, and turned and left.

Angelo was trying to get Molly to use the garden as her toilet rather than the rug in his study. There had been a significant regression over the last month in the puppy's training. He hardly knew what to do with her. The young woman he had employed to train her had come with great recommendations, but had created a press fest that he would have given anything to avoid.

He could only imagine what Natalie was making of it.

He had got through each day that she had been gone with a wrenching ache in his chest. It was much worse than five years ago. He had thought he had loved her then, but now his love for her surpassed that by miles.

He had thrown himself into work, but he had no enthusiasm for building an empire he couldn't share with her.

He didn't care about the children thing.

He just wanted her.

He had wanted to go to her, to beg her to come back to him, but he knew she could only be his if she was free to make the choice to be with him—not because she had to be, but because she wanted to be.

'Signor Bellandini?' Rosa appeared at the back door. 'You have a visitor.'

He frowned irritably. 'Tell them to go away. I told you I don't want to be disturbed when I'm at home.'

'I think you might like to be disturbed in this case,' Rosa said.

Angelo looked past his housekeeper to see Natalie standing there. He blinked a couple of times, wondering if he was imagining her. But Molly clearly didn't have any doubt. She barrelled towards her with an excited yap, ears flapping, tail wagging frenetically. He watched as Natalie scooped her up and cuddled her against her chest.

'She's missed you,' he said before he could stop himself.

'I've missed her too,' she said, kissing the puppy's head.

'So,' he said. 'What can I do for you? Do you want me to sign the divorce papers? Is that why you're here? You could have sent them with your lawyer. You didn't have to come in person to rub it in.'

She set the puppy down at her feet and met his gaze. 'Did you really mean it when you said you would never take me back?' she asked.

Angelo tried to keep his expression impassive. 'Why do you ask?'

She ran her tongue over her lips and lowered her gaze. 'I was just kind of hoping you only said that to make me think twice about walking away.'

'You didn't walk away,' he said. 'You ran away.'

Her teeth snagged her bottom lip. 'Yes, I know… I'm not going to do that any more.'

Angelo was still not ready to let his guard down. 'Why are you here?'

She lifted her eyes back to his. 'I wanted to say…' She took a little breath and continued, 'I wanted to say I love you. I've wanted to say it for ages but I wasn't sure how. I couldn't seem to find the words. They were inside me, but I had to find a way to get them out.'

He swallowed the lump that had risen in his throat. 'Why now?' he asked. 'Why not a month ago?'

'I've talked to my parents since then,' she said. 'It turns out my father wasn't making an important business call that day. He was calling his mistress.'

Angelo frowned. 'And he let you carry the guilt all this time?'

'And my mother,' she said. 'I'm not sure I can forgive either of them. I'm still working through that.'

'I don't think you should ever see or speak to them again.'

'They're my parents,' she said. 'I have to give them the chance to redeem themselves.'

'I wouldn't be holding my breath,' he said. 'You're likely to get your heart broken.'

She looked up at him with a pained look. 'I know you've got someone else,' she said. 'I've seen the papers. I just wanted to tell you because…because…'

'She's a dog trainer,' Angelo said with a little roll of his eyes. 'And not a particularly good one. I don't think she knows a thing about puppies, to tell you the truth.'

Her eyes started to shine with moisture. 'Dogs are easy,' she said. 'It's kids that are difficult. But I reckon a dog is a great way to ease yourself into it.'

He held out his arms and she stepped into them. He hugged her so tightly he was frightened he was going to snap her ribs. 'We don't have to rush into anything you don't feel ready for,' he said. 'I'm just happy to have you back in my life.'

'I'm so sorry for what I've put you through,' she said. 'I love you so much. I couldn't bear to lose you all over again.'

He looked down at her tenderly. 'This last month has been torture,' he said. 'So many times I wanted to pick up the phone and call you. I even drove halfway to Edinburgh but then turned back. I thought if you came back it would have to be because it was the only place you wanted to be. I felt I had to let you go in order to get you back.'

She smiled up at him. 'This is the only place I want to be. Here with you.'

He stroked her face, loving the way her eyes were shining with happy tears instead of sad ones. 'Do you think it's too early in our marriage to have a second honeymoon?' he asked.

She stepped up on tiptoe and linked her arms around his neck. 'Is the first one over?' she asked with a twinkling look.

He smiled as he scooped her up in his arms. 'It's just getting started,' he said, and carried her indoors.

* * * * *

INNOCENT IN THE IVORY TOWER

BY
LUCY ELLIS

Lucy Ellis has four loves in life: books, expensive lingerie, vintage films and big, gorgeous men who have to duck going through doorways. Weaving aspects of them into her fiction is the best part of being a romance writer. Lucy lives in a small cottage in the foothills outside Melbourne.

Innocent In The Ivory Tower is Lucy's first book!

For Martha

CHAPTER ONE

ALEXEI RANAEVSKY strode across the light-filled environs of his floating boardroom and picked up the newspaper one of his staff had been careless enough to leave behind.

He had made it clear he wanted to see no reportage of the Kulikov tragedy, but now the initial shock was wearing off he found himself drawn to what could only be described as the circus that was attaching itself to events. How to dismantle that circus was his current concern.

How to grieve for his closest friend would come after.

Events had moved to the third page. A picture of Leo and Anais at a race meeting in Dubai, Leo's head thrown back, laughing, his arm welded around Anais's slender waist. A golden couple. Alongside was exactly what Alexei didn't want to see: a photograph of the mangled car wreck. The 1967 Aston Martin—Leo's 'baby'—nothing more than steel and destroyed electronics. Leo and Anais's very human bodies hadn't stood a chance.

The commentary below—because you couldn't call it news—was adjective-heavy, full of references to Anais's beauty and Leo's work for the UN. Alexei scanned it for a few seconds, then sucked in a sharp breath.

Konstantine Kulikov.

Kostya.

There was something about seeing that name in print that made what had felt for days now like a nightmare fiercely, immediately real. At least there was no picture of the boy. Leo

had been intensely guarded about their private life: he and
Anais had been fair game for the media, but their family life
had been off-limits to anyone outside their circle. It was a sentiment Alexei admired him for. It was a rule he laid down in
his own life. There was the public man, and the private *fami-
lya*, and the fact that Leo had been that family for him made
his grief all the more stupefying.

'Alexei?'

His head snapped up, jaw hard, eyes emotionless.

For a second her name evaded him. 'Tara,' he said.

If she noticed the lapse it did not register on her stunning
face. It was a face that was currently making her several million dollars a year in beauty endorsements, in lieu of an acting
career that had gone nowhere.

'Everyone's waiting, darling,' she said smoothly, crossing
the space between them and pulling the newspaper out of his
hands.

It was the wrong thing to do.

He had never struck a woman in his life, and he had no intention of starting now, but every fibre of his body wanted to
lash out. Instead he froze. Tara lifted her chin defiantly. She
was nothing if not bold—and wasn't that what had drawn him
to her?

'You don't need to look at that trash,' she said harshly. 'You
need to pull it together and get out there and put a civilised
face on this whole debacle.'

Everything she said was everything he knew, but something—some important mechanism between his brain and his
emotions—had snapped. Many would say he didn't have any
emotions, not real ones. He certainly hadn't cried for Leo and
Anais. He hadn't even cried for his own dead parents. But there
was something surging through him that his brain wasn't going
to be able to control. Something that had its wellspring in that
child's name in black-and-white in newspaper ink.

Kostya.

Orphaned.

Alone.

Tara's 'debacle'.

'Let them wait,' he said coldly, his English coloured by his Russian accent. 'And what in the hell are you wearing? This isn't a cocktail party—it's a family gathering.'

Tara snorted laughter. It was one of the traits he had once found appealing about her, her lack of self-consciousness—as if her overwhelming physical beauty made it possible for her to say anything, do anything, be anything.

'Family? Give me a break—those people aren't your family.' She reached out and pressed her red-taloned hand to his waist, taut beneath the expensively tailored cream shirt. 'You have as much family feeling as a cat, Alexei,' she stated, face upturned, lips wet and red, her hand making its way down the front of his dark trousers. 'A big, mean, feral cat. *Very* big.' Her hand settled on what she found there. 'Not up to play today, darling?'

His body had begun to respond as long familiarity with the process had taught it, but sex was not on today's agenda. It hadn't been on the agenda since Monday, when his right-hand man, Carlo, had brought him the news in the early hours. He remembered the snapping on of the lamp, Carlo's murmured voice as he laid out the spare, basic facts such as they had been. Then he had been alone in that big flat bed, swimming in emptiness. Tara had been beside him, dead to the world under a blanket of whatever drugs she took to sleep. A body.

He had been alone.

I never want to have sex with this woman ever again.

He grasped her forearm and gently but with leashed force revolved her one hundred and eighty degrees to face the door.

'Off you go,' he murmured in her ear, as if imparting an endearment—only his voice was completely dead of feeling. 'Join them on deck. Don't drink too much, and here.' He picked up the newspaper she had dropped on the boardroom table. 'Dispose of this.'

Tara had been in the wide world long enough to know she

was experiencing the infamous Ranaevsky Chill Factor. She just hadn't expected to feel it herself, or perhaps not quite so soon.

'Danni was right. You *are* a cold bastard.'

Alexei didn't have a clue who Danni was—didn't particularly care. He just wanted Tara out of the room. Out of his life.

He wanted the people outside off his boat.

He wanted to turn the clock back to Sunday.

Mostly he wanted his control back. Control over the situation.

'How in the hell are you going to raise a child?' Tara snarled as she strutted out through the door.

Control. His dark eyes fixed on the Florida coastline, visible through the wraparound windows. He would begin by doing what he needed to do. Speaking to the people outside. Speaking to Carlo. Most of all speaking to Kostya, a two-year-old infant. But first he needed to fly across the Atlantic to do it.

"'The owl and the pussycat went to sea in a beautiful pea-green boat,'" sang Maisy in a soft contralto, her body arced over the small boy curled on his side in the crib. He had been sucking on the plump flesh of his fist, but as sleep claimed him his pink mouth closed and presently his barrel-shaped chest rose and fell beneath the delicate ribbed cotton singlet he wore.

She had been singing to him for a while now, after a full half-hour of reading, and her throat felt dry, her voice slightly hoarse. But it was worth it to see him like this, so peaceful.

Standing up, she scanned the room, checking everything was in its place. The nursery was as it had always been— a place of womblike security—yet everything outside it had changed. For this little boy, for ever.

Tiptoeing out, she closed the door. The baby monitor was on and she knew from experience he would sleep now until after midnight. It was her chance to get some food and then some sleep herself. She'd been awake so much of the past thirty-six hours she couldn't even gauge how much sleep she'd had.

Two floors down, the kitchen was dimly lit. Valerie, the Kulikovs' housekeeper, had left the spotlights over the benches on for her, and they cast an almost ghostly glow. Valerie had also left a dish of macaroni and cheese in the fridge to be re-heated, and Maisy silently thanked her as she slid the bowl into the microwave.

The older woman had been a godsend this week. When the news had come through of the crash Maisy had been in her room, packing for a vacation that was due to start on Tuesday. She remembered putting down the telephone and sitting by it for a full ten minutes before she even thought of what to do next. Then she had rung Valerie and life had resumed movement.

She and Valerie had both expected Leo and Anais's families to sweep in, but the house in the private London square had remained silent. Inside, Valerie continued to do her hours and return to her family at night, and Maisy cared for her charge and waited for the plea that had not yet come. *I want Mama.*

The press had been there for a couple of days, pushing up at the windows, clambering over the iron railings to drop to the basement. Valerie had kept the blinds drawn, and Maisy had only taken Kostya out once, to the private garden across the road. Maisy had worked for the Kulikovs since Kostya's birth, and lived in this house all that time. Leo and Anais had travelled frequently. Maisy was accustomed to being alone with Kostya for weeks at a time. Yet there was something—empty—tonight. The house felt too quiet, and Maisy found herself jumping as the microwave pinged, pressing open the door with a hand that trembled.

Get a grip, she told herself sternly, using an oven mitt to carry the bowl over to the big French provincial table. She didn't bother to turn on the main light. There was something comforting about the darkness.

Steam rose off the macaroni. She ought to be hungry, and

she needed to keep her strength up. Her fork made a cruise around the edges. In her mind's eye she could still see Anais in this very room a week ago, laughing in that full-throated way at a drawing Kostya had done in crayon on the floor tiles of a giraffe with a head like his mummy's. Anais had been almost six feet tall, and mostly legs, which had been the focus of her modelling career. It was clearly how her little son had seen her from his diminutive position.

Maisy remembered the first time she had met Anais. She had been a small, dumpy swot, detailed by her headmistress to introduce the skinny, impossibly tall Anais Parker-Stone to the rituals of St Bernice's. Anais hadn't known then that Maisy Edmonds was a charity girl, her place in the very exclusive girls' school arranged for her on a government programme. When she had found out, Anais hadn't changed her allegiances. If Maisy had been ostracised for her background, Anais had been victimised for her height.

For two years the girls had been close friends, until Anais dropped out at sixteen and four months later had started modelling in New York. Two years later she was famous.

As Maisy had matured she'd lost her puppy fat, gained a waist and some length in her legs, and her curves had become an asset. She had gone on to university but dropped out before the first term had even begun. Her only contact with Anais had been via the glossy magazines Anais stalked through. When Maisy had run into her at Harrods it had been Anais who'd recognised her—probably because she had hardly changed, Maisy thought ruefully.

Anais, all sleek blonde bob and three-inch heels, had shrieked with joy, thrown her skinny arms around Maisy's small shoulders and jumped up and down like a teenage girl. A teenage girl with a baby bump. Three months later Maisy had been ensconced in Lantern Square, with a newborn baby in her arms and a completely overwhelmed Anais weeping and threatening to kill herself and trying to escape the house every chance she could. Nobody had ever told her motherhood wasn't a job she could walk away from, that it was for life.

A far too short life, as it had turned out, Maisy thought heavily and stopped pretending to eat. She pushed the plate away. She had cried for her friend, and she had cried for tiny Kostya. She imagined at some point those tears would dry up. Right now it seemed they had.

She had more pressing considerations.

Any day now a lawyer for the Kulikovs, although more likely for the Parker-Stones, would land on the doorstep. People who would take away Kostya. Maisy knew nothing about the Kulikovs other than that Leo had been an only child and his parents were deceased. But she remembered Arabella Parker-Stone, who had seen her grandson once, a few days after his birth. It had been a brief visit, involving calla lilies and harsh words between Anais and her mother.

'I hate her, I hate her, I hate her,' Anais had wailed afterwards into a sofa cushion, whilst Maisy rocked Kostya in her arms.

Arabella had upset everyone. But her mind was failing and she was now in a nursing home. Kostya would *not* be going to live with his grandmother.

Nor will he be living with me.

Maisy didn't know how she was going to hand Kostya over to strangers. Wild thoughts of simply absconding with him had crossed her mind yesterday and today. It all seemed possible, with the world ignoring them, but once it paid attention how on earth would she manage it? She was jobless and her only skill was as a carer for the infirm, the elderly, or the very young. Her *vocation* was loving that little boy upstairs. He had become her family—but, more painfully, she was his. Somehow she had to find a way to stay with him. Surely whoever stepped forward would need a nanny? Would not be so cruel as to separate them...?

Maisy took a deep breath and pushed the hair out of her face. She reeled her bowl back in and, head resting on one hand, picked at a first mouthful of pasta, munching by rote. She needed sustenance; this would give it to her. Tomorrow she would have to go through Leo's office and phone people. Such had been his mania for privacy, very few outsiders had been in this house. Anais had never complained—she had merely gone out. Another excuse to leave her son. Maisy had never understood Anais's inability to bond with Kostya, but she had excused it.

And now it just didn't matter any more.

It was a movement, not a sound, that pulled her out of her miserable thoughts with an abrupt jab of adrenaline. Something shifted at the corner of her vision and her head jerked up, her shoulders pulling tight as twine.

Someone was in the house.

She froze, listening intently.

In that moment two men stepped out of the pooling darkness beyond the island bench, and as she processed their presence the room filled up with men. Three more came rushing down the stairs, and another two bursting through the garden entrance. That they all seemed to be wearing suits brought Maisy no comfort as the spoon dropped from her hand and she stumbled backwards out of her chair.

The shortest of the thugs came towards her and said, 'Hands behind your head. Get on the floor.'

But a bigger man—taller, leaner, younger—brushed him aside and said something brusquely in a foreign language.

Maisy stared open mouthed at him, shock rooting her to the spot and he swore.

'English, Alexei Fedorovich,' said another of the men, almost as terrifying with his height and bulk.

Oh, God, it was the Russian mafia.

The hysterical thought coincided with the younger man making a sudden movement towards her, and Maisy's body reacted to protect itself.

She grabbed the chair and threw it with all her might at him. Then she screamed.

CHAPTER TWO

'ALEXEI,' said a voice at his elbow. 'Perhaps we should wait.'

Alexei barely spared a glance for his factotum Carlo Santini. He didn't do waiting.

The first thing he'd noticed about the house was that the security code hadn't been changed. Clearly no one was in charge. The second had been the almost abnormal silence of the house. It was close on midnight, but there was a closed-up feeling to the rooms. His hackles raised, he'd headed towards a pale light gleaming from the stairwell leading downstairs into the basement. His godson had been alone for four days, and he wanted to see for himself the situation he was walking into. Although his security would move up through the house from basement to attic, he knew it would be easier to cut to the chase himself.

He had spotted her immediately—a shapeless figure hunched over a bowl, sitting in the dark. Good—staff. As he'd walked across the room she had seemed to sense him, because her head had come up and for a moment he'd been thrown by the vulnerability that softened her dimly lit features as she'd sought to make sense of his presence. He'd had a further impression of fragility and femininity, despite the clothes that enveloped her.

In that moment the French doors had exploded open in front of him and more personnel had come thundering down the stairs behind him. The woman had reacted like a loaded gun. They were protecting *him*, but she wasn't to know that.

The trigger for this overreaction had heaved her chair and

dived under the table, rolling herself into a ball. Now, Alexei cursed and shoved the table over a few feet, hauled her up into his arms, registering her real terror as she began to kick and struggle against him. Better him than one of his security detail, who would be less inclined to go gently with her.

His muttered imprecations and rough assurances of, 'I am not going to hurt you,' did little to stem her reaction—until he realised in his exhausted state he was using Russian. 'Calm yourself,' he said distinctly in English. 'No one wishes you any harm.'

Maisy jerked her head sideways and her eyes welded to his. They were deep blue, heavily lashed and stunning. His cheek-bones were like scimitars, and she recognised that faint up-sweep of his bone structure as Slavic.

He clearly hadn't shaved in many days, but otherwise he smelled good. Maisy's body recognised this as her mind strug-gled to keep up. His cologne filled her nostrils, along with the subtler but more enticing smell of him—warm, male flesh. She could feel the fight slipping out of her body as her senses told her this man truly meant her no harm, even as those same senses began to be overloaded with other messages.

Alexei sensed the change in her. She was no longer a vic-tim fighting back but a woman in his arms, waiting for him to make a move. He reluctantly set her down, but kept one hand fastened over her shoulder, holding her in place. He didn't want his security detail marching her off, possibly manhandling her. He didn't question why other men touching her filled him with the primitive urge to protect her. He was tired, and he hadn't had sex, and he was in the mood to tear down the house if he didn't get that child.

'Talk to her,' he said, the weight of his hand lifting from her shoulder.

Feeling suddenly adrift, Maisy looked up to face another man—shorter, slighter, perhaps a decade older and sharply dressed—who stepped forward and inclined his head rather formally.

'Good evening, *signorina*. I apologise for the intrusion. I am Carlo. I work for Alexei Ranaevsky.'

Maisy's head swivelled back to the younger man. He wasn't even listening. He had retrieved a phone from his jacket and was reading whatever messages it contained.

This was talking to her?

'Try Spanish,' was all he said, in a deep, gravelly voice she hadn't registered before when he had spoken in Russian.

Maisy sat through Spanish, Italian and interestingly Polish renditions of the same introduction. As the Polish rolled musically on she tried to marshal her racing thoughts. Her gaze kept creeping back to the man who had restrained her. He seemed to be the focus in the room, and he reeked confidence and control. Except when she had been in his arms for a moment there she had sensed something else. Something very much uncontrolled.

Maisy suppressed an involuntary shiver and his head came up, as if sensing her movement. His darkened eyes moved over her, settling on the pulse that was beating wildly at the base of her throat. It held his assessing gaze for a moment. Then he said abruptly, 'She's English.'

He despatched the mobile and gave her a measured look.

'I need to know where the boy is.'

Maisy's skittering pulse went still. Every hackle in her body rose.

Alexei saw the moment she shut down, and cursed himself inwardly. He didn't have time for this. When she didn't answer he lost patience. 'I'm taking Leonid Kulikov's son out of here. I need you to take me to him.'

'No,' she said.

No? *No?* Alexei made a soft sound of disbelief.

'I'm not letting you anywhere near the Kulikovs' child. Who in the *hell* do you think you are?'

The kitten could scratch. Despite himself, Alexei felt his libido give a little kick.

'I'm Alexei Ranaevsky, his legal guardian.'

Her gaze made an involuntary skate over the breadth of his chest and shoulders, then fastened on his face. He had dark hair, curling and close-cropped, and he was about as close to a fantasy as Maisy had ever had.

Yet her stomach twisted, even as she knew she ought to feel relief.

Someone had finally come for Kostya. But because no one was walking Kostya out of this house without *her*, this man had come for her too. Only he didn't know it. Something fluttered low in Maisy's chest and she recognised it was fear—quite different from the terror she had felt when these men had burst in on her. This was fear of the known.

Alexei had apparently said everything he was going to say to her, and turned around and headed for the stairs.

Maisy's anxious 'Wait!' didn't break his stride.

She chased him up two flights of stairs, all the while babbling about not waking Kostya, but he ignored her completely.

Why isn't he listening to me?

He'd reached the nursery landing when she launched herself at him physically. 'Please. Stop.'

Alexei paused midstride as female arms came around his waist. Bumping up against him, she grappled to take hold of his jacket. She was panting, and Alexei looked down to see some of her curls had come loose. With the colour high in her cheeks she was considerably more intriguing than she had been at first glance. She was also clearly very distressed.

But that was not his concern, Alexei dismissed irritably. She knew who he was. She was either trying to garner his attention or behaving irrationally. Either was of no interest to him. He moved and she didn't, and a very decisive ripping sound rent the air between them.

There was an awful moment as Maisy realised what she had done. His eyes locked on hers, whatever he'd been about to say giving way to a look of complete disbelief. Satisfaction at finally gaining his attention turned up the corners of Maisy's lips, and his stare dropped to the lush unpainted pink of her mouth and buzzed there.

Disconcerted, she lost her concentration for a moment, and something of this must have communicated itself because an answering smile hovered over his mouth. Struck, Maisy dropped her gaze and, making the most of her advantage in that moment, moved fast, scooting ahead of him and blocking his way as best she could.

'I am not letting you see Kostya until you tell me what's going on.'

His gaze ran the length of her, and his tone was an arctic degree cooler than his eyes. 'You're in full possession of the facts. I'm his legal guardian. Remove yourself.'

As if that was all he had to say.

'Or what? You'll get one of your bully boys to do it for you?' Maisy challenged. Some part of her brain told her this was *not* persuading him she was the right person to look after Kostya, but he was making her so angry with his high-handed attitude. It wasn't his house. Kostya wasn't his child. And she certainly wasn't his doormat.

'Do you cook here? Clean?' he rapped out. 'Because, quite frankly, I don't explain my actions to staff.'

'I'm the nanny,' she flung at him—which was close enough to the truth.

He swore under his breath, those blue eyes narrowing suspiciously on her. 'Why in the hell didn't you say so earlier?'

'I wasn't sure what was going on.'

It sounded lame even as she said it. She couldn't very well say, *You put your arms around me and I felt your body and I got thoroughly distracted, and then I saw your face and you reduced me to a puddle of wanting woman.* Because she darn well knew it probably happened to him every other day.

Maisy moistened her lips, drawing herself up to her full height of five feet four inches. 'I want you to hold on and explain to me exactly what you intend doing.' Her voice sounded high and breathless, and unlikely to get her a response from this hard man.

He didn't look ready to explain. He looked as if he wanted to shake her. He looked as if he couldn't believe he was having this—*any*—conversation with her. A child's wail broke the stalemate.

'Konstantine.'

'Kostya.'

They both spoke at once. Maisy dared him with her eyes to push her aside and he hesitated, clearly not wanting to let her pass but less sure about how gung-ho he should be with a two-year-old infant.

Maisy seized the opportunity and went first, but she could sense him close behind her all the way. She hesitated at the nursery door, then swung around and almost bumped her nose on his hard chest. His big body tensed and she cringed. She had to stop touching him. He'd think there was something wrong with her. Yet already a reactive shiver of response was running the length of her body and she instinctively took a step back.

'Listen,' she said, groping for composure. 'You will stay out here. He'll only be frightened if he sees a strange man.'

He inclined his head. 'I will wait.'

Maisy ducked into the room, dimly lit by a night lamp near the cot. Kostya was standing in the middle of the mattress, face red and wet as his cries died away on a last wail when he saw what he wanted. Maisy. His chubby arms extended trustfully towards her and Maisy closed the distance between them in an instant.

'Maisy!' he enunciated clearly.

She struggled with lifting him. He was big for his age, and in another year she would have difficulty carrying him in her arms. She felt for the armchair behind her and slid into it, cradling the warm little body in her arms.

Alexei stood watching them. He hadn't expected to be moved in any way by the sight of the child in a woman's arms. She seemed at ease in a way he knew he could never be with such a small child. He supposed it came naturally for some women, being maternal; it had certainly not been a natural function of any of the women he knew. In fact he struggled, now he thought about it, to come up with any woman he'd been with who was comfortable around children.

Which was something he had in common with them. He definitely had no interest in his friends' kids. He'd been god-father to Konstantine for two years and seen the child once: on the day he'd stood up for him in the Russian Orthodox Church here in London.

'I didn't know he would be so…small,' Alexei said quietly, not wanting to startle the child.

Maisy smoothed her hand over the back of Kostya's res-tive head as the little boy peered around to see where the male voice had come from. It was a voice that sounded somewhat like his father's, Maisy registered. A shade deeper, but with the irregular emphasis on vowels that revealed English was a second language for him.

'Papa,' he said uncertainly, in his clear, high child's voice.

'No, it's not Papa,' Maisy said softly, her tongue sticking to the roof of her mouth.

He came slowly towards them and dropped down beside the chair, so that his height and bulk were no longer frightening, and said in a grave voice, 'Hello, Kostya. I am your godfather, Alexei Ranaevsky.'

Some of the tension Maisy was holding in her body shifted and melted with those words. Kostya's godfather. Why hadn't she remembered? The day of Kostya's christening she had been in bed with a fever, but the au pair girl had brought back a gushing description of the *über*cool Alexei Ranaevsky, and here he was—in the flesh.

He lifted those megawatt blue eyes to her and said quietly, 'You will get him back to sleep and I will wait for you outside.'

The velvet of his voice brushed over her. Maisy recognised his words as a directive and wondered if Alexei Ranaevsky ever asked permission for anything.

When she emerged the house felt empty again. The security detail had evaporated, although Maisy doubted they were far away. She stood at the top of the stairwell, listening for movement.

'Here,' came a deep voice from across the landing.

Maisy followed it into her own room. She hesitated on the threshold. Alexei was standing by the window, somehow managing to fill the entire room with his presence. Amidst the delicately feminine decor of duck-egg-blue and white he looked absurdly out of place.

'Sit down,' was all he said.

'I'd rather stand…'

'Sit down.'

Maisy rolled her eyes and sat on her narrow bed. He began to walk around, lifting framed photos, knick-knacks, even examining an atomiser of the perfume Maisy usually wore. All the while his attention seemed to be on her, and it was disconcerting. His raw energy was starting to roll through her and Maisy shifted on the bed, wishing she hadn't sat down.

Alexei rubbed his chin ruefully and wondered why it was that after four days of abstinence, and a total lack of interest in sex for the first time in his adult life, it had all come roaring back the minute his body made contact with hers.

Looking at her now, it seemed she didn't appear to have a waist under all that wool, but he remembered the curve of it under his hands. In the same way he knew her breasts would be soft and round and her hips and bottom lush in his hands. Her hair was much longer than it looked—she had it all caught up—and it would be long and curling. He could bury his hands in it when she was on her knees to him…

He almost growled with frustration. What was it about death and sex? Maybe that was why his body had gone there and his head had followed. Leo was dead. Leo's child was now his lifetime responsibility, and he took his responsibilities seriously. Sitting in front of him was something both life-affirming and yet not serious at all. Sex with a real woman—not a sprayed, painted, waxed, plastic actress/model perfume commercial. Hell, she wasn't even wearing make-up. She didn't really need it, she had great skin, and that hair…

Suddenly she stood up. 'Mr Ranaevsky—'

'Alexei,' he offered.

'Alexei.'

She took a deep breath, and he registered she was about to make some sort of speech. That was never good.

'I didn't catch your name.'

'Maisy. Maisy Edmonds.'

Maisy.

'Sit down, Maisy.'

'No, I need to say this standing up.'

'Sit down.'

She sat. It was a good sign. Pliable.

She stood up. 'No, this is important. I want to come with Kostya. I don't know what your circumstances are, or what you have organised, but I want to stay with him until he's settled. And he doesn't know yet. When he's told, I need to be there.'

Alexei frowned heavily. 'He doesn't know his parents are dead?'

Maisy shook her head, the pain rushing through her.

'I had no intention of leaving you behind,' was his only comment. 'Do you have a valid passport?'

'Yes,' said Maisy. 'But why—?'

'Pack a bag. We move in twenty.'

'But—'

He gave her a brief, almost offended look. 'I'm not accustomed to explaining myself.'

To staff, added Maisy silently, biting down on a sharp retort.

Alexei registered her frustration, thinking wryly it was nothing next to his own. He had to get out of there before he did something stupid. He had overlooked momentarily who this woman was—a future employee. And he didn't bed his female staff. He left her to it, reaching for his pager as he plunged down the stairs to alert his men to the changed situation.

It took Maisy twenty minutes to bag up enough of Kostya's belongings for a week's stay. She assumed the rest of his life would come later. Her own would take considerably longer to assemble, but fortunately she still had that suitcase she had packed for France on Sunday. Only five days ago, but it felt a lifetime.

But before she took a step out that front door she was going to have a shower.

Downstairs, Alexei consulted his watch for the third time. Half an hour. It wasn't as if he wasn't used to waiting on a woman. He had yet to meet one whose 'five more minutes' meant anything less than twenty. But Maisy Edmonds wasn't in any way, shape or form a date, and he didn't have time for this.

He never dealt with the small stuff, and he could have sent someone up for her, but with his libido humming he realised he actually wanted her at his side. The sparks at least were keeping him awake and functioning.

Her bedroom door was slightly ajar. He gave it a push, half expecting to find her knee-deep in clothes. Instead he found a naked wet woman wrapped in a little white towel, with ringlets of damp hair cascading down her back.

Lust roared through him like a hot desert wind, obliterating thought.

She didn't cry out, or protest, or do any of the things an outraged woman should do in this situation—something that would make him turn around and leave her alone. She just gaped at him, clutching at the towel, her eyes growing wider, and then she actually stepped towards him.

He crossed the space between them, caught her around that surprisingly small waist and pulled her into his body, half dragging the towel off in the process. He was conscious of her making a noise as he hungrily took her mouth with his own, his tongue invading the sweetness inside. She was stiff in his arms, and he could feel her hands pushing at his biceps, but the rest of her was soft and pliant. Everything about her was everything he wanted in that moment; she was all feminine roundness and softness and warmth. He could bury himself in her and forget everything that had happened, everything that was going to happen. Sweet oblivion inside sweet Maisy.

Maisy could hardly form a coherent thought. Shock had turned to humiliation as she felt her towel shift and drop, and she was aware that at any moment she would be completely naked in a strange man's arms. This man was kissing her with a passion that went beyond expertise, as if his mouth and his tongue and his touch were desperately searching for something from her. And Maisy found something in herself was tentatively responding. The resistance melted out of her hands as she nestled closer to the source of this warmth that was spreading through her, seeking the shelter his arms offered, leaning into the strength that seemed so much a part of him. His hunger softened into something else as she began to respond.

It was almost too much. Her heartbeat was speeding out of control and his arms around her were almost too powerful, too possessive. She struggled a little, but only to drag his head back down to hers as he shifted in response, and she felt him laugh uninhibitedly against her mouth. He half lifted her and swept her up against the back of the door. It slammed with a thud, his forearm taking the brunt for her back, and Maisy felt his other big, callused hand smooth up her inner thigh. She grabbed it, muttered, 'No,' against his hair, and his mouth dropped to the pulse-point throbbing at the base of her throat. He licked her like a big cat, right there, his tongue rough and wet and hot.

Oh, Lord, thought Maisy, her body on fire. *I can't do this. I'm not ready to do this.*

'Lose the towel, Maisy,' he murmured hotly against her ear, his hands at her hips, moving around to cup her bare bottom.

'I can't,' she winced, embarrassment crawling through her.

And then it was over. It all happened in a moment. His mouth was gone, his hands were gone and she was leaning up against her bedroom door, clutching a towel to her near nakedness and staring into the eyes of a man who looked shell-shocked.

He rubbed the back of his hand over his mouth, as if removing the taste of her, and said in a low, fractured voice, 'That was inexcusable. I'm tired. I made a mistake. Forget it ever happened.'

Maisy's hazel eyes prickled. A mistake? Forget it ever happened?

Alexei knew he wasn't thinking straight. The girl in front of him was staring at him as if he was mad, and he couldn't blame her. He'd started something he couldn't finish. He'd left her high and dry, and the ache in his body wasn't going to go away any time soon.

What in the hell was he doing here? He had twelve security personnel scoping the property, a car waiting and a jet on the tarmac at Heathrow. And he, Alexei Ranaevsky, was tupping the nanny in an upstairs bedroom.

The goddamned *nanny*!

And doing a spectacularly lousy job of it.

Shoving aside the useless introspection, Alexei sized up the woman huddling against the door.

'You need to move so I can get out of here,' he directed. 'And for God's sake put some clothes on.'

Maisy flinched, but she still didn't move. She wanted desperately to be away from him, to be behind the bathroom door, to sink to the ground and wish away all her humiliation, but she knew the moment she stepped aside she might lose her chance.

She probably already had. He seemed so angry with her it was more than likely he had changed his mind. She should have shoved him off her to begin with. She should never have responded. She should have *remembered* Kostya came first.

Anais would be horrified if she knew what was going on, what had just happened—*in her own home*, just days after... Maisy felt so sick she actually thought she might throw up.

'Maisy.' He spoke her name abruptly.

'You haven't changed your mind?' she challenged, with what nerve she had left, strengthening her voice with the knowledge that Kostya came first. 'About me coming? With Kostya?'

For a moment he actually looked confused, as if she had said something completely out of left field when this was the only thing that mattered, wasn't it? Then he sighed and ran a hand over his unshaven face.

'No, I haven't changed my mind,' he muttered. 'God help me, I haven't changed my mind.'

She looked so lost for a moment something twisted inside him. He remembered her driven, *'No,'* when he had asked her to drop the towel, her hand like a trap on his when he'd sought to find the sweet wet place between her thighs.

But then why would she have left her door ajar if she hadn't wanted him to walk in?

Cynicism firmly in place, he took one last frustrated look at what he wasn't going to have and informed her, 'Get dressed. You've got five.'

It was the hardest walk Maisy had ever had to make. She hated him seeing her after what had happened—so much bare skin, as if offering herself up to him on a plate. He must have been watching her because she didn't hear her bedroom door close until after she'd shut herself in the bathroom and sunk onto the floor. Waves of humiliation rolled over her, and then she snatched her towel off and grabbed at the big fluffy bath sheet she should have been wearing. It wrapped around her like a hug, and she buried her face in its folds.

She'd been so uninhibited, so out of control. She'd felt his raw need, his naked desire, and she'd matched it with her own. Shame burned through her. This was not part of her bargain with herself and Anais. The last gift she could give her friend was a secure future for her son, and instead she had been wrapped around his godfather, seeking the comfort *she* needed, Kostya far from her mind.

It was the shock, she told herself. The grief. She would never have responded to him like that if she wasn't half out of her mind with misery and lack of sleep. But even as she formed the excuses she knew they were a lie, and it shamed her.

She had no choice. She must get up, wash her face, get dressed and go down there and face him. This volatile, unpredictable man was going to be Kostya's father to all intents and purposes. She must learn to deal with him.

Yet her fingers strayed to her swollen lips and she allowed herself a small shudder. That kiss. That *mistake*. It must never happen again.

CHAPTER THREE

The boy, the plane…and the nanny.

No, cancel that last appellation. The red-haired sex kitten, curled up in her chair and pretending to sleep whilst he endeavoured to make sense of the figures being pumped into his email from New York. No sleep, the altitude, and now the unexpected introduction of his libido into the equation meant he was in danger of making a mistake that could cost a great many people their jobs.

He gestured to one of the attendants—a young guy named Leroy. Alexei didn't hire attractive female staff any more for his private jet. They tended to lose focus on their job.

'Leroy,' he said. 'Miss Edmonds. Move her. I don't want her in my eyeline.'

Leroy looked from the sleeping bundle that was Maisy back to his boss. Alexei knew what the man was thinking but would never say, so he added tiredly, 'She's not asleep. She's faking it.'

Maisy gritted her teeth. She had heard every word Alexei Ranaevsky had uttered since he'd sat down over an hour ago. Usually in Russian, usually brief and to the point. He hadn't addressed a single syllable to her. It was as if she had simply ceased to be. But apparently she was distracting to his eyeline.

She lifted her head as Leroy approached her. He bent down and said in a soft voice, 'Miss Edmonds—'

'I know.' Maisy gave him a resigned smile, then yawned, ruining it. She stretched and gathered up her angora travelling

blanket, and climbed out of the luxurious seat. She looked
pointedly at Alexei, who had removed his jacket and was
propped with his feet up, scrolling through the information
on the state-of-the-art laptop positioned in front of him. He
didn't even acknowledge her, his amazing bone structure taut
under this artificial light. He looked more tired than she felt,
which was saying something.

'Put Miss Edmonds in a bed,' he said as she passed by him.

Alexei heard a faint, 'Thank you,' in that sweet, tangy voice
of hers, and felt his whole body shift instinctively in her direction.

Down boy. He growled. This wasn't the time or the place to
indulge his sudden craving for soft-eyed redheads. He'd had
six long months of not particularly satisfying sex with Tara.
Five months and twenty-nine days too long, in his opinion.
Although not in Tara's. She was telling the press they were
still 'good friends' two days after he broke up with her. Ironic,
as he'd never had a female friend—and if he did he wouldn't
choose Tara.

It was complicated. Maisy Edmonds was in his household,
for now. Although she was no nanny. She'd lied to him straight
up—another element to keep in mind. He had a fair idea who
she was: one of Anais's crew of hangers-on. Somehow she'd
inveigled her way into the house and into Kostya's life. If Leo
was alive he might have vouched for her—a single word would
have sufficed. But if Leo had been alive Alexei would never
have met her in such fraught circumstances, leading to such a
stupid indiscretion.

Which was bound to happen again.

The fierceness of her sexual response had taken even him
off guard. It had turned blind need into something more exciting, edgier. It had been he who was out of control, he recognised. Whilst she had met him every inch of the way, she had
also backed down fast. Meeting that resistance had saved him
from a very big mistake, and possibly a costly one. Because
there were always consequences.

He didn't do casual sex. And he didn't do sex full stop without a condom—which he wasn't carrying. He could only have her word on where she'd been. He wondered if Leo… Then he closed down that thought, because it suddenly made him very angry. An image of Maisy Edmonds in a towel, rubbing herself against a series of men, flashed through his tired brain, firing his temper, and he swore.

It wasn't going to happen—not in the coming days and weeks anyway. The dust still had to settle on Leo's portfolio, and more importantly there was his child.

Kostya had been unexpectedly lively earlier on the trip, but now was sleeping as if the world had ended. Alexei envied him that ability to completely shut down. He imagined he had possessed it once, many aeons ago, when he was an infant. A childhood rubbed raw by neglect and strife had worn it off. He rarely slept a regular eight hours. The past few days had robbed him even of that.

With the kitten safely put to bed, he could focus on what the screen was telling him. None of it was good news. His shares in Kulcor were merely window dressing. If the company foundered it wouldn't show up as a blip on his financial radar, but it was Kostya's inheritance—he had to hold it. It was the least Leo would have expected of him. Family came first. However, growing up with nothing but the clothes on his back had taught Alexei to value material security. When people let you down, abandoned you, and all you had was yourself, several billion in the bank was a nice bulwark against destitution.

Leo's son would never want for anything. He would make sure of it.

A bed. Not *the* bed—not the one and only bedroom on a private jet—but *a* bed. One of three. What kind of a man had three bedrooms on a plane? Maisy smiled helplessly at her thoughts. He had a private plane. The number of bedrooms was probably beside the point.

She sat down on the sumptuous bed, looking around at the

luxurious fabrics on the walls and furniture. She ran her hand over the silky bed coverings in deep purple and black. A man had definitely chosen the colour scheme, although she couldn't quite picture Alexei Ranaevsky spending much time with fabric swatches.

She could, however, imagine him on this bed, and her mind began to drift as she settled down under the luxurious covers, entertaining imagery mainly to do with him diving into bed with her. In the fantasy she didn't stop him; she was confident and even sexually aggressive. Part of her wanted to call a halt to the daydreaming—it wasn't healthy; she could never act on it. He probably wouldn't fancy her in the cold light of day... But another, darker part seized on his mouth hot on hers and his hand like a brand on her inner thigh. She shifted in the bed, irritatedly aware she was arousing herself, which only made it all worse.

She was never like this. She didn't fantasise about men to the point where she got hot and bothered. Her mind just didn't go there. Mind you, she hadn't had *time* to have a rich fantasy life, let alone an active sex life. Not with a baby. She wasn't even accustomed to air travel. She was the original stay-at-home girl. With the Kulikovs there had been several shuttles to the Paris house, but life with a new baby had pretty much shut down her opportunities to explore further afield than the Île de la Cité.

Her thoughts drifted from blue-eyed, hard-bodied Russian oligarchs to the more prosaic realities of her life. It had been impossible to leave Kostya for more than a few hours, and Anais had insisted no one had Maisy's 'way' with him. The deal had been she would have two days a week to herself, but the reality of a demanding infant had virtually turned Maisy into the mother of a newborn, with all the rigours that involved. The only normal life she had ever had was in those few months before Anais gave birth. Then they'd been girlfriends together, enjoying each other's company and all the fun opportunities London had to offer.

Leo had been home a lot then too, as Anais grew huge, and settled, hovering over her protectively, acting on her merest whim. Maisy had envied her friend that security, that devotion. Anais in turn had encouraged her to date, pushed her out through the door with a gaggle of Anais's other girlfriends into nightclubs.

For a few months she had lived like any other twenty-one-year-old girl in London. Those were the days when she'd had time to spend hours trawling clothes shops and dancing until dawn. She had met a couple of boys around her age and been in the awkward position of having to choose. Dan had worked at something in the music industry that apparently involved twiddling knobs, but he had been gentle and self-effacing and would sit up talking to her in little cafes until dawn drew her back to Lantern Square and Anais's barrage of delighted interrogation.

She had finally gone back to his flat near Earls Court and slept with him. It had seemed the right thing to do, moving the relationship along, except it hadn't quite turned out that way. She remembered lying there on his hard bed, staring at the pattern of cracks in the ceiling as Dan pushed into her virgin body, feeling self-conscious about their nakedness and wondering if she was doing something wrong. It had been quick and painful and messy, and not something she particularly wanted to repeat with him, and with that thought had came the utter certainty she had made a mistake.

She hadn't shared this with Anais—she hadn't told anybody. And a few days later, after an awkward coffee with Dan and an invitation to spend the weekend with him on a working trip, she'd ended it. The fact that he hadn't seemed too bothered had made her wonder if she was the only girl in his life.

Within weeks Anais had gone into labour, and Maisy's life as she'd begun to live it had been over. From then on, for two years, she had been the mother of a demanding baby boy.

It would have been impossible to make Alexei Ranaevsky understand the complexities of her relationship with Anais and Kostya last night. He probably would have been even less inclined to take her along. 'A friend of Anais's' sounded insubstantial—and, knowing many of Anais's girlfriends, she wouldn't have left a pot plant in their care, let alone a two-year-old.

No, *nanny* sounded sensible and professional and *useful.*

He needed a nanny, not a flighty girl with her head in a fashion magazine and her body on a beach in Ibiza. Yet deception did not sit easily with her. She wanted to be herself, not an imitation of whatever was expected of a nanny in this man's home. She hadn't even asked him if he had a partner or children. It would be shocking, given his actions last night, but not unheard of. Maisy had lived long enough in Anais's world to know adultery was a common coin and nobody blinked an eye.

What had happened tonight made no sense to her—from his perspective at least. He must have read signals into her behaviour, and she thought guiltily about the way she had visually eaten him up. She was less irresistible to him. He had been far more in control than she had. It had been he who had stopped it, owned it for a mistake.

He was clearly exhausted. The shadows under those beautiful eyes…the lines carved around his sensual mouth. Running on empty, Leo would say. Maybe she'd been available fuel, a willing female body. And she *had* been willing—shamingly willing. She had never felt that instant drench of attraction in her life. She still couldn't look at him without wanting to touch him, feel the solid heat of his body pressed up against hers. It was *wicked.*

She rolled onto her back, staring up at a ceiling starred with dozens of tiny pinpricks of light. Was this how Anais had felt about Leo? Was this like the wellspring of her friend's uninhibited passion for her husband, which had manifested itself as a longing for him whenever he was absent and a great deal of time spent in the bedroom, or the library, or on the kitchen table—much to Maisy's embarrassment as she'd come home unexpectedly one afternoon?

This was what she had been looking for, Maisy realised with a start. This passion. This excitement. This much man.

Except he was the wrong man.

Just as she was the wrong woman. The nanny.

Dawn was breaking over Naples when they hit the tarmac. Maisy had never travelled in a private jet, and the waiting limos were another shock to her system.

Alexei Ranaevsky was seriously loaded.

He was also not coming with them.

In the first limo with Kostya, Maisy gathered the courage to ask Carlo, who was travelling with them, why not.

'A chopper to Rome,' he replied briefly. 'London has held up several important meetings.'

Meaning his visit to Lantern Square. Perversely, Maisy felt a rush of anger towards both Carlo and Alexei. Kostya was not a *hold-up*. He was a little boy who had lost his parents. Surely Alexei could carve out more than an overnight flit to welcome the child?

Carlo gave her a wry look. 'Don't worry, *bella*, he'll be back. You'll see enough of him.'

Maisy stiffened at the familiarity of *bella*, and its implications. Plain enough words, but all of a sudden Maisy wondered if Alexei had spoken to Carlo, revealed what had occurred. It was too crass to bear thinking about, but Maisy's hands made fists in her lap and her whole body was on red alert.

She averted her face to the window and didn't say another word.

So this was where he lived.

The sixteenth-century exterior of Villa Vista Mare had not hinted at its sleek interior: soaring ceilings, glass everywhere, and blinding white surfaces. It was like stepping into the future. Maisy was accustomed to the shabby Georgian chic at

Lantern Square and the pretty comfort of the Kulikovs' other residence on the Île de la Cité in Paris. This sort of cutting-edge modernity and the money it took to fuel it was startling, and also troubling. Kostya's life was going to be here now. It screamed style and money and glamour. It didn't hold you in its arms and murmur 'home'.

Seven days later she was doing her best to install some of Lantern Square into Kostya's surroundings. She couldn't fault the nursery. Not unexpectedly, it was over the top. Alexei clearly believed the advent of a child into his life called for lots of *stuff*. The life-size pony on rockers was perhaps the worst of it. A sleigh for a bed was inspired. Over the week she had shifted the worst out and created a softer space.

Kostya was universally loved by the household; Maria the housekeeper, a handsome woman in her middle fifties, doted on him. But every morning Maisy woke with the expectation that today would be the day Alexei Ranaevsky would put in an appearance, and every morning she was disappointed. She couldn't make sense of his behaviour. He had spoken of his responsibility for Kostya, yet his actions spoke volumes as to where he saw Kostya in his life.

There was a room for the nanny off the nursery. It was utilitarian, with a view of the courtyard wall. Maisy tried not to spend any time in there other than to sleep, and she slept a lot. Alexei had organised a night nurse to be on duty, which meant she could sleep through the night for the first time since Kostya had been born. Six nights of uninterrupted sleep. She felt a hundred years younger.

Every day she took Kostya down to the beach in the morning, and read books on the terrace during the afternoon whilst he took his nap. In the evenings she would have liked to eat with Maria, but the housekeeper usually left at seven, after providing a solo meal. The rest of the skeleton staff seemed paid to be invisible. It was as if she was living in a palatial hotel all by herself.

On the seventh day she asked Maria if she might have a car to take down into the town. She had noticed a converted stable in the grounds securing seven sleek luxury vehicles.

'I don't want anything fancy,' she hastened to add. 'Just some beat-up thing I can motor about in.'

Maria laughed at her. 'You can borrow mine, Maisy. It's insured, and there's a child's seat in the back. I use it for my granddaughter.'

Maisy recognised that she was feeling a wild pleasure at the thought of getting out of the villa out of proportion to the lure of shops and other people. She ran upstairs and shimmied out of her T-shirt and shorts, replacing them with a green-and-pink floral sundress she had bought for her aborted trip to Paris. It was modest in the neckline, protecting her décolletage from the harsh sunshine, and fell just above her knees, but was virtually backless. She whipped her hair out of its ponytail and shook out her curls, solving that problem.

She got Kostya ready and strapped him into the car, giving Maria an enthusiastic wave as she rolled out of the courtyard and took off up the dusty road towards the highway that would take her down the hairpin bends and dips of the road into Ravello.

She had specific chores to undertake: organise funds from her English bank account, purchase a sturdier hat to protect Kostya from the fiery Italian sun, and stock up on trashy paperbacks. But it was impossible not to get sidetracked by the beauty of the old town.

Crossing the road after purchasing *gelato* for herself and Kostya, she spotted a beauty therapist's. The warm breeze caressed her bare legs and reminded her she was in desperate need of a wax. With Kostya sucking on his ice and occupied with a box of toys, she was able to deal with her legs *and* have her hair trimmed and blow-dried. Feeling infinitely more attractive than she had going in, Maisy strapped Kostya back into his pushchair and headed for the gardens she had spotted at the other end of the road.

Several cars slowed down, passing her, and a group of youths called out in Italian to her. She didn't understand a word but it was fairly clear it was appreciative. Maisy shook her head in disbelief. A pretty dress and 'new' hair and suddenly she was on display.

'Don't you grow up to be so silly, Kostya,' she said, ruffling the top of his fair head.

A screeching of tyres made her look up. A low-slung sports car was humming alongside the kerb. Maisy froze.

'Get in the car.'

Maisy released a deep breath, unaware she had been holding it. *Alexei.*

He was leaning over the steering wheel, his cobalt eyes hidden behind razor-sharp sunglasses. He looked what he was: cool, ruthless, very male.

She needed to handle this with the same cool. It was important not to appear eager or pleased or even furious that it had taken him seven days—*seven days*—to put in an appearance. It wasn't easy when any woman in her right mind would have leapt in that car with him without a second thought.

She glanced ahead at the gardens and then, deciding, put the brake on the pushchair and crossed the few steps to the kerb, leaning in.

'We're going to the gardens. I promised Kostya.'

She turned her back on his incredulous face, kicked off the brake and kept moving, making a beeline for the gates.

Alexei slotted the car into a space overlooking the sea and took off after Maisy on foot. When Maria had casually told him Maisy had just walked out of the villa and taken the boy with her he'd been annoyed his security team hadn't been alerted. The further information that she had taken Maria's old Audi had infuriated him. Those hairpin bends were suicidal if you didn't know them. But it was the sight of her in a flowery dress, with her arms and legs bare and all those pre–Raphaelite curls flowing down her back, being cat-called and ogled by Italian males that had sent him over the top.

Maisy wasn't sure if he would drive away and leave them alone, or come after them. What she didn't expect was for him to lay a hand on her elbow and wrench her almost off her feet. He whisked her around as if she were a doll. She had forgotten how big he was. The breadth of his shoulders and his musculature were outlined by the expensive weave of an olive T-shirt. Held up against him, Maisy felt warmth sweeping up into her cheeks, his proximity having the same upending effect on her senses it had had in London.

'What in the *hell* do you think you're doing?' he blistered at her.

The sunglasses meant she couldn't see his eyes, but she could feel them nevertheless—boring into her.

'Going into the gardens,' she answered, trying to pull her arm free. But he had a firm grip. 'For goodness' sake, let me go. I don't understand why you're so angry.'

Alexei took in her wide hazel eyes and soft mouth, the colour in her cheeks. She was a time bomb waiting to go off. He couldn't have this much woman living under his roof. He'd end up giving her anything she asked for.

She made a soft distressed sound as his hand instinctively tightened and he released her immediately, shocked by his own conduct. He had imagined—*imagined*—he could deal with her in a short interview at the house. Confront her with his investigator's report, set out the terms for her remaining with Kostya until he settled, and then ignore her. He was doing a good job of ignoring her. For six days and seven nights. Long nights—except for the sixteen hours he had slept under the effect of a sedative.

He wasn't unaccustomed to periods of time without a woman in his bed. There was something rejuvenating about the spread of a cool, empty king-size bed. But Maisy Edmonds had been there every night in his waking dreams, with her wild red curls and her lush, eminently squeezable bottom, and the spicy taste of her still tingling in his mouth. He hadn't misremembered her mouth—it *was* sweet and pink. The places he had imagined that mouth had been... To see it now, unmarked by lipstick, soft and innocent-looking, he felt like a sex-crazed brute.

'Leave my Maisy alone!' stated Kostya, standing up in his pushchair. He had managed to unclip his belt, and this held Maisy's amazed attention, whilst Alexei, deeply shaken by his reaction, faced her little protector with a tad more subtlety.

He instantly dropped down to Kostya's height. 'I didn't mean to upset Maisy. I'm Maisy's friend too. I came to bring you both home.'

'Don't want to go home. Want to be on holiday.'

'The villa *is* holiday,' explained Maisy, still looking at Alexei uneasily, as if he was liable to spring at her.

Alexei released his breath with a hiss and straightened up, extending his arms to Kostya. 'Come on, little man. How about I carry you for a bit?'

Kostya looked up at Maisy, and after a hesitation she nodded encouragingly, holding her breath as Alexei lifted the little boy into his arms. For a minute it seemed he might protest, but Alexei held him confidently, and Maisy saw the moment the little body relaxed into the man's shoulder.

It gave her a chance to observe him more closely. He was wearing jeans and they clung to him like a second skin. They also made him look younger, and it occurred to Maisy for the first time he was really only a few years older than she was. He couldn't be more than thirty and look at the life he led, the power he wielded, the level of sophistication he wore so casually. Maisy suddenly felt hopelessly out of her depth—and she was—but she had Kostya's wellbeing to fight for, and that gave her the added push she needed.

And the fact remained he had been gone for an entire week.

'Where have you been for the last seven days?' The words were out of her mouth before discretion could check her tongue.

He shrugged. 'What does it matter? I'm here now.'

He was here now. Maisy simmered on that for a few minutes as they resumed their stroll. She leaned into the pushchair that felt light as a feather now Kostya wasn't in it.

'How long will you stay?' she asked evenly, as if it were not the most important question.

'I've factored in three days.' He announced it with an air of magnanimity that stole Maisy's breath away.

Three days! She studied the man beside her. She was aware people were watching them, women were watching *him*. A couple of beautiful Italian girls perhaps her own age swung past them, sweeping Alexei's length with unabashed sexual speculation. Maisy blushed for him. Alexei, however, seemed completely unaware of anyone but herself and Kostya. In fact his focus was a little intimidating.

'Three days isn't very long,' she ventured quietly, carefully.

'It's all I have.' His tone was a warning to cease questioning him, to keep her mouth shut. She remembered his statement—*'I don't explain my actions.'* Certainly not to the nanny, she thought wryly.

'Explain to me why you borrowed Maria's car and made this very dangerous little trip into town,' he said in a quiet undertone clearly used to avoid disturbing Kostya.

He had pushed the sunglasses back through his hair revealing those incredible eyes that were every bit as intense as she remembered.

'It wasn't dangerous,' she replied, copying his neutral tone. 'I'm a good driver and I'm careful.' Then the truth surfaced and she made a frustrated sound. 'You try being cooped up in one place for a full seven days.'

He smiled slowly, knowingly. 'You were bored, *dushka*?'

Maisy was startled by the smile, the sudden intimacy of his tone. She shook it off with the suspicion he was probably like this with all women under thirty, unthinkingly working them up with throwaway charisma.

'Not bored, exactly,' she said uncertainly, wondering how honest she should be.

Your house is full of people who don't talk to me; Maria and the night nurse have taken over many of the usual calls on my time; I'm only twenty-three and I feel like I've been walled up alive some days.

'I just wanted to look around, get my bearings.'

'Yes, I saw you getting your bearings on the street. Half the male population of Ravello is going to be on the villa's doorstep.'

He spoke casually, but there was an edge in his voice.

'It's not my fault if Italian men are appreciative of women,' she replied stiffly. 'I didn't invite it.'

'That dress invites it.' His tone remained casual, but Maisy heard the censure and stiffened.

'Are you suggesting I'm trying to pick up?' she challenged.

Alexei's expression was taut, hinting at inner tensions she couldn't guess at. 'I'm Kostya's guardian,' he enunciated plainly. 'I expect you to behave like a lady and not flaunt yourself.'

Maisy didn't know what to say. In what way had she flaunted herself? What was wrong with coming into town for the day? What was wrong with her dress? All of a sudden the warmth and freedom of the day dwindled down to a cluster of doubts, and Maisy tugged self-consciously on her skirt. She couldn't help flashing back to herself in a towel, stunned by his presence in her room. Was that the impression he had of her? A woman who displayed herself to strange men for sex? She cringed at the thought.

The truth wasn't much better, and it wasn't fair. It was him. It was because of him she had responded so uninhibitedly. But how could she explain that to him without making even more of a fool of herself?

Kostya had slumped over Alexei's shoulder, taking in the view from this new height. He looked so comfortable up there Maisy only felt worse.

She had to rid herself of this stupid infatuation. It wasn't fair to Kostya, and it wasn't fair to her.

'You've gone very quiet,' Alexei said in a neutral voice.

'I'm sorry. I wasn't aware I was supposed to entertain you. I wouldn't want to be accused of flaunting myself.' Where had that bitter tone come from? She bit her tongue.

Alexei's eyes swept her body in a way that was disturbingly intimate, met her stormy eyes. 'You can have a social life here, Maisy. I just don't want you bringing men back to the villa.'

Maisy almost choked, forced to defend herself. 'What men? The only men I've seen for the past week have been in uniforms, and they barely give me the time of day!'

'Hence your little day out.' He spoke so quietly, so reasonably, Maisy could have hit him.

She stopped on the path, aware there were other people around and that Kostya, however young, shouldn't be overhearing this conversation. 'I think you've made it clear how low your opinion of me can go. I don't think I should have to defend myself when I've done nothing wrong.'

Alexei instantly felt like a jerk. He knew he was being tough on her, but she provoked him. She was so lovely even a sackcloth wouldn't stop men looking at her, and why it bothered him so much he was struggling to understand.

Because you want her, and if it backfires you're stuck with her, a cool, cynical voice intervened.

The child heavy in his arms was a reminder of how careful he had to be.

'I think we should go back,' he said gruffly. 'The boy has fallen asleep.'

Maisy didn't reply. She just jerked the lightweight pushchair around and headed back up the path ahead of him.

It occurred to him she was acting like a girlfriend, not the nanny. And he didn't have any experience of girlfriends.

Alexei took them back to the villa in his high-speed toy at a reasonable pace, handling the bends with such care and confidence Maisy realised he might have a point about the danger. Maria's Audi would be returned to her by a despatched member of staff.

There was a taut, tense silence in the car that was tying Maisy's stomach in knots.

She took a deep breath and examined his hard, uncompromising profile as he negotiated the road. An innocent trip into town had been turned into a man-trawling exercise on her part. He was clearly ready to believe the worst of her because it would make it easier for him to get rid of her when the time came.

Whatever I do, she thought a little desperately, *it won't be enough because he's decided I'm a party girl.* Which was so ludicrous she snorted.

His attention snapped to her. 'What is it?'

Maisy checked over her shoulder. Kostya's head was hanging; he was still deeply asleep.

She gave Alexei her best impression of Anais-like insouciance. 'I was just thinking, if all the men in Ravello are hot for me I'm going to need some evenings off to accommodate them. How about Fridays and Saturdays?'

It was a stupid thing to do, but he was *so* self-righteous. She wanted to show him how silly all his preconceptions of her actually were. Instead, the moment the words were out of her mouth she knew she had made a mistake.

The car shifted down a gear, slowed, came to a soft standstill on the side of the road. Alexei unsnapped his safety belt, glancing into the backseat at the slumbering infant. Maisy shrank back against the door, suddenly wary of what she'd stirred up.

'Wh—what are you doing?' she stammered.

'I need to make a call,' he informed her, head averted, scissoring the door open and closed.

Lacing his hands behind his neck, Alexei walked out his frustration along the verge, taking a few deep breaths. She was a very young, very provocative woman. She was taunting him because he'd offended her. She didn't mean to push his buttons. But she had.

He couldn't drive safely until he'd worked this through.

All the men in Ravello. He'd brought it up. He'd put the words into her mouth. He'd put the thoughts into her head. Maisy was clearly no more promiscuous than he was. Yet…images he'd never be free of flashed like a viewfinder through his mind. His mother's clients—sordid, terrifying for the child he had been. He let them flicker, then shut them off with abrupt practised closure, glancing back at the car. He could see her head bent, the gleam of all those fiery ringlets. He took a breath. This was Maisy—this was different. There was nothing more natural than his desire to take her to bed.

Maisy sat drowning in the sudden silence. She watched him in the rear-vision mirror as he walked slowly away from the car. Even through her shot nerves she registered his back view was every bit as scrumptious as the front, and he had an amazing taut behind.

She buried her hot face in her hands. *Me and my mouth*, she cursed. *What was I thinking? What am I doing? It was a joke—a silly joke. But of course he doesn't do jokes. This is all getting completely out of hand.*

She heard a click and felt the shift of weight in the car, dragging her hands away too late to find him beside her, watching her with the oddest expression. It was too late to hide her embarrassment.

Unsophisticated, foot-in-mouth Maisy.

'That didn't take long,' she blurted out, sounding uncomfortably breathless.

He was watching her and there was real, undisguised heat in his eyes. Maisy's breathing hitched and sped up. The buzzing atmosphere she recognised from her room was in the car. She had never felt anything like it, and with it came the memory of the feel of his mouth sliding over hers, the sheer force of his lust. You couldn't dress it up as anything else—they barely knew one another, and she had been with him all the way. Why wouldn't he think she would do it again?

'I decided I didn't need to make the call.' A smile sat tight on his lips as he turned over the quiet engine. 'Maybe you should reconsider all the men in Ravello, Maisy. I have a feeling you're going to be pretty busy.'

'With Kostya?' said Maisy by rote, her mouth dry, her throat closed.

'No.' He swung the sports car fluidly back onto the highway and accelerated ever so slightly, so that the breath leapt from her body. 'That would be with me.'

CHAPTER FOUR

BY THE time they drew into the courtyard she was a mass of nerves, but Alexei, in contrast, seemed completely energised. He already had Kostya out of his child's seat and was carrying him and the pushchair inside with the casual assurance that he would keep the boy with him for the rest of the afternoon—leaving Maisy to fumble with her shopping bag, feeling utterly swamped.

So much for looking after him. She was left with the shopping.

She could hardly credit what had happened. He had to be joking. He couldn't possibly be suggesting what it sounded like he was suggesting. She chased his words around her head as she went through the motions of decanting her purchases onto her bed and taking a shower in the modest *en suite* bathroom to freshen up. She was so distracted she almost doused her brand-new hair, just dodging the water stream in time.

This whole sexual attraction thing was inappropriate and dangerous. Alexei was like that car of his—high-powered. Things could veer out of control if she didn't handle him properly. She needed to tone it down, deflect him in some way. The problem was deep down she liked his approval—she liked that spark he got in his eyes. The woman in her did a slow burn every time he so much as looked in her direction.

Pulling on yoga pants and a long T-shirt, she told herself these clothes would firmly put the kybosh on any inclinations he had in her direction. Except, lingering in front of the mirror, she knew she was kidding herself. Deep down she wanted what she'd had in her room in London. She wanted him to look at her and lose control again. At the same time the idea terrified her, because it would involve tipping into a level of sexual intimacy she didn't know if she was ready for. A solitary horrible experience had not encouraged her in any way to repeat it, even if she had the opportunity. But for a week now in her darkest thoughts he had been there, lifting her, his mouth on her, the heat of his body being accepted into hers.

Her reflection in the mirror taunted her. Her skin felt tight, hot and her eyes as dark as she'd ever seen them, the pupils enlarged. Her body was giving her messages she was finding difficult to ignore.

Frustrated with herself, Maisy stripped and pulled on a soft knit top and her favourite jeans instead. They weren't obvious but they clung in all the right places. She told herself there was nothing wrong with enjoying a little male attention. She just needed to keep everything within bounds.

She could hear Kostya before she reached him. Alexei was sprawled on the floor with him in the entertainment room. Maisy hesitated, watching them. They were building blocks, and every time Alexei got eight up Kostya would knock them down, shrieking with glee. *Within bounds?* a dry little voice murmured in her head. *And whose bounds would they be, Maisy, his or yours?*

Alexei's head came up and she knew who had won.

'I can't win,' he said, his dark voice full of rich amusement. 'He's clearly experienced in demolition. I might employ him.'

Maisy took one step and then another into the room. She had not seen him so relaxed before and it made a spectacular sight.

Alexei made a round trip of Maisy whilst Kostya crawled about collecting his blocks. The scoop-necked knit top clung gently to the round shape of her full breasts and flared out over her hips. She was shaped like an hourglass—something he hadn't fully appreciated until this moment. If his hands were around that little waist of hers he was sure his fingers would meet. The jeans were like a second skin, tapering over her slender calves to her small feet.

Maisy exuded a soft femininity that had the testosterone pounding through him, obliterating any sensible thought he might have had about putting the lid on this attraction. Her curves, he recognised in a flash of clarity, made a nightmare of every sharp hipbone he had ever cut himself on.

Only one thought was pumping through his brain: where had this woman been all his life? His mouth was dry by the time she crouched down and brushed the curls from Kostya's eyes.

'He needs a haircut.' His voice was thick, darkened by the sexual impulses thrumming through his blood.

Her mouth tensed. He loved that she didn't wear lipstick. 'Not yet.'

'I'll get a barber in.'

'No.' A little frown line creased between her brows.

'Are you going to fight me on everything, Maisy?'

'If I have to.'

A very blatant image of Maisy naked, on top of him, assaulted his senses, and all Alexei could do about it was smile at her, wondering what magic words were going to break down whatever defences she had in place.

Maisy was making sure she looked him in the eye. He needed to understand when it came to Kostya she wouldn't let him steamroll her. But then he smiled that lazy big cat smile that made her tingle down to her toes and suspect they weren't talking about Kostya at all. She did her best to ignore the tingling.

'I don't think now is a good time for haircuts.'

Alexei sat up, the movement so abrupt Maisy almost jumped. He was sitting so close to where she was hunkered down she could have reached out and brushed the back of her hand along his lightly bristled jaw. She blushed at the thought.

'I spoke to a child psychologist on Monday,' he responded.

Right. Child psychologist. Good. Maisy moistened her lips. 'Maybe we can talk about it later,' she said jerkily, trying not to read too much into his close proximity. 'Kostya might be little but he has big ears.' She struggled to inject some normality into her voice, which seemed to have dropped an octave. 'Besides, it's the three Bs: bathtime, booktime, bedtime.'

Alexei could have punched the air in a victory salute. She was feeling him: the pink in her cheeks, the glitter in those cinnamon eyes. She was just a little nervous. Or it could be anticipation. He had no idea. She wasn't putting out obvious 'come and get me' signals, just little indicators she couldn't control.

'I can do that,' he replied, surging to his feet. Time to get this train on the tracks. He scooped up Kostya, who shrieked with excitement.

'No, no, you'll overstimulate him.' Maisy sighed as she clambered to her feet. She was feeling distinctly unlike herself. Her skin was prickling with awareness and she couldn't seem to get in enough air. Instinctively she stumbled back to avoid brushing against Alexei as he moved with Kostya, shoving her hands in her jeans' back pockets to disguise their trembling.

Overstimulation *was* in the air, Alexei reflected ruefully, looking down at her. Damn, she was sexy. He tried not to let his gaze drift south of her pretty mouth. It was very uncool. But he was enjoying that too—the sheer craziness of what was going on.

He followed her upstairs to the nursery, admiring the swing of her round, shapely bottom, knowing absolutely he was going to end tonight with his hands right there and Maisy's glorious red-gold ringlets spread over his pillow. The certainty stayed with him as he went through the bedtime routine. Maisy kept taking peeks at him when she thought he wasn't watching. He could read women's sexual arousal and he could feel Maisy's deep down to his bones. She just needed a little gentle handling and direction.

'Will you have dinner with me?' he said as Maisy grappled

with Kostya's nappy, and she gave him a wry look. Her nervousness had evaporated under the stress of managing a two-
year-old and she was getting mouthy with him. He liked that
too.

'Is that an excuse to get out of here whilst the going's good?'

'I can *handle* a nappy, Maisy.'

'The question is, will you in the future? Or are you going
to hire a dozen people to do the job for you?'

The criticism went home. Maisy observed his slight tensing
and was glad. It showed he did have an understanding of what
Kostya needed. The fact that he was here now, helping her, had
gone a long way to calming her fears. She had also managed
not to touch him, ogle him, or say anything that could be mis-
construed. In fact, she had behaved like a completely sexless
plant.

Perfect.

'Dinner, Maisy?' he repeated.

'I usually eat in the dining room at seven,' she said. 'Will
you join me then?'

Alexei dealt her a look of combined disbelief and complete
amusement.

'I think, *dushka*, we can do better than that.'

Dinner.

Maisy covered her hot face with her hands. She was going
to sleep with him. Maybe. It was good to be clear about these
things. She wouldn't think about next week or the month after
or the year after that. She would just go for it and damn the
consequences. Other women did it all the time.

She was a modern girl. She knew what was on offer.

She was kidding herself.

Maisy groaned and flopped onto her bed. Beside her lay the
two outfits she couldn't decide between. Her one cocktail dress
looked too formal and insubstantial, and clearly said, *Take me
now. I'm not even wearing a bra.* Definitely not suitable.

The strapless white silk frock was really for the daytime,

but she could dress it up with a necklace, some make-up, and do something fancy with her hair. The bodice was boned and did the work of a bra. Just about.

In the end she made up her eyes and mouth to stand in for the simplicity of her dress and clasped a gold filigree necklace around her neck. She used a clip to twist up her hair so that it toppled in disarray, the tips kissing the curve of her shoulder-blades. She slid her feet into a pair of very high silver heels and used the sliding doors to step out into the courtyard so as not to disturb Kostya.

She climbed the back stairs to the kitchen, feeling a little like Cinderella gearing up for the ball and going in the back way.

'Maisy, *bella figura*!' Maria exclaimed in Italian when she came into the kitchen, dusting off her floury hands and leaving the bread she was kneading to come and encircle Maisy, smiling broadly.

'Dinner with the boss, eh?' Maria folded her arms, shaking her head.

'To talk about Kostya,' Maisy answered primly.

The older woman gave her an old-fashioned look. 'He's a good boy,' observed Maria. 'But all these parties, these women.' She threw her hands up expressively.

Parties? *Women?* Maisy just knew she didn't want to hear any of this. Yet when Maria sighed and went back to kneading the bread she wanted to scream, *And*?

Maria's raisin-brown eyes slanted sideways at Maisy. 'What he needs is a good girl who can cook, raise the *bambinos* and keep him happy in the bed, yes?'

Maisy didn't know where to look. Cook, clean and heat up the sheets… Oh, and don't forget the baby-making factory. No, thank you.

'He might have learned the English, and he has the houses in Miami and New York, but he's European.' Maria leaned her floury forearms on the board and fixed Maisy with a steely determination at odds with her short, round little body. 'The

Russian men—they're like the Italians. They are traditional. Oh, times have moved on, and Alexei is what they say—*a modern guy*—but when he settles down...'

Maria straightened up with a sigh and wiped her hands.

'He doesn't particularly strike me as being ready to settle down just yet,' Maisy muttered, wishing they weren't having this conversation so close to her sitting down to dinner with him in a strapless dress.

'If you leave it to the men they'll *never* be ready,' said Maria. 'They always need the little nudge.'

Alexei would need some heavy earth moving equipment and possibly a natural disaster to shift him out of bachelor status, Maisy thought ruefully. He didn't strike her at all as the marrying type.

'You must be careful, Maisy,' said the older woman, her eyes settling on Maisy's flushed décolletage. 'He is the real man, and he will chase you, and you're a nice girl.'

The real man. That he was, thought Maisy, giving her bodice an upward tug in an effort to reinstate the 'nice girl'. Preoccupied, she made her way into the dining room. Alexei wasn't there, but one of his suits was waiting for her. Maisy recognised him as Andrei, the young man who had driven her here on the first day. He was friendly towards her in a way nobody except Maria had been since her arrival and, feeling nervous, she instantly engaged him in conversation about his day as she accompanied him upstairs and onto the roof terrace.

Alexei heard her voice before he saw her, and when she emerged he made the immediate decision never to send another man to fetch Maisy. In future he would undertake that task himself.

She was wearing some sort of frock, but it was difficult to register that when she moved, because the killer heels made her sway and he was pretty sure there was nothing between Maisy and that dress but air. The neckline was relatively modest—she wasn't spilling out of it, but the shape of her gave the impression she was. It was a dress designed to make a man think about what was poured into it. He was already planning how to take her out of it.

Maisy felt like a princess as he advanced towards her. Behind him there was a round table dressed in white and crystal, and there he was, in dark formal trousers and an expensive white shirt open at the neck to reveal the tanned strong column of his throat.

This wasn't a considered discussion about Kostya's future. This was a date.

'You always make me wait, Maisy.'

She looked up at him without understanding.

Up close, he saw she'd made a mystery of her cinnamon eyes and her lush mouth was a deep pink. There was a faint scent of exotic flowers clinging to her skin. She'd made an effort to be beautiful for him, he acknowledged. It meant *he* had to make an effort and not ravish her on the table before the first course.

He seated her and sat down across from her.

'You look beautiful, Maisy.'

She gave him a wry look. It wasn't the reaction he had been after.

'Do you always dine here, up on the rooftop?'

'Occasionally, when the mood strikes.'

He lifted the champagne and decanted some into a flute glass for her and then poured his own. Maisy watched the pale bubbles surge.

'It's so lovely,' she said, gazing around. 'I would eat up here all the time if I could. Is Maria preparing the meal?'

'I left that to the chef, *dushka*.' He looked faintly curious, as if her questions were not quite what he was expecting.

'She didn't mention it, that's all, and the kitchen was very quiet.'

'What were you doing in the kitchen?'

'Talking to Maria.'

Alexei gave her an odd look. 'Then you were talking to Andrei?'

She nodded. 'I didn't know you had a chef. Maria's been

making all my meals. She's a wonderful cook. I'm sure I'll put on ten pounds whilst I'm here if I don't start running again. Why are you staring at me? What I have said?'

'I hadn't realised you were so tight with the housekeeper,' was all he observed, sipping from his glass.

'She's been incredible with Kostya, and he's really taken to her.'

Alexei merely inclined his head, and suddenly Maisy understood the man sitting across from her didn't really care about any of this. He wasn't listening to her. He was *watching* her. He never actually looked directly at her breasts, but Maisy knew that he was *seeing* them because they had tightened, and suddenly the boning in her dress didn't feel anywhere near substantial enough.

Men didn't make a habit of looking at her like this. Especially men sitting across from her, pouring her champagne and looking as if they'd stepped out of a style magazine.

'Let's talk about Kostya,' she said, her high voice betraying a sudden rush of nerves.

'Drink your champagne, Maisy. You haven't touched a drop.'

Automatically she lifted the glass to her lips and took a sip. It tasted divine. She took another sip and sucked some of it off her lip. Premier champagne and pink shimmer lipstick—perhaps not the perfect combination.

Alexei watched her lip plump out, all wet and shiny from her tongue and the champagne. He would lick her there, later on, and then he would lick her further down, where she would also be plump and wet and wanting. He shifted in his chair as his body stirred to life.

Maisy put her glass down with a bump and he noticed her hands were trembling a little. Which was good. Hell, his weren't exactly steady. He lifted his eyes to hers, but instead of desire he saw a little worry line of concern drawing her lovely dark brows together.

'We really need to talk about Kostya,' she insisted a little more firmly.

Alexei made a frustrated but resigned sound in the back of his throat. 'Fine. We talk.'

Maisy folded her hands in her lap. She looked prim and proper—and that, he discovered, revved him up too.

'Do you intend for Kostya to live here in Ravello?'

As enquiries went it was pretty innocuous and reasonable, yet it was one Alexei knew he wouldn't answer in any other circumstances. He was so accustomed to guarding his privacy it had become habit never to respond to questions. Refusing to answer, however, wasn't conducive to persuading Maisy out of that dress, so he settled for neutral. '*Nyet*. Villa Vista Mare is only one of my homes.'

Maisy experienced a sinking feeling. 'How many do you have?'

'Seven,' he said briefly, as if it were of no import.

'Seven?' she repeated. 'What on earth do you need seven homes for?'

'Convenience,' he said after a pause.

At that moment a waiter appeared with their entrée—crab bisque—and Maisy smiled at him and waited as she was served.

Alexei wondered a little testily if she showered those smiles on every male she met except him.

'Does that mean Kostya will be travelling the world with you, to these homes?'

'*Da.*'

Maisy sighed deeply, looking past him into the flickering darkness, saying almost to herself, 'How is this going to work?'

Alexei gestured to her plate. 'Eat, Maisy. Worry later.'

She nibbled on some crab meat and finally gave him the full impact of her smile. 'It tastes of the sea,' she imparted, as if this were a wonder.

'It should,' he replied, enjoying her reaction. 'It came out of it this afternoon.'

The main course received the same enthusiasm and he watched her eat, itself a rare event. Most of the women he sat down at a table with picked their way around a plate and drank like fish. Maisy hardly touched her champagne, but cleaned up her plate.

'I've spoken to a child psychologist, as I told you earlier,' said Alexei as their plates were cleared. 'He informs me Kostya needs to feel secure here before he's told about his parents.'

'I agree completely.'

Her cheeks were flushed now—a combination of the spices in the main dish and her single half glass of champagne. Alexei knew they had to get this thorny question of Kostya's welfare sorted before he could dance with her and feed her *gelato* and watch her lick it off the spoon, and then off his tongue. He also had to get his body under control before he stood up.

'I'm dreading it,' she confessed.

He experienced a measure of guilt for his lascivious thoughts. He needed to focus on this. It mattered.

'He hasn't asked for his parents?' he said slowly.

Maisy folded her napkin. 'No.'

There was a long silence. He was clearly waiting for an explanation, but Maisy didn't know where to start without being disloyal to Anais.

For once he didn't push her, and Maisy heard herself saying, 'I don't know how it is in Russia, but often in England in high-flying families the children can be overlooked.'

Alexei went very still. 'You're telling me Leo was a neglectful parent?'

Maisy suddenly felt uncomfortable, realising she had stepped unwarily into dangerous territory. She wasn't the only person at the table protective of the Kulikovs' memory. Alexei wasn't going to like what she had to say.

'It depends on your definition of *neglect*.' She decided to talk to her plate. It seemed the easiest thing to do. 'He was a busy man—you know that. He wasn't always around.'

'Kostya is an infant,' Alexei said with some assurance. 'It's natural his mother would be his primary caregiver.'

'Anais had some difficulties.' Maisy released the breath

she had been holding. 'She was very young—only twenty-one when she had him. She wasn't particularly close to her own mother. It's hard to explain. Anais didn't spend a lot of time with Kostya.'

There—she'd said it. It was out there. She looked up to find Alexei was staring at her, and it wasn't a look she was accustomed to from him.

'What sort of concoction is this, Maisy? You're trying to make me believe Leo Kulikov wasn't a good father?'

'It's not a concoction, and I'm not saying they were bad people,' she insisted. 'I'm just trying to make you understand what's going on in Kostya's little head.'

'I don't need you for that, *dushka*, I've got a child psychologist who will deal with that problem. What I'm more interested in is why you're so keen to make me think the worst.'

'I'm not,' Maisy protested. 'You wanted to know—' She broke off, upset by the contempt she could see forming in his eyes.

'I know how much Leo loved his boy,' said Alexei, in a voice that brooked no argument.

Maisy pushed the remainder of her plate away. 'I'm not hungry any more,' she said in a low voice.

Alexei leaned towards her. 'Listen to me, Maisy. I don't want to hear these stories. They don't do you any credit. I wasn't going to bring this up with you, but I've got some questions about your background I'd like cleared up before we go any further.'

'My background?' She hated the nervous tremor in her voice. It made her sound guilty of something.

'Daughter of an unemployed single mother, yet privately educated, and you'd never held down a job until you appeared in the Kulikov household two years ago.' He wielded the facts as if they were accusations.

Maisy flinched from them. He'd brought back so many memories she had hoped to leave behind for ever. She didn't want them here tonight on this Italian rooftop. She wanted to be the woman she was in the process of becoming. She wanted him to be the man she had imagined him to be.

All of a sudden she felt the past was very close to the surface.

'How did you find out all that?' she asked, gathering herself together.

'It's my business to know. What? Did you think I'd just let you in the door without a background check? Give me a break.'

'You could have asked me,' she said, with no little dignity.

'Yes, but would I believe you,' he replied silkily.

The unfairness of his accusation hurt. 'Probably not. You seem to think I'm a liar, but to what purpose I have no idea.'

He was looking at her as if she had done something unforgivable—as if she'd crawled out from under a rock somewhere. It would have been easier to make up some story, she realised sadly, tell him the same lies everybody else had expected from her: Leo and Anais were a super couple, with a super life and a super baby. But the truth was—like everyone—they had been flawed, and because they'd been larger than life their flaws had enlarged accordingly.

'Tell me,' said Alexei with deceptive calm, 'why do you think I invited you to have dinner with me tonight?'

Maisy knew she was walking into a trap. She would answer and he would say something clever and she would look a bigger fool. So she didn't say anything. She stared endlessly at her half-empty champagne glass as the seconds ticked by.

'Did you think, Maisy, we were going to talk about your employment contract? With you in your strapless frock and me pouring you champagne?'

Don't say it, she willed him. *Please don't say it.*

'Or did you think I was going to take you to bed and keep you in the style to which you've become accustomed?'

His words stripped her of cover. She had nowhere to hide from them because it was true. She had wanted to go to bed with him. She had worn her best dress and her laciest knickers. She had drunk some of the champagne for Dutch courage.

Kostya's future had come second to her desire to draw Alexei to her.

For the first time she had put the little boy second and herself first, and now she was going to pay for it. He'd set her up. She wasn't fit to look after the needs of a young child. She was a sex-crazed bimbo.

Swallowing hard, she lifted guilty eyes to meet his icy scorn. Her dignity lay in shreds around her. She felt the same way she had when huddled behind the bathroom door at Lantern Square. He *did* this to her.

'Are you going to send me away?' she asked hollowly.

Their eyes locked.

'Don't be ridiculous.'

There was a fraught silence.

Alexei suddenly wanted to smash the last five minutes and go back to where they'd been before. She was looking at him like a deer caught in the headlights—that same lost look he remembered from London. It made him want to gather her up and shelter her from the harsher realities of life, including his own. But she'd pushed all his buttons with that crack about Leo. It was absurd and it was wrong, he told himself.

'Kostya needs you.'

Maisy frowned. He said it as if the idea was distasteful to him. As if she was everything he said she was. It gave her the nerve to push out her chair and get up.

'If your stupid investigator had done a better job he would know I never *worked* for the Kulikovs. I went to school with Anais. We were best friends. I would have done anything for her. And I won't let you wreck her little boy's life. I'm one hundred per cent sure if Anais had known the future she would have named *me* Kostya's guardian. You're Leo's work. *Leo* made the mistake. Kostya shouldn't have to pay for it.'

She took a deep sustaining breath, taking some satisfaction that he looked pale and tense, but also horribly aware she had said some cruel things. But he had too. He had said she wanted to go to bed with him for *money*. He had *hurt* her.

'You lucked out, Alexei. I don't want anything from you. I thought I wanted to make love with you, but now I've never wanted anything less.'

Swaying a bit on her heels, she didn't look at him. She just walked away. He didn't try to stop her. Lust didn't override loyalty. Family came first. And Maisy, however inviting, was just a woman. Women were everywhere, he thought cynically.

'That dress,' he said coolly after her. 'Nice for a nanny. Leo must have paid you well. I expect you're *very* expensive to keep, Maisy.'

'No one has ever kept me,' she defended herself over her bare shoulder.

'I bet.' It was a crass thing to say, and Alexei instantly regretted it.

His throwaway line hit Maisy square in the solar plexus. He made her feel like a whore in her pretty dress and her make-up. All the *effort* she'd gone to… She spun around, determined not to let him have the last word, only to find he was already on his feet and coming towards her, his expression contrite, as if he'd realised he'd gone too far. But she'd moved too quickly, and her spindly heels wouldn't support the shift in her weight, and she went sprawling, jarring her shoulder as she tried to break her fall with one arm. Pain speared up her arm, making her cry out, and then she was lying on the ground, holding her arm and sucking back tears.

Alexei was on his knees beside her instantly, his arms coming around her. But as he touched her shoulder she cried out again.

'Let me help you,' he said gently, his anger no longer evident.

Maisy was too shaken up to protest, but as he lifted her she was thrown into immediate physical intimacy with him and it robbed her of breath. She could feel his biceps hard beneath her back, his big hand fastened around her thigh. He had to do these things to carry her, she reasoned wildly, but after the terrible things he had said to her the shivery reaction running through her body felt shameful. She averted her face from him, determined to block him out. If he saw how much he disturbed her it would just be more fuel for his accusations.

He carried her across the roof to the access door and down the stairs, as if she weighed nothing. Pain was pulsing through her shoulder, but the sheer awfulness of how cruelly his taunts had gone home overwhelmed it. He thought she was a liar, a party girl who spread her legs for anybody with enough cash, and he didn't want her looking after Kostya.

She wanted to cry, but she couldn't show that weakness.

She had just made the biggest fool of herself in the history of her life, and now a man who couldn't stand her—moreover a man who was an utter pig of an unreconstructed idiot, who couldn't see simple truths if they hit him in the face—was carrying her into…

His bedroom. Maisy's heartbeat sped up despite the pain.

And wasn't this what you were hoping for at the beginning of the night, Maisy Edmonds? a little voice niggled at her.

His bed was large and plain and masculine, with expensive dark blue linen. Fresh sheets, she registered. Had he been planning to seduce her here? Everything he had said to her came home, and she knew with every inch of her body she didn't want to be in here. It was too humiliating.

She began to struggle. 'Put me down. Put me down *now*!'

He was forced to release her and she slid to her feet, holding her arm folded over her chest. It was throbbing, but she had no intention of playing victim.

Alexei didn't say a word. He just made a phone call whilst she stood there, not sure what to do. He finished the call. 'A doctor's coming up to the house,' he said heavily. 'Where is the pain coming from?'

'I don't know. I think I jarred it,' she answered, swallowing hard. 'I'll go and wait in my room, if you don't mind.'

'Maisy, you had a nasty fall. Lie down here and let yourself to be checked out, okay?'

It sounded so reasonable, and the pain was pumping through

her body. But she kept seeing the look on his face when she'd told him the truth about the Kulikovs. It shouldn't matter so much, but it did.

In the end the pain won out and she sat down awkwardly on his bed. Alexei did something surprising. He dropped to one knee and reached for her foot, sliding off one shoe and then the other. There was something about seeing him silent on his knees in front of her that made her say, 'It's not your fault I fell. I did that to myself.'

'How's your arm?' he asked quietly, not making a move.

'I think it's going numb,' she said in a small voice.

'You landed at a bad angle.' He lifted his hand, hesitated, and then gently smoothed the tangle of curls that had been disturbed and now fell over one side of her face. Maisy swallowed. 'I'd give you some painkillers, but I think we should wait until the doctor has a look.'

'Okay.' The truth was she didn't want to be alone—not when her body felt as if it was in shock. And it wasn't only the fall. The implications of everything he had thrown at her were beginning to sink in.

The doctor was an urbane older man who clearly knew Alexei. He was scrupulously polite to Maisy as he examined her shoulder and prescribed painkillers, which he handed over to Alexei with instructions. Nothing was broken. Sleep and time would heal her.

'I'm a fraud,' she said tiredly. 'Nothing broken after all.'

Alexei sat down beside her on the bed. 'Take these, Maisy,' he said, and pressed two white pills against her lips.

More physical proximity she couldn't handle. Maisy drew them in with her tongue, brushing against his fingers, blushing. He'd think she was coming on to him.

He poured a little water into her mouth and she swallowed them down. His thumb lingered on her bottom lip and Maisy gazed back at him, startled, feeling heavy and tired and numb. She shifted awkwardly as the boning in her bodice dug hard.

'I need to get my dress off,' she said uncomfortably. 'I can't sleep in it.'

'Right.' He reached behind her, his fingers starting on the dozen tiny fabric buttons. His touch whispered down her back and Maisy shut her eyes, wishing everything was different. 'That's the problem with couture,' he said in a deep voice. 'No zips.'

'Anais gave it to me. I didn't know it was couture,' answered Maisy dully. 'I never looked.'

She caught her bodice with her good arm as the dress sprung free. She sat there, huddled in it, looking anxiously over her shoulder at him.

'If you turn your back I can stand up and drop it and then get into bed,' she explained awkwardly. She waited miserably for him to make some crack about it being a lousy attempt to seduce him.

Instead he said quietly, 'Of course.'

He was so formal she could only stare at him as he stood up and turned his back.

Maisy got off the bed and dropped the frock. Self-consciously she stepped out of the dress and kicked it away, shifting back onto the bed, pulling the cover up to her neck.

'Thank you,' she said awkwardly.

The pillow felt blissful beneath her head. She could feel the drugs beginning to take effect. Alexei scooped up her beautiful dress.

'I'll leave you now,' he said, in that oddly formal way. 'If you need anything just call out. I'm in the room across the hall.'

Maisy closed her eyes, damming up the tears that were brimming. She sensed the moment the lights went out.

'This wasn't how I envisaged the end of our evening,' she heard him say in a low voice from across the room.

I know, she thought miserably.

CHAPTER FIVE

MAISY opened her eyes in the vast bed to a low-grade headache and a great deal of self-recrimination as the memory of last night swamped her. She thrust her head under the pillow.

Of *his* bed.

She bolted upright, panic setting in as she realised she didn't have a shred of clothing to wear. She was trapped in his bed in her lacy knickers. After everything he had said to her last night the last thing she wanted was to be accused of angling for sex. Because that was what he'd come out and accused her of—being some sort of bimbo on the make, cavorting in couture. Ridiculous as that was.

Oh, Lord, where was her dress? The last she'd seen of it he had been carrying it away with him. Surely there were some clothes in this room?

Wrapping her arms across her bare breasts, she ran to some double doors. They opened onto a walk-in wardrobe and she spotted his shirts immediately, grabbing the nearest one and sliding her injured arm carefully into one sleeve, then the other. She had trouble with the left side buttonholes, but eventually got it done up decently enough. The shirt tails dangled almost to her knees. She went into the bathroom and washed the raccoon make-up off her face, running a hand through her unruly hair. She had to admit she didn't look that bad, all things considered, and the pain in her shoulder was now just a dull ache that should fade in a day or two.

All that had really got hurt last night was her pride.

Other thoughts intruded now. She remembered how gentle
he had been with her when he'd realised she was hurt, how he
had looked after her and how good that had felt. She had made
the mistake of opening up to him a little, but he didn't want to
hear it. She needed to remember that. Leo's death was still too
raw for him. Only the knowledge that Alexei's feelings for his
friend ran that deep gave her any comfort this morning, and
that was in regards to Kostya.

As for what he had said in regards to *them*, she probably
should thank him. At least now she wouldn't make an idiot
of herself over him. He wasn't going to kiss her again. He
might have—he might have done a great many things. Until
she opened her big mouth and brought up Leo and Anais. Now
he thought she was a liar, and apparently angling to be a kept
woman. If it wasn't so offensive she would be laughing about
it. Damn him, he owed her an apology.

Maisy glared at her reflection. She was going to get one.

Alexei felt like twenty kinds of bastard this morning as he
pulled on a pair of jeans and nothing else.

He'd been so focussed on sexual conquest last night he'd
barely appreciated Maisy's company, but a long night with only
his thoughts had replayed her laughter and her absurd commentary about his lifestyle and made him sorry he hadn't tried to
open her up a little more. But he'd closed all that down, sling-
ing insults at her as she just sat there, completely defenceless.
He had pretty much called her a whore, with nothing to support that accusation.

In fact he was starting to suspect Maisy's sexuality was as
artless as the rest of her. She wasn't selling something, and—
surprise, surprise—he didn't want to buy her. He didn't know
exactly what it was he wanted from her, but he knew a beautiful girl in a stunning dress shouldn't be pushed so far, end up
so distressed, she lost her balance trying to escape his cruel
taunts. She was lying in his bed in pain because he couldn't
deal with his goddamned issues.

This wasn't him. He didn't lose control like that. Especially with a woman. Especially not this woman. Maisy's uncomplicated sweetness was what he needed right now, so why was he pushing her away?

Barefoot and bare-chested, he crossed the hall. He lifted his hand to knock as his door swept open. She was standing there in one of his shirts, face scrubbed, amazingly beautiful.

'I want to know why you have such a low opinion of me,' she said bluntly.

The shock of seeing her like this, clearly strong and ready to take him on again, put him off balance. The combination of bare legs and *his* shirt made it difficult for him to think straight. Yet he was compelled to mutter, 'I don't have a low opinion of you.'

She stared back at him as if butter wouldn't melt in her mouth, although her eyes were all over his bare skin. 'Then maybe you could be a little nicer to me.'

Nice? She wanted him to be nice?

'How's your shoulder?'

'A little touchy, but I don't want to talk about my shoulder.'

'Neither do I, but it's good to know.' And in one movement he heaved her up over his shoulder and with his foot kicked shut the door behind them.

Oh, my.

'What are you doing?' she managed, although it would have been fairly clear to Blind Freddy what was going on. He was going to finish what he'd started in London right now, here, on this bed that was suddenly under her, and she was looking up into his laser-blue eyes and every one of her fantasies was pulsating to life.

'Yes or no, Maisy. Your decision.'

Yes, screamed her body, shifting from zero to a hundred in under two seconds. *But you hardly know him. Nice girls don't do this. Anais made Leo wait three months...*

Then he ran his thumbs gently over the inside of her wrists, lifting one of her hands to press his mouth where his thumb had been. Maisy made a soft little sound and he lifted her arms up over her head so that her breasts lifted and her body stretched out for him. He lowered himself down over her, hovering, his weight on his forearms, overwhelming her with the sheer size and strength of his body.

She broke the connection of their gaze to sweep a comprehensive look down his body, poised above hers. The faint press of his ribs, the slabs of muscle across his chest and shoulders and back, bunched as he bore the weight of his own body. It all combined to make her feel small and soft and feminine, and she wanted to touch him so badly her palms were burning.

'What do you want, Maisy?'

His scintillating blue eyes were so deep in hers Maisy found it hard to gather her words. Her heartbeat was so loud she was being deafened by it.

'I want everything,' she confided, her breath catching in her throat. 'I want you.'

Something flared in his eyes that caused a tug deep in her pelvis, and she half rose up off the mattress to meet him as he lowered his head to kiss her, long and slow and with a deep satisfaction. As if they had all the time in the world. But he kept her arms pinned so that she felt vulnerable to him in this position, her breasts rubbing slightly against his chest, her nipples sharpened with nerve endings and pressing against him shamelessly.

It felt incredibly good, yet when she tried to shift her arms his hands slid over hers and made it impossible for her to move. The more she strained against him the deeper he kissed her, her breasts sliding and pushing against him. Then he released her.

Stunned, Maisy lay alone on the bed as he leapt up. For a moment she didn't know what was going on, until full morning sunshine rushed into the room. Alexei had activated the blinds on the windows, letting in some light on the subject. Maisy blinked furiously as it hit her in the face. She brought her arms down, pressing on her good elbow as she struggled to sit up, confused and wondering exactly what she was getting herself into.

Alexei stepped in front of her so that she was forced to remain seated, gazing up at him. For one simmering moment he just stood there, looking down at her, those jeans sitting tantalisingly low on his lean hips. His abdomen was so ripped she longed to trace her fingers along the fine delineations of muscle. He was that close. A light smattering of dark chest hair covered him before arrowing down and disappearing into the V of his taut pelvic cradle. Maisy followed it with her eyes, her mouth running dry as she registered the distinct bulge. He surely didn't want that? Now? Did he? Was she supposed to start confessing everything she didn't know about the male body?

'Stop thinking, Maisy,' he instructed her, his voice warm with humour. 'Shift over, *dushka.*'

Feeling off-centre and decidedly gauche, Maisy scooted over into the centre of the bed, wondering if she should say something—if she was supposed to be doing something a more sophisticated woman would just know in her bones how to do. But he was coming down over her, blocking out the sun, and suddenly all she could see and feel and inhale was him.

He brushed his lips over her mouth, and when she instinctively responded he moved away to drop butterfly kisses along her jawline. Maisy began to sense he was playing a game with her, one of advance and retreat, as if tightening his hold on her each time. She didn't want London, she didn't want out-of-control, but nor did she want to play a part in any sort of game. She wanted simple, she thought nervously as her body responded despite her jangling thoughts. She wanted honest. She just wanted *him.*

Maybe she should tell him.

Then his breath was hot in her ear and he began to promise her things…wicked things, sexual things…and then he shifted slightly, and she was pinned under the heft of his body, and she felt every inch of what he wanted to do with her.

Oh, my.

Maisy lost her ability to think, the wicked images he had put in her head heating her blood. She wrapped her arms around his neck to anchor him to her and made her own soft, satisfied sound under the impact of his mouth on hers. She winced as her shoulder gave a sharp tug and he instantly rolled onto his back, his arm around her waist, to pull her over on top of him.

For an instant she felt a wave of disappointment. Was he going to pull away from her again?

Instead he framed her face with his big hands. 'Better for your shoulder,' he muttered against her mouth, lifting to kiss her again, and a rush of real warmth ran through Maisy because he was looking after her.

Being on top also allowed her to set the pace. She fused her mouth to his, tasting the salt and spice and goodness of him, her hands meshing in his hair as she swept her tongue into his mouth. She had absolutely no idea what she was doing. She knew the mechanics, what went where, but her single dismal experience had left her with very little understanding of what he was going to like. She hoped if she pleased herself it would please him too.

His hands were on her back, searching for the ends of his shirt and rucking it up. He spread his fingers over her cool bare skin, sweeping his hands down over her hips until he had the little scrap of lace clinging to her bottom beneath his fingers. He squeezed the lush weight of her buttocks and her knees dropped instinctively to either side of his hips. The impressive erection contained in his jeans was nestled in exactly the right spot for her, and he groaned as Maisy gave an experimental wriggle, then settled over him. He obliged, using his hands on her hips to work her rhythmically against him.

Maisy began to pant, making little gasping noises, and Alexei thought the sound alone was going to undo him. It was incredible. He felt like a teenage boy all over again, barely able to keep a leash on the urges rushing through his body. It was all Maisy—the feel and smell and look of her, and the way she used his body to satisfy herself. Something had tipped in her favour early on in this encounter and he had lost the upper hand. If he'd ever had it. He began to growl her name and her thighs clenched around him.

That deep note in his voice always pulled on her inner muscles, and combined with the friction of him under her it lit the match and Maisy moaned, body taut, as her core dissolved into liquid sunshine. Unable to believe what had happened, she pressed her mouth into the base of his throat, face blood-red, and trembled on top of him with tiny aftershocks. Oh, God—she had used him as a sex toy.

Alexei was sitting her up, moving her on past the moment, so that she was virtually straddling his lap. His bigger body made her feel small and delicate in his arms, vulnerable to him in this position. Stripped to the waist, the spread of his chest was available to her hands and she began touching him, marvelling at the strength beneath the hot skin, meshing her fingers in his light chest hair, nuzzling him with her nose and mouth, running her tongue over his flat nipples until he hissed. The sound surged through Maisy's body, giving her a much needed boost in confidence.

His hands were actually shaking as he got busy at the buttons of his shirt.

'Okay, Maisy?' His eyes sought hers again as his fingers kept on moving down the shirt.

She swayed against him and their mouths met, mingled. Maisy got a little lost in the kissing until his lips left hers, and then she looked down and saw the deep valley between her breasts had come into view. Alexei's stunning hot gaze did not shift from that moment on as he peeled the shirt open.

Alexei said something under his breath and then his big hands were splaying over them, catching up her nipples. He bent his head to take one into his mouth. His bristle-roughened chin abraded her sensitive skin as he suckled and fondled and nuzzled her, ignoring her efforts to touch him in kind until she was unbearably anxious to feel him inside her. She had not imagined in her wildest dreams she would feel this driven. It wasn't in her nature, wasn't in *her*—until now.

She put her hands on his waistband but his hands were already there, pushing her away.

'Not yet, *dushka*,' he rasped, lying her back flat on the bed and kissing down her belly to the scrap of white lace she was wearing.

She could feel her whole face suffusing in a hot blush of reaction. He edged off her knickers so slowly it felt like for ever. She was almost relieved when they were off. Then he went sliding to his knees on the floor, dragging her legs after him, so for a moment her knees hooked over his shoulders.

Maisy stopped breathing. It was an unbearably intimate position—especially when she looked down—and she wriggled, a wave of embarrassment passing over her. Then she felt him begin to blow air over the moist core of her, and she bit the fleshy part of her hand to keep from crying out.

Dan hadn't done this. Dan hadn't been anywhere near down there with his mouth. She'd read about it, but the reality was liquefying.

When he parted her and she felt his fingers slide into her she keened, and when his tongue ran over her clitoris her hips began to undulate on the bed. She didn't care how loud she was being. It didn't take long until her inner walls were tugging on his fingers as he slid them out of her, and his tongue dragged over the sweet centre of her one last time before he stood up, unhooking his jeans with suddenly clumsy fingers.

Maisy lay there watching him, her cheeks red, her eyes bright, her body unbelievably lush in his eyes. From her softly rounded arms to her breasts, the curve of her little waist to stunningly flared hips, the solidity of her female thighs and the taper of her calves down to her pretty feet. She was a pink-and-white study in eroticism, with the golden fire of her tumbled curls and the red-gold at the apex of her thighs a touch of genius.

An artist would give a great deal to paint her like this; a

man would give his soul just to look upon her. That he was getting it all sent Alexei into overdrive. He didn't want to be out of control with her, but he could already feel himself slipping and sliding towards mindless pleasure. The things he could do to her—the places he could take her if she would let him. And he knew she would let him. And every primitive male instinct in his body charged to the fore.

She sat up slowly, as if knowing not to rush her movements, and replaced his clumsy hands with her own, gently popping every last button.

He had a look of incredible concentration on his face, and as his jeans hit the floor Maisy's mouth made a perfect circle of wonder. *This* was not what she was used to. She ran a fingertip along the heavy veined shaft, wondering how on earth they were going to fit. He put his hand over hers and drew her fingers over him, around him, up and down, giving her voiceless instruction on how much pressure he needed, the speed.

Just watching him made her tremble. The force of him, the weight of his desire was almost too much. Maisy knew she had just hit the deep end and could no longer feel the bottom. He unwrapped her hand but kept hold of it, anchoring her back on the bed, coming over her. He kissed her with the full force of his mouth, his hands sliding down under her lush behind to lift her and position her.

'I want you under me the first time,' he muttered into her mouth, as if she needed telling.

Maisy felt him brush at her entrance, his blunt tip penetrating her. She reached up to stroke his face, wanting him to be looking at her, seeking a connection with him. He went a little further and then swore under his breath, pulled out of her, drew back, stood up.

'Don't move,' he instructed.

Alexei was tearing open a foil packet, and she watched as he dealt with the necessities, sheathing himself at speed, so that she was reminded he had done this far too many times. *Whilst I've only done it once*, she thought, her heart pounding.

He hadn't taken his eyes off her, and as he positioned himself over her again he paused to lean in and kiss her again—a kiss that told her he knew who she was.

He sank slowly into her, moving with stealth, as if relishing the surprisingly tight clasp of her. Maisy began to lift her hips to coax him, bring him into her. Bring him home. Her eyes flared wide as he fully seated himself. His shoulders were braced above her, the muscles heavy across his shoulders and chest. He looked down at her with the intent expression of a man who knew absolutely what he was doing. He framed her face with one hand.

'Okay, Maisy?' His voice was strained, his whole body tensed above her.

It was the second time he had asked her that, and she liked it. She liked it so much she thought her chest might explode with feeling. It showed he cared about her. In answer she wrapped her good arm around his strong neck and brought his mouth down to hers.

Her body had taken over now, and that tiny doubt planted in that grimy room in Earls Court was exploded in the time it took Alexei to fully penetrate her. *This* was her man, the right man. He knew exactly what to do, and her body responded in kind. He drove her higher and higher, until she was hanging over the edge of a cliff with her fingertips. When she fell he came with her, and she clung tight to him as he thrust again and again, her brain on hiatus as she gave herself over to the sheer joy of being a part of him.

When he sank forward, his head pressed to the curve of her neck, she held him as tightly as he would let her for as long as he would let her, and when he pulled out of her and rolled onto his back he rewarded her by taking her with him.

'I don't usually do this.'

Alexei couldn't think. But that wasn't surprising, given he was still coming down the other side of an incredible orgasm. He knew his brain would flick the functioning switch in a

minute, but right now all he could do was say her name—
Maisy—and run his hand happily down the full round flank
of her bottom and thigh. Her head lay on his chest—all those
long ringlets cascading over them—her smooth thigh rested
on his hair-roughened front quad muscle, and he could feel
the hot wet centre of her pressed against him. There were so
many things he wanted to do with her, and just anticipating
the weeks to come made his blood hum.

But she was saying something. She was sitting up, and managed to pull the sheet around her as he watched her. 'What
don't you usually do?' He didn't want to move, but he wished
she would drape herself back across him.

'This. Have casual sex.'

The words sounded a bit harsh. He was thinking *incredible*
sex. Surely he'd covered all the bases? She'd definitely come
apart in his arms. She should be purring like a kitten, but instead she was sitting there, huddling in a sheet, talking about
casual sex.

Then the other shoe dropped. Of course. She wanted to
hear that he respected her, that they would be repeating this
regularly—for a while—and then she'd drop the sheet and
crawl back into his space.

He could do all that. He would, once his brain clicked into
gear. But some other part of him said, with a sincerity he didn't
recognise, 'Nothing about this is casual, Maisy.'

She had the softest eyes in the world, he thought, arrested
for a moment by the expression on Maisy's face. And somehow he had said exactly the right thing, because some of the
tension had run out of her and she looked both shy and hopeful.

How in the hell was she shy after what they'd just done?
What they were going to do? With her face flushed, her round
hazel eyes dilated, she looked like a woman who had enjoyed
very satisfactory sex. She also looked a little embarrassed.

It was sweet. He reached for her and she came to him, soft
and warm and accommodating. Exactly what he wanted from

her. He laid his hand between her legs, easing them apart as his fingers found her sensitive part and slid in and out of the hot wet core of her. His eyes never left the expression on her face as he built her orgasm out of the remains of what had gone before.

CHAPTER SIX

'I HAD wild uninhibited sex in broad daylight. I had *lots* of wild, uninhibited sex in broad daylight,' Maisy confided to the pillow, as if this were a secret, and Alexei laughed. The sound was so reassuring Maisy subsided into the vibrations of his chest, wanting to stay curled against him for as long as possible. His large, tight-muscled frame took up more than half the bed, but she didn't mind.

Alexei ran a possessive hand over her hip, now covered by a single sheet. He had so thoroughly explored her body in the last two hours he couldn't imagine a freckle or dimple he wasn't familiar with, but she insisted on covering herself, revealing a modesty that oddly touched him.

He pulled her tighter into the shelter of his body.

He never did cuddling.

He performed, he took his pleasure, and then he showered and dressed and left.

Maisy curled against him, as if heat-seeking, her closing lashes soft on her round cheeks. He'd exhausted her, and the thought satisfied an entirely primitive, unreconstructed part of himself.

The more sophisticated part of him was planning ahead. How to fit her into his schedule; how to set the parameters of their relationship...

She has no idea who I am or what I require of her, he thought, and it was an oddly charged feeling—one he didn't want to relinquish yet. He couldn't quite put his finger on it, but for a time he had felt a barrier come down. He'd felt free to just luxuriate in this closeness. Soon enough they would have to get out of bed and harsh reality would intrude. He didn't want clingy, didn't want emotions, didn't want a *relationship*. He wanted sex. In return he would give her anything she desired.

Foremost, he didn't want her to nurture any illusions about him.

Then why did it feel as if he was shutting her out and in the process shutting down a part of himself?

He bedded glamorous women for a reason. It had nothing to do with their allure. Hell, he doubted they were even his *type*. But they came with a pack drill. They knew what they were about, they knew what they wanted, and they knew what he was offering. There were limits to these liaisons. Tara had been a perfect example.

But just the thought of her this morning ran a chill through him, and he tightened his arms around Maisy. Tara was a reminder of why Maisy had snuck in under his radar. This uncomplicated sweetness was what he wanted—probably needed. Maisy had come to him with nothing but her wonderful, warm, accommodating body.

Peace was what he was feeling, and in answer to it he rolled her onto her back and settled himself across her, cradling his head on her belly.

It would be good for them both. She clearly hadn't had much of a life, from what she'd told him with her mum and the gig with Anais's baby. He could offer her luxury, travel and a speed dial for her sexual repertoire. He in turn would get this much joy and sweetness in his bed.

And he would not let himself be weak and mistake it for anything else.

He shoved that thought aside and luxuriated in the feeling of her. After everything that had gone before it was like being reborn. He needed six months of Maisy. In fact if he was a doctor he'd recommend it.

She smelled so good—warm female skin, the faint traces of the tangerine soap she used, and sex. She hadn't rushed off to wash herself and it was nice, just lying here with her, feeling the rise and fall of her breathing under his head, knowing she wasn't going anywhere.

She sat up, dislodging his head. 'Kostya,' she said.

Realising a response was required from him, Alexei gazed up at her, a smile of disbelief on his slumberous face. 'Relax, Maria will get him up.'

'I always get him up,' Maisy protested, swinging her legs off the bed, trying to drag the sheet with her.

Alexei had no intention of moving. 'Come back to bed, *dushka*. Maria can look after him today.'

Even as he said it Alexei registered Maisy's disapproval.

She made a dash for his shirt and thrust her arms frantically into the sleeves, covering herself as quickly as she could. She didn't say anything, and the longer that went on the more annoyed Alexei was feeling. The baby was *fine*. *He* needed a bit of attention. Where in the hell was she going?

'Maisy!' He didn't like the bark in his voice, and Maisy clearly didn't either. She swung around, hair flying, frowning at him as if he had offended her. 'Please come back to bed,' he said with studied patience.

Maisy shook her head. 'I can't,' she said.

'Fine.' He bounded off the bed and headed for the bathroom. He was going to shower and start the day. Maisy needed to know who was in charge.

'Where are you going?' she said.

'The entertainment is over. I need a shower and a shave,' he shot back at her.

Maisy paled. Her anxiety to get downstairs to the nursery dulled as the impact of that word pinned her to the spot.

Entertainment.

She stood staring at the open bathroom door. She felt as if he'd slapped her. He couldn't mean it. She wanted to run after him and tackle him, demand he take it back, but there wasn't time.

Kostya.

She kept moving, her heart pounding as she skittered along the hallway, praying no one appeared around the corner to find her naked except for a man's shirt. Alexei's shirt. Everyone would know what they had been doing, if they didn't already. It wouldn't matter so much if it was the beginning of some sort of a relationship; it mattered a great deal to her if he thought of her as providing 'entertainment'.

Her heartbeat began to slam inside her chest, heavy and dull, as reality laid a cold hand on her shoulder. All the drama of last night came rushing back. He'd said some pretty hurtful things and he hadn't taken one of them back. As if sex cancelled it all out. Although for him it probably did. He seemed very pleased with himself. And why wouldn't he be? One meal and she was on her back. What sort of girl jumped into bed with a man so quickly?

Emotions were roiling through her and she could barely keep a lid on them. Oh, God. It was all too clear. She had made a huge leap of faith, and he had had a one-night stand.

She had to walk through the nursery to get to her room. The realisation brought her to a halt. She couldn't walk in like this—not if Kostya wasn't alone.

Trying not to think about the humiliation to come, she retraced her steps. She could hear the sound of running water. She took a deep breath and walked into the luxurious bathroom. Alexei was standing under a waterfall of water, head down, shoulders hunched. His beautiful long lean body took her breath away, still. Knowing he was an absolute bastard didn't change that.

He looked up as he sensed her presence, his lips parting. He cut off the water. 'Changed your mind, *dushka*?'

There was something about that endearment, that *casual* endearment, that twisted the knife. Maisy blocked the truckload of pain she could feel coming and said, 'I need my dress. Where did you put my dress?'

'A little cold in the shirt, Maisy?' He grabbed a towel and began drying his hair, completely unselfconscious about his nudity.

Maisy focussed her eyes on a spot across the room and repeated, 'I need my dress.'

'I heard you.' He casually wrapped the towel around his lean hips and knotted it. 'It's safe to look, *dushka*. Although I've got no idea what's spooked you, Maisy. It's not as if you haven't been introduced.'

She wanted to hit him.

That did it.

Maisy stepped up to him and for a moment she fancied he actually looked expectant—as if she was going to launch herself into his arms after everything he had said and done.

Bastard. She slapped him as hard as she could across his face. His head jarred slightly to the right and then slowly came around again to stare down at her. Maisy took a backward step.

He brought a hand slowly up to his jaw and rubbed. 'Feel better?'

'No.'

'I'll get your dress.'

It was all over. She could still feel where he had been inside her and yet it was over, Maisy registered. She couldn't believe she had hit him. He was cold, arrogant, self-centered, and she was…on the premises and…happy to oblige.

That was how it was, wasn't it?

Yet as the seconds turned into minutes she began to lose her ground. Maria would be with Kostya, as she was every morning. The realisation had stolen up on her even before she'd walked in here, and now it bloomed with full force. She had overreacted. She had been lying in that bed, suddenly feeling alone and self-conscious, terrified of what was to come, what this sudden new intimacy meant, and she had run away rather than face it. Somehow she had convinced herself that if the sex stopped he wouldn't want her in the bed, and she'd felt too raw to face that so she had jumped out. He might be angry with her now, but that didn't mean everything was over before it began.

Alexei had reacted appallingly, but at least he was fetching her dress. Dan hadn't even given her the taxi fare home.

A soft gust of bittersweet amusement at her overreaction made her drop her head. She was hopeless at all this men stuff, but she would get better.

His arms came around her from behind and she was drawn up into a bear hug that turned her insides to mush. 'I'm sorry,' he muttered against her ear.

Maisy turned and burrowed deep into him and hung on. Relief made her limp.

Alexei rested his chin on the top of her warm head and released a deep sigh. 'Go and see Kostya.'

It was, she recognised, a magnanimous gesture. He wasn't used to making room for other people in his life, yet here he was making space for Kostya, putting his needs first. Maybe accommodating *her* a little.

I'm being considerate, thought Alexei, enjoying the results of a clinging Maisy. *I'm attuned to her feelings.* Wasn't that the current jargon? But something in him regretted having hurt her.

Maisy reacted predictably for once, turning up her face to be kissed and reassured. He knew the drill. But there was no kiss. That little crease was back between her brows.

'What am I going to tell Maria if she asks where I've been?'

Maria? Who cared about the housekeeper? 'My sex life is not Maria's business.'

The little crease deepened. 'Not you—me.'

'Maisy, I chased you down to Ravello yesterday. I had dinner with you on the rooftop. Everybody knows.'

She blushed.

She blushed—after two hours of lying naked under him and over him.

But there were certain things she didn't do, he registered,

and when he led her in some directions she did not come with him. It hadn't mattered—he'd been so caught up in the sheer impact of being with her.

It was unlikely, but he had to ask.

'Maisy, were you a virgin?'

'I can't believe you asked me that.' She tried to wriggle out of his arms, but suddenly Alexei could think of no better way to spend the next five minutes than drilling Maisy for some personal information.

Women usually spilled their guts on the first encounter— gave him well-edited potted histories of their empty lives until he and his billions walked into their world. One Hollywood actress had tried to persuade him she had never enjoyed sex until him. He might have been flattered had he not seen her by the pool of his home in Florida intimately entwined with another woman.

He watched Maisy squirm, her round cheeks hot and pink, her red-gold curls a tangled out-of-control mass. She was using it to hide her face from him. He knew he could never let her know about *his* former life. She would be horrified. Little hot-to-trot Maisy had a great deal of girl-next-door in her.

He'd known it yesterday afternoon, when he'd climbed back into the Ferrari and seen her mortification. She wasn't a gold-digger. She was just a little out of her depth. When he'd lowered the levels she had risen to meet him. He'd been rewarded with the most incredible sex he had ever had.

Be nice to me. Even the sound of her voice stoked him. She loaded the simplest words with carnal meaning. Yet here she was blushing, embarrassed.

He'd read her wrong. Again. Not only was she a good girl, she was a romantic.

'How many men, Maisy?'

He knew he should have framed that question more sensitively, but he didn't *do* sensitive.

'How many women, Alexei?' She jerked up her face, embarrassed, but with that edge he was beginning to look forward to.

'Too many.' His answer surprised even himself.

She made a wry face, but he saw a flash of hurt in her eyes.

She must never know. It would tear a big hole in that romantic little soul of hers.

Stunned, Alexei wondered where that thought had come from. Pushing it aside, he gave her chin a gentle pinch.

'How many, Maisy?' he pressed.

'Just one. Once.'

She looked almost defiant as she said it, as if daring him to comment. Alexei, rocked by that little announcement, did his best to disguise it. He hadn't thought for one moment she was a virgin, but now he knew she might as well be.

'Could you tell?' she framed awkwardly as his silence stretched on.

He pushed the hair out of her eyes. 'I think I'm very lucky,' he said genuinely.

It was clearly the right thing to say.

Maisy sprang up and squeezed him around the neck. She was happy. He had made Maisy happy for the first time since they'd climbed out of bed and everything had gone pear-shaped. There was a lesson there. Keep her horizontal as often as possible.

But there was Kostya to consider.

'Kostya,' she said, right on schedule.

'I'll go.' He didn't know why he volunteered, but he was beginning to understand any chance of uninterrupted play with Maisy could only be engineered if he loosened her grip on Kostya.

Besides, it was time to build a relationship with the boy.

Maisy was fastening herself back into her white gown when there was a knock on the door. She froze.

'Miss Edmonds?'

She recognised the voice and went to open the door. It was one of the girls from the kitchen. She merely held out an armful of supplies: some fresh clothes and her bag of toiletries.

Maisy accepted them wordlessly, then remembered her manners and thanked the girl. Jeans and a T-shirt and plain cotton underwear. Alexei had not chosen these for her. She knew him now. She also knew he was not going to be discreet about any of this.

Well, Maisy, in for a penny, in for a pound.

She emptied the toiletries bag and found bubble bath. A bath. She was going to have a bath.

She filled Alexei's big tub, carefully hung up her dress, and submerged herself in warm sudsy water. Her spirit felt light. For the first time in a long time she felt young and desirable, and for the moment free of any responsibility except for herself. She stretched out her legs and draped her arms along the sides of the tub. Her body ached in an unfamiliar but entirely satisfying way.

Alexei had behaved as if he couldn't keep his hands off her and she had gloried in his obvious enjoyment of her body. He had been so tender with her, putting a lie to that 'entertainment' crack. Yet she couldn't ignore it. He had made it for a reason.

She sensed that, as much as he wanted her, his instinct was to push her away. Strange as the thought was, it was as if he had a wall around him. She'd felt it back at Lantern Square—how untouchable he seemed. Something had changed in the park yesterday. She'd seen the real man behind that wall when he'd hunkered down to Kostya's level to reassure him. That same sweetness had been in the way he had removed her shoes last night. In these moments he had been reachable, human, vulnerable.

But she sensed these glimpses were involuntary. He didn't want the closeness she sought. Even as he had kept her snug

in his arms, she had instinctively known this was as much as
he was offering.

She needed to be very careful. She needed to guard her
heart.

Kostya was pleased to see Maisy. He got up and toddled across
the terrace to throw up his arms for his morning cuddle.

Alexei noted approvingly that a cuddle was all he required
and then he was struggling to be put down. He ran back to
his pedal car. Observing the child this morning, he had been
aware of what Maisy had said to him last night about Leo's
absence and Anais's inability to cope. But Kostya appeared to
be a well-adjusted little boy—no signs of clinginess or insecurity. Her claims just didn't add up. A huge part of him was
relieved, but it worried him that she had lied. It didn't align
with the girl he was beginning to know.

Alexei remained where he was, with a pile of newspapers
from around the world, his smart phone and a strong espresso.
It was a morning like any other when he wasn't working—
except for Maisy. She had pulled up her hair into a ponytail and
wore jeans and a V-necked T-shirt. He didn't want clingy—he
didn't *do* clingy—but Maisy had taken it *way* in the opposite
direction. Clearly they were pretending not to know one another. Interesting. He decided not to react to her, waiting for
her to come to him.

Sipping his espresso, he idly thumbed through his schedule,
lining up his phone appointments for the day.

Maisy poured herself a glass of orange juice from the buffet
and approached the table uneasily, waiting for Alexei to look
up, to speak, with half of her attention attuned to Maria—who
must *know*. He'd turned up yesterday and this morning she was
bouncing out of his bed. It was one thing to be a sexually independent woman. It was another thing to have an audience—a
traditional Italian audience.

Before she sat down he half rose from his chair, his manners clearly so ingrained that even when he was ignoring her

he behaved like a gentleman. Maisy settled herself, still waiting to be spoken to. Nothing. She looked around. Maria was clearing the buffet. Steadying her nerve, she watched Kostya for a while. She was constantly aware of Alexei, typing into his phone, stabbing with his thumb, and Maisy experienced his uninterest like a well-placed kick to her fledgling sexual self-confidence. It was exactly like the aftermath of her sleeping with Dan. She had dressed in the cold whilst he had answered emails, his back to her. Except this was worse—because as she had buttoned herself up she had known she didn't care for Dan and had no intention of repeating the experience.

This time she wanted to climb into Alexei's lap. Her insides seemed to light up when she had his attention. Even now, as he fiddled with that stupid device, she couldn't strip her eyes off him, was wishing he would just look up and acknowledge her. But she knew he wouldn't. It was the equivalent of dressing in the cold.

All of her insecurities came rushing back. Maybe he had changed his mind. She might have been able to attract him but she couldn't hold him. Her mind went helplessly back over events, trying to find the flaws in their lovemaking. Had she done something he didn't like? Had she not been responsive enough? He had wanted her to take him in her mouth but she hadn't felt confident enough. Maybe that was it?

She tried to sip her orange juice, but she was so tense it went down the wrong way and she ended up in a coughing fit.

Alexei looked up as she set down the glass with a bump and choked. Tears of reaction had sprung into her eyes, sparking the deeply held pain she was nursing, and more brimmed and slid down her cheeks. She swiped at her eyes, hoping he wouldn't realise she was crying because of him. It would put the nail in the coffin of her humiliation for him to see how deeply all this was affecting her.

She pushed back her chair noisily, not looking at him.

'Where are you going?' He sounded genuinely surprised.

'I'm disturbing you,' she got out rapidly. 'I'll just go.'

'You haven't eaten any breakfast.'

He had noticed? She hadn't thought he'd even registered her presence.

'I'm not hungry.' She had to get away from him. She walked blindly down the terrace, blinking rapidly.

Then she heard Kostya's high little voice. 'Maisy!' And she had to go back for him.

However broken up she felt inside, she was all Kostya had. Funnily enough, he was all she had too. And as she hurried back the child met her halfway, arms extended to be lifted, cuddled, assured of her love. He was heavy, so she sank down onto the ground with him and rocked him in her arms, mustering a smile and reassuring chatter. She might be an abject failure with men, but she knew how to be a good mother to Kostya.

'You have to leave him with me today,' Alexei was saying. He was sauntering over, smart phone and papers abandoned, looking unaccountably edgy.

Maisy looked up, her eyes still wet so that her lashes had a starfish effect. Alexei tried to block the accompanying flash of emotion as he remembered how uninhibitedly she had given herself to him. Now she was acting as if she wanted to be anywhere but around him.

His first instinct was to reassure her, but it was clear she was carrying a bucketload of regrets. Well, tough. He wasn't going to apologise for enjoying her body so thoroughly. Maisy was built for a man's pleasure. Everything about her—from her wild glossy ringlets to the serious curve of her waist to the fulsome round of her bottom—sang to his libido. After too many women with borderline eating disorders, the curves and valleys of Maisy's small yet womanly body reduced him to drooling, uncontrolled lust. He fully intended to keep her and have her again and again.

He could deal with her regrets with jewellery. It always worked a treat with women's moods. Experience told him put a diamond pendant in the valley between those magnificent breasts of hers and she'd soon cheer up. He'd organise Carlo to have a selection sent down tomorrow.

Except deep down he knew jewellery would probably upset her.

But for now he had a small child to wrest from her arms. A thought which didn't make him feel particularly proud of himself. Especially with Maisy looking so incredibly vulnerable. It would be too easy to gather her up into his arms and soothe that edginess in her away. He'd played it cool this morning, aware of the staff observing them. Any other woman and it wouldn't have mattered, but Maisy had unaccountably befriended a good many of the people who worked for him. Those seven days he had left her alone here had backfired on him. Shy as she was around him at times, she clearly had no trouble drawing other people to her and holding them.

Everyone liked Maisy. Which was fine. Except it made *him* liking her slightly more awkward. He didn't know why, but he felt a distinct vibe of disapproval from Maria this morning. It was ridiculous. Maisy was over twenty-one, and she was a sexually active young woman—it made sense they'd ended up in bed together. He wouldn't be fulfilling his function as a fit and healthy twenty-nine-year-old male if he didn't drag her off to bed.

Yet that wasn't exactly how it had been. Maisy wasn't just some girl, and it hadn't felt like a function. It was the beginning of something—he just couldn't quite grasp what it was that was making him so uneasy. And this morning had been eminently worthwhile. In fact it had been a revelation.

Still, he had to separate this woman from this child, and do it with the least amount of trauma to either of them.

But Maisy was sitting there, being all that was motherly with Kostya, and it affected him. She was incredibly feminine—something he suspected was playing havoc with his usual defences in this kind of situation.

He would have had to be blind this morning not to see how relieved she was to have him confirm their encounter was not casual. And now she was everything soft and tender, cradling the child in her arms, looking exactly like the kind of woman a nice guy would want to protect and cherish and probably marry. Hell, she had 'wife material' written all over her. Absolutely off-limits to a guy like him. Yet he'd gone ahead and infiltrated her affections anyway.

It was about time he made sure she understood. He didn't want her to nurture any illusions about him. He was a bastard, and Maisy needed to understand that before she started confusing what he was offering her with happy families and swamping them both in unnecessary and dangerous emotion.

The thought assailed him that he wasn't exactly clear on what he was offering her, and for one tiny moment he allowed himself a glimpse of just what a relationship with Maisy might look like.

Which was probably why he didn't pull any of his next punches.

'Maisy, if you're worried about Maria stop it now.'

'That's easy for you to say,' she muttered.

'Maria is accustomed to female guests coming down to breakfast in a great deal less than you're wearing, *dushka*. I wouldn't let it bother you.'

He knew it was a brutal thing to say. Something flinched inside as he actually witnessed the moment she took his meaning. Her eyes flew to his, and then flashed away as she turned her face into Kostya's curls.

Alexei felt cold to his stomach. *Congratulations*, he thought, *you're a bigger bastard than you thought*.

With the rug pulled from under her, Maisy scrambled for a foothold in this strange new world. How on earth was she going to stay here with him and pretend to be okay with all this? A little voice reminded her he wasn't *trying* to insult her—he was just telling her how it was. It wasn't as if she'd imagined he lived like a monk, but for him to actually *tell* her she was one in a queue was probably the hardest thing she would ever have to hear from him. Until he said goodbye. Which, clearly, would be sooner rather than later.

But the truth wasn't what she wanted this morning. She wanted a show of affection and his hand in hers…and a little reassurance.

What she got was a man who had put in the time for sexual gymnastics first thing, but was keen to put it all behind him now the day had begun.

'So, will you be spending the day with Kostya?' Maisy was proud of how level she sounded—as if the waves of pain crashing over her were being deflected by a larger sense of self-preservation.

'Why don't you spend it with us?'

He actually sounded gentler, but Maisy couldn't bring herself to look at him. She started when he reached down to lift Kostya from her arms, and felt a twinge of regret when Kostya went so willingly. Maisy didn't know what to do now. She felt awkward sitting at his feet, with images of the intimacies they had shared shredding the atmosphere between them. She couldn't go back, she realised, panicked.

'I think I want to be alone for a while,' she said stolidly.

Stupid girl, stupid girl, stupid girl.

She clambered to her feet, feeling ungraceful and at a disadvantage, and walked as fast as she could across the terrace, not aware of where she was going, just conscious of wanting to put some distance between herself and the rocks on which she had shipwrecked herself.

CHAPTER SEVEN

ALEXEI watched her go. Why had he opened his big mouth? Why hurt her like this? It had barely begun and he was tearing shreds off her.

'Want Maisy,' wailed Kostya, clinging to his shirt front.

Alexei looked down at the infant's ominously reddening face. He was clearly reacting to all the tension. *I've stuffed this up*, Alexei thought flatly. 'I want Maisy too, *malenki chelovek*.'

She had reached the end of the terrace and he watched her hesitate, circle, looking for a way out. But this terrace led nowhere, and the glass doors were locked. For a moment he watched as she pushed at them, and then he saw her shoulders drop, saw her shake her head and lose heart.

That was enough.

He strode towards her, watched her face come up—her pale, lovely face—strained and tense. And *he* had put that tension there.

He hadn't meant to push her this far. He'd been trying for disengagement when all he was feeling was passionate connection. He hadn't meant to hurt her.

'Maisy, we need to talk. I'll hand Kostya over to Maria and then you're coming with me.' He reached for her hand, but she pulled away, eyes flashing.

'You're too late, Alexei,' she slung at him fiercely. 'I don't want to hear anything you have to say.'

Kostya released a huge cry and scrambled for Maisy. She

took him into her arms, flashing daggers over his curly head. 'Now look what you've done,' she breathed.

Alexei made a very male European gesture with one hand and pinned her with his incredible eyes. 'If you want to do it in front of the boy—fine. Here's the deal, Maisy.'

He spoke in a low, firm voice—the one she imagined he used in another life that didn't involve crying children and emotional women who refused to vanish after sex.

'This morning was incredible. I want to repeat it. Often. I want you in my life. Is that clear enough for you? Does that sort out the problem?'

Incredible. Repeat it. He wanted her in his life.

Maisy was sure he was wondering why she wasn't cheering. Instead his coolly delivered words struck a flint of anger inside her. 'I'm sure that works with all those other *female guests* of yours, but I require a little bit more finesse, Alexei, so I'm turning you down.'

'Fair enough.' He shrugged, and Maisy's face fell so fast it should have amused him. It didn't. 'I should have dragged you back to bed and manacled you to the bedpost,' he declared. 'But I don't bring women here. The handcuffs and paraphernalia are in my Rome apartment.'

Maisy huffed, trying to cover Kostya's ears. 'You're disgusting!'

'You weren't saying that around dawn, *dushka*. How in the hell are you still blushing?'

'I'm not used to stripping naked and bouncing around on a bed in broad daylight,' she snapped.

'Something that does incredible things for my ego,' he replied complacently.

Maisy huffed again.

He gave her an arrested look. 'You are adorable, Maisy.'

She suddenly couldn't wrest her eyes away from his. What was it he'd said about not bringing women here?

'We can't have this conversation in front of Kostya. Where's Maria?'

'*Now* she sees sense,' Alexei murmured, stroking the back of Kostya's head, managing to caress the back of Maisy's hand. She didn't pull away.

Kostya distracted with strawberry yoghurt in the kitchen, Maisy walked with Alexei down into the garden. As they lingered before a stone fountain amidst the greenery Alexei said, in a dark, suggestive voice, 'We could go back upstairs.'

'I won't answer that.' She turned her face away, but a little smile was tugging at her lips.

'We could do it here.'

Maisy gasped. 'I'm not making love to you in a garden. Anyone could see.'

He smiled slowly at her. 'You're right. I'm very possessive, Maisy, as you'll learn. I don't want any other man seeing you when you climax.'

'You're so confident I would?' she whispered, unsure they wouldn't be overheard. She suddenly imagined dozens of men hiding in the bushes.

'Would what? Wrap those lovely legs around my waist or climax?'

'Both,' she snapped.

'I can't force you, Maisy, but I can guarantee the climax.'

He was outrageous. Maisy loved it. She bit her lip. She didn't want to forgive him so soon, but her heart was racing and her skin was prickling and suddenly all she wanted was to wrap herself around him and not let go.

But she couldn't do it. He was going to break her heart.

He was playful with her now, attentive. But how long was that going to last? Until the next time she said no or didn't fit in with his schedule, or demanded what she knew he couldn't give her: a loving relationship.

She had to grow up and set some boundaries of her own.

'I want to be with you too, Alexei. But I think it's important to be pragmatic.'

'Pragmatic?' He didn't like the sound of that, although half an hour ago it had been exactly what he was after.

'When Kostya is settled I will need to go. It would be disastrous for him if he were to begin to think of us both as his parents—which is what would happen if…if I was in your life.' Maisy knew she was being sensible. She knew she was putting the interests of the child above her own, and she knew he couldn't argue with her on this. But, oh, she wished he would.

Alexei was silent. The playfulness had evaporated.

'He can't see us being…affectionate together in front of him,' she elaborated.

'Affectionate?'

'I know it's not really affection, I know it's just…sex. But he's so little he'll just see it as grown-ups showing love to each other, as we love him, and he'll think we all belong together.'

Alexei swore in Russian. Maisy blinked. His anger was evident, but it wasn't directed towards her. It was strange, but she sensed he was looking inward.

'I'm not an idiot, Alexei, I know how the world works. It's bizarre that we even met, let alone that I'm here. I think what's happened has happened because of the Kulikovs. We're both grieving and it gives us a bond. We've been thrown together, and it was…inevitable.'

'It *was* inevitable—I'll agree with that,' he replied, looking at her oddly. 'So what are your terms, Maisy?'

The question was blunt and to the point, and it hurt.

Terms? She had no idea. 'What—what usually happens when you're with a woman? I mean, how does it work?'

'I put her on the payroll and give her bonuses when she really performs.'

Maisy blinked again, and for an aching moment Alexei realised she wasn't sure if he was joking or not.

'Do you really think I'd do that? Listen.' He stood in front of her and tugged on her hands. 'That bed upstairs. It's mine. I don't bring women here. At all. Ever. This is my sanctuary.'

'No "female guests"?'

'Only a few, very firmly attached to their husbands. This is where I bring family.'

For a moment Maisy experienced an overwhelming explosion of belonging, even as common sense told her he was referring to Kostya. She was here because of Kostya. She wasn't a part of this family of his. But she was his first woman here.

'So what am I supposed to do?' She aimed for casual, but it came out needy.

Unexpectedly his thumb pressed against the frown line between her winged brows.

'Don't fret, Maisy. I'll make it easy for you. You live with me, you travel with me, you dodge the paparazzi with me. You'll be written up as "a mysterious redhead" until they dig out your details—and they will dig them up, dirt and all. Anything you want to keep hidden you can forget about. So, any bank robberies I need to know about?'

Maisy stared at him. Surely he was joking? No, not joking. 'Nobody will be interested in me. I'm not anybody.'

'Everything I do seems to attract some sort of interest. I'm hoping because you don't have a profile it will blow over.'

He'd thought about it. The realisation zoomed through Maisy's faltering confidence and made her feel a little stronger. Alexei had considered how she would fit into his life before now. Then she remembered all the security: in London, at the airport. Only here it seemed to have evaporated. It hadn't occurred to her before, but Alexei led a somewhat high-octane lifestyle.

What was that going to mean for her? More importantly, what would it mean for Kostya when she was gone? And she *would* go. She had told Alexei that much and he hadn't argued with her.

It made it easier for him. It made it terrifying for her.

He slid his big hands around her waist, sitting on the rim of the fountain and drawing her between his legs so that they were on eye level.

'Kostya is severely going to cramp our style,' he said, with a smile in his voice.

'No, he's a wonderful little boy,' protested Maisy loyally. 'And he's so taken with you.'

'I agree wholeheartedly he's a great kid. But this "no affection" rule is going to be a bore.'

'There's no choice,' she said solemnly.

'There are always choices, *dushka*. You've exercised yours. Can you live by it?'

Maisy swayed into him. In his world there were choices— rich men always had choices. Unless by some miracle a leopard changed his spots and he fell head over heels in love with her…no, she didn't have a choice. She only had an inevitable outcome.

Alexei's arms came around her and he laid his head on the soft warm curve of her breasts. He released a lovely, deep, satisfied groan.

'What is it?' she asked, smiling at the sound.

'I've been wanting to do this all morning,' he revealed, looking up and flashing that killer smile. 'Your breasts are a gift to mankind. Well, to me—and at a stretch I'll share with Kostya.'

Maisy snorted and began to laugh.

'And now they're jiggling. I'm in heaven.'

'Stop it.' She smacked his shoulder lightly. 'You didn't answer my question before. Are you going to spend the rest of the day with Kostya?'

'Absolutely.'

'Can I have the day to myself?'

'You and Kostya?' he asked.

'No, I agree it's better if I'm not in the picture.'

Alexei set her back, hands linked behind her waist. 'There's a spa just outside of town. Why don't you spend the day there?'

Maisy didn't want to leave the circle of his arms, let alone go to a spa. But he was being sweet, offering her something she might like.

'I'll arrange it. A car will take you. What's that crease for?'

He gently smoothed her worry line with his thumb. 'What are you thinking now, little Maisy?'

'I don't know,' she said, suddenly breathless, wishing so much of this was different. If she had met him under different circumstances. If they had *courted*... Such an old-fashioned word. Maybe *dated* was better. She would have liked to be dated. Instead they'd set *terms*. 'I wish...'

'What do you wish?'

His voice had taken on that low timbre she liked so much, and her whole body began to speed up. *That we could be together, just the two of us, with no one else around.* 'I wish I had more clothes to wear,' she said instead, and that was true too. 'I think I'll go shopping.'

Alexei's arms released her. His expression was indulgent but somewhat cooler than what had been there earlier in his eyes. 'Excellent decision. Shop in the morning, spa in the afternoon.'

Maisy tried not to throw herself back into his arms. She couldn't very well pick up his hands and hold them on her waist. 'What will you do with Kostya?' she asked.

'Guy stuff.'

'He's two.'

'Guy stuff with training wheels,' he amended, and Maisy couldn't help smiling at the image. He really was trying with Kostya. It made her feel better about leaving him for the whole day.

'Whatever you do, remember to take his nappy bag and his water bottle. I'll pack it for you. And he needs his hat on at all times. He's so fair he burns in a trice.'

'I can do this.'

He suddenly looked so completely out of his depth that Maisy couldn't help herself, and launched herself into his arms. She wrapped her arms around his neck and inhaled the lovely male smell of him that she would keep with her for the rest of the day.

Alexei's hands landed gingerly on her waist, as if he was

startled by her sudden missile launch of affection. 'I'm hugging you,' she told him, her voice muffled by his shoulder. His arms tightened around her nicely and Maisy smiled contentment.

Alexei frowned into the middle distance. He hadn't expected any of this: the time it was going to take to build a bond with Leo's little boy, the emotional investment. Yet what choice did he have? There were two other couples waiting in the wings to take responsibility for him; it would perhaps be the most sensible course to hand the boy over to one of them. Yet Leo had named *him* Kostya's guardian. Leo didn't do anything without a reason, and Alexei didn't back down from a challenge.

But he hadn't expected Maisy, who was presenting her own unique challenge.

The minute they'd hit the bed this morning every one of his tightly held tenets about women and sex had flown out of the window. It was probably to do with her innocence, which was playing havoc with the traditional Russian male he'd thought he'd done a good job of burying deep enough that he hadn't thought about marriage and children and a future in years. Not since he'd made his first million and women had become easy and their expectations primarily mercenary.

Maisy, with her long glossy ringlets tickling his chest and her soft sweet mouth trading slow kisses, eyes shut, expression dreamy, as if he was every one of her fantasies rolled into one, had seemed much more absorbed in making this morning romantic than in the sort of sexual marathon it turned into. That was *his* doing. He hadn't been able to get enough of her. Her subsequent reaction to him meant he'd have to be deaf, dumb and blind not to realise she was investing her emotions in this, in *him*. But what was confusing him was that he was virtually *encouraging* it.

He'd put it down to the ego-stroke of having a woman more interested in his attention than his bank balance, but he knew he had to put matters on a more fiscal level. Once he was keeping her the whole aura of romance would dissolve, and the little touches of sweetness, her insecurity about his feelings, would be smoothed over by regular cheques.

Hell, the sheets upstairs were barely cool and she was planning a shopping trip. Maisy was a sweet girl, and she was heat itself between the sheets, but at the end of the day why should she be any different from anyone else? And why was he even entertaining notions of what it would be like if she was?

Feeling as if she had run an emotional marathon, Maisy came down the main stairs, checking her purse. Credit card, passport, the Italian currency she had bought yesterday. She was all set to go shopping, and she wouldn't be a card-carrying woman if the thought of a few hours looking at clothes didn't pique her interest. The added bonus of a little pampering this afternoon put a smile on her face.

Alexei had made an appointment for her in a spa in the hills at two, giving her a few hours to trawl the shops. Andrei would be driving her, which was the best news she'd had. All Maisy wanted to do was prop herself up at a window, watch the scenery drift by and daydream like a teenage girl about Alexei. She knew it was silly, but she hadn't been able to think of anything else but him since he'd burst into that kitchen at Lantern Square. Now her thoughts had a vivid sexual imagery that scorched her cheeks but kept a little smile triggered on her lips.

She was smiling as she reached the mezzanine and Carlo Santini came out of nowhere. She hadn't realised he was even on the premises, but given the size of the place that was probably a moot point.

'Miss Edmonds?'

Maisy tried not to look worried.

'Alexei asked me to pass on these items to you. This is the security key that gives access to all areas of the villa. If you ever require a motor car, as you do today, there will be a driver always at your disposal. Just phone through to the house office and it will be arranged. Here is the number.'

He held out a smart phone and unwillingly she took it. She had no idea how to use it.

'An account has been opened in your name. Here are the details, and your cards.'

'A bank account?'

'*Si.*' He smiled at her then, and she didn't like his smile. 'Did you think you would not be paid, *signorina*?'

Maisy's whole being ground to a halt. She remained silent. His smile was definitely not pleasant. She hadn't imagined that.

'Now is your chance to spend up, Miss Edmonds. Mr Ranaevsky is a very generous man.'

Maisy stayed where she was a long time after Carlo had left her, the smart phone heavy in her hands. She looked at the clear plastic wallet of cards through a blur of tears.

It was *stupid* to be angry, stupid to be hurt. This was how he did things. This was what she had agreed to. But knowing that and really *understanding* that she wasn't special, she was just part of the way he ran his life—his empire—bit hard.

He was showing her very clearly the *terms*.

But Carlo Santini had looked at her as if she were some sort of woman to be paid off.

Those weren't *her* terms.

Shoving everything into her handbag, she barrelled down the remaining flight of stairs. She'd show him. She wouldn't spend a *cent* of his stupid money.

Four hours later Maisy was blissfully prone under the experienced hands of a masseuse, all the knots and tension in her muscles worked away. She hadn't realised how much she had needed this—not just the massage, but time away by herself. And she didn't feel guilty—not about leaving Kostya, who was in safe hands, nor about this morning and what she and Alexei had done in that big bed. Twenty-four hours ago she would have had a hard time disrobing for a massage, but now she was lying naked on her belly, a towel draped discreetly over her lower body, content to be pummelled and oiled and taken care of.

What a difference a day made—or rather a very satisfying morning.

Bundled in a white robe, her hair wrapped in a treatment, Maisy thumbed through a pile of glossy magazines, her thoughts on what she should wear home from her new purchases. She wanted Alexei to see the full impact of the results all this pampering yielded, but mostly it would be so lovely to just feel beautiful. There hadn't been much time or space in the past two years for feeling beautiful.

She flipped a page in the social events section of a glossy US magazine and her thoughts came to a stuttering stop.

It was Alexei. He was on a boat, at a party, his arm around the waist of Tara Mills. Maisy didn't have to read the caption to recognise her face. It had been on a billboard at Naples airport when they'd flown in. More than a model, she was a brand.

Finding it difficult to draw in enough air, Maisy began to read the paragraph below.

Has Tara met her match in Alexei Ranaevsky, Russian oligarch and all-round bad boy? If the diamonds around her neck are anything to go by, Ranaevsky is serious.

It wasn't the silly words penned by a journalist that froze Maisy, it was the reality of Alexei's past that threw her. Alexei had dated Tara Mills?

Calm down, she told herself, tossing the magazine aside. He was allowed to have a past. But she couldn't help it. She picked up another and started flipping through to the social pages, and then another. Alexei was everywhere, arm around a different woman, all of them with skyscraper cheekbones, mile-long legs and the attitude to go with it. Blondes, brunettes—it didn't seem to matter.

I'm the redhead.

He had told her about this—that his life was the subject of

media scrutiny, that she would be written up, that there would be little privacy—and she hadn't paid enough attention. Well, she was paying attention now. She was looking at the evidence of exactly *why* Alexei was a media darling. He was wealthy and powerful and gorgeous, and he paraded women like the sports cars she had seen lined up in the converted stables at the villa.

How on earth has this happened to me?

Not in a million years had she ever imagined this would be a lifestyle she would be stepping into. She took a good look around her. She had wondered over the cost of this spa treatment when she'd stepped from the car and been greeted by an attendant, and been impressed by the luxury surrounds—another converted villa—but had not fully appreciated how exclusive the spa might be. This was a spa with guests—virtually a hotel—and given she was the only client in the facilities she had a fair idea that personalised, discreet service for wealthy patrons was the name of the game.

Without even realising it she had landed in a fantasy. Except it wasn't *her* fantasy. She didn't want to be photographed and written about. Not that there was anything to write other than *Alexei Ranaevsky slums it with naive redhead.*

Maisy felt as if a huge lump had taken up residence in her throat. Even after her hair was blow-dried to glossy silk, her nails French polished and her face delicately enhanced with some colour, she looked in the mirror and all she saw was a fool.

Maisy was home.

Alexei brought his conference call to a grinding halt, leaving a shocked Carlo Santini to mop up the mess. Every sensible cell in his head was telling him to let her come to him, but every instinct was dragging him down those stairs.

He found her standing in the entrance hall, surrounded by shopping bags—a couple from boutiques he vaguely recognised, the rest clearly retail.

'Bravo.' He stopped on the bottom step and commenced a slow hand-clap. 'You've bought out the Amalfi Coast.'

Maisy looked up, and for a moment she didn't say a word. She just looked at him as if she was seeing him for the first time. Then a parody of a smile broke out on her pink-painted lips and she said, 'I should be exhausted, but I'm not. I had so much fun.'

Her enthusiasm was so palpably false Alexei just waited for the punchline.

It didn't come. She began gathering up some of her bags and Andrei, who had driven her around all day, scooped up the rest, earning one of Maisy's sunny artless smiles. Alexei found himself crossing the floor rapidly, intervening, deciding on the spot to organise a different driver to transport Maisy around. He didn't like the way the younger man's eyes lingered on Maisy's face. He'd be sprawled on the floor if that gaze moved anywhere else on her body.

Maisy preceded him up the stairs—at least her bottom hadn't changed. Shapely, still moving like a pendulum when she walked, then charged ahead to the nursery, almost running from him.

He'd fix that.

'I've shifted your room.'

Maisy slowed, turned. She looked distinctly disturbed.

'I had no idea you were sleeping in a broom closet. I've put you in the room next to mine. The one I slept in last night.'

'Oh.' Maisy looked as if she'd wanted to say something but had thought better of it.

'But you'll be sleeping in my bed,' he added.

On receipt of that little announcement Maisy clung on to her shopping bags like life rafts. What in the hell was the matter with her?

'Is that a problem?

'No,' she said stiffly, 'of course not.'

Clearly it was. 'I didn't think it would be.' He didn't mean to sound clipped, but she was already moving away from him, heels clicking. She really had the most endearing walk in heels—as if she hadn't quite mastered them.

Maisy kept going. If she could just get to her room and shut the door, get herself together before she had to face him again, it would be all right. But he was undoing her with every word.

Of course he followed her into her room. She wasn't going to get any time alone. With her head in overdrive, she was wondering just how she could bring up the spectre of a million other women and not sound like a jealous shrew?

'Can I have a minute?' she asked, her voice light and thin.

'I haven't seen you all day, Maisy. Didn't you miss me?' He had closed the door and was leaning back against it, all lean, muscular grace. His stunning blue eyes were not on her, however. They were on the bags.

The room had a whole wall of glass facing onto a terrace. The view was breathtaking. But Maisy turned her back to the water, setting down her bags on the floor. 'I haven't had much time to miss you,' she replied stiffly. 'I was so busy. Did you have a lovely day with Kostya?'

He gave her a tight smile, and she realised her odd behaviour was impacting on him. He pushed away from the door, coming towards her with an intent that made her step back. If he touched her now she would hit him. He merely dumped her bags on the bed.

'You *have* been a busy girl. A complete wardrobe overhaul?'

'No,' Maisy said slowly, 'just a few new dresses. I packed for Paris, not Italy, and it's very warm, and I thought—' She broke off, wondering why she was explaining herself to him.

Defending herself.

'I got Kostya some overalls and the sweetest pair of pyjamas,' she barrelled on, determined to steer the subject into more neutral waters.

She caught her breath as Alexei snagged a lingerie carrier.

Suddenly, knowing what she did and in this mood, she didn't want him to see her purchases. She had made them when she felt loved-up, and she was feeling distinctly frozen out right now. Amazing what being at the end of a long line of sensationally attractive women did for an ordinary girl's ego.

'No—don't,' she said, reaching for the bag. But he whipped it out of her reach.

'You can't disappoint me now, *dushka*. I mean, you hardly made this little purchase for yourself.'

And he shook out all the frilly nothings she had indulged in over the bed.

He zeroed in on an ivory satin negligee with lace inserts. Maisy put a hand to her temple. She could hardly pretend now she hadn't made these purchases for him.

Alexei didn't know what he'd expected to find. The satin slid through his fingers like water. It was a classic negligee. His gaze went to the bra-and-knicker sets on the bed. All classy, in pale colours. Nothing outrageous, nothing overtly sexy— everything to remind him Maisy had been wearing plain white knickers with just a bit of lace this morning.

Suddenly he knew he'd blundered. He couldn't see a price tag on any of this, he just saw understated elegance, and he was given the strong impression of a woman who had come into his life without any intention of seducing a man. He could have told her all she needed to do was smile at him and he was hers.

'I like this,' he said gruffly.

'I don't think they have it in your size,' Maisy said tartly, surprising him, reaching out and snatching it out of his hand. She added assertively, 'I didn't buy this for you. I bought it for me.'

He smiled slowly, watched the wariness in her eyes turn into something else—something closer to where they had been first thing this morning. He liked it when she was like this: ready to stand up for herself, willing to take him on. Few people did it in his world. He liked it when it was the woman in his bed.

Which reminded him. 'Wear it tonight,' he said, more abruptly than he'd meant.

She frowned. 'Is that an order or a request?'

'And wear your hair down,' he said, as if she hadn't spoken, crowding her. He couldn't help himself. She smelled like sandalwood and bergamot, and that indefinable Maisy-smell he'd had tattooed on his skin this morning.

Maisy opened her mouth to give him a piece of her mind, but he picked up one of her ringlets and bussed the end of her nose with it.

'Don't look so dire, Maisy. It's just sex.' And with that he bent and brushed his mouth over hers, effectively silencing her.

She tried to tell herself he *hadn't* just given her the real terms of their arrangement, but something curdled deep in her belly. First the money, and then all those other women. She would never mention the other women to him—she had too much pride—but by God she would tackle him over the money.

She pushed her hands up against his chest and gave him a shove.

'Maisy?'

He actually sounded disconcerted. She shook her head disbelievingly. 'I thought we'd sorted this out. I thought we had an arrangement.'

'Okay.' He backed up. 'What's the problem? You've been like a cat on a hot tin roof since we got up here.'

'You put me on your damn payroll. I thought it was a joke, but it's not. You got that awful Carlo Santini to give me money!'

'I'm not allowed to spend money on you?'

'You're not spending money on me. You're *paying* me.' She shook her head. He just didn't get it. 'And for your information I have my own money.'

'No doubt. But life is going to get expensive for you, Maisy. You're with me now.'

'Am I?' She doubted that. The problem was she didn't feel as if she was *with* him—and how could she after a single day? She felt like a fraud. The girl who *accidentally* ended up in Alexei Ranaevsky's bed whilst he was on vacation from his models and his actresses and his Euro trash. She added the last to make herself feel a little better.

Alexei closed in on her again, his hands closing over her arms. 'Don't make it a big deal, Maisy. Let's just play it as it goes.'

'You think less of me because I've never held down a job,' she blurted out, not sure what she was saying any more.

'Where did that come from?' He angled a frown at her.

'You said so last night—'

'I said a lot of things last night, *dushka*. I want you to forget them and just focus on the here and now.'

'I have a job. Looking after Kostya,' she ploughed on, refusing to be diverted. 'And I can tell you, caring for a young child is a hundred times more difficult than buying up companies or cruising the stockmarket or whatever it is you do!'

Alexei's mouth quirked at Maisy's dismissive summing up of his hard-won business empire.

'I agree,' he said. 'It is more difficult and in a completely different way. But I'm here now. That life is over, Maisy. Time to let it go and face up to a few facts of life.'

'Facts? Such as?'

'Life has changed for you. The horizon has widened. Your little purse, *dushka*, isn't going to bear the strain.' He smiled slowly, his eyes stroking her. 'Let me spoil you, Maisy.'

That line usually worked a treat.

Maisy's mouth formed an ominous little line. 'Does that mean I get a diamond necklace?'

Alexei's eyes hardened, his hands falling away from her. 'You've been reading the tabloids.'

'No, just upmarket magazines. You're a bit hard to miss.'

'Is that what this is all about? Don't you think that's a bit beneath us, *dushka*?'

He actually sounded impatient. Maisy's temper went into overdrive.

'You're a real piece of work, aren't you?' she exploded, giving him a good shove, frustrated that even when she put all her effort behind it she couldn't shift him an inch. 'A different girl for every day of the week. Well, I'm not going to be one of them, Alexei. I have my own money. I have my own jewellery. All I want from you is—' She broke off, scrambling for a neutral term.

'*Da*? What is it you want from me, Maisy?'

'Sex,' she snapped. 'To quote you. *Just sex.*'

'Now we're talking.' His gaze did a run of her body.

Maisy stiffened all over. She couldn't imagine what he saw in her. And that was the problem. She knew it was her own insecurities—but, damn it, why couldn't his former women-friends be a little less polished, a little more…ordinary?

But she was looking at the reason why. Spectacular bone structure, height, lean muscular build and a mind like a steel trap. He was a prize. But not one granted to girls like her. It was on the tip of her tongue to ask him why. But that would have been too humiliating.

He in turn was studying her like a puzzle. She backed away from him and began shoving the underwear back into the carrier, refusing to look at him. She felt like such a fool, going to all this effort to look pretty for him, spending money she couldn't afford on lingerie that was probably laughably tame compared to what he was used to.

Out of her depth didn't even cover it. *Don't make it a big deal.* Those were his words. Because it clearly wasn't a big deal to him.

'I'm convinced I should have tied you to the bed this morning,' Alexei muttered, expression shuttered.

Maisy turned her back on him and marched into the wardrobe. When she re-emerged he was gone.

Just sex, he'd said. So now she knew.

CHAPTER EIGHT

MAISY was almost done feeling sorry for herself, but her shoulder was starting to ache and it was making her tetchy. She told herself all she wanted was to crawl into bed—her own bed. But that wasn't what she had signed up for. She had Kostya to bathe and read to and put to bed, and then it would be time to front up to entertain the man who put diamonds around the neck of Tara Mills. Mr *Don't Make It A Big Deal*.

But it was a big deal. She just knew she wasn't going to be able to get past the knowledge of all those other women. Not because of who they were—each individual blurred into one glossy, silicone-enhanced mass—but because it made no sense at all why he was with her now.

She kicked off her heels and padded barefoot to the nursery. It was after six, and Kostya was fractious after his long and exciting day. He babbled about ponies and kept mentioning another boy, one of Maria's grandsons, but mainly he talked about 'Alessi', who was clearly a big hit. As he should be, Maisy thought wearily as she ran his bath and collected the assortment of plastic toys he required.

He was splashing and Maisy was wilting when Alexei put in his appearance, hair damp, freshly shaved, smelling faintly of luxury cologne and male skin. Maisy was suddenly immensely grateful she had spent her afternoon being doused in oils and potions that gave her hair and skin a gleaming intensity her sinking spirits did not match.

The immediate rapport between man and boy sent her into

the corner, perching on the washing hamper, whilst Alexei conducted the Royal Navy in the bathtub.

'I'll put him to bed,' Alexei assured her over his shoulder. 'Go and fix yourself up and I'll fetch you for dinner.'

Fix yourself up. Maisy eyed the soap dish. Could she crack his skull with it if she applied enough force?

'Maisy?'

'I heard,' she said, not bothering to disguise the irritation in her voice.

What in the hell was wrong with her now? Alexei watched as she leaned down to kiss Kostya's downy curls, her ringlets sliding forward. She was very sweet with him. He found himself leaning forward as Kostya reached up and tugged on one of her curls and held on.

Alexei saw a flash of the old Maisy, laughing a little as she detached herself from Kostya's tenacious grip. He hadn't fully realised she had gone until she'd laughed, her expression softening.

It threw him. He'd been so busy justifying his own behaviour he'd forgotten this sweetness, this warmth that had drawn him in to begin with. He wanted this Maisy back—the one who had greeted him at his bedroom door in just his shirt; the one who had wrapped her arms around him this morning in the garden.

If Kostya wasn't here he'd have her stripped and gasping under him on the bathroom tiles, all arguments and all anxieties over how she'd fit in his life erased by mind-blowing sex. But mind-blowing sex wasn't going to fix the problem with Maisy, because the problem *was* the mind-blowing sex. She had blindsided him this morning. Last night he'd planned a practised seduction, a little recreational sex with a pretty girl. He could actually pinpoint the moment it had stopped being familiar territory and started being something entirely new: when she'd leaned into his car and told him she wasn't going to do as he told her and powered off with that pram, a swing in her hips. She said no at every turn, to a man who rarely if ever heard the word and when he did, manoeuvred his way around it. She'd been defying him ever since, going her own way even when it left her trapped on a terrace or spending money she probably didn't have on lingerie to seduce him.

So he'd sent Carlo to her with that credit card. He'd arranged a bank account for her. He'd done all he could to force her to conform to the stereotype he'd constructed to *handle* the women in his life. To neutralise relationships.

If he'd planned to push her away he couldn't have done any better.

He caught hold of her hand as she straightened up and she looked startled. He pressed his lips to her palm. It was a gesture designed to reassure her, but her eyes just flared wide— as if she thought he was going to launch himself at her here and now.

Irritation at the gulf between his expectations and her experience must have made itself known in his expression, because she jerked her hand free as if he'd scalded her.

Releasing a deep sigh, Alexei said, 'It shouldn't be this hard, *dushka*.'

Maisy tried not to load his words with meaning, but as she dressed she couldn't douse the suspicion that she'd managed this afternoon to severely damage whatever connection they'd had in bed that morning.

She stood in front of the mirror, checking herself from all angles in her heels and her new underwear. The image in the mirror was disconcerting. A taller, voluptuous, sex kitten Maisy. The one she'd known existed deep in her fantasy life but who had never been given the kit to play dress-up in and come into being. She hadn't really bought this underwear for him, she realized. It was for herself. To make her feel confident.

Everything she had done this morning, everything Alexei had done to her, played itself over in Technicolor as she lifted her black satin dress over her head. It slid like water down her body and she felt her pulse leap lightly as her silhouette meta-morphosed with the aid of her expensive lingerie.

I look good, she thought, feeling more confident. She carefully ran a brush through her ringlets, slicked her lips with the glittery lipstick she had purchased at the spa. They looked fuller, and with her eyes made up she looked as beautiful as she had felt this morning, when Alexei had been moving inside her and she'd had his whole rapt attention.

That was what she missed, she realised, and she didn't know how to get it back. She was puzzling over it when a rap on her door broke the spell.

Alexei was leaning on the wall across the hall from her door. He was dressed up. Dinner shirt, jacket and dark pants. Muscles and testosterone and moody blue eyes. Maisy's pulse picked up, overriding the morass of feeling that was swamping her tonight. She almost forgot how different she looked, but was reminded as Alexei came away from the wall, his sullen mouth widening into a decidedly elemental smile.

He said something in Russian. It sounded beautiful—all rolling 'r's and hushed vowels. Then he said something else, and it sounded dirty.

'Suddenly I don't have an appetite,' he finally said in English, crowding her. 'Let's skip the food and get down to business.'

She closed the door quietly behind her, then folded her arms in a self-protective gesture that wiped the smile off Alexei's face.

'I was joking, Maisy. The helicopter's waiting. We've got a table booked.'

'We're going out?'

'It's usually the idea when you dine with a beautiful woman.'

Natural colour swept into her cheeks and Alexei relaxed. He watched her arms unfold, some of the tension flow out of her shoulders and her spine lift.

'I can't believe we're going out in public,' she marvelled. 'On a proper date, like normal people.'

Alexei stared at her, wondering if she was actually going to clap her hands and jump up and down.

'Except for the helicopter,' she added, smiling.

'I can do normal,' he asserted roughly. He was starting to get the hint that what worked for Maisy were the traditional aspects of relations between men and women. He could do that. He suddenly wondered if he should have brought her flowers. Instead he obeyed a sudden instinct and bent and kissed her gently on the cheek, took her hand.

Maisy lit up like Christmas in response, and floated after him.

Afterwards she didn't know where she'd found the nerve to climb into the glass fishbowl he called a helicopter, but she got to cling to him in the dark, which made it all worthwhile.

It was a magical night. The exclusive restaurant was in Naples, and Maisy would never forget slipping out of the limo with Alexei and walking hand in hand the rest of the way through the old city. They had a private room, but Maisy had the thrill of walking across a room full of people on his arm. She discovered she had an appetite, despite her long and event-ful day, stealing bits off Alexei's plate and feeding him the anchovies she couldn't stand. As she licked up her dessert—a meringue and cream fantasy with tiny pink crystals that melted on her tongue—she knew for once exactly what she needed to do tonight to make everything perfect.

Alexei had brandy and coffee, watching her eat with obvi-ous pleasure. She extended her spoon to him and he obliged, taking a sweet mouthful he didn't want just to make her smile.

'I don't want this night to end,' she confided as he draped her cape around her shoulders.

'Would you like to go dancing?'

Maisy turned up happy eyes. 'I would.'

Alexei took her to a supper club where he could slow dance with her. Maisy wrapped her arms around him, wanting to tell him this was the first time she'd danced like this. He was her first in so many ways. She shivered in reaction.

'What is it, *dushka*?'

His voice had dropped to a low pitch that thrummed in her belly.

Speaking before she could lose her nerve, she replied, 'I want to make love with you.'

She actually felt Alexei's breath hitch in his chest beneath the press of her hand. It was gratifying, and thrilling. For the first time since they'd met she felt as if she had taken the reins.

'Shall we go home?' she suggested.

Alexei didn't argue.

Something had altered. Maisy felt the change come over Alexei as they entered the house. All the lights were glittering in the many windows, and the place looked like a fairytale castle, but Alexei strode across the mezzanine and up the stairs as if on a mission.

Maisy struggled along behind, no longer holding his hand but being shackled and dragged. So much for taking the reins. But she didn't mind all that much. If he wanted to behave like a caveman she was happy to be what he was dragging back to his cave.

To her annoyance, Carlo Santini stepped out of the corridor at the top of the stairs. Alexei swore when he saw him. A volley of vitriolic Russian intruded on Maisy's dreamy state.

Alexei made a silencing gesture with one hand, then turned with elaborate politeness and said in English, 'A small emergency has arisen, Maisy. I may be some time.'

He didn't touch her. He didn't kiss her. He just walked away. And Maisy, disappointment settling over her, very slowly bent down and removed her shoes, sinking back down to ground level.

In her stockinged feet she returned to her room. She felt alarmingly keyed-up, but had no intention of decking herself out on his bed on the faint chance he would return and want her on tap. The moment had passed.

She didn't know why, but seeing Carlo Santini had reminded

her of the type of relationship Alexei had set down for them. He had his life, his work—which he was now attending to—and he had a woman for recreation. Which happened to be her.

It didn't go a long way to making a girl feel special.

Maisy stripped herself of all her clothes but didn't take a shower. She spent a long time scrubbing her make-up off until she was barefaced. She hesitated over the negligee. Something was niggling—something that told her if she donned it and waited for him she would be playing right into his stupid mistress scenario.

So she dug out her old sleepshirt instead. It was just a long white T-shirt with a cartoon mouse on the front, soft from hundreds of washings. It felt so familiar she was assailed with an overwhelming longing for a simpler life, and the less complicated girl she had once been.

I need Anais, she thought sadly, curling up like a snail on her bed. Anais would read Alexei like a book and provide footnotes. *To me he's just a seething mass of testosterone and conflicting messages. I can't keep up.* She yawned and snuggled into her pillow, hugging it to her. Her bed felt huge and empty, but it wasn't as if she wasn't used to sleeping alone.

She surfaced to consciousness with a sigh. A large male hand was on her inner thigh and she jolted, rolling backwards to thud into his big, solid body.

'Alexei. You gave me a fright,' she mumbled groggily.

'I apologise, *dushka*, I didn't mean to wake you.' But he was kissing the back of her neck in the way she'd learned she liked, and her bottom was pressed against what was clearly on his mind.

'I can't do this,' she protested, but he was already lifting her T-shirt, peeling it up her body. She squirmed and pulled away. 'No, stop it.' She kicked out at him. 'I need to sleep.'

'Sleep?' Alexei sounded incredulous.

'Yes,' she muttered. 'And so do you if your mood's anything to go by.'

A very big part of her wanted him to pull her into his arms

and override her objections. Instead Alexei literally thrust himself away from her, rolling onto his back, sweeping aside the covers.

'Where are you going?' she demanded softly, struggling to sit up.

He jack-knifed out of the bed. 'I need a shower, if that's all right by you. A cold one.'

Maisy pulled the covers back over her, but as the minutes went by she felt herself shivering. It only grew worse as the time ticked by. She heard the shower being switched on and off. Any minute now he was going to walk through here and out of that door.

She heard the door open, shut. Maisy rolled over to watch him in the moonlight coming through the window. He was picking up her clothes.

'What are you doing?' she framed softly.

He didn't reply. He draped her gown over the armchair in the corner, and then her bra, her stockings and barely there cami-knickers. All the bits she had strewn carelessly over the floor. Maisy had never met a coat hanger she liked.

She watched him silently, still shivering but feeling strangely moved. His gestures were so precise they seemed to have meaning. Now he would leave, she thought, as he ran out of items. Except he didn't. He climbed into bed beside her and there was only the sound of his breathing, steady and deep, and hers, uncertain and shallow.

'Your emergency,' she said uncertainly. 'What was it about?'

Alexei was silent for so long Maisy didn't think he was going to answer her. His words startled her when he did speak. 'It was to do with a timber company.'

'Nothing serious?' She had an excuse now to roll over.

Alexei was lying on his back, naked, one arm hooked behind his head. He was staring up at the ceiling and didn't look at her, but she could see the tiredness in the set of his profile and for the first time it occurred to her how work never stopped for him.

'I've dealt with the bare necessities. There's nothing that can't be cleared up tomorrow.'

She realised he had left things unresolved to return to her. Before she could enjoy the feeling she remembered Carlo Santini. She remembered all the women.

Yet here he was, in bed with her.

Maisy drew the covers more securely around her neck. She was so cold, and it wasn't going away. She felt cold to the bone.

'I had an amazing time tonight,' she said quietly into the dark. 'I want to thank you.'

Alexei's head shifted. His eyes welded with hers. 'You were happy,' he said. It wasn't a question, it was a statement. Then he frowned. 'You're shivering.'

His whole body shifted then. He lifted the covers and literally dragged her into him, and she was engulfed in Alexei. Cold shower or not, his body was like the sun. He exuded heat and comfort, but she couldn't relax.

'Talk to me,' he murmured into her hair. 'Tell me about how you came to be at the Kulikovs'.' When she was silent he prompted, 'You met Anais at school?'

Maisy didn't want to go near the Anais and Leo question. He had reacted so strongly the other night she didn't want to risk it. But with her cheek pressed against his firm, warm chest she felt a little safer to talk about it. It wasn't as if he'd tip her out of bed, would he?

'Anais came to St Bernice's when we were fourteen. She was a skinny beanpole and I was a chubby little swot.' She said it lightly, but it was forced.

Alexei smoothed his palm over the curve of her hip. Maisy felt something inside give a little, because he'd made it extremely clear since they'd met that the womanly aspects of her body were what he found desirable.

'You were close?'

'I was bullied a little, because I wasn't from the right sort of background, and Anais fought those battles for me. I'll always be grateful to her for that.'

'So what happened at the end of school?'

'Anais went modelling and I—' Maisy took a deep breath. She had never told a soul this story and it felt strange doing so now. But the dark helped—and the heavy solidity of Alexei wrapped around her. 'My mum got sick. I looked after her.'

'I see.'

But he didn't see. He couldn't know what a slow descent those two years had been. She'd been on the verge of her adult life and it had all been taken away.

'Your mother is dead.' He said it bluntly.

Maisy looked up at him. 'How do you know? Oh, the investigators.' She tried to put a little room between them but he refused to let her budge.

'No, I didn't get them to dig that far. I know because you haven't made any phone calls to England. All girls call their mothers at some point.'

'Even if my mum was alive I probably wouldn't be ringing her,' said Maisy frankly.

'She did a job on you?' He propped himself up so he could watch her telltale face.

'She was a single mum. She was only sixteen when she had me. She always told me I'd ruined her life. Then she got cancer and she needed me.'

Alexei rubbed his thumb over the pulse at the base of her throat. 'Then what happened?'

'I ran into Anais in a department store in London. It was just weeks after Mum's funeral. I was—numb. And suddenly there she was. She was pregnant with Kostya and she wanted me to move in with her and help. She didn't have any sisters and her mum was a bit of a nightmare.'

'You had that in common.' He was brushing the hair out of her eyes. She loved it when he did that, felt cherished by him. 'And you stayed with her thereafter?'

Maisy was silent. She suddenly felt tremulous. He was straying very close to dangerous ground.

'You never thought about going back to school?'

If there was an implied criticism in there she couldn't detect it, and it gave her the courage to answer honestly. 'After Mum died I thought about university. I'd got in, but I couldn't go because of Mum. And then Anais appeared and I made my decision. I can't regret it.'

'Surely Leo could have got you a job in one of his companies? I know you, Maisy. You're a smart girl.'

It wasn't the use of the description 'smart' that pleased her. It was the assertion *I know you*. He didn't, but the assurance he had that he did made her feel warm inside. Wanted.

'I had a baby to look after. It doesn't give you much room for a social life, let alone a job.'

'So tell me about this one lover, one time.'

He spoke so casually, just slipped it in, his fingers sliding gently through one of her long curls. But Maisy wasn't fooled. He was marking his ground.

Maisy *really* didn't want to discuss Dan with Alexei. It made her feel pathetic, and she desperately didn't want him to see her as that.

'Were you in a relationship with him?'

'Of course I was,' Maisy answered unthinkingly, then stiffened. She had jumped into bed with Alexei quickly enough, and this wasn't anything like a relationship. There was no *of course* about it. She waited for him to react, but he was observing her as if what she was saying was fascinating. 'I don't really want to discuss it,' she said quietly. 'It happened. That's it.'

'You were in a relationship, you lost your virginity and that was it? No repeat performance?'

'I called it quits.' Suddenly the stitching on the edge of the bedsheet became the most interesting thing in the room.

'How long were you seeing each other?'

'Six weeks.'

'So a long-term thing?'

Maisy felt her temper stir and lift. 'Okay, you've made your point. I'm not sophisticated, and I had crappy sex with a crappy boy in his crappy bedsit. But look—now I've come up in the world. Better sex with a better boy in a better bed.'

'Better sex?' He chuckled, the sound a gravitational pull that had her edging back in against him. 'This is fantastic sex, *dushka*. The best I've ever had.'

Maisy spun for a moment on that assertion. He couldn't be serious?

'And for your information, Maisy,' he murmured, his breath warm in her ear, 'I'm not a boy. I'm a man. And there's a difference.'

Maisy knew that. Alexei had made it very clear what that difference was since day one.

'I wish I'd known you then,' he inserted softly.

'You wouldn't have given me the time of day.'

There—she'd said it. Her throat was aching with unexpressed emotions she was finding it difficult to keep repressed.

She felt the change in Alexei's body and it was like a kick to her belly. He didn't want to hear her insecurities, but they were all she felt tonight. The day had been too volatile; too much had happened to her. And now she couldn't sleep. She could only lie pinned to him, baring her soul to a man who probably wanted nothing less.

'I would have taken you to a luxurious hotel and taken your virginity with a great deal more care than some bloke in a bedsit,' he said with rough assurance.

Maisy pressed her temple against his chest. For a moment she allowed herself to believe him. He was touching her, his palms and fingertips moving over her waist and back and hips in circular movements, but not in a sexual way. At least she didn't think so. He was just warming her.

'Alexei…' she murmured.

'Hmm?'

'I wish it had been you,' she confessed. 'I know we're just having a fling. But I wish it had been you.'

Alexei's hands had stopped moving and it felt as if he'd stopped breathing.

'It's how I feel,' she said nervously, wondering what the stillness meant.

His big hand tipped her chin up and he brought his mouth down on hers, hard and hot and possessive. She had the fleeting thought, *This is just like London.* And it rocked her.

His hands were suddenly under her T-shirt and around her breasts. Maisy felt her body rev to speed without a second thought. She was still shivering, but she couldn't *not* respond. He was still hers. She could already feel him at her core, and she was wet for him. He tore her old shirt in two, baring her breasts. He entered her with a single thrust and she rocked into him, not caring about anything but the fury that was driving her upwards. She'd gone from virtually zero in the physical department to Alexei's level in the span of a day. God knew what he had created. Maisy didn't even know who she was any more.

She splintered into a thousand pieces so quickly she could have wept, but he was still moving in her, and Maisy clung to him, digging her nails into the slabs of muscle behind his shoulders, feeling it build again. His mouth kept contact with hers, his eyes pinning her so that when she climaxed again he was with her. But it was different this time. She felt him pour himself into her. Sweat glistened on his shoulders where Maisy pressed her mouth, and then he was sinking heavily on top of her. He stayed inside her, not moving. Her heartbeat began to thrum to the rhythm of his and she closed her eyes, the tears rising and choking her.

'It's not a fling,' he muttered. Then he lifted himself up on his forearms and fixed her face in place with his hands. He meshed their mouths. 'It's not a fling,' he repeated.

Just in case she hadn't heard him the first time.

Alexei gave Kostya his promised three days. He introduced him to the sea, held his tiny barrel-shaped body in the gently breaking surf as it creamed the shore and built sandcastles for the sea to destroy.

Maisy sheltered under a huge hat and a billowy sheer

shirt—the sun had never been kind to her—and feasted her eyes on Alexei in a pair of low-slung board shorts that did nothing to curb her X-rated thoughts. His golden tan made a mockery of her pale, lightly freckled skin. She could blame the heat of the day for her hot flush as he strode up the beach to where she sat under an umbrella, her trashy novel fluttering in the breeze, but his gaze told her otherwise, locking on the sumptuous curves of her breasts and hips in the flattering fifties-style bikini.

Last night had shifted something in their relationship. The tensions between them seemed to have evaporated, and on this private beach, in the full glare of the late-afternoon sun, Maisy felt an enormous clutch of contentment and the wicked stir of her body. It was as if her body was suddenly fully awake after a long sleep, and like Sleeping Beauty she was in thrall to her prince. Her gloriously built prince, with his slumberous smile and Tartar eyes eating her up as she fumbled in her bag for sunscreen to reapply to Kostya's sand-encrusted nose.

It was her rule that they shouldn't show physical affection in front of Kostya, but it was a rule she was regretting as six and a half feet of Russian male stretched himself out on the lounger beside her, his long, lean body glistening with seawater and sand, his lashes wet and black, framing his brilliant eyes. He lay there watching her, looking immensely relaxed and happy. The grim, tense Alexei had been banished. She had fallen asleep in the arms of a looser-limbed, becalmed man, and so he remained.

Kostya settled on the sand within the circumference of the umbrella and dug with a stick, making comments about the ant he was tracking. Alexei extended his hand and Maisy broke her rule, giving him hers. The peace and serenity of the moment settled very deeply over them.

It was, Maisy realised, sanctuary.

'I have to fly to Geneva on Friday,' he told her, his voice a register deeper, tugging on those muscles deep down inside her. It made her smile, and a response flared in his eyes. 'I want you to come with me.'

'I think Kostya and I should stay here,' she answered reluctantly. 'He's just starting to settle in. It would be wrong to disturb him.'

'Maria can look after him. It's only for a couple of days and a night.'

The night. He wanted her for the night. Maisy's toes curled with delight.

'A night too long.' She bit her lip, wishing it could be different. 'I can't leave him, Alexei.'

'No.' He looked out at the blue horizon, but Maisy knew he wasn't admiring the view. 'No,' he said again, his chest heaving in a deep sigh.

'You don't mind?' She wished she didn't sound so anxious. It made her sound needy and insecure.

'I mind, but I understand.' His thumb was running up and down over the palm of her hand. 'Leo didn't have parents for the first eight years of his life. It might explain why he didn't have as much time for his son as he probably should have. I won't make that mistake.'

Maisy stared at him. She hadn't known that, but Alexei's admission went a long way to healing the wound his words the other night had opened. So he *did* believe her—or was giving her the benefit of the doubt.

'But I travel a lot, Maisy. Kostya is going to have to get used to that.'

She tried to ignore the absence of herself in that statement. After all, what was between them wasn't for ever. But it was life for Kostya. 'Maybe in a few weeks, when he's secure?' she suggested.

'A week. He can have a week. Then I want you with me. I can't bring my life to a standstill, Maisy. It doesn't work that way.' He softened his tone. 'Besides, you'll go crazy here on your own. You need me to keep you entertained.'

'How entertaining will it be if you're working?'

'New York, Paris, Rome, Prague. Don't you want to see those cities?'

'I want to be with you,' said Maisy simply, because it was the truth.

He didn't answer her, but his hand remained secure around her own, and for all the tenuousness of her situation Maisy felt he would continue to hold her hand through this whole experience. She wouldn't think about it now—how it would be when he finally let her go.

CHAPTER NINE

'You smell so good.' They were in the apartment he kept in the fifth *arrondissement* of Paris. It had spectacular views, taking in the Seine and the spires of Notre Dame. It was the first time Maisy had been here and she was not a little overwhelmed by it all. She had expected sleek lines and into-the-future modernity from Alexei, but all around her was restrained Louis XVI cream-and-gold luxury.

It was like stepping into Paris in the eighteenth century. She loved it.

'I'm not wearing perfume.'

'Whatever.' He inhaled deeply as he nuzzled her neck.

Prickling all over in a good way, Maisy heard herself babbling, 'I just use this tangerine soap. That's probably what you smell…'

'I smell you, Maisy,' he growled in her ear, his big hands splaying over her waist as he dragged her in against him.

It was early morning and they had landed at Orly only an hour ago. Alexei had a long day ahead and they had both been up since 4:00 a.m. Admittedly she had slept on the plane and in the limo. Now she was wide-awake, her body starting to climb as his need for her made itself known.

'You smell good to me too,' she admitted, turning in his arms.

'Aftershave and soap,' he countered. 'Nothing fancy.'

But everything about him was fancy, thought Maisy, feeling utterly adored in his arms. He screamed wealth and good taste and leashed power—except when he was with her, in bed, and that was when she had him on her level. It was a strange alchemy of him being stripped to the essential bone, of him just being a male—albeit a very fine specimen—and her losing all of her everyday 'Maisyness' and becoming his equal, the woman he wanted.

The curves she despaired of back in London were all he wanted in his bed. Nothing she said or did with him in bed was ever wrong. His praise and response to her had given her such new-found confidence. Yet the rest of the time she didn't feel quite right.

They were constantly moving from Naples to Rome to Moscow to Madrid. She was always in limos, by herself or with Kostya, entering empty suites or apartments he kept in so many cities. Alexei sent stylists and personal shoppers to prepare her for dinner, usually in out-of-the-way places. He certainly didn't flaunt their relationship. Some evenings she ate alone. He claimed she would be bored at business dinners, and she was too unsure of her position to press the point. She now had clothing and jewellery brought to her by strangers to be worn for his pleasure. None of it was hers. She was always very careful. They didn't belong to her. She didn't want to damage them. She didn't know how to ask Alexei in the cold light of day what she should do with them.

So on this, her day in Paris, with Alexei tied up in talks and Kostya booked in with the children of friends of the Kulikovs, who were overjoyed to see him again, she hit the pavement in comfy flats and went shopping for herself.

She was footsore and faintly depressed on her return at seven. The personal shoppers had made it seem so easy, but the experience of trying on endless pieces that either didn't fit or made her feel dumpy or wrongly shaped or both hadn't been quite the fun she had anticipated.

Alexei was disconcerted that he had arrived home early, intending to surprise her, and learned she had gone out. He regarded the shopping bags on the bed as if they were alien.

She dragged out a pair of jeans and some comfy T-shirts, putting them in a neat pile, then produced the lovely fuchsia silk dress that had been the stellar purchase of her day, holding it up to show him.

'The shows are on next week, *dushka*,' he asserted dismissively. 'I will take you.'

Maisy hung on to her silk dress. *That* was his comment?

'I can't afford couture,' she said in an undertone.

He frowned.

'I mean, I know you want me to dress that way, and I appreciate it. But I wanted to get some clothes for myself today. It's a bit weird, always wearing borrowed clothes.'

'Maisy, the clothes belong to *you*. I got them for *you*. The clothes, the jewellery—whatever. It's yours.'

Maisy sat down on the bed, holding on to her dress. 'Oh.'

'Most women would be pleased,' he said.

It was the 'most women' that did it. Maisy smoothed out her new dress. 'Is that how it worked in the past? You dressed the women you were with?'

It was the first time she had raised the subject since the villa at Ravello, and Maisy experienced a wave of vertigo at the immensity of what lay underneath her question.

'No…' Alexei spoke slowly.

'Tara Mills, Frances Fielding, Kate Bernier.' She rattled off the names as if she were reading them from the tag on the back of her dress, because that was where her eyes were. She couldn't look at him. 'I don't suppose any of *them* needed help dressing up.'

'How in the hell did you get those names?'

The tightly leashed aggression in his voice brought her chin up. She wasn't backing down now. She had a right to know where she stood. He shouldn't be so defensive in telling her.

'I read about them in magazines,' she answered truthfully. 'It's okay, Alexei, everyone has a past. I'm not going to go postal.'

'I don't appreciate you researching me, Maisy. If you want

to know about my life, you only have to ask me.' He spoke in a perfectly reasonable tone, but his eyes were as cold as flints of ice.

She had crossed a line, Maisy realised with a sharp twinge of reaction. These were the limits to their relationship. She dressed for him, waited for him, slept with him, but she didn't ask him personal questions. Whatever he said.

'I seem to remember you had an investigation done into me,' she replied jerkily.

'Yes, because you were looking after my godson.'

Maisy squeezed the silk under her fingers as she made fists in her lap. 'And I read up about you because I am having sex with you every night.' And morning, and sometimes in the afternoon…

'I would rather you didn't look for information about me in the tabloids.'

'Fair enough,' she conceded. 'So, if you didn't dress them, why do you dress me?'

'I imagined it would make things easier for you.'

Yeah, right. This was about him being ashamed of her. 'I think I need to buy my own clothes,' she said, her voice amazingly calm given how shaken she was feeling. 'Buying me a wardrobe isn't a gift. It's…impersonal.'

'Impersonal?' He sounded as if he was trying out the word.

Maisy took a step into the abyss. 'It's kind of like you're buying me.'

Then he said absolutely the wrong thing. 'I've never paid for sex in my life.'

The aggression coming off him kept Maisy seated. 'I—I was talking about our relationship,' she faltered. All the while another voice was saying, *What relationship, Maisy? It's sex. He's always said it's sex. He just said it's sex.*

'I live a semi-public life.' He paced out, as tense as she had ever seen him. 'You need to be dressed for it if you're going to be with me.'

If. *If you're going to be with me.* Maisy's eyes were

starfish-wide as she cottoned on to what he was saying. Struggling to catch up, she recognised it for what it was. An ultimatum.

'You can't wear that—' he made a dismissive gesture at the pink silk puddled in her lap '—whatever it is. To dinner tonight.'

She hadn't been planning to. It was a dress for the daytime. But after all he'd said she was starting to feel completely surplus to his needs—had been feeling that way since they'd started travelling. And it was making her both terrified and very, very angry.

'There's nothing wrong with this dress,' she stated between her teeth.

'I want you in the champagne silk you wore in Rome.'

'No.'

'Fine.'

He turned away from her, removing his watch, his cufflinks. She watched him tumble them onto the bedside table. He headed for the walk-in wardrobe.

'Where are you going?'

He didn't answer, but a minute later he reappeared, naked. 'Shower,' he said briefly.

'I'm going to wear what I want to wear,' she defended herself. Why didn't he say anything?

'Do what you want,' he replied. 'The invitation is withdrawn.'

Maisy just gaped after him. What did he mean, the invitation was withdrawn? They weren't going to dinner? She couldn't believe what had just happened. Was he angry with her because she had bought her own clothes and refused his?

She heard the shower go on. Fine. She stood up too quickly and the room shifted slightly, so she sat down again. It had been such a long day—but, damn him, she wasn't going to be a pushover. Giving herself a few minutes to calm down, she fetched her brush and toiletries and marched into the bathroom. He was towelling himself dry and seemed a bit thrown to see her. But Maisy ignored him, shaking her hair out of its pins and pulling the brush through it with rough strokes.

'I'd like some space, Maisy.'

'Tough,' she replied, grabbing her spray conditioner and letting fly.

He wrapped the towel around his hips and left her to it. Maisy pushed down the pain and kept going, taming her curls into a neat chignon and then making up her eyes and mouth. When she emerged into the bedroom Alexei was dressed in trousers and was buttoning up a tailored white shirt. It clung faithfully to the wide expanse of his shoulders and chest like a sleeve, making him seem both overwhelmingly male and yet elegant at the same time. He was going out, she registered. Without her.

'Where are you going?'

When he didn't answer she hurled the brush she had in her hand at him, aiming for his legs and missing entirely. Her brush bounced on the luxurious carpet. He merely gave her a quelling look as if to say, *That's the best you can do?*

Not quite knowing what she was doing, but powered by the unfairness of it all, Maisy stripped off the simple shift she had been wearing all day, unhooked her plain cotton bra, slid off her knickers.

She kept her back to him. She had never undressed in front of him in all these weeks. There was something unfailingly intimate about it. Once she was in bed with him it was different. But the act of actually going about her daily robing and disrobing made her feel vulnerable, and she didn't need more of that.

She emptied out the bag of frothy nothings she had bought to wear for him, picking up a sheer black bra and knickers that had cost more than her pretty dress. The knickers had little bows at the side to be tied, and the bra had a bow at the front. Neither was at all practical for wearing anywhere other than in a bedroom to seduce a man.

Which had been her intention when she'd purchased them. Right now she had no idea *what* her intention was.

She adjusted her breasts into the cups, making sure they were secure, then cast a look at Alexei over her shoulder. He had got no further with his buttons from the moment she'd started stripping.

'Come and help me,' she requested, sounding petulant.

He didn't hesitate, which fired her confidence, and when he was only a hand-span away from her she turned around and untied the bow, so that the weight of her breasts tugged the bra cups apart.

'Do me up,' she instructed.

His hands moved obediently to slide under the fabric, his thumbs circling her nipples so that her head fell forward onto his chest. 'That's not helping me,' she murmured.

His voice was gratifyingly a register lower. 'You started this. I'll finish it.'

A lick of lust moved over her and she grabbed hold of his waistband, her hands trembling so that she was woeful at disengaging the buttons. But it didn't matter. He lifted her and she wrapped her bare legs around his hips. Ignoring the bed, he propelled her back against the wall, yanking the bows on her knickers free, testing her readiness with his fingers, lifting her again to slide his erection into her, his back and shoulders bunching up under her hands as he took the strain of doing it slowly and steadily and completely.

Maisy's head flopped forward, her hair cloaking them both as he buried his face in her neck and began to thrust into her with little finesse but a great deal of energy. Maisy couldn't stop the noises that were answering his rather effective grunts as she lost herself in the flashing pleasure.

That it could be like this startled her. That he could do this to her was almost overwhelming. No condom, she thought presently, straining against him. It must have hit him at the same time, because he seemed about to pull away from her, but his body continued to thunder forward and won out. Yet as he slid her down the wall and her feet touched carpet he pulled free and came over her bare stomach, holding himself with such an expression that Maisy never thought she had ever seen anything so beautiful. She felt like a goddess, all of her anger spent, all of him on her.

He was apologising to her, leaning against her, his head heavy, bent low, his breathing laboured, those big shoulders heaving. Maisy loved this. Loved the way she could do this to him. It made everything that had gone before somehow meaningless, as if this thing they shared overwhelmed the prosaic realities of the life they were living together.

Alexei was still in his shirt. He had stepped out of his boxers and trousers and Maisy had pushed the shirt back over his shoulders as they'd grappled. It hung suspended halfway down his back.

'You didn't come,' he muttered in her ear.

'Doesn't matter.' She wound her arms around him, burrowing, needing that closeness.

'You can wear what you want to dinner. We'll eat here. Whatever you want.'

Maisy hung on to him, but she had gone very still and quiet inside. Her instincts were telling her something and she didn't want to hear it right now. Easier just to take him at his word. But those words settled like stones in her belly.

This was her power over him. This was what she used for leverage. She had just manipulated a situation her way with sex. Those games he had tried to play with her early on and quickly given up she had now instigated as her own, however unconsciously.

But something about this relationship—probably to do with how it had started, the imbalances between them and Alexei's history—was changing her. Changing them.

She didn't want to be this woman. She didn't want to be this way with Alexei. She wanted honest, and real, and for him to love her. The realisation flashed with neon clarity across her mind. She was in love with him.

She wanted him to love her as she loved him. Had loved him from the moment she tore the lining of his jacket and he had looked at her, really looked at her, and she had seen him and recognised in him something she needed very much.

And right now all the danger signs were flashing red.

The first night they were back in Ravello Alexei dreamt of St Petersburg.

He was eight years old and on the streets. He ran in a pack of kids, all of them living hand-to-mouth. He couldn't remember his father, but he could still see his mother's stunning face, cosmetically enhanced, bending in and blowing alcohol into his lungs. Promising she would return for him in a few days but never coming back.

He woke bathed in sweat, shaking. Blackness was all around him and he was alone.

Maisy woke to the sound of a shout. She sat up, no longer disorientated when she woke in the night to find herself in a vast bed. Falling asleep every night pinned by Alexei's arm had made what was once so novel an integral part of her everyday life.

Alexei was awake. It was too dark to see his face, but she could feel the startled reaction running through his big warm body. He'd had another one of those dreams. She reached out in the darkness and laid her hand on his chest. It was hot and hair-roughened and rose fast under her hand.

'Are you okay?' she whispered.

He rolled away, dislodging her hand and presenting the bulk of his back and shoulders to her.

Maisy was wide-awake now. She didn't know what to do. The other time he'd woken in the night like this he had pretended to go back to sleep, but they both knew he had lain awake most of the night.

'Alexei,' she whispered, 'talk to me.'

He made that grunting noise she recognized, which told her she could wrap her arms around him but not expect much communication. So she did, lying down and wrapping her arms around his middle. Alexei sought her hands, knotting them with his and lashing her against him.

He could feel her breath against his back, the soft brush of her wayward hair, the sweet rub of her smooth calf over his. It soothed.

He said, half to himself, 'Kostya will be all right.'

His voice was hoarse and Maisy was instantly on high alert. Something was very wrong.

'Of course he will be.' She spoke feelingly but she felt uncertain. A couple of weeks had passed now since Kostya had been told of his parents' deaths. Alexei had been amazing with him, giving both her and Kostya the strong bulwark they both needed in those awful fragile days as the tiny child groped for security.

Maisy had broken her rule on those nights, having Kostya in bed with her to soothe his night terrors. Alexei had volunteered to take the other bed but Kostya had wanted his beloved Alessi too, and what Maisy had most feared had come to pass. They were a facsimile of a family, huddled together in this vast bed that had once seemed so alien and threatening but was now where all the happiest times of her life were spent.

'I'll protect him,' Alexei asserted.

'I know.' She stroked his back.

He tried to clutch on to the human warmth of her touch, but he was being swamped by his own fears from the past and they were fast dragging him under. It coalesced the longer he lay there, beginning to tense under the feel of her touch. He had allowed her to get too close and he knew the terror he was feeling was a warning. She too would leave. It was inevitable one of them would abandon what they had. He had to reinstate proper distance. He could not allow his own fear or weakness to dislodge the grip he had on his emotions. He had to do it now.

Abruptly he shifted, dislodging Maisy's hold, and reached up, flicking on the lamp.

'I can't protect him from you, can I?'

He watched her blinking blearily in the unexpected light, covering her eyes with her hands. Defenceless. But he needed to be brutal. She needed to hear this.

'What are you talking about, Alexei?'

'I'm talking about you leaving, Maisy. Because we both know there's an end date.'

She stared back at him, appalled. A slow cold trickle of dread made its way down her spine.

'Why are you attacking me?' she whispered. 'It's the middle of the night.'

Then he said the words she had been dreading in the darkest part of her soul. 'I can't do this any more, Maisy.'

A tiny, endlessly hopeful, naive part of her had imagined a future with him—one involving a white dress, a picket fence and babies. The things she'd longed for when she was a little girl and the world had been a much more black-and-white place. But she knew now that wasn't going to happen. Not with this man.

Weeks of living with him, sleeping beside him, welcoming him into her body, and she understood she hadn't really touched anything beyond his surface. These dreams she sensed were a gateway into whatever darkness was eating away at him, but even lying in bed with him, privy to their ragged effect on him, she was not invited inside.

'I see.' It was all she could think to say, although she didn't see at all. But it was three o'clock in the morning and he was ripping her heart out and she hadn't even seen it coming.

Although in retrospect the signs had all been there. Despite the travel, they had essentially been alone. She hadn't minded a bit, because she'd had Alexei and Kostya, but it said volumes for where he saw her in his life. She remembered those photographs in the magazines, those women on his arm. That would never be her. He had never intended that to be her. She was like some sort of secret he kept.

Deep down she'd known this day was going to come. But it

made no sense—not at three o'clock, not just hours after she'd fallen asleep in his arms, her body still bearing the traces of his lovemaking. He couldn't be tired of her yet. He was just shucking off the effects of his nightmare. If she stayed very still and very small he might just go back to sleep and forget about it. But she wasn't that girl any more. She had changed. She had grown up.

She watched a deep breath shudder through him, and he said almost hopelessly, 'Are you happy with me, Maisy?'

'Yes.' *I've never been so happy. I've never felt so right in my whole life.*

'You never go anywhere. You never see anyone.' He propped himself up against the headboard.

'I see you,' she said. 'I see Kostya.'

He was trying to persuade her to leave.

'We can't keep this up. It's starting to get on my nerves.' He looked down at her. 'We need to be with other people, out in the world, or this is never going to be normal.'

What on earth was he talking about? Maisy wanted to shake him, but she sensed half of this was about his pain and the strange hour and the stillness. If she kept quiet he might just say something revealing, something that would let her in just a fraction.

But she couldn't help murmuring, 'You want to see other people?'

'Maybe you need a job,' he said instead. 'You need a life of your own.'

It hurt. 'I have a job. I look after Kostya. I have a life.'

'For how long?' He turned his head and she was shocked by the tension bracketed around his mouth and eyes. He looked older, tired.

'I think that rather depends on you.' There—she'd said it.

'If I had my way we'd never leave this bed.'

But his expression didn't soften and he was done talking. She knew there would be no revelations tonight. She knew she should push, but his words were pounding in her head: *we can't keep this up; we need to be with other people; you need a life of your own.* And it all contained the same message: *you're not enough any more.*

'Can we go to sleep?' She voiced the last thing she wanted to do.

He stretched across and the light went out. Maisy waited for him to reach for her, but he didn't. He remained upright, sitting still and silent in the dark.

Rolling over, making herself as small and unobtrusive as possible, she stared into a bleak future without him and she too didn't sleep.

'There's a boatload of people turning up at noon. I thought I'd put them on the yacht instead of dragging them through here, but there's a small group who will be staying overnight. Do you think you can handle that?'

Alexei delivered this with the unconcern of a man who issued orders on a daily basis. It was just he had never issued an order to *her*, and Maisy didn't quite know how to react.

He looked amazing this morning, in an olive-green polo shirt and tailored chinos, freshly shaven and no doubt smelling of tangy aftershave and male skin, but Maisy didn't know because he hadn't so much as bussed her cheek since their early-morning discussion.

Now he was springing this on her. People were coming? He hadn't said a word.

'I'm usually quite good with people,' she ventured. They were eating breakfast in the dining room. Maisy never felt entirely comfortable, perched at the end of the long table. Alexei's place was set beside hers, but he had managed to set his chair back and Maisy didn't feel their usual morning connection, when he sat so close she could hook her foot around his ankle and rub up his calf. She wasn't rubbing anything this morning.

'I know. I've seen you in action. The staff love you.' He sipped his espresso as if it held his attention. But Maisy wasn't fooled. His highwire brain was on the job. 'However, after

today it'll be official. People will want to know who you are.'
He turned his head slowly, fixed her with those blue eyes.
'What do I tell them?'

I'm your girlfriend, Maisy wanted to scream at him. *I love
you. I've loved you for every minute of every hour of every
day since I laid eyes on those handmade Italian shoes. You're
everything to me. You bring the day and you hang the moon,
you stupid idiot.*

'Tell them I'm Maisy Edmonds and I look after Kostya,'
she said, kicking back her chair, feeling furious with him and
sick to death of herself. 'And that when I'm done supervising
his meals and making sure he gets enough sleep, I look after
you.'

She made to stalk off, and it would have been a great exit,
but he reached out and leashed her wrist, dragging her onto
his lap. She sat stiff and affronted, refusing to look at him.

'I'll send a car for you at one. Carlo will come with you on
the launch.'

'I *hate* Carlo,' she said with a passion, not sure why she'd
chosen now to tell him.

'What has he done?' Alexei's gaze sharpened on her.

'He's a pig. He thinks you've bought me. Ever since you
gave me those stupid cards and that smart phone.'

'I've never seen you use it once.'

'I put it in a drawer. I don't need it,' she dismissed, annoyed
they were talking about gadgets instead of what mattered: her
and him, and where they stood. 'I don't need any of it.'

'The money is there for you to spend, *dushka*. I want you
to enjoy yourself.'

Maisy sighed heavily. He was never going to understand
how she felt. 'I've told you, Alexei, I don't want your stupid
money.'

He'd given her a bank account, but he'd never so much as
given her a bunch of flowers. Everything was rising to the surface today, and now she had to face a host of strangers, and be
introduced as what? Alexei's latest accessory?

'Can you be ready at one?'

'Do I have a choice?'

He stroked the curve of her jaw, encouraging her to look at him.

'I think I told you once before, *dushka*, you always have choices. You made one when you decided to be with me, and now I need you to abide by your choice a little longer.' He dislodged her from his lap. 'Off you go. And I've organised a little help for your dress.'

Maisy puzzled over this enigmatic statement until midmorning, when a stylist arrived at the house. She was sorting out Kostya's washing when Maria let her know over the intercom, and she came down in jeans and a stained T-shirt, her hair pulled back in an elastic band.

The woman had clearly been paid a good deal of money, because she barely raised a perfectly groomed eyebrow, but Maisy was whisked upstairs immediately. Apparently two hours was going to be pushing it to get her ready.

It was gruelling. She was plucked, waxed, polished, made up, brushed, stripped, and dipped into a hot pink silk and chiffon dress that fell from spaghetti straps from her shoulders, skimmed her breasts and flounced over her knees. She stepped into silver sandals. Her hair was elaborately plaited and pinned, tendrils artfully brimming around her made-up face. Her eyes looked like mysterious pools with all the kohl, and her mouth was as fresh as a pink rose.

Maisy could categorically say she had never felt beautiful in her life.

And she felt beautiful now.

'*Bellissima,*' murmured the stylist's assistant.

Maisy blinked rapidly. Tears were going to ruin the effect of her eyes.

'I've never had a client cry before,' said the stylist, gently dabbing Maisy's lashes.

Except she wasn't emotional about the dress, the make-up,

the look; she was thinking that if Alexei saw her looking like this he might keep her a little longer, that she might stand a chance against his lifetime ingrained habit of treating women like expensive toys.

She didn't want to end up like her smart phone. In a drawer, out of sight, out of mind. Redundant to needs and circumstances.

Maisy stayed below deck to protect her hair from the wind during the high speed trip in the motor launch to the floating palace that was called *Firebird*.

It was her first visit to the yacht, although Alexei had pointed it out to her with binoculars. He had casually commented he used it mainly for entertaining, and as he hadn't been entertaining anyone but her there had been no need to go there.

Clearly her entertainment value was on the wane.

There was something about seeing the sleek lines of the yacht and experiencing its vast size up close that had Maisy once more thinking about what this opulence must do to someone's sense of self. Yet for all his wealth Alexei was remarkably down to earth. It was a big part of why she had fallen in love with him.

The yacht was buzzing with activity. Another tender was arriving as she stepped aboard, and Maisy felt an unexpected flutter of nerves. She was naturally shy, but had worked very hard to practise her social skills, so that she could usually make friends wherever she went. But these people were Alexei's friends, and that thought sent her over the edge. She needed to pull herself together and remember there was no reason why they wouldn't like her, that there was nothing out of the ordinary in her situation. In this world mistresses were an *expected* addition to a successful man. And, although Alexei had never used that word, Maisy now understood he believed it was the only position in his life a woman could occupy.

As she was escorted into the main salon she saw people on the foredeck actively craning their necks to get a glimpse of her. It was an odd sensation, and Maisy wasn't sure she liked it. The attendant with her knocked briefly on a door, then nodded to Maisy and retreated.

'Enter.'

Maisy felt very odd, waiting for permission to enter Alexei's presence. He was applying cufflinks to his suit and he dropped one of them as he looked up and fastened his eyes on her.

She went to pick it up but he caught her hand, raising her up. 'I want to look at you.'

His approval should have been gratifying, but Maisy was finding it difficult to enjoy it.

'You look so different,' he said, his accent thicker than usual.

'It's the hair and the make-up,' she dismissed, trying to make light of it. 'It's still me underneath the scaffolding.' She tried not to seem too eager, but couldn't help asking, 'Are you going to kiss me?'

'Of course.' He brushed his lips over her cheek.

Disappointed, Maisy tried to justify his coolness. She was wearing lipstick; they were both dressed up; he probably didn't want to reek of her perfume...

'You look beautiful,' she said impulsively, touching his jacket, straightening what was already straight.

'That's my line,' he replied, subtly drawing away.

But it hadn't been his line. *Different* had been his line.

'I'm nervous,' she blurted out.

'Don't be. They're only people.'

'They're your friends.'

'No, Maisy, for the most part they're just a crowd. You'll enjoy yourself. I'd ask you to keep a lid on the Kostya situation, if you would. People are curious, but it's none of their business.'

The Kostya situation? 'I don't quite understand.'

Alexei scooped up the gold cufflink. 'Simple. I'll be blunt. Don't tell people you're the nanny.'

He gave her a brief taut smile, as if trying to take the edge off his words.

'No,' Maisy said quietly, 'I wouldn't do that. It would be humiliating for me, considering my circumstances now.'

'We're not going to have an argument right now, are we, *dushka*?' He was smiling but his eyes were hard. 'So close to showtime?'

'No, no argument.' She focussed on his hands, fumbling with his cuff, and instinctively reached out and took the cuff-link from him, fastening it to his sleeve in silence. She could feel him breathing so close to her. She stroked his wrist with her fingertips and his breathing hitched. It was the reassurance she needed. She lifted his hand and pressed her lips to his palm. It was then she realised why he had been having so much trouble with the cufflink. His hands were shaking.

Yesterday she would have asked him why. Today she gave him her best smile. 'No one will notice lipstick on your hand, and if they do—' her smile faltered only a little '—you can tell them it's just a token of affection from your mistress.'

He didn't correct her.

CHAPTER TEN

MAISY had felt overdressed as she was sped towards the yacht. Now, amidst so much luxury and Alexei's guests, she was glad of her clothes and hair and insubstantial sandals. Some of these women were utterly breathtaking. The men were all cool and sharp and controlled. She recognised the type. She had been living with a prince of the blood for several weeks.

She desperately wanted to cling on to Alexei's hand when she came out into the sunshine on his arm, but she knew deep down any sign of vulnerability would bring her closer to the edge of their relationship. She really didn't want to fall today. Not in front of all these people.

Yet her fragility threatened to undermine her with every step. The heels on her sandals clicked on the teak decking, the silken underskirt of her dress flowed over her hips and thighs like cool water, yet her skin felt hot and tight and her throat ached from everything she was holding inside her.

Alexei had completely metamorphosed into a cool stranger and she was out of her depth. They were back to where they had been at midnight on that strange night weeks ago in London. It was as if all that had happened between them had been a feverish dream and at any moment he was going to look down at her and demand to know who in the hell she was.

It shocked her when he suddenly sped up, let go of her hand, and crashed into a bear hug with another man. It was genuine. As was his greeting to another equally imposing man. The women with them flashed smiles and a lot of jewellery, and kissed him joyfully in the European fashion.

Maisy tried not to gape. They all spoke in Russian at once, and as the seconds ticked by she felt more and more excluded, although they were all darting looks at her, waiting for Alexei to introduce her. If she had felt more confident she would have enjoyed his clear enthusiasm in the moment, but instead it only underlined how differently he was treating her.

'Hello,' she said abruptly to the woman standing closest to her. 'I'm Maisy.'

'Stefania,' said the girl, beaming at her, then darting a look at Alexei.

'Maisy, this is Valery and Ivanka Abramov, and Stiva and Stefania Lieven. Maisy Edmonds.'

'Alexei has told us absolutely nothing about you,' said Stiva, giving Alexei a curious look.

'Well, I'm sure we can get to know her now,' interposed the brunette Ivanka.

She gave Maisy a wink, and instantly some of the tension in Maisy's shoulders eased.

'Your dress is gorgeous,' Stefania joined in. 'Who designed it?'

'I don't know,' Maisy said, darting a nervous look towards Alexei. 'Sorry.'

She could have kicked herself. She sounded like a complete moron. But the other girls were chattering on about designers, and the two men, although speaking to Alexei, kept glancing her way with reassuring smiles, helping her feel welcomed to their inner circle.

She appreciated their effort, but everything about these two couples screamed 'married' and it only made her feel more isolated. Not to mention the fact Stefania kept being roped back into Stiva's arms, giggling and blushing. Anyone with eyes in their head could see they were in love. And, whilst Ivanka was more circumspect, there was an easy quality between her and Valery. All she and Alexei had was this wall, and she couldn't see over it, had no idea how to begin scaling it, and doubted it was ever going to come down.

After half an hour Ivanka drifted away to make a phone call regarding her children and Alexei moved Maisy on, although she could see he was reluctant. These were clearly his friends, and the people he had spoken of who would be staying at the house. The rest were the crowd. Yet he made his way dutifully through them and Maisy trailed him. Whenever he smiled at her or touched her it was for public consumption.

He detached himself from her after several introductions, making sure she had a glass of mineral water in her hand, brushing her fingertips with his lips—once more for show, she realised sadly. Fortunately she managed to drift and be drawn into one group or another. Everyone wanted to speak to her. Was she enjoying the Amalfi Coast? Alexei had gone unusually AWOL, and now everyone knew why. And who could blame him? This was a theme with few variations. It embarrassed her and she didn't know what to say. She was offered champagne and took it. As she was propelled from one knot of people to another there was always another glass.

Then at last she was sitting down by herself, protected from the hot sun by an awning. She felt fuzzy from the champagne she had consumed for Dutch courage. Was it three glasses? Four? She'd lost count. Her glass had never seemed to be empty and she'd just kept sipping. Her shoes pinched and her face hurt from smiling.

'You must be Maisy.' A tall, slender woman in an almost transparent white shift was standing over her. Her black hair fell in a faultless waterfall to her shoulders. She was vaguely familiar. 'We haven't been introduced. Tara Mills.'

Maisy accepted the hand that was offered.

'We have Alexei in common,' she said, sitting down, crossing impossibly long and elegant tanned bare legs. Maisy drew her pale ones in under her. 'You don't mind, do you?'

Perhaps another woman would have thrown the contents

of her drink in Tara's perfect face, but Maisy was feeling distinctly generous. So this was the former mistress.

'I need another drink,' she replied instead, looking around.

Tara merely lifted a hand and a waiter arrived with a tray of them. In any other circumstances it would have been funny. Tara and Alexei were perfectly matched. A snap of her fingers and the world came to a halt and then turned on its axis for Tara Mills.

Tara held out her glass and clinked Maisy's. 'To our mutual friend.'

'He may be your friend but he's not mine,' she said without thinking.

'Trouble in paradise?' Tara placed a slender hand on Maisy's bare knee, drawing Maisy's attention to its round curve in comparison to Tara's bony leg.

'No.' Maisy felt driven to deny it and took a deep swallow. The alcohol buzzed through her system and she knew without a doubt the day was going to end badly.

'You're to do with the Kulikov baby, aren't you?' Tara set down her untouched glass. 'He was obsessed with rescuing the little thing.'

'Rescuing?' Maisy echoed, letting down her guard.

'Oh, you know what they're like, the hyped-up brotherhood. As soon as news of Leo's accident came in they were all lining up to adopt the boy. Alexei won. Alexei always wins, doesn't he?'

Maisy tried to process this jigsaw of information. Alexei was Kostya's godfather, but what on earth was the brotherhood?

'What I'm *dying* to know—and you're going to tell me, Maisy—is where you come into the picture. A little bird tells me you were the *nanny*, but that can't be right. Alexei's got too much class to sleep with the nanny.'

'I don't know,' Maisy said fuzzily. 'He slept with you. His standards must be pretty low.'

Tara didn't blink. 'Oh, Maisy, you're a funny little thing.

Make sure he puts your goodbye package into shares—they'll last longer.'

Suddenly Maisy was so very glad he had never given her any jewellery. All of that stuff she'd worn she considered on loan. Tara was wearing a single sapphire pendant that hung low between her small high breasts, but all Maisy could see was the diamonds she had seen in the magazine photograph. He had bought Tara. Just as he'd bought this luxury yacht.

He didn't buy me, she told herself. *That's the difference. He didn't buy me.*

Tara stood up. 'Just one more word of advice, Maisy. Today? He invited me.'

Maisy spilled her champagne. She stared blankly as the liquid soaked into her expensive lap, darkening into a wide stain.

'Oh, honey.' It was Ivanka, instantly at her side, putting the glass to one side, sliding a maternal arm around her waist. 'We need to fix you up. Can you walk?'

Maisy nodded, unable to speak because she needed all her concentration to keep herself together and take a step, and then another. She was grateful for Ivanka's sturdy arm around her waist and her knowledge of the yacht. When they reached one of the staterooms Ivanka led her straight to the bathroom.

'Take off the dress. We need to soak the stain.'

As Maisy hesitated Ivanka grinned at her. 'You really are a sweetheart. I'll fetch you a robe.'

Stripped, Maisy waited in her knickers, arms crossed over her bare breasts. She ventured out into the stateroom, feeling distinctly woozy. For a moment she couldn't move because a man was standing in the doorway. He said something in a foreign language and Maisy made a sound, stumbling back into the bathroom and slamming shut the door. She leaned against it, terrified of what was going on. She didn't know how long she waited, heart pounding, before there was a brief knock on the door.

'Maisy, it's Ivanka.'

Maisy slid away from the door. She wrapped the robe around

herself gratefully. 'There was a man in the doorway,' she said shakily. 'He saw me.'

Ivanka swore quietly. She squeezed Maisy's hand. 'You're okay?'

'I think I'm drunk.'

'Yeah, I saw Baba Yaga casting her evil spell. Don't believe anything she told you, Maisy. She's had a hard time adjusting to life post-Ranaevsky.'

I can imagine, thought Maisy drearily. She was feeling distinctly light-headed. The room was beginning to spin.

'I think I need to lie down,' she revealed shakily.

'Right.'

Ivanka got her to the bed, and the moment Maisy's head touched the pillow the whole room started to lurch. She groaned. 'Don't leave me,' she pleaded.

'I've got your back, honey.' The mattress sank a little as Ivanka perched beside her. 'You don't drink, I take it?'

'No.'

'Well, Tara Mills would drive anyone to it. You know…' She stroked Maisy's temple. 'I think he picks them because they're the last women in the world who'll get under his skin. Which makes you a freaking miracle.'

Maisy suddenly wished she was a million miles from drunk. This woman knew the secrets of the universe, and this was her chance to make sense of them.

Ivanka smiled at her, as if sensing her unspoken need to know. 'My husband Valery—you met him earlier,' she prompted. 'He and Alexei go right back to the orphanage.'

Orphanage? Maisy's eyes snapped open. 'Is this something to do with the brotherhood?'

'Brotherhood? Oh, Tara strikes again. There is no brotherhood. It's just the four boys—well, three now that Leo's gone.' Ivanka crossed herself reflexively.

Maisy's tired brain did some quick turns. Orphanage in Russia. Four boys. Suddenly Alexei's life opened up before her and darkness rushed in. The dreams. Last night. The way he was behaving today. Maybe it wasn't about her. She thought she was the centre of his life because he was hers. But it wasn't about her.

An orphanage?

He never talked about his family and she had never asked, afraid he would ask about hers. Now she wished she had—wished she had shown more courage.

'I didn't know,' she said heavily.

Ivanka smiled, looking at her curiously. 'He hasn't told you? I'm not surprised. I didn't get the entire story for a year—a full year, might I add—into my marriage. It took me a difficult pregnancy to get it out of Valery. And Alexei's a whole different kettle of fish. Need-to-know basis.'

'I need to know.' Maisy tried to sit up, but Ivanka laid a gentle hand on her shoulder.

'Lie still. You'll only feel worse. Here's the deal. The boys met up in an orphanage as kids. You can't know what Russian orphanages are like, Maisy. It's not like here or in England. It's pretty primitive. The story goes Alexei broke them out and the boys lived independently on the city streets, sleeping in parks, cemeteries, anywhere they could. Basements of public buildings in the long winters.'

Maisy did sit up now. 'But what about the authorities? Wasn't anything done?'

'No one cared, Maisy. Homeless children are everywhere in my country. Valery says if it wasn't for Alexei they'd all be dead. He had that "survival of the fittest" instinct even at eight.'

'Eight?' Maisy framed the word, not quite believing it. 'And no parents?'

'Oh, Alexei had parents. I think that's what made him as tough as he is. His father took off when he was very young, and his mother just came home one day and told him she was going on a little break for a few days and would be back for him. She never came.'

'What happened to her?' Maisy asked, aware she wasn't going to like the answer.

'Who knows? Probably a new man, a better opportunity. She'd have been finding it hard to ply her trade with a seven-year-old boy around her neck.'

'Her trade?'

'She was a prostitute.'

Maisy suddenly really didn't want to be having this conversation with Ivanka. She didn't know her. She knew Alexei would consider what she was doing a betrayal, but what choice did she have if he wouldn't talk to her about any of this?

His mother had abandoned him. A seven-year-old. Instantly a much younger Alexei flashed into her mind—a little boy with innocent blue eyes and long lashes and a frail child's body, trying to survive those Russian winters without anyone to protect him. It was that stark. And it suddenly made absolute sense that he would storm Lantern Square with a truckload of security. He was doing for Kostya what nobody had done for him.

'How did they survive?'

'Cunning, street smarts, not knowing anything else.' Ivanka gave a little shrug, but Maisy could see how much it affected the other woman to talk about it. 'Valery and Stiva ended up back in an institution, but then Alexei and Leo got lucky. The Kulikovs took them in. They made Leo their son.'

'And Alexei?'

'They had other children. It was decided Alexei was too far gone. He'd be a bad influence.' Ivanka spoke matter-of-factly. 'He was running a cigarette scam for a local crime boss by the time he was eleven, Maisy. I don't blame Marfa Kulikov one bit. But she always opened up her home to the boys on holidays, gave them all a break from the relentlessness of their lives. Probably saved Alexei's life. I know for a fact he still lights a candle for her on her saint's day.'

Something hard and fast lodged in Maisy's chest.

'But Alexei's always been the smart one. He knew he'd end up getting swept into some serious violence if he didn't find something legit. That's when he got the boys organised with the boats. He started up a boat-hire business when he was fifteen on Lake Ladoga. It gave all four of them their start. None of them have done too badly.'

'I don't know what to say,' was all Maisy could murmur.

'Just don't tell Alexei I spilled. It would cause all sorts of problems between him and Valery. Leo's death has hit them all hard, but Alexei hardest. They were the closest, those two. I always got the impression Alexei looked after Leo, but Leo gave Aloyshia the emotional support he needed and didn't get elsewhere.'

Aloyshia. Maisy flinched at the casual affection in that name. Years. He had known these people for years. They were his blood and his bone, his family. These were the people he confided in.

He had told her nothing. But then, she hadn't asked.

'Now, before we both start crying, how is little Kostya? I'm dying to see him. Whenever we saw Anais and Leo he was never with them. I suspect he was at home with you.'

'Yes, I looked after Kostya for two years.' Maisy didn't see the point of evading the truth.

'Which is how you and Alexei met. You're very young to have been raising a child. I got the impression Anais didn't spend very much time at home.'

Maisy had no intention of defaming her friend, but Ivanka seemed to understand this and laid a warm hand on hers.

'Leo chose a highly strung racehorse and wondered why she didn't turn into a brood mare when he got her in the stable. They're Valery's words, not mine. I'm a brood mare, Maisy, and happy to be one. I've got two boys of my own—Nicky and Sasha—you'll meet them tonight. You, on the other hand, seem more like a filly to me, which makes it hard to imagine how you manage a two-year-old boy. Actually, I don't know how you manage the thirty-year-old one.'

'I don't. Not very well,' Maisy confessed. She was finding Ivanka very easy to talk to.

'Tell me how you and Alexei met.'

'He attacked me in the Kulikovs' kitchen.'

'Okay—so far, so not Alexei.' Ivanka laughed. 'Do tell, Maisy.'

So Maisy started at the beginning, picking her way through the rubble of the past few weeks, explaining about Anais and looking after Kostya, and the outrageous way Alexei had stormed into the house.

'That's Alexei—never does things by halves,' was all Ivanka said.

Maisy edited out herself in a towel, him throwing her up against the door, and moved on to coming to Ravello. 'And then I fell in love with him,' she said simply. It was the first time she had said it aloud, and the fact that it wasn't to Alexei, that it could never be to Alexei, opened the floodgates.

She cried. For herself, but mainly for the little boy who had been abandoned by his mother and left to fend for himself. Ivanka stroked her head throughout, until a strange sort of peace invaded Maisy's body. And with it the nausea rose. She just made it to the bathroom in time.

And that was where Alexei found her.

'She's drunk.'

Alexei sounded incredulous, and in the old days—the days before today—Maisy would have laughed. But she was too busy being gloriously ill into a mercifully pristine toilet bowl.

Ivanka said something in Russian. Something that silenced Alexei. And in the silence Maisy slid onto her bottom, shutting her eyes against the suddenly clear certainty that she had disgraced herself.

The problem with nausea was that now it had passed she felt a reprieve—enough to realise how appalling her situation was. She awkwardly got to her feet, flushing the toilet and refusing to look at Alexei as she struggled to the sink, filling a glass with cold water and rinsing out her mouth. The mirror wasn't kind: she looked white, her fancy hairstyle beginning to come apart. The robe gaped open and she sashed it tightly, her eyes going anxiously to his.

Alexei's whole body told the story of how angry he was with her. His arms just hung at his sides, and he was tense and frozen to the spot.

Ivanka was gone. Wise woman, thought Maisy, drawing her arms about her waist. She needed a hug, and Alexei wasn't going to provide it.

It was hard to feel sorry for him when he was towering over her, all two hundred pounds of Russian machismo, judging her.

'Are you all right?'

He was *very* angry, she recognized. His accent was so thick she had to concentrate to understand him.

She nodded. 'Ivanka helped me. She's very kind.'

Alexei said something under his breath.

'How much did you drink?'

'I don't know.'

'You don't drink.' He sounded almost helpless.

Maisy met his eyes in the mirror. 'I didn't do a lot of things until today,' she muttered, leaning into the sink.

'Where's your dress? Why are you undressed?' He framed the question roughly.

'I spilt champagne on it. Ivanka took it to soak.' She took a shuddery breath. 'I think a man was here and saw me. When I didn't have any clothes on.'

'I heard about it.' The last scrap of colour left Maisy's face. He made a European gesture with his hands. 'Don't look like that,' he said urgently. 'I've taken care of it.'

'What do you mean?' she whispered.

'Everyone's gone. I've emptied the boat.'

'Oh.' *Oh.*

Alexei shifted on his feet. He wasn't angry with her, Maisy registered. Something else was going on.

He had emptied the boat. Because of her. Was he taking care of her?

'Did he speak to you? Touch you?'

Maisy shook her head. 'I shut myself in here. I didn't leave the door open even a crack.'

His expression altered. He took a step towards her. *Why isn't he holding me*? her nerves were shrieking.

'I don't regret that,' he said in a driven undertone. 'I refuse to regret London, but I'm sorry if I made you feel manhandled.'

Manhandled? Maisy wrapped her arms around her waist again, knowing someone had to hold her. 'It didn't feel that way,' she answered honestly, wondering why they were back to talking about London again, and then another wave of nausea crashed over her and with a moan she zeroed in on the toilet bowl.

'Go away,' she got out, before she began retching on an empty stomach. She felt Alexei's hands on her shoulders, hovering. 'The glamour of being your mistress,' she mumbled, wiping her wet mouth with the back of her hand and not caring. She slumped on the floor, head and shoulders down. She didn't want to see anything like disgust on his face.

To her astonishment, Alexei hunkered down beside her, his face close to hers, his eyes haunted, his features stark in the pallor of his strained face. In a moment of blinding clarity Maisy realised he had looked this way all day, only it was worse now. He was *suffering*, and all she had done all day was worry about herself, her feelings, her misery.

And now she knew his.

'It's all right,' she said, smoothing her hand over his jaw instinctively. 'I'm here.'

But it wasn't the right thing to say. He flinched, then covered it by offering her his hand. When she didn't take it he scooped her up as if she were a little doll. Maisy didn't even bother to fight him. She was feeling all sorts of empty. He might as well carry her shell wherever he wanted to put it.

'You're not well. You need to lie down.' It was not an instruction or even a declaration. He was just speaking aloud. He wasn't having conversations with her any more. He hadn't been all day. His brief fracture in the bathroom had healed over. There was no sign he even cared about her any more.

'I want to get off this boat,' she said in a low voice. 'I want to go home.'

He laid her on the bed, speared a hand through his hair, looking out of the window at the smooth blue water. It was late afternoon—that lazy, warm time in early summer. He didn't even see it. He felt cold. He'd felt cold all day. Sixtieth-parallel-cold—the kind of chill you only got in a St Petersburg winter.

Seventeenth of May. He always spent this day on this boat, surrounded by people. Well, the people had gone, and there was only Maisy, looking so pale and wounded, and struggling with him over inanities. She didn't have a clue. He'd dragged her around all day but he hadn't actually absorbed anything she had said or done or asked of him.

But he wasn't going to forget how he'd felt when one of his male guests, the son of shipping magnate Aristotle Kouris, had made the mistake of telling Stiva that 'Ranaevsky's mistress' was cavorting naked in one of the staterooms. The fear had torn through him. If Valery hadn't been there he would have killed Kouris. But first he'd had to get to Maisy. Valery had called a halt to proceedings and he had bulleted down here, to find Maisy in bed all right, but not being attacked, being comforted by Ivanka, who had given him an old-fashioned look he didn't want to analyse right now.

And she was drunk and sick and vulnerable. And ashamed. He felt her shame like a palpable thing. It was about all that he *was* feeling.

He had to tell her, he realised. He had to say something. At least it might give both of them a reprieve.

'Maisy, I'm a bit toxic at the moment. You need to give me a wide berth. Can you do that?'

She had dragged her legs off the bed, the robe had come open, and she was struggling to make herself decent. In a far off part of his brain the rueful thought occurred that despite everything she was still shy about her body, still modest... And without warning it all played out in his head. London. He had been thinking about it all afternoon.

London.

She had never invited him in. He had invaded her privacy, overridden her modesty and *taken* her. Snatched and grabbed and *manhandled* her. Just like every man who had come trudging through that one-room apartment, hitched up his mother's dress and done his business. Then left money on the kitchen table. Money for her drink and her clothes and her drug habit. If it hadn't been for the neighbours he would have starved.

Maisy moistened her dry lips. 'For how long do you want me to keep away from you?'

'Just today. Give me the rest of today.' His voice was deep and black and lost.

She bent her head. There was nothing more to say.

Except an image of a small boy with brilliant blue eyes seared her mind's eye and she lifted her head.

'No,' she said.

Maisy stood up, her eyes never leaving his.

'No,' she repeated.

He actually looked panicked. Cool, oh-so-sure-of-himself Alexei Ranaevsky looked panicked. She stepped towards him and he backed up as if she was armed and dangerous. Maisy stopped.

'Ivanka told me about the orphanage.'

Something flickered behind those magnetic eyes, then closed down and Maisy found herself looking into obsidian. She swallowed, watching Alexei's familiar features harden with every passing second, his cheekbones more pronounced, his Tartar heritage never more obvious as his eyes narrowed on her.

'Ivanka had no business doing that.' His voice was hard.

'Maybe not, but you'd never have told me. Alexei, you were seven years old!'

He didn't even flinch.

She couldn't bear the bleakness in his eyes.

'What's the significance of today?'

He continued to look through her and Maisy felt her resolve slipping. But she had to try. Knowing even as she closed the distance between them and slid her arms around his waist that he would push her away, she did it anyway, feeling him stiffen in her arms.

But he didn't push her away. He didn't shift an inch. She tightened her arms around him and pressed her cheek against his chest. She could feel his heart beating. Thudding.

'May seventeenth is my birthday.'

A simple statement, but one Maisy felt soul-deep. *This* was what he did for his birthday. *This* was how he celebrated. Nobody even knew.

'I wish you'd told me,' was finally all she could think to say.

'It's just another day, Maisy.'

'But it brings back the past for you.'

It was the wrong thing to say. He took her by the elbows, physically setting her back from him.

'Listen, I know you mean well, *dushka*, but I don't need this.'

'This? Confiding in me?'

'Sympathy.' He gave her a crooked smile. 'I'm a big boy, Maisy.'

Yes, the little boy she wanted to comfort was all grown up. This was the result.

'Your sympathy is misplaced,' he said with finality. Then he turned away. 'I'll have some clothes sent down to you.'

'I'm not offering you sympathy,' she asserted shakily. 'Don't go like this, Alexei. Why won't you let me in?'

But part of her already knew why. She had never *really* been part of his inner circle to begin with.

'Maisy—' His big shoulders dropped and he swung around, a familiar rueful smile tugging at his mouth as if he was finding it difficult to be assertive with her.

It was then she recognised something that had been staring her in the face for a long time now if only she'd had the eyes to see it. She was the only person he did this for. Waited, listened, smiled. With everyone else it was clipped or cool or *über*sophisticated. The facade. With her he was like this… gentler, more human. She conjured up the Alexei she had first come up against in Lantern Square, hard as nails, taking no prisoners. Certainly not listening to her.

Well, he listened to her now. He'd been listening to her for weeks. She just hadn't been asking the right questions.

'Sometimes I feel I know next to nothing about you,' she admitted. 'Those men, Valery and Stiva, they're your family, aren't they? You must love them very much. And Leo—you must miss him.' She swallowed hard, took a deep breath and plunged in. 'But I'm here.' She paused to let that sink into his thick skull, then tunnelled on. 'I met Tara Mills this afternoon. I had this silly idea all your ex-girlfriends were perfect goddesses, but Tara was just…cold and angry. Boy, is she angry with you.'

'I didn't invite her, Maisy. She came with Dimitri Kouris.'

Alexei inserted this so fast Maisy almost smiled, and then reassured him she wasn't going to break into a jealous tirade.

In the end she shrugged. 'It doesn't matter either way.' And saying it made it so. 'But it made me think you couldn't have been happy with her, and you've seemed happy with me until today.'

'I am happy, Maisy.' He sounded so sincere, but he didn't make a move to touch her and his actions spoke louder than words.

She put her head to one side, studying him. 'You look about as happy as I feel, and that's saying something. You're an amazing man, Alexei Ranaevsky. I don't think I've stopped long enough to smell the coffee on that one. To have come to where you are, when someone like me wouldn't have had the resilience to even survive, it makes you pretty special.'

'So now I'm your hero?'

He gave her that cynical smile she'd seen him use on other people. But it didn't work on her. She *knew* him—or was coming to understand him. She loved him, and he was running scared from it. His past was so bleak he couldn't even recognise what was staring him in the face, but he sensed it, and it had him on the run.

'No, you're my boyfriend.'

That wiped the smile off his face. And there it was. The stretch between what she needed from him and what he was willing to offer.

She attempted to deflect his predictable reaction. 'Don't look so worried, Alexei. I know today's hard for you and I haven't made it any easier. But you could have confided in me just a little. I mean, who would I tell? Kostya?'

He cleared his throat. 'I didn't mean to isolate you.'

'You haven't. It's been nice, just the three of us, but I understand it's not enough for you, and I like your friends—or what I've seen of them. Ivanka has been very kind to me.'

'What's not enough for me?' Alexei zeroed in on the one thing she'd hoped would get lost in her rush of words.

'The three of us.' She swallowed. 'Me.' She hurried on. 'I didn't realise until today how different your life must have been before us. Leo and Anais lived very quietly at home. I didn't see this side of things. I mean, there were famous people on this boat, Alexei.'

Alexei's expression softened, some of the tension leaving him. 'They're just people, Maisy, and not particularly interesting for all their fame or money.'

'"A crowd" you called them. Why do you invite them?'

'Honestly, Maisy, after today I've got no idea. What a disaster.'

'I'm sorry I wrecked everything. You didn't need to empty the boat.'

'You didn't wreck anything,' he asserted in a driven undertone. 'I was a damned fool, dragging you along to this. I had an insane notion I could keep everything as it was, but that's impossible. You don't fit into this life, Maisy. You never did. And

I'm sorry you had such a lousy day. I take full responsibility for it.'

Maisy stared at him, trying to make sense of what he was saying above the roaring in her head. What did he mean she didn't fit into his life? Okay, she needed to get over this. She needed to put him first right now. Ignore the panic scrambling for a grip in her head and just focus. She'd been doing a good job of it. Dropping the ball now would be disastrous.

'I made an idiot of myself without any help from you, Alexei.'

'Nobody thinks you're an idiot, Maisy.' He closed the space between them and did what she had been wanting him to do all day. He framed her face, bent and kissed her. Gently, sweetly, far too briefly. 'I'll make it up to you tomorrow.'

Tomorrow. The future they didn't have.

She caught at his hand as he moved to step away. 'Where are you going?'

'You need clothes, *dushka*, and we need to get going. I've got guests, remember?'

Maisy flushed. Not *we've* got guests, just him. His guests. And she was holding him up.

'Maisy?' He captured her face between his big hands. 'This isn't about you. It's my problem. Okay?'

'No, Alexei, it's about *us*.' She pulled away from him. 'But I can say it till I'm blue in the face. You don't want it to be us. You're happier on your own. Go on, let me get dressed. We've got a long evening ahead and I'm not very happy with you right now.'

Alexei had the grace to lower his head. He looked about wiped out, Maisy realised, but he was right. He was a big boy. She had wounds to lick. He could look after himself.

CHAPTER ELEVEN

WHILST Maisy dressed Alexei returned to the boardroom to make a call in privacy to Valery at the house. He hadn't been in here since that dreary day when they had all gathered aboard *Firebird* to discuss Kostya. It felt like a lifetime ago.

Bursting into Lantern Square had changed his life irrevocably and there was no going back. He wouldn't want to go back. Maisy had changed everything.

You're my boyfriend. Those three words had summed up her simple, uncomplicated assessment of their relationship.

And, God help him, he'd been behaving like a boyfriend from day one in that park in Ravello, when she had snapped and crackled at him and, like the sucker he had never been, he'd followed her—tame as an alley cat offered food and a lap for the first time.

He'd convinced himself it would be casual sex to scratch the itch, but from the moment he'd seen her in his shirt, clear-eyed and standing up to him, casual had gone out of the window.

She'd known. Instinctively she'd known he wasn't the kind of man who would stick around. Every time they'd made love it had been behind her eyes. The question.

And finally all of it had come home to roost—what he had taught her to believe with his string of well-publicised affairs and his defensive habits. He'd thought he was protecting her, but all he'd been doing was protecting himself.

You don't want it to be us.

But, God help him, he did—and that was the black irony of

it all. He wanted a lifetime with Maisy. He'd just been on his own so long he didn't know how to go about it.

It was good to take her dampened dress off, her flimsy sandals, and just lie in a tub of clear warm water, her hair loose and submerged, her eyes closed. Downstairs there were guests to entertain, but Ivanka had assured her they were family and she was to have her bath, not worry about anything, and come down when she was ready.

Maria brought Kostya to her whilst she was dressing, and he helped her pick out a dress. She chose the cocktail dress she had brought from London.

The dress fell to her ankles, but was so sheer that no matter how she stood or moved it clung to her figure like a second skin. She waited to feel self-conscious but the feeling didn't come. Alexei had taught her the curvy body she had hidden under layers was sexy—no longer a source of unease but something to be celebrated.

There was a knock on her door. 'Come in.' She had expected Maria, looking for Kostya, but it was Stefania. She had swept her shoulder-length blond hair up and was wearing a glamorous seventies-style caftan, dripping in gold jewellery. Maisy loved the way these Russian women went completely over the top. It must be liberating.

'Wow, you are *so* not wearing that around my husband.'

Maisy turned in surprise, but Stefania was laughing.

'Oh, the baby!' She'd spotted Kostya.

Maisy introduced them, and Kostya allowed himself to be scooped up and admired.

'He's so beautiful, and you're a natural, Maisy. I don't know how I'm going to manage when I have one. I know everyone has a nanny, but I think Ivanka's on the right track. She does it all herself.'

'She's crazy,' said Maisy honestly. 'Everyone needs help.'

'But you brought up Kostya yourself. Alexei was just telling the boys you did it on your own for two years.'

Alexei?

Maisy was digesting this information when Stefania said critically, 'You need something around your neck. Show me your bling and we'll pick something out.'

'I don't have any bling,' Maisy confessed, trying to keep her voice light.

'You're kidding me? Alexei hasn't thrown open the gates of all the best jewellery stores? Maise, I'm gonna talk to that man.'

'No!' Maisy groaned. 'Please, Stefania, I honestly don't want jewellery.'

Stefania looked at her as if she had said *I don't need to breathe air.* 'Okay,' she said slowly, 'but you have to wear something, Maisy. Let me lend you one of my strings. I promise nothing over the top—something simple, ladylike. You do ladylike. I can tell.'

Within minutes Maisy was wearing a strand of pearls so pure they were iridescent. It would be hard to give them back.

Stefania smiled like a cat that had the cream at their reflections—herself so fair and slender, Maisy voluptuous, her long red-gold hair caught up in a single clasp. 'We look good. The guys will go off.'

It was seven o'clock when they went down, and past Kostya's bedtime, but Maisy knew instinctively part of the reason the Abramovs and Lievens were here was to see Leo's little boy. Maisy led him into the drawing room by the hand. She had dressed him up in his best royal-blue pyjamas suit, and with his angelic blond curls he looked delicious.

The glass of whisky in Alexei's hand slid from his grasp. He just caught it in time as Maisy strolled into the room holding one of Kostya's hands, Stefania the other. Maisy was elegance personified. She was wearing something white and it moved like water on her body, showcasing every curve. She'd pulled her titian hair up, which only made him want to take it down, and it drew attention to the delicate bone structure of her face. The artless, sunny girl he had first known might be lurking under the glamour of her evening dress, but it was a knowing woman whose eyes clashed with his across the room, then looked away to concentrate on his guests.

Her movements were unhurried as she smiled at everyone, answered questions about Kostya's development and hovered over him. Every shrug of her bare shoulders, every extension of a slender arm, turn of her head was seductive, drawing him across that room to the perimeter of where she held court, kneeling on the Aubusson rug, impossibly elegant even with a two-year-old squirming around her.

Valery and Stiva were riveted—and it wasn't to what Maisy was saying. When had she become this sophisticated woman? Had he not been paying attention? Or was it that it suited him to see her as sweet little Maisy, the girl he had collected from Lantern Square? Nothing ever stood still, and her words came back to smack him up the side of the head: *To have come to where you are, when someone like me wouldn't have had the resilience to even survive.*

Maisy underestimated herself. She had something he'd been lacking all his life: the courage to give of herself to others. He watched her—not only with Kostya, the child who wasn't her own yet whom she had taken into her heart, but with his friends, cheerful and generous despite her appalling day.

He'd been an absolute idiot.

Maisy kept an eye on Alexei as the evening wore on, but she didn't go out of her way to approach him. He needed to come to her, but as time wound away she was starting to feel as if that would never happen.

It was a revelation seeing him with people he cared about. This was how he had been with her and Kostya in these last weeks—generous and warm and loving. He got Sasha and Nicky, Ivanka's boys, set up with a games console in the entertainment room, and he scooped Kostya up to fly him through the air and fed him grapes, all the while carrying on a discussion with Valery about some American baseball team and a foolproof betting system.

He had a whole life she was only getting a glimpse of.

Well, he might not think she fitted into this life, but she had no intention of letting him go that easily.

After dinner, Maisy excused herself as coffee was served and sought the seclusion of the terrace. She could only hope Alexei would have the sense to follow her out—although given his unpredictable behaviour over the past couple of days she couldn't be sure.

Leaning against the railing, she took in deep sustaining breaths, trying to concentrate on the enviable view of blue sea. *Lap it up, Maisy,* a little voice taunted. *It's not going to last. Your days are numbered.*

Not without a fight, she responded, fisting her hands on top of the stone.

'Maisy.' His deep voice washed over her and she almost slumped with relief. She shut her eyes, wanting the peace to last, wanting him to be part of that peace but knowing he couldn't be.

He was too scared to love her.

'Go inside, Alexei. You've got guests.'

'Why are you out here on your own?'

'I just wanted some time out, okay?' She opened her eyes and made herself look at him. He was at least a metre away, arms folded, typical I-am-an-island stance. It was the same stance he had taken so many weeks ago, on that strange night when he had burst into her life. It was as if the past weeks had never happened. As if they had never even been lovers.

'Fine.' He didn't shift.

The cold sea wind had picked up and Maisy shivered. She could feel Alexei looking at her body, not very modestly wrapped in white silk and nothing else. She knew her nipples were prominent. She felt self-conscious about it now that his desire for her had so obviously cooled. Goose flesh had risen on her arms and she rubbed them.

Alexei shrugged off his jacket with a single movement and drew it around her shoulders, but otherwise he didn't touch her.

Maisy released a shuddery sigh, wondering why his gesture should touch her so deeply.

'You should be wearing more clothing,' was all he said, his head bent, his eyes intent upon hers.

Suddenly the wind was gone, the view blotted out. There was only Alexei, blocking out the world, and Maisy was thrown back to Lantern Square when she had stepped into his arms and he had picked her up and branded her. There was no other way to describe it, and she was still wearing that brand. She was his. From then on she'd always been his.

'Please talk to me, Alexei.'

'It's not the time or place, Maisy.'

Her temper snapped. 'Too bad—because I've got a few things to say. First of all, I love you. I'm in love with you. And I'm stupid with it—because, honestly, any other woman would have seen the writing on the wall long before I did.'

He was silent. Maisy almost swore.

'You don't have anything to say to me?'

'This "stupid" love…' his voice was low, almost fractured '…did it make its appearance after Ivanka told you my sob story or before? Don't tell me you fell for me when I burst into the kitchen at Lantern Square and terrified the life out of you?'

How on earth had they arrived back at that? Maisy shook her head. It was either that or shake him.

'Right now I have no idea why I love you,' she slung at him heatedly. 'Maybe it's the multiple orgasms.'

His savage laugh ripped through the tension holding Maisy in place.

'I know you *think* you love me, Maisy,' he said, with a smile that didn't reach his eyes. 'I'm basically the first man you've been intimate with. It's understandable you imagine you feel this way.'

Think. *Imagine*. She wanted to claw his eyes out.

'Basically?' she said, stony cold.

Something flashed through Alexei's expression, leaving his eyes almost feral. 'He didn't give you an orgasm.'

Maisy rotated her fists. 'How do you know?'

He moved so fast she didn't even have a chance to resist. His hands were around her arms, pinning her, his mouth hot and hard, demanding a submission she wasn't going to give him. But the shock of it, the longing to be in his arms and provoke a response from him, undid her. She gave a soft little moan and kissed him back.

He drew back, satisfied, releasing her. 'That's how I know, *dushka*. Only me.'

'And when did you realise that, Alexei?' she flashed back at him, wiping her mouth and gaining satisfaction from the narrowing of his eyes. *Yes, Alexei, look—I'm wiping your low-down kiss off me.* 'Today? Yesterday? Last week?'

'Seven weeks ago,' he growled. 'You've been in my bed six weeks, five days.'

He surprised her with the knowledge he had kept count. A tiny flicker of hope formed in its wake.

'It took me a full seven days to make my move,' he continued. 'Slow, considering I could have had you that first night in London.'

The light went out. Maisy struggled to keep her nerve, but he had never been like this with her before. He could be cold, but he had never been crass.

'What do you mean?' She hated the note of desperation that had crept into her voice.

He heard it. She saw the bleak satisfaction enter his hard eyes. 'You heard me. I seem to remember you kissing me back, Maisy, your legs around my waist. You were there all the way.'

'No, that's not true. You're twisting it. I was so ashamed. I couldn't believe I'd let you do that—' She broke off, seeing triumph flash painfully across his face.

Idiot. She had blundered and said what he had been pushing her to admit. She'd allowed her own vulnerability to him to distract her from what was at issue. Maisy suddenly realised what this was all about and she shut her mouth.

'*Da*, you were so ashamed you couldn't wait to dive into bed with me the day I turned up here. It must have been hard, *dushka*, all that waiting. Explains why you were so easy to warm up the minute your back hit that mattress.'

Maisy made herself stay expressionless and stone-still, all the while silently repeating, *He doesn't mean it. He doesn't mean it.*

He was waiting for her to respond. Waiting for her to do something. But Maisy held her ground. And the longer she stood there, staring stonily back at him, the more pronounced the ticking of the nerve below his jaw became. He was *so* stubborn, she thought, and *hard. Harder than me*, thought Maisy desperately, and he could so very well win because of it.

Cursing in Russian, he cut the air with a frustrated gesture of his hand, reeling around and walking away from her. Then he spun and said harshly, 'This is who I am, Maisy. I'm the one who turned your life upside down, who railroaded you into a sexual relationship—who drags you all over the continent and dresses you up like a doll, parades you on a boat as if you're a goddamned trophy.'

Maisy could only stare at him and listen and ignore what he was saying.

He was shouting at her now. 'I'm a class-A bastard, Maisy. That's my reputation. You seem to be the only person on the planet who isn't aware of that.'

She had never seen him like this. He had been angry before, but always in control, always measuring his response. That control had splintered, but the anger wasn't directed at her. She knew him now. It was directed at himself.

But she had some of her own to serve up.

'Listen to me, you stupid man. For your information, I would *never* have let things go that far that night in London.' Her voice rose strong above the hum of the wind and the ocean. 'The only reason I ever slept with you here was because *I* wanted to, and it was everything I dreamed of—because you were sweet and kind and considerate, everything you claim you're not. But I'm tired of being on the outside of your life, and I will never, *never* forgive you for throwing my feelings back in my face unless you get down on your sorry knees and beg my forgiveness, and then work your behind off making it up to me.'

Face flushed, body trembling Maisy took a backward step. 'Starting right now.'

Then she swung away and headed inside. She'd had her say. At last. Whatever happened next was up to him.

It occurred to her that his friends had probably heard a great deal of what had been said—especially the last part where she'd been shouting—but suddenly she didn't care. She felt almost light-headed with emotion. If strangers thought she was a fool, what did it matter? She was fighting for the life and the man she wanted, and she refused to be ashamed of that.

She accepted a glass of iced tea from Valery as she sat down, who murmured, close to her ear, 'We're rooting for you, Maisy, and by the way I love the dress.'

Maisy went red to the roots of her hair, but the adrenaline enabled her to smile and shrug.

'Valery, stop flirting with Maisy,' said Ivanka mildly.

Alexei had come into the room looking like thunder, hands hooked into his pockets. He stood at the end of the sofa, staring at her.

Maisy shrugged off his jacket and threw it at him.

Stiva clapped his hands and dropped into the chair opposite Maisy. 'Now, *this* I've gotta see.'

'You're toast,' said Valery, handing Alexei a glass of brandy.

Alexei ignored it. 'Maisy, upstairs—now.'

'No.' She crossed her legs and concentrated on her drink. She could literally *feel* Alexei breathing. 'But if you're the— what was it?—*class-A bastard* you claim to be why don't you just drag me out of here by my hair?' She blinked innocently up at him, her fingernails scoring her palms.

She heard Stefania's sharp intake of breath, and then the

solid warmth of Ivanka's leg and hip as she slid onto the sofa close up beside her. She remembered her assurance— 'I've got your back'—on *Firebird*, and wanted to tell her it was fine. Alexei wasn't about to do anything so primitive. Except she really didn't know.

And the not knowing sped up her heart.

Alexei towered over her, laser-blue eyes fixed on her alone.

'You really want to have this out here and now?'

There was a warning in his eyes even as his voice remained cool, direct. Public voice, private eyes.

She flashed back to that morning when he had towered over her as she'd sat on the terrace, Kostya in her arms. Literally crushing her heart with his careless assertion about other women.

Except it hadn't been careless. He had used it as a weapon to keep her at a distance and more importantly, it hadn't been true.

Was he lying to her now? Was he doing it to push her away?

'Alexei thinks I'm too good for him,' she said out loud.

'Yeah, because you are,' said Stiva jovially.

'Stiva!' Ivanka glowered at him.

'He tried to make me his mistress, but I'm not. I'm his girl-friend. Not that he's ever even brought me a bunch of flowers.'

'Or bling,' put in Stefania.

'I don't mind about the jewellery. I told him I didn't want any. I didn't say anything about flowers, though.'

Maisy was talking to her glass. She knew in revealing what was between them before others she was taking a chance with this most private and closely guarded of men. These people were his family, but that probably made it worse. Yet what choice was he giving her? And what had she to lose? She needed to push him. For him to see he was surrounded by people who loved him. *She* loved him. She wanted him to love *her*.

'A single rose from the garden would have done, or maybe some wildflowers from the roadside—' She broke off as her glass was snatched from her and then big familiar hands closed around her waist.

He plucked her from the sofa and she wound her arms around his neck and let him carry her, as docile as she had been that morning when he had come to seduce her.

'Like I said,' Valery commented dryly, 'toast.'

Maisy threw an anxious look at Alexei's face so close to her own. He wasn't angry. He was determined, but it wasn't anger he was radiating—it was something else. Something that made her instinctively cling to him.

'Where are we going?' she demanded, although it was clear he was taking her upstairs.

'Why can't we have fights like that?' Stefania's high voice floated after them.

Maisy suspected she was about to be ravished on that big bed upstairs and little else. A miracle would have to take place to get Alexei to talk, and she was just about out of pulling miracles from her sleeve.

Maria appeared at the top of the stairs and Maisy struggled to be put down, but Alexei held fast.

'I have bad news for you, Alexei,' she said simply. 'The *bambino* wants his *mamma*.'

Alexei paused on the threshold of the nursery, expecting a difficult struggle to calm Kostya down. It was going to take many months to convince a child of this age his parents weren't coming back. He'd been through it all with the psychologist.

The boy was with the night nanny, his little face red and screwed up with crying. It had been a long, awful day, but it was the first time Alexei had felt truly hopeless. He couldn't communicate with Maisy, and he couldn't protect Kostya from this.

'Mama!' He sniffled, big eyes latching onto Maisy and not letting go.

She moved swiftly to him, took the child into her arms and

settled into a chair. His cries subsided almost instantly as he buried his hot face in her neck and clung.

Alexei swore softly under his breath. He'd been blind. It wasn't Anais the boy wanted. It was Maisy. She had taken the role of Kostya's mother from the beginning.

It had always been Maisy.

It was peaceful in the nursery, but Maisy knew what awaited her outside. She'd forced this confrontation and now she was going to get it. Ready or not.

Alexei was watching them, arms folded over his chest, leaning against the bureau. He hadn't turned tail and run in the face of the infant's tears. For a man with no experience of children he'd adapted quickly and irrevocably to the fact he had one in his life. It was clearly just *women* he had a commitment problem with.

Kostya's body was sleep-heavy, and Maisy knew the moment had arrived. She moved reluctantly to stand.

'Here, let me take him.'

Alexei's deep voice had the volume turned down, but its impact shuddered through Maisy as she gave up the baby to him. He lifted Kostya from her arms with a practised move that caught at Maisy's raw emotions. His eyes flickered to hers. They had done this so many times, she realized. Like a tag team—*like parents*. She saw acknowledgement of this in his expression for the first time.

Shaken, Maisy fetched Kostya's favourite blanket, draping it over his sleeping body, and then without saying a word or sparing a glance for Alexei she slipped outside.

She was halfway down the hall when she heard the nursery door click shut, and then Alexei's hushed voice whipped her around. 'Not so fast.'

In that instant Maisy realised she was actually running away from him. She was behaving like a scared little mouse—the timid girl who had started at St Bernice's all those years ago and looked to Anais to fight her battles. She was a grown

woman now, and if anything the past few weeks had taught
her she could handle one large, moody Russian male—except
this time she needed to do it without sex muddying the waters
and confusing the issues.

He stalked towards her, the down lights on the walls throwing his shadow so that he seemed to increase in height as he
stood over her.

Maisy's trembling hands automatically found her hips. 'If
you think I'm going to jump into bed with you and have mad,
passionate, angry sex so you can put this behind us and just
go on as before—'

'We've done that, Maisy, and moved on from it,' he interrupted.

The fact that he was on the same page with her brought
Maisy up short.

'What I want to know is what was that about downstairs?'

Testosterone was pounding out of him, and Maisy was so
distracted by the urge to press herself up against him she had
trouble concentrating.

'The stuff about the jewellery,' he clarified, his accent clot-
ting up the words.

Maisy shook herself. She was doing the very thing she had
warned him against.

'I'm sorry for embarrassing you,' she answered. 'But I was
very angry—'

'You didn't embarrass me, Maisy,' he broke in impatiently.
'I want to know what it was about.' He seemed to close in
around her. 'What do you want from me? I'll bring in a jeweller tomorrow—you can have whatever you want.'

'I don't *want* jewellery!' she exploded. 'Oh, how can you
be so ridiculously obtuse?'

'*I'm* obtuse? You made it very clear in Paris that anything—
anything—I bought for you was payment. Can you blame me
for being wary about putting anything around your neck?'

'So it's all *my* fault? I don't know what I'm doing, Alexei.
Have you ever thought about that? It's not like I've ever been

a rich man's mistress before. Forgive me if I make mistakes. You never gave me a rule book.'

'You're not my mistress,' he said firmly. 'I have never, *never* treated you as a mistress.'

'You dress me; you chauffeur me around in limos; you keep me separate from your working life. Until now I've never met any of your friends. What else am I?'

'I'm looking after you. You and Kostya. The three of us.'

'No, Alexei,' she said softly, sadly. 'It's just you.'

Her words fell like stones into the silence. Maisy's emotions trembled with the weight of the impact of what she had said. He looked so lost, her big, steely take-no-prisoners Alexei. *He needs me so badly*, Maisy realized, and it gave her the courage to go on.

'That's what you do, Alexei, to protect yourself. You shut yourself off. You choose women who pick you because of what you can give them—*stuff*, luxury and publicity—and that way it's never about emotions. And God forbid anyone asks for more than that—falls in love with you because you're so scared to be vulnerable to someone, to trust and lay yourself open to being abandoned and hurt again.'

Alexei said something harsh in Russian. The sound of it was enough to dry up the words in Maisy's mouth. He was very pale and very menacing in the down lights, his shadow pressing down on her.

'I *know* I would never abandon a child who needed me,' she pressed. 'Anais never bonded with Kostya. It was all I could do to get her to be there in the morning when I got him up. I *do* know what it is to be abandoned because I watched it happen to a child I love. It made it impossible for me not to do everything I could to care for Kostya. And you clearly felt the same way—because you came and rescued him, because that's how you show love. You offer protection. But I don't need your protection. I'm not two years old. I need you to open yourself up to me and trust me not to take advantage of you, not to hurt you.'

'What is it you want from me?' he said in a low voice. 'Name it and I'll do it.'

He still wasn't prepared to risk himself. Maisy felt the weight of the only choice left to her bearing down. She had to leave him and go back to London. She had done all she could to make Alexei see what was standing in front of him. She loved him, but she didn't know if he was ever going to change. Nothing she had said seemed to have made a whit of difference.

She needed to protect herself emotionally or he would destroy her. It was the only way forward for both of them. It meant she could very possibly lose him, but what choice had he left her?

She had to risk herself, because he wouldn't. 'Anything?' she whispered.

He turned, his features entirely Tartar, menacing, miserable. It broke her heart.

'Let me take Kostya back to Lantern Square.' Her voice dropped an octave as she felt the world shift and tumble away from her feet. 'Let me go.'

He flinched as if she had struck him. 'Kostya is my responsibility, not yours,' he said, in a strained voice she barely recognised.

'I can't leave him,' she whispered.

He turned away from her. She could see all the muscles in his shoulders converge on that one point at the nape of his neck where she used to link her hands. Those shoulders rose and fell.

'You're the only mother he's ever known,' Alexei said in a low voice, as if speaking to himself. 'It took me until tonight to recognise that.'

Maisy felt time stop as he turned slowly, his blue eyes so dark in the down light they seemed black. His eyes held hers, as if in challenge. 'All things considered, I think going back to Lantern Square might be exactly what you need, *dushka*.

But I am in Kostya's life. You're never going to be free of me whilst you're with him.'

'I'm packing now,' she answered, swallowing hard. 'And I'm going first thing in the morning. Can you organise that for Kostya and me?'

'*Da*. But this isn't over, Maisy.'

She shrugged, her throat clenching with the effort to keep her emotions in check. There was nothing more to say. She'd said it all. It was up to him now.

CHAPTER TWELVE

MAISY heard the bells chime over the door. No clients had been scheduled today, so she expected it was Alice, back early from the school run.

She put down her pen and got up to put the kettle on, pouring Earl Grey tea leaves into the pot. Her eyes were a little sore from peering at the laptop screen, but Alice would be pleased when she heard her good news. She'd managed to source French *valenciennes* lace and get it under price.

Alice's little shop was a dream come true for Maisy. After landing back in Lantern Square, her first week had been absorbed by resettling Kostya back into a routine and organising a crèche for him before she got stuck into looking for a job.

It had been whilst she was filling in forms with a couple of the other mothers at the crèche around the corner that she had got talking to Alice. With her youngest now at school she had taken her millinery business off the internet and into a store, and hadn't been looking forward to toiling through the pile of applications she'd received for an assistant's job. Maisy had seen her chance and taken it.

All the role required was sourcing materials, a little bookkeeping work and chasing up orders three times a week. It was perfect.

It also kept her busy. Today was a record day for her. It was the first morning she'd woken up and her first thought hadn't been of Alexei. No doubt she'd think about him some time today—slide into a little reverie, maybe even soak her pillow tonight in tears—but it had only been a month, and she didn't expect to get over him any time soon.

What mattered was that during the day she was her own woman. She had already established a small circle of friends through Kostya's activities and her own work here in the shop. She went out to the cinema, she shopped, she met other people for coffee. It was simple and restrained, but it suited her. That lifestyle of limos and hotels and personal shoppers had never sat well with her. This was on her own terms, and if it didn't include Alexei it wasn't through any lack of trying. She'd told him what she wanted from him. It was becoming eminently clear he couldn't give it to her.

She turned to make room at the table for Alice, and almost tripped. Standing in the doorway was not slender, elfin-faced Alice but six and a half feet of Russian male—the same male she had been alternately longing for and cursing over for four long weeks. He was wearing simple and expensively tailored dark trousers and a white shirt open at the throat, and he looked every inch of what he was: a ruthless, sophisticated guy. So out of place amongst the lace and frou-frou of a ladies' hat shop it was almost humorous.

Almost.

Alexei noted the wide eyes, the pink cheeks, the shock, and took immediate advantage.

No sense in wasting time.

He had known Maisy had garnered herself a job virtually the minute she'd walked back in the door of Lantern Square. He knew she was rarely home, that she took Kostya with her here to the shop when he wasn't in the crèche, or on play dates to various addresses over London. She preferred the bus to expensive cabs, and she went to the cinema most Thursday nights.

The millinery shop was within walking distance of the house and Alexei had come on foot, turning over the bare facts of Maisy's existence since she'd vanished from his sight.

It all sounded completely ordinary, and he knew Maisy must love it.

But *this* he hadn't expected. The small, elegant shopfront, the tinkle of bells as he entered, the subtle fragrance in the air that reminded him of daisies and blue skies. He was rendered overgrown and slightly clumsy in this rarefied atmosphere, and he wondered with a smile if *any* man had dared step inside.

According to his report Maisy worked here on Thursday afternoons until four. He could hear somebody moving around at the rear of the shop and he strode across the shiny black and white parquet, sidling around the counter, noting the lack of security cameras or any security devices at all. He frowned.

She was standing with her back to him, head slightly bent. From the top of her bright head down to the elegant pale blue sheath dress, cinched at her small waist and clutching her rounded hips, down the seams of her pale stockings to the pretty French heel of her shoes, she was all lovely lines and femininity.

Then she turned, and those cinnamon eyes flared, and her face happened to him all over again.

But she didn't do any of the things he might have expected her to. A gasp, a frown, or more preferably throwing herself into his arms. She simply stood there, slender arms at her sides, bright titian ringlets framing a solemn expression tinged with a little wonder. She didn't make a move towards him, but nor did she move away.

It shouldn't have come as a surprise. She'd been magnificent in those last couple of days they'd had together, lifting the bar on their relationship so high he'd been unable to cross it. Exerting her own will, matching it against his. Few men had the guts for it, but she hadn't blinked. Then again, those men didn't burrow up against him in bed and lift soft eyes that turned all his intentions her way.

Yet, unlike every other woman he'd come across, she hadn't used sex to manipulate him. She'd given him an ultimatum, and she'd stuck by it. He hadn't known she'd had it in her. All he'd seen was the sweet, artless girl he had fallen in love with on sight. But, damn, he respected her for it. And she'd been right.

'Alexei.'

'Hello, Maisy.'

Looking up into the familiar, beautiful lines of his face, she struggled to find the man whose wretched eyes had haunted her dreams for weeks now. He had returned to being the hard-edged, sophisticated guy who had come bursting into her kitchen and changed her life for ever. Except when his eyes rested on her a little smile she recognised tugged on the corner of his lips, and his blue eyes softened on hers with a question.

Alexei Ranaevsky didn't ask questions. He issued directives.

Everybody knew that. But Maisy knew differently.

It hadn't been that way between them from the moment he'd seized hold of her arm in that park in Ravello. She remembered how his body had actually been vibrating, and in her ignorance she had thought him angry. It hadn't been anger, and it had been more than desire for her. He had felt the connection and it had thrown him as much as it had thrown her, and they'd both been tumbling down the long hill of it ever since.

Maisy knew where she wanted to land, but it had been almost a whole month and he hadn't called her—he hadn't let her know how he was doing.

Every night he spoke to Kostya on the phone. It was a regular six o'clock routine. She would pick up, would hear his voice, deep and caressing, saying, 'Maisy,' and she would reply, 'Kostya's right here,' not trusting herself to even say his name. She would sit beside the little boy as he chattered exuberantly, the faint sound of Alexei's voice all she'd allow herself. There was always the temptation as Kostya said his goodbyes not to press 'end' and to speak to him herself—but what would she say? *I love you. I want to come back to you.* But it wasn't her call. Alexei was a smart guy. If he had something to say to her he would have rung her and said it.

Actually, knowing the man as she did, he would have hopped on a plane and said it to her face.

And here he was.

In those last days together she had taken command not only of herself but of whatever was between them. Having him suddenly here, filling up the tiny space with his presence, it felt as if Alexei had seized it back, and Maisy felt slightly on the back foot.

'What are you doing here?' She sounded breathless to her own ears.

'I've been to Lantern Square to check the security.'

It wasn't what she'd expected him to say, and something small and bright that had lit in her mind at the sight of him went out.

'I had it changed whilst you were with me in Ravello.'

He made it sound as if those two months had been merely a holiday. Next he would make some comment about her tan fading—that was if she'd even had a tan. Maisy stopped gazing up adoringly and pulled herself together.

'I really don't think it's necessary,' she said, as coolly as she could manage. 'I don't think Kostya's in any danger.' But even as she spoke she could have kicked herself. She knew exactly why he was so security conscious. Every time he looked at Kostya he saw himself and what he had never had.

'Not just Kostya. I want you to be safe, Maisy.'

'Me? Why would anyone want to hurt me?'

'I don't think anyone wants to hurt you. I just—' He broke off, running a hand through his hair as he smiled at her ruefully. 'I'm doing that thing you say I do. I'm showing you how much I love you by protecting you.'

Maisy was glad she had a table behind her to steady herself against.

'I'm on my knees, Maisy.' His voice was a whole octave deeper. 'I'm begging you to forgive me. I want to take you and Kostya home with me to Ravello, where you both belong. I want us to be a family.'

Maisy's mouth had run dry and she moistened her lips. 'It took you almost four weeks to decide this?'

He was suddenly filling the tiny private space, and Maisy had nowhere else to go.

'Has it been so hard without me?'

'No,' she lied.

'I haven't been able to breathe,' he confessed roughly. 'It hurts every time I do.'

Me too, her heart whispered.

'Four weeks, Alexei.' It came out jerkily.

'And look what you've done with it.'

He smiled at her then, that slow smile she loved so well. She wanted to smile back, but she felt if she did her entire life would go land-sliding towards him and she didn't want that quite yet.

'You were too scared to love me,' she risked saying.

'Precious little scares me, *dushka*, but you had me on the back foot from the moment we met,' he confessed—so candidly she couldn't help edging towards him. 'That day on the yacht, Maisy, it all came apart. When we were travelling together it was easier to keep you tucked away, out of sight. I understand you felt marginalized, but that's not what I was thinking. You belonged to me—a better me—not the man who keeps all the financial balls spinning. I didn't want to let the air in on that rarefied atmosphere we had. It was so precious to me.'

Maisy had gone very still. She hadn't considered it from that angle before. It had never occurred to her that *she* was the good thing in his life. All she had imagined was her inability to fit in.

'I wish you'd told me,' she answered softly.

'Hell, I hardly framed it as an idea to myself. I was running on instinct, Maisy. But I knew it wasn't fair to you, so I decided to use *Firebird* as an introduction.'

'Except it meant then that in everyone else's eyes I was your mistress.' It still stung, and she wasn't going to hide that from him.

Alexei's blue eyes sought hers earnestly. 'The people who mattered didn't think that, Maisy. Anyone with eyes in their head could see how much I loved you.'

He'd said he loved her. Twice. Maisy couldn't help reaching up to lay her hand against his chest. The heat and solidity of him felt like utter security.

'I realised I was pushing you away when all I wanted was intimacy. I just didn't know how to protect myself and still have everything with you.'

Maisy touched him with her other hand, just resting it on his chest, her fingers slightly curling around the fabric. He seemed to feel so guilty, and she didn't want that.

'I knew I'd made a colossal mistake,' he said roughly. 'But that meant re-evaluating everything I knew and I was struggling with it. When Leo died I was lost.'

His heavy sigh had her hands tightening on his shirt.

'Nothing felt right,' he said simply. 'And then I found you and it all fell into place.'

His eyes hadn't left hers once. His sincerity was making it difficult for her not to respond, yet she wanted to hear all of this. Desperately.

'Watching you with Kostya, seeing how much of a mother you've clearly been to him from birth, and then having you open yourself up to me. We're both very lucky males to have you in our lives.'

Maisy bit her lip.

'It just took me a little time to adjust, and you kept pushing,' he confessed with a half-smile, then reached out and gently thumbed the line puckering between her brows. 'I'm glad you did, *dushka*. You made me face a few home truths. It was only when you made it clear what you wanted that I realised I'd been kidding myself.'

'I didn't think I had much to lose,' she confessed. 'You would have pushed me away anyway. You didn't want me to love you.'

He framed her face with his big hands. 'Maisy Edmonds, as fast as I was backing up, I had no intention of losing you.'

'You sent me back here.'

'You asked me to. I gave you what you wanted.'

'If you'd argued with me I would only have resented you,' she admitted honestly, more to herself than him. 'I needed to find myself again, Alexei. I needed to see if I could do it on my own.'

'Look at you.' He gave her that slow smile that made her thighs turn to water and everything tingle. 'The working girl.'

'Damn right.'

Alexei was tangling one hand through her curls. 'Now I've come for what I want.'

'You're very sure of yourself,' Maisy murmured, thrilled.

'*Da*, but you like me that way, *dushka*.'

'Bossy.'

'Taking you over, not giving you a choice.'

He leaned in and kissed her, and his tenderness was the undoing of her.

He drew back enough to say, 'But you've got all the choices now, Maisy. Come back with me, be a family with me; share your life with me. You can have it all, *dushka*.'

Maisy gripped hold of his shirt front, making a mess of the sleek tailored lines.

'I want to be with you, Alexei.'

It was an echo from another time, another place, and he recognised it immediately. By a fountain in a garden, when they'd both been reeling from the impact of what being together might mean.

He knew exactly what it meant. The rest of his life was standing in front of him.

Gently disengaging her hands, he dropped down onto one knee and looked up at her. 'I love you, Maisy Edmonds. Would you do me the honour of becoming my wife?'

Maisy stared at him for what felt like the longest time. He was in love with her and he wanted to marry her.

'Oh, yes, I'm sure I can do that,' she responded, a big smile breaking out across her face.

Maisy's eye caught the glitter of the ring he had produced and she swallowed hard.

'Take a deep breath,' he murmured. 'I know you're not that keen on diamonds.'

She had a hard time not snatching it from him. Then she realised the ring was glittering because Alexei's hands were shaking.

Alexei slid the ring onto her finger. It fitted almost perfectly.

'It's so beautiful,' she whispered. '*You're* so beautiful.'

'That's my line, *dushka*.'

He was on his feet, gathering her into his arms. The relief on his face was almost as touching as his sweet, old-fashioned proposal. Maria had once told her that underneath all the surface swagger Alexei was as traditional as they came, but she hadn't listened.

She was listening now.

'I love you, Maisy.' His eyes deep in hers, his voice was heartbreakingly sincere. 'Let's go home.'

* * * * *

FULL SURRENDER

BY
JOANNE ROCK

Joanne Rock is the author of over fifty books for a variety of Mills & Boon series. A three-time RITA® Award nominee and former Golden Heart winner, Joanne is a frequent speaker at writing conferences. Bolstered by the kindness of other authors in the writing community early in her career, Joanne enjoys paying back that generosity by helping aspiring writers today. When she's not writing, she is most often found at sporting events cheering on her three athletic sons. Learn more about Joanne's books by visiting her website, www. joannerock.com, or www.millsandboon.co.uk.

To all the compassionate and giving souls who make the world a happier place for animals, and in particular to the folks at Safe Place who take in animals in need. Bless you for your hard work and I wish you much success in your mission.

_1_

THE USS _BRADY_ cruised into Norfolk, Virginia, at 10:00 a.m. EST, right on schedule. The navy destroyer ship had been deployed for six months, but for Stephanie Rosen, the homecoming had taken five long years.

A military marching band played at the front of the pier, near the ship's ramp. Flags and banners fluttered in the late summer breeze while overexcited kids crowded the gate for a first glimpse of their arriving moms or dads. A refreshment tent overflowed with reuniting couples and families. But Stephanie had yet to spot the man she'd been waiting for. The man who had no idea she'd be here today.

"I've been crying all morning," a woman next to her confided, dabbing at her eyes with a tissue. Smiling through the tears, the older lady searched for her grown son, a fact Stephanie had discovered during the long wait for the sailors. "It's crazy to cry, but I'm so happy I can hardly stand it."

Touched, Stephanie squeezed the woman's arm. She felt more comfortable waiting with a mom than with some of the wives who were dressed in their sexy best despite the early hour. It was apparent a lot of the re-uniting couples had seduction on their minds.

"Happy tears are the best tears." There had been a time when Stephanie hadn't been able to cry at all, her emotions closed off after a long, mind-numbing ordeal. These days, she was grateful for the return of her emotions.

Now it was time for the return of her snoozing sen-suality, the final phase of her recovery from that dark time five years ago. And there was only one man she trusted with the job. A man who'd been honorable and courageous well before his navy days.

Daniel Murphy.

"Oh, my God, there's my son!" the woman next to her shouted, her voice hoarse with emotion as she launched toward a handsome seaman in dress whites.

Leaving the pair to their reunion, Stephanie stepped closer to the front of the pier as the crowd thinned just a little. She'd noticed that, while some families lingered to enjoy the festivities, most hastened to their cars to catch up privately at home. She had an exit strategy to combat the traffic just in case she could convince Danny to come home with her.

Nervousness fluttered in her belly at the insane plan. She hadn't spoken with him in years. She wouldn't even have known his status now—still single, thank you, God—except that she'd gathered her courage to call his mom in Cape Cod for an update, begging Colleen Murphy's discretion about her inquiry. But his mom had been totally gracious, saying she was grateful that someone would be on hand to greet Danny when he docked in Virginia while his family prepared a reunion for him back home in Massachusetts.

Adjusting the red hibiscus in her hair, she lifted a hand to shade her eyes and scanned the faces of the last few officers exiting the ramp. She didn't expect an overly joyful reunion with a man she'd only known for all of five days before she went overseas for her former career as a camerawoman. After all, she and Danny had agreed their relationship would be short-term from the moment they'd met. He'd probably wonder what on earth she was doing here.

"Danny, where are you?" Stephanie asked herself, wandering aimlessly through the happy crowd, the full skirt of her polka-dot dress swishing around bare calves. Her outfit was a nod to Donna Reed in *From Here to Eternity,* the fifties film that was the extent of her navy knowledge.

And then, just when she decided he must have flown back separately, Stephanie saw him.

She didn't need to see the details of his face even though he stood almost two stories above her on the ship deck. An officer in dress whites moved to the top of the ramp, possibly the last man off the USS *Brady.* White wheel cap on his head and ribbons on his chest, he walked with more power and purpose than the laid-back guitarist she'd met five years ago at a house party. And yet she somehow recognized the way he moved.

Or maybe she simply recognized a bolt of lightning when it hit her, just as it had so long ago. Her skin tingled. Her body froze in place. She doubted her ability to speak.

It was him.

The man—or the memory of him—who had gotten her through hell and back even though he didn't know it. Now, she just needed one more favor from Danny Murphy, and it promised to be the most awkward request of her life.

DRESS SHOES CLACKING on the steel bow ramp, Danny Murphy barely saw the crowd of people still milling around the pier below. He'd waited to disembark in the hope of avoiding the worst of the scene. Most of his buddies were hooking up within an hour of arriving back home, the sprint to their women almost laughable if it wasn't so damn relatable. Imposed celibacy was a drag, but right now Danny told himself he was most interested in sleeping for seventy-two hours straight. His family knew he liked a few days to himself to acclimate to life on land before he had to be social, and for the first time in his naval career they'd respected his wish.

Of course, half the reason they'd been so accommodating was because they were busy getting ready for a Murphy-family wedding back home in Cape Cod. In the last year, his brothers had all found true love.

He wasn't looking forward to treading through their happy world as a single guy. A single guy still messed in the head thanks to…

Stephanie?

He nearly tripped, ass over fancy white cap, at the sight of the hot brunette at the ramp's end. A woman who'd materialized the instant he'd thought of her. It was the woman he'd been fantasizing about. Right here in Norfolk.

She looked so good, he figured she must be a mirage. She wore a sexy black-and-white polka-dot dress that showed off her tiny waist. Wide shoulder straps and a modestly low neckline framed a heart-shaped locket more than her cleavage, but then again, her curves weren't exactly disguised. She'd pinned a big red flower in her hair, the bloom tucked behind one ear so that a petal brushed her forehead.

"Hi, Danny." The vision spoke as he got closer, making him certain she wasn't a mirage.

All vestiges of tiredness fell away.

He reached the end of the ramp and couldn't go a step farther unless he wanted to wind up in her arms. Which he did. But he would not allow that to happen no matter how good she looked right now.

"Stephanie." He'd dreamed about holding her again. Mostly, he'd just dreamed about *seeing* her again.

She'd gone to Iraq with his cousin, a reporter, to film a series for an online news magazine. But she'd been kidnapped and held captive for six weeks.

Sometimes he still woke up thinking she was still

over there and he had no way to find her. His legs would be tangled in his sheets and he'd be sweating like a son of a bitch. Memories of her, and leftover guilt that he hadn't been able to help, had sabotaged every relationship he'd had since.

Even now, he wasn't sure if he trusted that she was here. He sure as hell didn't trust his knees to keep him on his feet.

"I…um." She backed up a step. "I hope it's okay I came to meet the ship. I know it's been a long time."

"Yeah." He couldn't think of a damn thing to say to her, but he didn't want to scare her off, either. "It's fine. I mean, of course. It's good to see you."

Eloquent as a damn elephant, that was him. He tried to shake off the shock of her appearing out of the blue.

"You, too." She smiled and five years fell away.

It was almost like meeting her for the first time, back before the nightmare of her abduction started. That is, until a new fear clocked him between the eyes.

"Are you, er, looking for someone?" He glanced around the pier, wondering if she was seeing a guy who had served on the USS *Brady* with him. What if she was meeting someone else?

"I was looking for you." She bit her lip and now she was the one whose gaze darted around the people nearby. "Unless *you're* meeting someone? I don't mean to get in the way of anything."

"No. God, no." He shook his head, relieved that she was here for him. But damn. Why would she seek him out now, after all this time? "I'm just surprised you'd be in Virginia. Last I knew, you were living in Long Island."

He'd been to her town house there, in fact. After they'd met at a friend's house party in Brooklyn, Danny had gone home with her and spent the next four days at her place. They hadn't been apart for more than five minutes at a stretch during that crazy, awesome time together. They might have had a future if she hadn't been headed overseas for an extended assignment. Instead, they'd just parted ways, wishing each other well, never realizing how her life was about to implode.

"I moved to D.C. a couple of years ago, so I'm not all that far from here. I started a new pet-photography business out of my home. I just…really wanted a fresh start."

She didn't need to say why. The memory of seeing her face on the news a couple of months after she'd gone to Iraq on assignment was burned into his brain. It had taken every ounce of self-restraint he could manage to join the service instead of trying to board a plane with a weapon and hunt down her captors himself.

For a moment, the old fire raged inside him, the fury and resentment that had driven him long after she'd been released. But he wrestled that into submission for her sake, since she was right here in the flesh and talking to him. He knew she'd volunteered at a counseling center for a while afterward, but he hadn't known about the new photography business.

"I have a car close by," she was saying now, pointing behind them. A few trinkets jingled on her bracelet and he realized they were all silver charms of different dog breeds, no doubt inspired by her work. "I heard that returning sailors like to eat good food as soon as they return home, so I…" She cleared her throat and tucked her hair behind the ear without the flower. "I wondered if you'd like to have lunch with me and catch up."

Around them, a military band played, volunteers handed out balloons to kids, and families wept and hugged. Danny was aware of his surroundings, but didn't really hear anything, the rest of the world operating like a silent film in the backdrop of the main attraction. Stephanie Rosen. Returned stateside four and a half years ago.

Returned to him…just now.

He wanted to wrap her in his arms, to see if she smelled the same, felt the same. But he knew he'd never be able to let go if he touched her now. Instead, he'd play it safe until he found out what she wanted.

"Sounds good," he managed to say, dropping his bag onto the pier. He couldn't imagine why she'd seek him out after all this time. He'd tried to get in touch with her once, but his efforts had been met with radio silence on her end. "My car is probably closer, though. I had a buddy park it nearby last night. I know all the shortcuts out of here to beat the traffic."

"Sure." She nodded as she accepted a blue balloon from a clown whose white makeup ran in streaks down the side of his face where he was sweating. "No problem. But first…" She opened her arms wide. "Welcome home, Danny Murphy."

The simple gesture humbled him so fast his throat burned with old emotion. Christ, he should have found a way to be there when she came home so he could have welcomed her. But he'd already been in the service, property of the U.S. military and unable to leave his duty station, determined to make sure no one else suffered the way she had.

It took all the strength and discipline he possessed to rein in his feelings now and give her a hug without crushing her. Folding her carefully in his arms, he buried his face in her hair, breathing in the clean scent. She squeezed back with surprising strength. Her body was so delicate, tall but slender. It was easy to forget it since her personality was big enough to fill a room.

Or at least it had been. Most people who went through that kind of ordeal were changed by it. Who wouldn't be?

And with that ice-cold reminder, he found the courage to release her.

"Thank you." His gaze locked with hers for a moment, the scent of her still in his nose.

"My pleasure." She smiled up at him, holding her balloon. "You look kind of dashing in white." She smoothed a hand over his chest, skimming his ribbons and kicking up his temperature. "And not at all like the laid-back rock 'n' roll dude I met five years ago."

Did she have any idea what her abduction had done to him? She wasn't the only one who'd changed.

"It's been a long time," he acknowledged, hoisting his bag onto one shoulder and using the other hand to steer her toward the pier's exit. Yeah, it was dicey to touch her when he still wanted her. Had always wanted her. But his feelings for her were more complicated than that now. Stephanie wasn't just some woman who'd knocked him for a loop with the best fling of his life.

She was…someone he respected for all that she'd been through. Someone who deserved to be protected.

"Only a handful of years," she countered, sidestepping a couple of toddlers dressed in sailor suits. Her voice was throaty and sexy. He'd forgotten that about her. "The guy I knew could never leave his band behind for six months at a time."

He could barely remember what he'd been like back then. It surprised him that she wanted to talk about the past. Talk about *them*. He didn't know if he could handle a trip down memory lane. Tough enough just keeping a hand at the small of her back without pulling her against him.

A kid's cry sounded behind them and she turned to look back at the stragglers still visiting on the pier. He turned, too, sticking right with her. One of the sailor-suit kids had lost his balloon, the spot of red floating higher and higher while the little boy's lower lip curved into the fiercest frown Danny had ever seen. Stephanie rushed back to hand him her balloon, the magic of a replacement popping the kid's mouth right back into a smile while the parents thanked her.

The action drew some attention from lingering sailors on the dock. Single frigging sailors from the way the guys looked her over. Danny wrapped an arm around her waist and shot them the evil eye, torqued off at them when he had no right to be.

If she was surprised by the sudden close contact, she didn't show it. She fit against him just as perfectly as he remembered, her hip the ideal height for him to rest his hand on as they walked.

And in no time, he was thinking about how else they fit together. Memories bombarded him like rogue torpedo fire.

"So where are we going?" she asked as they left some of the crowd behind. "Is it far?"

"No." He could see the Gran Torino already, parked in a private lot behind his favorite local restaurant. "There's my ride. Looks like my buddy had it washed, too."

She murmured appreciatively. "I remember you telling me about this vehicle. You were restoring it yourself."

He swallowed hard, recalling that conversation. It had taken place in the huge claw-foot tub in her condo. Her on top of him. Naked. Sated. Covered in bubbles.

"Yeah. I don't put many miles on it since I'm hardly ever home." He'd kept it garaged at his folks' place up until this past spring. Then he'd moved it to Norfolk so he could use it when he wasn't at sea.

"Looks like you outdid yourself." She hurried a step ahead of him to get a closer view. "Nice wheels."

She eyeballed the 1972 classic while he popped the trunk and found a pair of shoes he kept in the back. He could deal with the dress whites, except for the damn shoes that went with them. He set his cap in the trunk, too, and then went for the buttons on the tunic.

Stephanie's whistle stopped him cold. She stood there, at the back of the car now, her eyes roaming over him while her lips quirked in that wry smile he recalled from their first meeting long ago.

"Undressing already, Danny?" She cocked her hip and fanned herself with one hand. "This lunch is going to be more fun than I thought."

2

As SEDUCTIVE EFFORTS went, it wasn't much. But Stephanie needed to get the ball rolling and she was mega rusty when it came to flirtation.

Still, she'd expected more reaction than the frozen stare Danny gave her now. Fingers stilled on the buttons of his white shirt, he didn't move a muscle. His body was so tense he might as well have been carved from marble.

Damn it, this had been a bad idea. She was about to withdraw her comment and change the subject when his green eyes went a shade darker. His strong chest rose and fell, his jaw flexing. A handful of subtleties made her realize he felt the same heat as her. He was just a whole lot better at hiding it.

"Uh, that is, sorry," she apologized hastily, stepping away from the trunk to admire the vintage Ford instead. She wasn't sure why he'd want to suppress an attraction, but she hadn't meant to put him on the spot by assuming any kind of connection still existed between them. "I didn't mean to invade your space."

She forced her gaze to the car's burgundy-colored paint, admiring the way the metallic flecks caught the light and hoping she hadn't overstepped too soon and too much. Her skin felt as hot as the sun-warmed metal looked, her pulse throbbing so fast she felt it vibrate right through her skin.

"I don't have any sense of personal space after sharing a 500-foot ship with 300 people for 180 days," he said slowly, the soft swish of fabric assuring her he'd started undressing again. "But if I did, you'd be more than welcome to it."

Oh. Warmth smoked through her, chasing away the embarrassment with another kind of heat—the kind she never seemed to feel anymore. Yet Danny Murphy could call forth that delicious response in no time flat.

Apparently, she'd come to the right person to re-awaken her libido. Now, if only she could convince him to sign on for the mission she had in mind.

"Thank you. I didn't mean for that comment to slip out, but I guess for a minute it felt like old times." She couldn't help the smile that started in her heart and worked its way to the surface. And she couldn't stop smiling, even as he came over to her side of the car and opened the passenger door. He wore a gray T-shirt and a pair of loafers with his white uniform trousers. "I think I'm probably putting the cart before the horse to flirt with you when I don't know your official relationship status. Danny, are you seeing anyone?"

His mom hadn't mentioned anyone special in his life in their brief phone conversation, but then again, it seemed as though Danny kept some distance from his family these days. A lot could happen in six months while the USS *Brady* stopped in ports all over the Atlantic.

He stood in the open door after she got in, his green eyes briefly skimming her legs while she adjusted her skirt around them.

"I'm unattached." The way he said it lent the words a slightly ominous quality.

Or had she imagined that?

"Me, too," she admitted, her voice failing her a little at the thought of how *very* unattached she'd become in the last handful of years. Some days, it seemed that she connected more with the pets she photographed than actual human beings.

Danny lowered himself so that he was eye-to-eye with her.

"Do you mind waiting a minute while I run inside and finish changing?" He held a pair of khakis in one hand. "The restaurant doesn't open to the public until noon, but I know the owner and he's got something for me."

"Sure." She nodded, hypnotized by the sight of him after so long. With the partial change of clothes, he looked more like she remembered already, except perhaps for his clean-shaven face. When they'd met, he'd worn a dark soul patch trimmed beneath his lower lip and the shadow of short hair at his chin.

She still remembered exactly what that scruff of bristles felt like against her when he kissed her. What would he feel like now?

"Good." Rising, he pressed the old-fashioned lock on the door. "You should keep the doors locked even though this is a good neighborhood, okay? I'll be right back."

She tried not to think about that small protective gesture as he slammed the door shut and jogged up the back steps of a dockside restaurant. The day had started off so well. She didn't want to lose the pleasantly flirtatious vibe by remembering the time she *hadn't* been behind a locked door and a man had grabbed her right off the street, yanking a bag over her head....

Panicking, she rolled down the window for fresh summer air. Claustrophobia was more of a problem right now than the likelihood of getting kidnapped two blocks away from a huge U.S. military installation. She dragged in deep breaths, trying to calm herself. She refused to end up like her mom—perpetually nervous about everything. And, thinking of her mother's constant worries, Stephanie checked her cell phone to make sure it was off. Phone calls from a nervous parent were not welcome when she was trying to seduce a man.

"Hey," a familiar voice called from nearby, sooner than she expected. "Are you okay?"

She watched Danny descend the wooden steps, his white trousers in hand now that he wore a pair of faded khakis that conformed to muscular thighs. He also carried a couple of huge take-out bags, one of which was topped with three baguettes that stuck out of the paper sack. Hauling in one more deep drag of the salty sea breeze off the harbor, Stephanie wiped a little sweat from her forehead and gave him a thumbs-up.

"I'm good to go," she called back, not wanting to ruin this reunion with stupid stuff from the past that did not rule her life anymore. "And I'm dying for a ride in this baby."

She patted the side of the Gran Torino through her window. Then, recalling he was still locked out, she leaned over and popped the door on his side.

"Fair enough." He slid in beside her, tossing the take-out bags and his extra pair of pants in the backseat. Then he dropped a set of dog tags into the console with a bunch of coins. "But will you be disappointed if we eat lunch at my place?" He started the engine and then jerked a thumb toward the bags of food. "I've had an order in at this place for six months and I hate to miss out on homemade manicotti."

By now, the scent of basil-laden tomato sauce wafted her way. She peered back at the huge bags and frowned.

"I don't know. Are you sure there's going to be enough food for me in there?"

He laughed and the sound soothed her like a hug. The last of her claustrophobia disappeared, carried away by the warm breeze drifting through the windows as they drove past pawn shops and pizza joints toward the main road.

"Jerry packed enough grub to feed six people, which should be about right for the two of us."

He cranked the radio and lowered his window. She realized the song playing was one his band used to cover, a ballad with hard-core guitar harmonies and a screechy lead vocal. For a moment, the years rolled away, a weight lifting from her chest. It had been easy to be with him five years ago, too. He could be charming when he wanted, but more often he was quiet. She'd liked that about him because she was the same way with a public personality and a private one. And both sides of her had felt comfortable around Danny.

She lifted her voice to sing along while he drove. On a quiet stretch of access road before they met the highway, he stuck his head all the way out the window, letting the wind whip through his hair. She was tempted to copy him, it looked so fun. When he ducked back into the car, his dark hair stood straight up in the center, as though he'd been through a wind tunnel.

They took turns singing on the way home, maybe because it was easier than talking. Sometimes that public party persona was simpler to deal with than the moodier private one. But she half dreaded asking him to have a fling. Something told her he wasn't going to jump in with both feet the way he had five years ago. He struck her as more serious now, for one thing. She'd seen it in that powerful stride when he'd walked down the boat ramp, felt it in the way he'd tensed when she'd flirted with him.

Half an hour later, they were on the far side of the

Chesapeake Bay Bridge, rumbling over coastal roads. They passed a sign welcoming them to Cape Charles.

"It's beautiful out here." She'd grown up on Long Island, but it had been easy to forget you lived anywhere near the water with the dense urban sprawl from the city. Here, the scent of the bay hung in the air and patches of beach were occasionally visible through the trees. Blue water sparkled under the early afternoon sunshine.

"When I left Cape Cod, I tried to choose a place that felt like home. My house here is a pretty good compromise." He hit his turn signal just then, pulling into the driveway of a gray, cedar-sided house that would have been lovely even if wasn't overlooking the water.

Perched on the beach as it was, she couldn't imagine what the Nantucket-style home had cost him.

"Oh, wow." She'd known that his family was wealthy. But she hadn't really pictured this. "If this is a compromise, I can't imagine what the house you were raised in looks like."

He turned off the engine and tugged the bags out of the backseat.

"Before my dad formed Murphy Resorts, he was a real estate developer at a time when property rates were growing exponentially. So yeah, my folks live well these days." He hit a button on a key-ring remote that lifted a garage door off to one side. Two weathered Adirondack chairs sat on a deck off the room over the garage.

"Do you have someone take care of things while

you're away? It must be hard to leave such a beautiful place." She followed him into the garage, which was empty except for a bicycle and a scooter as big as a small motorcycle. He'd left his car outside.

"A property manager has it cleaned and watches it while I'm gone." He used his keys to open an interior door that led them into a modern kitchen full of white-washed cabinets and stainless-steel appliances.

But her eyes didn't stay on the kitchen. The open floor plan drew her attention to a huge family room with a wall of windows that overlooked the water.

"This is incredible." She walked toward the windows, drawn by the view. "I can't imagine how relaxing it must feel to come home to this."

The beach was empty even though a few boat ramps were visible down the shoreline, suggesting other houses were nearby through the trees that lined the property.

He dropped the bags onto the counter and shuffled through the take-out lids, so she returned to the kitchen to help.

"After growing up near the water, I get a little stir-crazy if I can't see it now." Turning on the oven, he slid some foil containers inside to reheat. "Would you like to take a walk out there while this warms up?"

"That'd be great." She wanted to feel the sand between her toes, but walking out on that shoreline with Danny would be the ideal time to come clean about what she wanted from him. Her heart rate jumped into a higher gear as an attack of nerves set in.

"This way." He nodded toward the French doors off the living area and they walked past overstuffed blue couches to reach the patio.

Stephanie took her shoes off and left them on the wooden deck before she followed him down the few steps to the beach. Sea grass bent in the breeze on a couple of low dunes close to the house. Beyond that, a few patches of dried black seaweed clumped in piles while the surf rolled onto the shore with a rhythmic *whoosh*.

"My dogs would love this." She tipped her face into the salty air.

"You have pets?" He stretched his arms over his head and arched his shoulders like he was working out some kinks.

She tried not to stare. But then again, how could she not? It had been a long time since looking at a man incited the kind of sensual interest she felt right now. That spark of excitement made her feel alive. Healthy. Whole.

"Yes. A couple of cats." Her voice cracked, her throat dry. She licked her lips and tried again. "I meant the dogs I photograph would have a blast out here. I love taking pictures in natural settings like parks, or at the owners' homes. But I'd get some great shots if I had this in my backyard."

Water really brought out the personality of some dogs. Labs and retrievers. Newfies, Porties… And maybe if she kept thinking about her job, she'd forget about what she really needed to discuss. The oh-so-awkward reason she'd made the three-hour drive from D.C. to Norfolk.

"I'd like to see your work sometime." He toed off his loafers and socks, then headed into the shallow surf. "But first, I've got to ask—"

"Uh-oh." She waded in after him, gathering her excess skirt material in one hand so that it didn't blow in the breeze off the water.

"What?"

"I know what you're going to ask, but I'm still working up the nerve to answer." She flexed her toes into the squishy sand, which fell away beneath her feet as a wave rolled back out to the bay.

"Are my questions that obvious? We haven't seen each other in five years and you're already reading my mind?"

"It doesn't take a mind reader to guess that you'd be curious about why I popped up out of the blue today."

He frowned. "That wasn't what I was going to ask, but now that you mention it, learning that is actually a high priority for me."

Crap. Crap. Crap.

Why hadn't she let him just finish his thought? Because she was nervous and antsy and...oh, God. This was a stupid idea.

Nevertheless, she'd been imagining this moment for a whole year and she'd hate herself if she chickened out now.

"Are you familiar with the idea of—" she cleared her

throat "—sexual healing? You know, recovering lost mojo by having sex with someone you trust?"

Silence met her question. Can you say…awkward?

Danny looked as if she'd hit him with a two-by-four. But there was no turning back now, so she took a deep breath and summed it up for him.

"Well, my mojo hasn't been the same since…you and I were together last. I've been waiting for you to return from your deployment so I could proposition you. What do you say to re-creating our affair?"

DANNY WASN'T SURE if he stood there for ten seconds or ten minutes after Stephanie posed the question. He couldn't have been more stunned if a rogue wave rose out of the bay, knocked him on his ass and dragged him out to sea. In fact, he probably would have recovered faster if that was the case.

"Danny?" Her voice sounded far away because of all the thoughts that came rushing into his head. She stepped closer, her hand landing on his wrist.

Her request echoed in his mind on an endless loop. He didn't know whether to pump his fist in victory or cry that she needed to ask. Yeah, knowing *why* she wanted that kind of healing ripped him raw. In her public account of her abduction, she'd denied being… assaulted. She'd written a book about the experience afterward, and he'd read the whole thing cover to cover a few times. But he had no way of knowing the deeper damage of what she'd really been through—the things she hadn't put into print.

If she was brave enough to ask him for something like that, however, he was humbled to be the one she went to. He'd damn well do whatever she wanted. Even if it ripped apart the crappy patch job he'd done on his memories of that whole time.

"Come here." He would have gone to her, but he was still a little numb. He was also wary of spooking her by showing her how much he wanted this. "Please. Will you just come here?"

Between her uncertain step forward and his arms reaching out, he caught her. Drew her against him. She stumbled a half step, but then she was tucked tight to his chest, the top of her head just below his chin where he could rest his cheek and breathe in the scent of her hair. Her arms went around him and her skirt wrapped around his legs in the sea breeze.

He held her that way for ten steadying beats of his heart before his body reminded his brain what she'd just asked of him. All that numbness evaporated. Like a fireball shot into an oil spill, there was sudden ignition everywhere and a tremendous rush of heat.

"Is this your way of letting me down gently?" Stephanie wiggled free of his arms, backing up a step. The flower that she'd stuck in her hair was starting to wilt, no doubt a little crushed from when he'd held her. "Because if this is just a nice attempt to say no—"

"Yes." He bit out the word more sharply than he'd intended. "I say hell *yes*. I have to leave in three weeks for another six-month deployment, so I won't be in town for long. But if you're cool with that and don't mind that this is short-lived…I want to be with you."

He straightened the red flower, tucking the stem more securely behind her ear and trying like hell to smother the inferno threatening to consume him from the inside out.

Her eyes went wide. A smile started, but she lifted her hands to her face, hiding it.

"Seriously?" She sounded happy. A little breathless. "I hope you're not saying that just because you feel bad for the awkward girl who sucks at seduction. It's just that I feel safe with you and—"

Danny kissed her. No hesitation this time. His blood still simmered for wanting her, so it wasn't exactly a chore to seal her lips with his and cut off that line of thinking in no uncertain terms.

She sank into him, her body pliant and warm. She tasted like cinnamon, her lip gloss as edible as the woman. Her soft, yielding mouth reminded him of other kisses, other times she'd given herself to him. And as much as he loved those past days together, he wanted this kiss to be all about the present for both of them. A moment belonging so fully to the here and now that they'd never confuse it with the past.

Edging back, he whispered, "Not a chance." He stroked up her spine to thread his fingers through her hair, the water swirling higher around their legs as the tide came in. "This is about me and you and new beginnings."

"Yes." She nodded fast, obviously liking that idea. "A do-over."

"Exactly." They'd be safer that way, he thought. The more they focused on the present, the easier this would be for both of them. "Are you ready to leave the past behind and enjoy the moment?"

Using her hands, she steadied herself on his shoulders as a wave rolled past them, splashing up to his knees.

"Very ready." Her affirmation was all the encouragement he needed.

Lifting her against him, he tipped his forehead to hers.

"Here's to a clean slate," he said softly.

He twirled her in the surf with him, her damp skirt twining around his legs. Too late he saw a high wave speeding toward them. He turned to shelter her and take the brunt of the water on his back, but the force was too great, pulling them down, submerging them both in the Chesapeake Bay.

3

As THE WATER CLOSED over his head, Danny kept Stephanie pressed tight to him. He hadn't meant to haul her into the surf without warning. But Stephanie had always had a sense of adventure and spontaneity, just like him.

Or so he thought until she started to struggle in his arms.

Blasting straight to the surface, he pulled her high out of the water, arms locked around her waist and shoulders.

"Are you okay? I didn't see that wave coming until it was too late." He scanned her face, trying to get a read on what was wrong. "Is it too cold?"

Water sluiced down her face and shoulders, her dress straps sagging on her arms. Her flower had disappeared and her dark hair was plastered slick to her head. What scared him most was how pale she'd gone.

"I'm fine." Her eyelids fluttered. Her heartbeat

throbbed fast in the blue vein that stood out sharply against her pale throat. "I just... It was dark and I couldn't see for a second."

He frowned. Fear of the dark?

She'd never been freaked out by not being able to see before. So it only made sense something had happened between now and then to give her that kind of phobia. No doubt it had to do with her abduction. In trying to distance them from the past, he'd unwittingly thrown her right back into it. It would kill him thinking about how she might have developed that new fear, but he'd be damned if he'd ask her about it now, when they were supposed to be focused on a fresh start.

"I'm so sorry," he muttered against her forehead. Being with Stephanie was going to be filled with landmines for both of them. "I should have gotten us to the surface faster. I didn't realize..."

It never occurred to him she might panic. He cursed himself for his insensitivity.

"It's all right." Her pupils were wide despite the sun still high in the afternoon sky. She wrapped her arms around herself, her teeth chattering. "I was just surprised."

"Come on." He draped an arm across her shoulders and steered her toward the shore. "You can dry off inside."

"Thanks." She wrung out a fistful of wet hair as they trudged toward the shore, soaked clothes weighing them down. "I promise I'm not usually spooked that easily. I love the water."

Yeah. He remembered that about her. They'd taken midnight swims in the pool at her town house those days they'd spent together on Long Island. Sat in the Jacuzzi tub for hours.

"Maybe we can hit the beach sometime when it's not such a surprise." He scooped up his shoes as they reached the shore, then guided her back toward the patio and into the house. "Let me get you a towel."

He saw a blanket on the back of the couch and grabbed that instead. Wrapping her up in blue fleece, he assessed the damage. Her eyes were focused. Clear. Her color seemed better. And he would make damn sure it stayed that way.

"You want a shower while I put the food on the table?" He gestured down the hall while they dripped on the rug near the French doors. "There's a bathroom off the spare bedroom on the right. It connects to a walk-in closet that has some extra clothes. You can grab a T-shirt or whatever you need out of there."

"Sounds good." She gave a firm nod, as if she was as determined as him to put the incident in the water behind them. "Thank you."

Her gaze roamed over his face, slowing at his mouth, lingering there. Was she thinking about that kiss they'd shared, too? He still couldn't believe what he'd agreed to out in the bay with her. In a perfect world, they'd take things slow and easy. Not rush into anything. But if she kept up those long looks of hers…he'd find it hard to be the sensible one.

SLIDING INTO ONE of Danny's T-shirts, Stephanie paused to bury her nose in the cotton at one shoulder. Granted, she probably only smelled laundry detergent. But there was something about wearing a man's clothes that made her feel sexy and safe at the same time. Like having some of Danny's strength around her 24/7.

Wouldn't that be addicting if she wasn't careful?

She pushed the wicker basket full of clean shirts back into the closet cubby, reminding herself that part of the reason Danny seemed like a safe choice right now was that he'd only be home for a few weeks. She hadn't known that his stay would be quite that short, but she'd realized it was inevitable he'd go back to sea for his job. No chance of getting in over her head with a guy due to leave before the month's end.

Pulling through her tangled hair with a wide comb she'd found in a drawer by the sink, Stephanie peered into another wicker basket and found a stack of running shorts. She dug deeper until she spied a gray pair with a drawstring waist that might cinch enough to fit. Her underwear was soaked, so she'd have to go commando. Which might be fine down below, but up top? She stepped from the closet back into the bathroom and checked her reflection. A second T-shirt was definitely in order if she wanted to give the girls halfway decent coverage.

Snagging a second white T-shirt, she pulled it over her head, determined to enjoy her time with Danny from this moment forward. She'd freaked out in the water, but she was done with that now.

Yes, she'd been traumatized when her assignment in Iraq had turned hellish. The family who'd grabbed her and reporter Christina Marcel had been coerced into doing so. Apparently, the family had angered Iraqi insurgents the week before when their oldest son had met with Christina to be interviewed for a story on the effects of the war on the Iraqi people.

Furious that the young man had talked to American reporters, insurgents had killed him and demanded the family use their connections to abduct and hold the reporters or risk seeing another one of their sons gunned down. Her captors hadn't been as cruel as seasoned rebel soldiers might have been, but Stephanie had still been terrified of them, knowing they would do whatever the insurgents wished.

She hadn't been raped, although she'd been beaten when she was first taken, to keep her from trying to escape. She'd been scared to death and she still had nightmares about being kept in the dark.

But she'd dealt with it. Put it behind her. And now, years later, she was finally ready for this. For Danny Murphy, the last great memory she had before she went to Iraq. Keeping that in mind, she padded through the hall toward the big, open kitchen.

"It smells fantastic," she observed lightly, hoping to get this day back on track. She'd survived the worst of her awkward request of Danny, so now she only had to enjoy the fruits of her embarrassment.

He'd said yes, after all. She shivered just thinking about what that meant.

"I hope you brought your appetite." He stood by the coffee table, arranging plates and glasses on the heavy plank top so they could eat on the sofa. Steam wafted from the plain white dishes loaded with manicotti and red sauce. Salad bowls were heaped with fresh greens and grated cheeses. And a bread basket held several slices of the baguette, some that were plain and some slathered with butter and lightly broiled.

He'd changed into dry shorts and a worn black concert T-shirt for some obscure band, the lettering peeling. His dark hair was still damp and sticking up in a few places as if he'd just used his fingers to shove it out of his eyes.

Her mouth watered for the man as much as the meal.

"I didn't realize I was hungry until now." She edged around the sofa to take a spot in front of the low table. "The view is pretty great, too." Realizing she happened to be staring at him at the moment, she pointed hastily out the window. "I mean, of the bay."

He sat beside her on the sofa.

"I like the view, too." He never took his eyes off her. While that comment sank in, he lifted a glass of water and handed it to her, then raised his own. "Here's to old friends."

Her heart beat fast. She resisted the urge to tug at the layered T-shirts she wore, knowing her body would be sending obvious signals about how much he affected her. The soft cotton created a pleasurable friction against her breasts.

"Cheers to that." She clinked her tumbler to his and

sipped the water, hoping it would help cool her off. "Don't let me slow you down, Danny. You must be starving."

She gestured toward his plate and he grinned.

"I'll try not to inhale it," he said as he picked up a fork and dug in.

Following suit, she tasted the manicotti and promptly realized what he liked about the simple dish. The cheese filling was light and amazing. The pasta obviously homemade. And the sauce—yum. She'd polished off half of it before it occurred to her that, delicious as the food was, she wasn't coming close to fulfilling her real hunger.

Setting her fork down, she wondered how to move things forward with Danny.

"So…" she began, watching him help himself to more of everything. "I don't mean to sound overly practical about this, but I wondered what you thought of the logistics of…er…you and me?"

He eyed her over a forkful of pasta.

"I may have been out to sea for six months, but I've still got a pretty good idea of how the logistics work."

His wolfish grin stirred her more than the earnest touches of her last—and only—boyfriend after what had happened in Iraq. She had thought something was wrong with her for months while she'd dated Josh, a guy who worked for the agency that had helped with publicity for her book and that vetted the responses she still received on her memoir. She'd thought she wanted to pursue a real relationship with him and had blamed her lack of sensual interest on her ordeal. After all, she had shut down emotionally in a lot of ways afterward.

But maybe the truth was that spark just hadn't been there with Josh. Not the way it was with Danny. She got back to hammering out the details for a fling, hardly daring to believe it was really going to happen after all this time.

"I mean, where should we conduct this liaison? Here? Or would you like to come with me to my place in D.C.? For that matter, we can find a neutral location if you want to go out of town for a few days."

He seemed to ponder the idea while he ripped off a piece of bread.

"Can you take some time off from your work?" He passed the bread basket to her, but she couldn't eat another bite.

"I'm in a good position with work. A friend is filling in for me at the studio and I cleared my personal appointments for a couple of weeks." She finished her water and then realized how that sounded. "Although, I was also giving myself a vacation. I don't expect you to hang out with me all that time. I know you must have things to do here since you're not home all that often."

"Actually, I promised my folks I'd head home in a couple of days. I'm spending ten days back in Cape Cod so they can invite all the family and throw a big shindig for me the weekend before my brother Jack's wedding. It's the only reason they didn't meet the ship when I came home."

"So you don't have much time." She bit her lip, wishing she had him to herself a little longer. Plus, knowing he'd only be here a few days put an awful lot of pressure on her to get this affair off the ground in a hurry. "Unless we could do this after you get back to Norfolk?"

She was already mentally rearranging her schedule. Beside her, Danny put down his fork on his empty plate.

"Why don't you just go to the Cape with me?" He finished his water and set the glass on the table, his full attention back on her.

"With all your family? For a wedding, no less?" She knew a little about the Murphys thanks to her friend and former coworker Christina, Danny's cousin— Stephanie and Danny had met at Christina's house all those years ago.

The Murphy family was huge, with five biological brothers and a sixth who they'd fostered. They were also wealthy beyond her imagining, owning a hotel conglomerate with interests that spanned the globe. Danny's father was a Fortune 500 executive, and he'd always expected Danny to go into the family business. She'd read a little more about the Murphys in the past year, which was how she'd worked up the nerve to phone Danny's mom a week ago. No matter that his dad sounded like a driven business guru, the articles online had depicted Colleen Murphy as a dedicated humanitarian and down-to-earth person.

"Why not? There's lots of room back home, so it's not like we'd be right on top of everyone else. I usually stay in the gatehouse, so I've got some privacy while I'm there. And two of my brothers have places nearby so they wouldn't be underfoot anyhow." He propped an elbow on the back of the couch, facing her. "They're not a bad group. Competitive as all hell, but they're good guys. And the thing is, I hear they've all got women in tow now. So if you don't go, I'd be the only stag Murphy in the bunch."

"They've got women *in tow?*" Stephanie wondered if she should be offended. "Will I be in tow?"

"Okay. Poor choice of words. Technically, I've got two brothers engaged, one getting married and two more sapped out over women they're dating." His hand strayed close to her shoulder and she imagined its weight on her skin. Its warmth smoothing over her bare flesh. "I haven't even met Kyle's or Axel's new girlfriends so that'll be a trip."

"Won't it be a lot of pressure for you to show up with me?" She wasn't sure she was ready for family scrutiny when she'd only just barely worked up the courage to reclaim her sleeping sensuality after all this time. "I mean, will people expect us to be a real couple?"

"No one is going to expect anything." He frowned. "But if it makes you uncomfortable—"

"No." She didn't want to miss out on the time with him. Family or not, she preferred to have more time with Danny since she didn't expect to solve her intimacy issues overnight. As much as she wanted to test the waters with him, she worried she might take two steps forward and one step back. "I'd love to go to the Cape with you. Thanks for asking."

"Great." He settled deeper into the couch cushions, his fingers finally straying closer to her shoulder. He smoothed a touch along her upper arm, just below the seam of the white cotton fabric of the T-shirt. "That settles that. Now we just need to figure out what to do for the next couple of days until we leave."

Was it her imagination, or had his voice grown softer? Seductive. The hooded look he gave her revealed nothing, but it sure heated her insides.

"I can go back to Norfolk." She knew it was a foolish offer as soon as she made it. She'd asked him to re-create their affair, hadn't she? Why back away like a scared rabbit now that he'd said yes? "I mean, I don't want to infringe on your downtime if you'd like a few days to rest and...whatever."

"I think it would be great if you'd stay with me. Right here." His thumb circled a small patch of her skin, giving her goose bumps everywhere else.

"Ooh." She cleared her throat to cover her sigh of pleasure at his touch. "That would be nice. I left my car back near the base, though. My bag is in the trunk."

"Do you keep a spare key in the wheel well or somewhere underneath?" His fingers skimmed higher, hitching up the seam on her T-shirt to touch the top of her shoulder.

"No." She couldn't help the shiver that went through her. "Why?"

"I have a friend who would drive it up here if I let

him take my boat out in return. That is, if you don't mind someone else driving your car."

She had all she could do not to stretch like a cat under his lightly stroking hand. Why was it that she could let her guard down around him so easily when she'd been tense and agitated every time Josh came near her back when they'd dated? Was it that another year had passed? Or was it one hundred percent Daniel Murphy?

"Actually, I have one of those models where you can call the company and they'll bounce a satellite signal down to make it unlock or some crazy trick like that. Although I guess that won't help him start the car." She frowned, wishing she could have taken him up on the offer. The trip from D.C. had been more than enough time behind the wheel for her in a day.

"Umm…this guy's a ship mechanic. I give him ten-to-one odds he can hot-wire your car with his eyes closed. I'll have him pick it up in the morning, unless you really need your things tonight." His whole hand cupped her bare shoulder now and that seemed to be the only thing she could think about.

With no bra to get in the way, he could be touching her bare breast with the slightest movement. Better yet was the realization that she really, really would like that.

"Yes." She tipped her neck to one side, giving him all the more room to touch her. "That would be perfect."

He quit touching her.

"You want me to have it brought here tonight?" Danny reached for his phone on the coffee table.

She shook her head, confused for a moment until she recalled what he'd asked. "No. I don't need the car."

"You're sure?" He still held the cell phone when she wanted him to hold her.

"Positive." She left the rest of the words unspoken, the request for him to put his hands back on her.

"Okay. Cool." He set the phone down again and met her gaze.

She could have sworn that heat flared in his eyes for a second before he scrambled to his feet.

"I'd better put the food away." He picked up the dishes and glasses, whisking them into the kitchen while she tried to recover from the sharp bite of longing she hadn't felt in years.

Seducing Danny could take a little more ingenuity than she'd thought if she had intimacy issues and he was going to insist on taking things slow. Just because she'd received an invitation to spend the night didn't mean she'd be sleeping in his bed.

ACCEPTING STEPHANIE'S INVITATION didn't mean he could fall on her like a sailor on dry land for the first time in months. He would restrain himself because she deserved better. Hell, she might not even be ready to be with him like that given the way he'd freaked her out back in the water. As much as she might be sending him the green-light signal, chances were good that she didn't know exactly what she needed.

Which was why he would be a gentleman if it killed him. Which was also why he cleared the dishes and cleaned up the kitchen with a speed and dedication he usually reserved for his job.

He had no idea how things would go between them tonight, but his blood still simmered. He'd be back out in the bay to cool down if he couldn't get himself under control.

In the living room, Stephanie wandered around checking out his book collection on one shelf and old CDs on the other. He'd chased her out of the kitchen twice, mostly because he needed the space to get his head on straight. He looked over again, and saw she was scrolling through his iPod playlist while the device was docked in the stereo. When she cranked up a Doors tune, the house filled with dark, moody music. She sang and twirled absently, occasionally running her finger down a book spine or drifting past the open French doors to breathe the fresh air.

Seeing her like this, full of song and a bounce in her step, brought him right back to that night they'd first met....

MUSIC STILL POURED through him, the echo of his show in the city humming in his head. Danny had booked the gig in Manhattan three months ago, knowing his band had what it took to make it on a big stage. And sure enough, the well-connected club owner had declared their show a success. The other guys in the band had expressed doubts about his level of commitment to music given the prominence of his family—and his dad's seemingly never-ending thirst to expand Murphy Resorts, Inc. while strong-arming all his sons into corporate positions. But maybe the fact that Danny had set up this gig would quiet his detractors.

His bandmates certainly looked happy enough as they mingled at a house party hosted by Danny's cousin, journalist Christina Marcel. The timing had been nice for him since Christina was headed overseas for a six-month-long news feature on the war in Iraq and she'd wanted to throw a little going-away party for her and her camerawoman, Stephanie Rosen. She'd been more than happy to expand the event into a reception for the musicians.

"You were awesome!" Christina threw herself into Danny's arms as soon as he walked out onto her balcony, her energy a formidable thing. "You've got to cut yourself free from the resort business and pursue your music, Dan," she whispered in his ear. "You're so talented with that guitar."

"Thanks." He kissed her cheek, liking the view from her Brooklyn apartment. The city glowed across the water, reminding him his dreams were all right there for the taking.

Except that, more than music, he wanted to follow Christina over to Iraq. He hated sitting at a desk job and carrying on, business as usual, while a war unfolded. He needed to get involved. To use his smarts for something beyond making another dollar for the old man. He liked music, but even that had been making him feel restless.

"Have you met Stephanie?" Christina asked, oblivious to his dark thoughts as she blew kisses to someone who had just come out onto the balcony.

Danny turned to see one of his older brothers, Jack, who'd made the trip to New York with him. Danny couldn't help but think that Jack was his designated watchdog this weekend. In a family full of high achievers, Danny had always been the crazy one, whereas Jack was Mr. Responsible. Long ago, the guy had been charged with watching over the younger brothers while the oldest learned the ropes of the resort business.

"No." Danny looked around the balcony, more than ready to meet anyone that wasn't related to him. Sometimes, when you had a big family, it was damn tough to escape their expectations. "Is she here yet?"

"Are you kidding?" Christina laughed and tugged him closer to whisper in his ear. "She's been looking forward to an introduction ever since your first set back at the club."

Danny waited while Christina waved her hand over the crowd.

And summoned a woman who damn near floored him.

It wasn't just one thing about her. It was everything. Pale and delicate with wide blue eyes and fairy-tale dark waves that hugged her shoulders, she looked as though she belonged to another era. Except she wore a red silk scarf, tied pirate-style around her forehead, and her lips were quirked in a wry, knowing smile. She danced her way over to the jazz tune piped through an outdoor sound system.

"*Hola,* Christina," she greeted his cousin, toasting her with the drink she held in one hand. Then, never taking a sip, she set her glass down on the railing twined with pink-flamingo-shaped decorative lights, which surround the balcony. "And *hola* to you, Daniel Murphy. I've been anxious to tell you that you play guitar like a god."

She didn't say it like a groupie. She said it like someone who genuinely loved music. And then she launched into an air guitar riff, her head thrown back and her fingers flying over imaginary strings. Danny was surprised, charmed and yeah, totally taken with her.

And he'd known her for all of two minutes....

HOW THE HELL WOULD he ever be able to resist her now? He'd been a sucker for her then, before he'd ever touched her. This time, he knew exactly how good they were together. More importantly, she'd finally sought him out after all this time. When she'd ignored a couple of phone calls from him a few years ago, he'd left her alone, figuring she'd moved on. But now?

She needed him.

So what was he doing in the kitchen drying the same glass for the last freaking five minutes?

He set the tumbler on the counter with a force that threatened to shatter the thing on the granite. Stephanie peered his way.

"All done?" She took a step in his direction but paused at the stereo to turn the music down a few notches.

No. He was only just getting started.

"Yes. I have been for a while, actually." He tossed the towel on the breakfast bar and met her in the middle of the living area. "I've just been looking at you and wondering...where to go from here."

She hugged her arms around her waist and shrugged. Her blue-black hair was glossy in the sunlight that streamed through the windows that lined half the room. Her eyes sparked with some of the old light, the mischief he'd always liked about her. She had a playful spirit that really worked for him.

Or at least, she used to have a playful spirit. Protectiveness surged through him at the thought of anyone daring to take that from her.

"Funny you should say that, because I've been over here thinking the same thing." She combed a strand of hair away from her forehead with one hand.

"Really?" He told himself to take it slow. No matter how she flirted with him, he was going to take this easy. One day at a time. "For the woman who set this whole thing in motion, I'm surprised you don't have some idea what to do next."

She quirked an eyebrow at him.

"Yes. Well. Like you, I remember the logistics, even if it's been a while." She tossed his words from earlier back in his face, an irrepressible smile drawing him into the sphere of her spell.

And yeah, he could call it that because she had that kind of power over him.

"Would you like some help figuring it out?" He sifted his fingers through the dark waves curling around one of her shoulders and twined a lock around his thumb.

"I'm all ears," she assured him, swaying closer.

His heart slugged so heavily in his chest it felt like an alien force trying to fight its way out. He wanted her. Badly.

"We could try the kiss again," he suggested, his voice dipping into a predatory rumble no matter how he tried to keep things light. "Maybe this time, we could christen the do-over better than what I managed out in the bay."

Bright blue eyes shifted downward, her glance settling on his mouth.

"I'd like that." Her hands found his arms and gripped them lightly. She dragged him down to the couch to sit beside her.

Every instinct he possessed urged him to wrap her against him and hold her there. He'd let go of her five years ago and lived to regret it sorely. How the hell could he resist squeezing her tightly to him now?

But the battle raged inside him and he wrestled that hungry beast to the ground, giving Stephanie the barest brush of his mouth on hers. She tipped her face higher, providing him with more access, so he increased the pressure slightly.

Slowly, he learned the taste of her all over again.

Recalled the nuances of her kisses and the way she arched into him for more. His soap on her skin didn't dilute the more feminine essence beneath it—her fragrance, her lip gloss, her everything. He cradled her face in his hand, enjoying the moment.

That would have been enough for hours. For days even. Except that she closed the space between them, pressing her breasts to his chest with nothing to separate them but his T-shirts—one on him and two on her. She wore nothing underneath his clothes. He'd thought as much earlier when he'd watched her move around the living room. Even before that when he'd touched her shoulder and didn't feel a bra strap there.

But now, knowing for certain how easily he could cup the gentle swell of her breasts in his hands…

Slow and easy went out the window.

Sliding his arms around her back, he hauled her against him and hoped he never had to let go.

4

SWEET SENSATIONS FLOODED her so fast, Stephanie couldn't begin to appreciate all the ways Danny's touch made her feel…extraordinary. His lips on hers were gentle, thorough, stirring a need that she'd been running from for years.

Now, she welcomed it.

Nerve endings came to life virtually everywhere as she inched closer to him on the couch. Pleasure spiraled just below her skin, a soft tickling up the backs of her thighs and a small shiver down her spine. Her breasts ached at the feel of his hard chest, her nipples so tight with need there was no way he could miss her response.

She felt sexy. Sexual. And yes, safe. Nothing could touch her when Danny held her. It was a soul-deep surety that made her relax and let her guard down. That knowledge, along with her trust in him, made everything else easy. Pleasurable.

God, she should have found him a long time ago. She needed him.

The iPod soundtrack switched from the Doors to Elvis Costello, the late afternoon sunlight slanting through the French doors to warm her shoulders while Danny warmed all the rest of her. She cupped his face, keeping his lips to hers so she could savor every teasing stroke of his tongue.

His hands smoothed down her back, pausing just before her hips and starting the slow journey up again. Broad palms and long fingers left no square inch untouched. Better yet, the slight pressure molded the rest of her closer to the unyielding muscles of his chest. She could still remember how it had felt to be naked against him. To trade touches and sexual favors, their moments together all the more frantic and precious because they'd known they wouldn't last....

"What's wrong?" He pulled back, green eyes instantly clear. Alert.

"Nothing." She shook her head, fingers skimming his shoulders. She wanted to lose herself in him. "Why?"

He tipped her chin up, as if to see her better. "It's hard to explain. You drew back somehow. I didn't know what you were thinking and I don't want to upset you, like back in the water."

"No. That won't happen again." She brushed a hair out of her eyes. "I won't let it."

She wouldn't allow the past to rob her of one more day. Not one more minute. She'd already rebounded in every way except this…the whole intimacy thing. And the time had come to conquer that, too.

"It's okay." Danny's fingers roamed the top of her shoulder, breezing along the neckline of her T-shirt, where the pad of his thumb rasped over the tender skin at the base of her throat. "We can take this easy."

"Easy doesn't sound like the best approach to me." She tilted her head to one side, freeing access to her neck, where an echo of his touch lingered. "I think a proactive strategy is better. Something a little more aggressive."

He studied her for two ragged breaths, the only sign that holding back was costing him.

She knew a moment's regret that she'd brought her request to his doorstep on the same day he came home from a six-month deployment. No doubt he was wired and very deserving of long hours of uncomplicated sex. But what was her alternative? Wait a week to come see him so he could hook up with someone else first? The notion bugged her so much she took a deep breath and slid onto his lap. Damn it, she would provide for his needs this time.

She seemed to have effectively overridden his gentlemanly instincts. He banded an arm around her waist and another at her shoulders as he kissed her again. His aftershave smelled like cedar and pine, the scent vague and deep in his skin since he was already wearing a five o'clock shadow that abraded her chin. Stephanie didn't care. She liked everything rough and he-man about him, from his callused fingers to the dark hair on his arms.

Melting into him, she allowed the kiss to carry her away. He cupped her hip, exploring her curves through the cotton fabric of the gym shorts. She wanted to touch more of him, too, but his mouth moving in rhythm with hers mesmerized her so that it was difficult to remember her own name much less how to seduce him.

The kiss kindled a fire deep inside her, the slide of his lips over hers so overtly sensual that she felt a phantom imitation of it in the most sensitive of places.

"Oooh. Right. There." She savored the gentle nips. The soft bite of his teeth along her lower lip.

Her whole body tensed, the years of abstinence making her incredibly sensitive. It wouldn't take much to push her over the edge, to take all that sexual potential and turn it into wave after wave of fulfillment.

"Lie down for me," Danny urged between kisses, leaning her back into the sofa so that he came down on top of her.

The weight of him was gone in an instant as he edged off the couch and onto the floor, never breaking the kiss. She lay sprawled on the cushions while he knelt beside her, his hand splayed over her waist where her T-shirts rode up from the shorts.

She yanked her eyes open, sad at the loss of his body against hers. But the intensity in his forest-green eyes told her she needn't have worried. He didn't seem to have any intention of stopping yet.

Reassured, she watched him hook a finger in the

hem of her shirt and lift it higher. His dark head bent over her pale skin, tracing the path of the shirt with kisses. Then, as he neared the undercurve of her breasts, his tongue took over the task. She squirmed beneath him, her breath coming fast. She was so tense. So ready for more.

Yet it touched her that he took his time and showed such care with her. Unable to hold back, she took the hem of the shirts she wore and lifted them all the way up. Off. She lay on the discarded white cotton like a pillow, her hair still tangled in the neckline while her bare breasts rested mere inches from his mouth.

Danny studied her. Assessed for all of five seconds before he turned his full attention to what she'd un-veiled. He closed his mouth over one taut nipple, swirl-ing his tongue around the ache until she arched into the kiss. She lifted herself up enough to yank at the fabric of his T-shirt, wanting to feel his naked chest against hers. Heck, she just wanted to see him. Feast her eyes on all that maleness.

"Stephanie." He broke away, his eyes passion-fogged and his hair tousled. "If any more clothes come off, I'm not going to be able to think. That's why you're up on the couch and I'm on the floor. That position promotes blood flow to the gray matter instead of… yeah." He tipped his head forward in defeat, not fin-ishing his sentence.

"But I've been imagining what it would be like to find you again for almost a whole year. I didn't just decide to show up and see you last week. I've wanted this for a long time. It'll be okay if we don't think for a little while." She dipped a hand beneath his shirt, smoothing her fingers up the side of his chest and running them down his back.

His muscles danced beneath the caress, responding to her touch in a way that made her want to feel more of him.

"But I haven't had that much time." He reached beneath her and tugged out the white T-shirts she'd been wearing, untwining them from her hair. When he freed the cotton, he laid the fabric over her sensitive breasts.

"I thought you were on board with this idea?" She let go of him to clutch the material to her chest.

"I am." He rested his elbows on the couch beside her. "You have no idea how much I'm on board. But I don't want to mess things up."

"It seemed to me like things were going really well." Her skin still burned where he'd touched her, her lips swollen from his kiss.

He stroked her hair where it lay tangled on one shoulder.

"But you're in a better position to judge than me. You came here talking about healing and lost mojo, so I know some things have gone wrong for you. But it's been a long time since we've been together, so I'm not sure what that means."

The fire inside her cooled in a hurry. She edged back on the sofa, scrambling to sit up straighter, one arm still clinging to that shirt in front of her.

"The whole world knows things have gone wrong

for me, Danny. I didn't think I needed to spell it out."
The abduction and the aftermath were the last things
she wanted to talk about now. Hadn't she just got done
thinking her past wasn't going to rob her of another
minute? "If you want the full story, I poured my heart
into an account of my experiences in Iraq. Too bad the
media decided I was 'selling out,' using my captivity
experience to make a buck, and panned it before half
of them even read it."

"I've always wondered if you held anything back
in the book. If they hurt you—if you were sexually
assaulted—I need to know." His voice hitched when
he asked, the small slice of emotion touching her more
deeply than anything they'd done together so far.

He tugged a blanket off the back of the couch and
covered her with it, gently tucking the edges around
her.

"No." She shook her head. "I was honest in my written account of the experience. The people who held me
were too emotionally devastated to abuse me like that.
Actually, they weren't bad people in the first place.
They were just…grieving. As helpless as me in a lot
of ways. They didn't even know they'd have to keep
Christina and I in their home all that time. The family
thought that after they kidnapped us, the rebel forces
would come and take us away, but they never did. Later,
some military officials told us they guessed the rebels'
numbers were just too thin to come back for us, which
I thank God for."

Finally, the family had released them six weeks

later, once they'd made plans to relocate their sons to relatives in the south of the country, where they would be safe from retaliation.

"Me, too." Danny shook his head. "Sorry to bring that up now, Steph. But thank you for telling me."

"That's okay." She folded her legs under her, retreating from him. "As long as we're talking about that, is there anything else you'd like to know?"

"Honestly? Yeah. What happened after you came home?" He rose up off the floor to sit beside her on the couch. Close, but not touching. He stared out at the bay, the sun fully set and the sky streaked with red in its wake. "I wrote to you. Called you."

"Oh." She hadn't been expecting that. At all. "If you did, I don't remember. I changed phone numbers frequently to avoid…everyone. After the book came out, I hired an agency to deal with the letters because there were a lot of irrational accusations about not being supportive of the war, or using the war to further a media agenda." She waved away the still-painful memories, half wondering if her former boyfriend, Josh, had ever seen a communication from Danny. It was his job to go through the letters, after all.

Would it have made him jealous? Or had the agency merely discarded the communication, deeming it too personal? "I still receive hateful letters, in fact. But I'm sorry if I missed a note from you. It was a dark, miserable time."

Danny's chest tightened to think she'd been harassed.

He'd waited a whole year after she'd been released to try contacting her, knowing she'd need time to recover. Besides, he'd been in training for his first assignment and then he'd been on board the USS *Brady,* working long hours thousands of miles from home. It hadn't occurred to him the fallout from the book she'd written would bring her so much grief.

"I understand. I just wondered." Danny had read her book, but he didn't think he could talk about her abduction experience now without giving away how much he'd fallen for her five years ago, or that he'd kind of gone off the deep end when she'd been held hostage. "That was part of the reason I was surprised to see you today. Not just that it's been a long time. I figured you didn't want anything to do with me."

She wove her fingers through the fringe on the blanket he'd draped over her. "I'm sure the kisses just now told you nothing could be further from the truth."

Glancing his way, she gave him that mischievous smile he was crazy about.

"You did seem awfully agreeable." He dropped a hand on her knee. She was wrapped in the woven fabric as if in a cocoon, but he could see the outline of her leg. "I just want to be sure I don't cross a line and send you running again."

"You should trust me to know what I can handle." She toyed with the fringe. He could see the tops of her breasts through the gap in the weave since she'd let go of the T-shirt.

"It's me I don't trust." He was seriously pushing his

boundaries to look right now. He wanted her in his bed and he wanted her all night long. But no matter what she said about being ready for this, she didn't have a clue what he wanted from her.

Sexual healing was only the beginning. He was going to show Stephanie that she belonged in his life, safe in his arms, forever.

5

RELUCTANTLY, STEPHANIE retreated to the guest bed-room alone.

She didn't know why she'd expected her new affair with Danny to follow the same course as their wild encounter five years ago. But that was kind of what she'd hoped for. They'd fall into each other's arms and have sex until they couldn't see straight. Spend every waking moment together—and every sleeping moment, for that matter. And she'd be a new woman when it came time for him to leave Norfolk again.

Brushing her teeth with one of the spare tooth-brushes Danny had pointed out, Stephanie stared into the cedar-framed mirror over the pedestal sink and knew she'd been naive to think an affair could unfold like that now. For one thing, they were both older. She'd known going into this that she was more world-weary, more cautious. That was half the reason she'd had a tough time with relationships.

But she hadn't really considered that *he* would be more wary, too. As she pinned up her hair and washed her face, she reminded herself that he wasn't the same fun-loving rocker who could take a week off from his father's business because it was a family company. Danny was a navy lieutenant, a surface warfare officer with people who depended on him. He'd walked away from the lucrative Murphy holdings to join the military, no doubt taking one hell of a pay cut. For that matter, he'd walked away from his rock band, as well.

They'd gone on to make it big without him. He'd signed away the name and his rights to the group, and his bandmates had taken a song he'd written to the top 100 four years ago. Stephanie felt sad hearing that song on the radio, knowing it should have been his guitar on the studio track instead of some fill-in imposter.

Why hadn't she asked him about that? Or about what had made him Mr. Serious since they'd been together?

Tugging a flannel bathrobe off the hook inside an armoire Danny had shown her, Stephanie slid it on and padded across the hardwood floor to find him. It was only eleven o'clock.

And it wasn't as if she was planning to seduce him. She just wanted to know.

Too bad he wasn't in his bedroom. The door across the hall was open wide, the room dark. A light still glowed downstairs, so she followed it, listening for any sounds in the still house. The only thing she heard was a creaking sound from the flooring as she made her way into the kitchen. A bottle of whiskey stood open on the counter—that hadn't been there earlier. Curious, she picked it up as if it could provide a clue to his whereabouts.

That's when she heard the strains of a guitar floating through a crack in the French doors. Following the music, she stepped out onto the patio to find Danny on the edge of the planked deck, his feet in the sand. A shaft of light spilled out into the dark, the only illumination on the moonless night.

She didn't say anything since he was in the middle of a blues riff, the chords sad and sweet at the same time. Sitting beside him on the patio, she wrapped the robe tighter around her legs and stared out at the ocean while he finished his song.

"It's great to hear you play." She'd forgotten how much she liked hearing his fingers working the instrument strings. "I remember you had a guitar at my house. It was fun to hear snippets of music while I was folding laundry or taking a shower."

There'd been something intimate about that. Not just the romance of feeling as if she was being serenaded. More like a small pleasure in knowing his habits. She'd enjoyed that glimpse into his world and discovering he would strum a guitar while he watched the news on TV or while he waited for his coffee to cool down in the morning.

"Playing relaxes me." He danced his fingers silently over the strings, as if he practiced some chord progression.

The water swooshed against the shore nearby, the

sound calming after an emotional day. In the distance she heard a dog barking, but the houses nearby were silent.

"It's odd that I found you playing the guitar since the reason I came looking for you was to ask you about your music."

"Yeah?" He reached toward her and at first she thought he meant to touch her, but then he gently tugged the bottle of whiskey from her hand.

She'd forgotten she still held it. He uncapped it and poured a short measure into the empty glass beside him. Then, instead of sipping it himself, he passed the drink to her.

"I always wondered why you gave up your band." She tipped her face into a light breeze that blew off the water and wrapped her fingers around the glass. "You seemed to enjoy music so much."

"Playing is an outlet for me. I never wanted it to feel like work." His fingers tripped through a simple melody that she realized was a nursery school staple— "Twinkle, Twinkle, Little Star."

She smiled. "It's definitely good to have a part of your life that feels like playtime. But wouldn't it be even better if your work felt like play?"

"Maybe someday." He strummed idly for a minute before swapping into a bass line. "But I wanted to make a more tangible contribution to society first."

For a moment, she simply sipped the fiery whiskey and watched his lower fingers keep the rhythm line while the others picked out a harmony on the strings.

"I'm just surprised you joined the military so soon after we met. I thought you were going to encourage the band to take their music to the next level."

He continued the song for a moment before his fingers quit moving all together. The silence felt discordant.

"They did take it to the next level," he reminded her. "I signed over my stake in the band so they could do just that when I joined the navy."

Somehow, she knew better than to pin him down on this, even though his answers only gave rise to more questions. Like—why did he join the navy right after she left the U.S.? Instead, she handed him the glass and waited while he took a slow drink.

"I signed my contract a few weeks after you were taken." He set the glass down, but he kept the guitar perched on one thigh. He didn't play it now, his elbows resting on the polished body of the instrument.

Her heart ached at the admission. She'd wondered about the timing before, but she'd written it off as a coincidence. Now, she wasn't so sure.

"I knew I wasn't going to personally locate you or anything like that," he said with a quiet seriousness she'd never heard from him before, like a note out of synch with the rest of the song. She suddenly sensed she didn't know this man half as well as she thought she did.

"But you didn't join the navy because of...*that,* did you?" She'd been about to say "because of me," but she could hardly dare to formulate the idea in her head

much less ask out loud if it was true. She couldn't bear
to think her ordeal had had such a profound effect on
him. It was bad enough she and Christina'd had to en-
dure it. That their families had worried themselves
sick—literally. Stephanie's mother had suffered a nervous breakdown that had led to hospitalization, leaving
Stephanie to come home to a much-changed family.

And, oddly, more than a little guilt for her mother's illness.

"It wasn't like I came up with the idea on the spot."
Danny eased off the guitar and lifted it into an open
case on the deck behind him. "Coming from a family
with so much has always made me feel guilty somehow.
Like I'd won a cosmic lottery and hadn't really done
anything to deserve it. Plus, I never enjoyed the time I
spent behind a desk, even though I went to school for
architecture."

She'd vaguely recalled that he held some kind of
technical degree. Perhaps that had been another sign
of the navy lieutenant lurking within the easygoing
rocker, but she'd been so busy enjoying his fun and
spontaneous side that she hadn't really taken the time
to understand the whole man.

"So you'd been thinking about going into the military before then." Relief flowed through her. She took
another tiny sip of the whiskey to keep her warm as
the night air turned cooler.

"Yes." He slid closer to her, draping an arm around
her shoulders. "But when I heard you and Christina
were being held prisoner..."

He tensed and she wished she hadn't asked about this. Not tonight when he'd just come home and it should be a happy occasion.

"I didn't mean to bring this up," she blurted, even knowing she couldn't undo words already spoken. "That is, we don't have to talk about that time if you don't want to."

"If you're going home to Cape Cod with me, it's better you know about this now anyhow." His hand rubbed along her shoulder and down one arm, warming her. "My family all remembers that you were a big part of the reason I went into the navy. I wouldn't want you to be caught off guard by anything they might say. Not that anyone would have a reason for bringing it up."

DANNY WATCHED Stephanie's face as she processed the news. Her profile was shadowed, the glow spilling out onto the deck from the house not providing much light. But he could tell she was surprised. Upset.

A furrow creased her forehead, her lips pursing into a frown.

"I never meant to put anyone in danger for my sake." Her voice was thready. She rubbed at the goose bumps on her arm.

He knew she wasn't just thinking about him and his service. He'd read her book. Remembered her mother had had a breakdown that led to severe pneumonia while Stephanie had been held captive. She'd come home to find her mom hospitalized and near death. While her mom had lived, he wasn't sure what their relationship was now. When he'd known Stephanie, they hadn't been close.

"You didn't do anything," he reminded her gently as he pressed her nearer to warm her up. "I was pissed off that a foreign situation was so hazardous that members of the media could be snatched off the street. That warranted getting involved and made me sorry as hell I hadn't signed the paperwork sooner."

Those few weeks after she'd been taken—before he'd entered the navy—had been a nightmare. His family had convinced him to try diplomatic channels. Financial channels. They'd used their international business leverage to try to get answers. They'd offered money to shadowy figures who might have leads. And all the while, Danny had seethed. He'd broken most of his knuckles during those three weeks, punching doors, walls and even—he sorely regretted—his younger brother's nose. Poor Kyle had barely commented on the situation.

Even now, Danny had to unclench his fists as he remembered the paralyzing inability to help her.

That helplessness was a feeling that he refused to ever experience again. Because any help she needed now, he planned to provide. In spades. And yet, instead of taking her to bed with him earlier, he'd shown her the guest room and turned to the guitar, scared spitless of screwing things up with her.

"Then thank you, Danny." She turned toward him suddenly, planting a kiss on his cheek. "Thank you for fighting for me. For other foreign travelers overseas.

I'm so grateful for the job you do after seeing what it's like over there."

His grip tightened on her shoulder, keeping her pressed to his chest.

"You're welcome." He closed his eyes, inhaling the clean scent of her mingled with the night air. "It was the best thing for me." He would have gone off the deep end otherwise, but he didn't tell her that. Not after what she'd gone through with her mom.

But it was true. The service had saved his ass and given him a sense of purpose when he'd wanted to go Rambo on Stephanie's captors.

"Can I ask one more question before I leave you to play your guitar in peace?" She peered up at him, the flannel robe she wore gaping a little at the lapels so he could glimpse the thin cotton T-shirt she wore beneath.

Was it still layered over a second? Or had she stripped one off as she'd gotten ready for bed? The thought heated his blood in spite of the topic of conversation—one he'd avoided discussing with anyone for years. But with Stephanie asking the questions, he couldn't feel defensive. He only wanted her to be safe. Happy.

"You can ask anything." He meant it. For her, he'd tear down defenses he'd spent five years building.

"When you wrote to me after my book came out…" She seemed to weigh her words, laying a hand on his chest, right over his heart. "What did your letter say?"

Crap. Sure she could ask him anything. That didn't mean he'd be able to answer.

"It was a long time ago." He didn't mention that he could probably recite the thing verbatim since he'd spent more time composing it than he had on original music for the old band. "But I was basically checking to see how you were doing. Ask if you wanted to... get together."

All of which was true.

He braced for her reaction. He'd put more of himself on the line with her today than he ever had before.

She shivered against him and he lifted her onto his lap, settling her across his thighs.

"I was so mixed up then, it's probably just as well I didn't see you," she confided, her blue eyes more visible now that she was turned toward the scant light coming from the house.

He didn't mention that her reluctance to see him made it easier for him to spend months on end at sea. No other woman had come close to Stephanie, and a couple of years ago, he'd put some effort into trying to find someone.

No one fit in his arms like this. No one rocked an air guitar like she did. When they'd parted ways before she left for Iraq, he'd always imagined he'd pick up the phone and call her after her six-month stint to explore the attraction. Neither of them had seen the need to make some big commitment before she went abroad, but they'd been young and had never imagined the way her trip would change both of their lives.

He couldn't tell her that it had damn near killed

him that she'd never acknowledged his efforts to get in touch with her.

"So it wouldn't have been a good idea to see me then, but now it's okay?" He smoothed a few strands of her hair that had separated from the knot at the back of her head. The silky locks glided over his skin, another reminder of how delicate she was. How soft and tender.

"Back then, I couldn't handle any reminders of that time in my life. I didn't see Christina for a long time, either." Her husky voice rasped in the cool air, the admission easing some of the ache he'd felt at her rejection of that old letter he'd sent her. "Being with you would have just triggered a whole mess of emotions I wasn't prepared to deal with."

His heart slugged his chest, slow and steady. He watched her mouth move as she spoke. Stephanie might not be ready to let him into her life, but she'd come here because she wanted to be with him. Maybe that physical connection would have to be enough until he could convince her they deserved more than that.

"And now?" He could feel the whiskey burn in his chest. Or at least he told himself that was what accounted for the fire he felt inside.

"Now, I have too many hang-ups to let my guard down and be with anyone else. I went into pet photography because the animals give unconditional acceptance. I do fine with them, but with most people… not so much." She traced the seam of the collar on his T-shirt, unaware of how much she affected him. "Since I never had any problems with you, however, I thought it would be a good idea to see if I could still—" her fingers walked down his shirt, lightly skimming his chest "—find release. You know. Still lose myself completely in the moment without freaking out."

The warrior in him demanded to know why, if she hadn't been assaulted, she would "freak out" during intimacy, and who he needed to castrate as payback. But he understood now that he should take care of her first and think about the rest later.

"So this is a test of sorts." He focused all his thoughts on her. The present.

"For me more than you," she assured him, her hand splayed along his ribs. Her thighs shifting lightly against his.

"Then we'd better go study." He scooped her up in his arms, one arm beneath her knees and the other under her shoulders. Standing, he left his guitar in the case on the deck, knowing the salt water would trash it but willing to make that sacrifice for something far more precious. "We're both going to ace this one."

6

FOR A MOMENT, Stephanie's nervousness melted away. After months of waiting, she was really going to be with Danny again.

She wrapped her arms around his neck as he strode across the deck toward the French doors to the house, allowing herself a dreamy sigh of satisfaction before her nervousness returned. And she knew it would. She'd pinned so much on this reunion with him that it was inevitable she'd be wound up about it.

"What about your guitar?" She looked back over Danny's shoulder at the case resting on the patio outside, her heart beating fast as he carried her into the house.

"I have others." He never broke stride as he strode down a hall off the kitchen. "And if you're thinking about the six-string—" he paused as he flicked on a light in a big, modern laundry room "—then I'd better give you something else to occupy your mind."

"We're going to do laundry?" She peered around at the stainless-steel front-loader washing machine and the old-fashioned drying rack standing beside a matching dryer.

"Hardly." He turned so she could see the other side of the room, where a small, inset stall looked like a minishower with a big grate on the floor that covered a drain. "I thought you'd want to wash the sand off your feet."

He set her on top of the grate and removed a handheld showerhead that had been installed at waist level.

"Cool." Her bare feet were definitely gritty, as were his. "It's a foot shower?"

"No. It's a spot to wash the dog I don't own yet." He turned the water on, but pointed it down into the drain until he was happy with the temperature. Then he handed the showerhead to her. "I designed the house myself, and I figured this setup would be nice to have in the future."

Stephanie sighed with pleasure at the hot water between her toes.

"And helpful when your feet are sandy. How clever." She worked on the other foot while Danny grabbed a towel from a stack in a basket above the dryer. "I'll be anxious to take a closer look at the rest of the house to see what you've done."

Stepping onto the towel, she traded places with him so he could wash off.

"Tomorrow," he said firmly, shutting off the water. He stepped onto the towel before coming toward her.

"Right now, I think we have an experiment to conduct. A test to take."

His green eyes fixed on her.

Her mouth went dry. Nervousness spiked, but not nearly as much as her desire for him. All her hopes for this night—this moment—made her tremble.

The force of the attraction made her launch herself into his arms. She kissed him with years of pent-up longing, allowing herself to show him how much she wanted him. She'd held back earlier, unsure of his response. But now, there was no need. He understood what she wanted.

What she feared.

His lips were soft and slow against hers, his deliberate control of the kiss helping her to relax and just enjoy it.

When he broke away from her, his gaze dropped to her mouth.

"I'm going to take you upstairs now."

It wasn't a question. But then, she'd signed on for this the moment she propositioned him. She nodded, her lips tingling from the scorching look he gave her as much as the kiss.

"Let's go." She offered him her hand, ready to follow him anywhere.

DANNY SWALLOWED HARD as he led her through the darkened house. Up the stairs. Into his bedroom.

Last night, when he'd thought about returning home after six months at sea, he'd never in a million years envisioned her here with him. She'd given him some-thing so special and unexpected that he wanted to make this perfect for her.

In fact, that's how he was going to keep his head on straight tonight—thinking about her and what she wanted. This wasn't about him and how much he'd dreamed about her. Feared for her. Wanted to avenge her.

This was just about Stephanie and what she needed. He'd already made quick work of his own most basic needs after he'd settled her in a spare bedroom for the night. That was one of the reasons he'd suggested they retreat to their own beds originally—he hadn't been able to think about anything but sex until he took the edge off a few times on his own. The self-gratification didn't take away from how much he wanted her now. But he hoped it would help him be patient enough to take good care of her.

He let go of her hand and turned on the dimmer switch, casting the smallest glow over the room so she could observe everything around her. He'd understood her fear earlier—not being able to see—and wouldn't let that happen again.

She remained in the middle of the room, halfway between the bed and the sitting area, right where he'd left her.

"I like being able to see you." He met her there, the two of them spotlighted by the glow from a wrought-iron chandelier. "That way I know I'm not dreaming that you're really here."

"I spent too long waiting for you to come back home to leave now."

He wished she'd been waiting for him for more reasons than her need to recover her sexual confidence, but he would enjoy whatever she gave him.

"That's so damn good to hear." He lifted a hand to a silver pin in her hair. "I'm going to take this down now, okay?"

He didn't want anything to catch her off guard. No surprises.

As she nodded, he slid out the pin and her glossy dark mane unwound onto her shoulder. Pocketing the clip, he sifted his fingers through the silky mass.

She arched her neck as if she liked that. He had to be careful not to breathe her in too deeply or he'd lose himself in the feel of her.

He steadied her by the shoulders, or maybe he was steadying himself. Either way, he had her clasped close to his chest, absorbing the warmth of her skin through flannel and cotton.

"What would you think of me taking off your robe?" He ran a finger down one lapel, pausing shy of the *V* between her breasts.

Her pupils dilated until the blue became a thin rim around the dark center.

"I'd like that." Her husky voice was as intoxicating as a caress up his thigh.

He tucked a finger into the knot at her waist and tugged it free. The flannel tie fell away, opening the robe so he could see the T-shirt and the cotton shorts

she'd put on after her shower. She looked beautiful.
Touchable. With no makeup on and no complicated
clothes to unhook or unzip, she was utterly natural
and so different from other women he'd known. She
didn't pout her lips or bat her lashes. Didn't toss her
hair or giggle.

As he stared, her breasts pressed against the white
shirt, the soft shape of her curves outlining the shadowed tips of nipples that demanded his attention.

"I'd kill to kiss you here." He tugged on the hem of
the shirt so the fabric rubbed against the taut peaks.
"I don't even need the shirt off. I just want you in my
mouth."

Her eyelids fluttered and then closed. "Yes."

Wrapping an arm around her waist, he steadied her
back as he helped her arch toward him. He bent over
her, closing his lips around one dusky tip. She shuddered hard. A throaty cry edged up her throat, vibrating in his ear while he shaped the tight crest of her
with his mouth.

He drew on her, not caring about the fabric between
them as long as she was on the other side of it. The
steamy heat of the kiss turned the material damp, making the cloth cling to her. Her fingers clutched at his
shoulders, her hips cradling his.

Hunger roared in his veins. She couldn't miss the
erection that she'd pinned between them. The friction
of her body there was as potent as if she'd stroked the
naked length of him with her hand. His temperature
spiked to feverish levels, his vision narrowing to her.

"I'd like to see more of you." He breathed deep to cool himself down, but every lungful of air contained the feminine scent that went deeper than any fragrance and clung to her skin even after a dip in the ocean and a shower, intensifying with the heat of her body. He wanted to lick every inch of her until he found the source of it.

"Then we're even because I'm dying to get you naked," she whispered, spearing her hands beneath his shirt to span his abs. His chest.

Just that simple touch had him seeing stars.

"And while that sounds…incredible—" he struggled to rein in the need for her, which was quickly spiraling out of control "—I think it's a risky proposition."

"I don't care." She flexed her fingers against his flesh, her nails digging gently into his skin. "I've been waiting so long for this."

"All the more reason to make sure nothing spoils it." He couldn't trust himself to the same degree once his shorts were off. "Come here."

He led her toward the bed and gripped the hem of her T-shirt. Taking his time, he skimmed the fabric up and off, tossing it aside.

The sight of her half-naked body left him speechless. Her breasts were high and round, perfectly formed. She was pale and smooth everywhere, right down to the curve of her hips, where she had the running shorts cinched. The waistband dropped a little near the drawstring, exposing her stomach well below her navel.

His mouth watered to kiss her there and work his way down.

"If your hands are half as thorough as your eyes," she murmured, "this is going to be fun."

"I'll make sure of it." He didn't allow any room for doubt. He swept a hand over her hip and hooked a finger on the shorts. "Ready?"

"Danny." She gripped his wrist, an urgent expression on her face.

Was she backing out?

"What?"

"I want this so badly, it scares me." Her fingers trembled where she held him. "Don't stop, okay?"

"I'm not stopping until you see stars." He brushed a kiss along her temple. Maybe keeping her distracted would help. More touching. Less talk.

Untying the drawstring, he let the shorts fall. And damned if his knees didn't nearly drop along with them. She was naked beneath the cotton. No panties, no thong, no nothing. Just a tiny patch of dark curls shielding her sex.

The throb in his cock was nothing compared to what it would be by the time he was done. He wanted her, but he had no intention of taking her tonight. Not when she just needed to climax. He wasn't going to rush this thing between him, even if it killed him. By the punch of blood in his veins down below, it damn near might.

"Beautiful," he praised her, lowering his mouth to hers. "Open for me."

Lips parting, she let her head fall back, giving herself over completely. He took his time savoring her, stroking and nipping until they were both out of breath. She wrapped her arms around his waist, pulling him close. Feeling her hips against his was like setting a detonation device in an armory. If she kept moving against him like that, he stood no chance of honoring his good intentions. For that matter, if he hadn't kept his shorts on, he'd be inside her already.

Steeling himself to the heaven she offered, he lifted her up and laid her out on his bed. He reached for an extra pillow and dragged it down to where she lay, crossways on the king-size bed. He tucked it under her head, propping her up, while he began a slow descent of her body. He paused at her breasts—her low moan made him linger there. He cupped her, lifting each breast to his mouth in turn.

It was all he could do to keep his hips away from hers—he was drawn to her like true north. He smoothed a hand down her side to her hip. Lower.

When he grazed her thigh, sweat popped along his brow from the effort to hold back. Her soft sighs and breathy cries were making him crazy, the need for her all but taking over. His hands trembled by the time he dipped one between her legs. Parting her thighs, she arched her back when he drew hard on one nipple.

"I want to touch you," he warned her, fingers sliding higher. Closer to where he wanted to be most.

"Please. Please. Pleeease," she chanted, twisting under his touch as if she could guide him where she needed him.

He lifted his head to watch her face when he touched her sex, partly to make sure she was okay with this. Mostly because he couldn't take his eyes off her.

When he stroked a finger along her slick folds, she shuddered against him.

"Oh, yes, Danny." Her fingers speared through his hair, holding him closer while she moved against his hand.

She was so ready for him. He forced himself to close his eyes for a minute because seeing her was pushing him toward his own release. Just the feel of her could send him over the edge, but by cutting out the visual—if only temporarily—he gave himself a fighting chance of staying in control.

Of course, it also meant he wouldn't see right away if she hesitated over anything. The thought wrenched his eyelids open again. Imagining her going into another panic, like in the water, helped to level him out.

He could feel when she neared her climax. Her body stilled, her expression softening into a kind of frozen wonder. He kept up the rhythm of his hand and wrapped his lips around a taut nipple, drawing her deeply into his mouth.

At once, she flew apart. Her hips thrust, her heels digging into the bed. Needing to feel just a little of it, he dipped a finger inside her. She clawed lightly at his shoulders while the soft convulsions of her feminine muscles squeezed him again and again.

He'd expected a tough time holding back, but in the aftermath of her orgasm, he felt more grounded than what he'd imagined he might. He wanted her, of course. Badly. But he'd given her the kind of experience she needed to start feeling more confidence again, and that felt incredible.

Hell, just watching her reach that pinnacle was an experience he'd never forget. That fulfillment helped him as he began the battle to will away the mother of all hard-ons. But this had to be about her.

They held each other in the glow from the dim chandelier for long minutes. He pulled a blanket over them and listened to her breathing until it went back to normal. The sound of her soft sighs provided a kind of ease he hadn't known in forever.

He was almost able to draw a whole breath again when she shifted beside him, her smooth thigh grazing his leg as she rolled closer. On cue, his body returned to full-on happy mode, ready to take care of her every need.

Damn it.

"This isn't a one-way street," she whispered against his lips, her hand coming to rest on his chest. "I'm more than ready to return the favor."

His blood pounded in his veins, the need for her turning into a throbbing ache all over again. But as much as he wanted to bury himself inside her, he didn't want to rush the progress they'd made.

"There is nothing to return," he assured her, kissing her eyelids so that he wasn't mesmerized by those wide blue eyes. "I got to see you find release and that was...so much more than I ever would have expected tonight."

The high road never killed anyone, right? Although the pain in his balls after this self-denial would probably come close.

"Are you sure?" She frowned and opened her eyes again, clearly concerned for him.

And that, as much as getting to touch her, made him a happy man. If she cared about him like that, there might be hope for something more down the road.

"Positive." He dragged another blanket over them along with the first. "Do you want me to leave the light on?"

She bit her lip, her indecision so palpable that he remembered why he was holding back. No doubt she was still battling some demons from her past.

"If you don't mind, that would be great." She smiled gratefully over her shoulder while she lay down on her side.

Danny tucked her against him, careful to keep his hips out of the equation.

"No problem." He stroked her back long after she fell asleep in his arms.

Yeah, the light on was no big deal. But the fact that she needed time to trust again, coupled with him leaving in twenty-one days, was going to be a hell of an obstacle.

7

TWO DAYS LATER, Stephanie had to pinch herself to be sure she wasn't dreaming.

She was finally sitting next to Danny Murphy again after waiting and waiting for him to come back to the States. He'd proven to her—several times since that first night together—she could hit her sexual peak with him and everything was in good working order on that front. Now, she mulled over the selection of wines stashed above the wet bar of the Murphy Resorts corporate jet on the flight to Cape Cod for Danny's welcome-home party.

It was a dream come true, if only she could convince Danny she was ready to take the next step physically. But it was tough to ask for more from a man who kept bringing her to heights of pleasure she'd forgotten existed.

"I can't believe your father sent a company plane to pick you up," she mused while she ran her hand over bottles of Tempranillo and Beaujolais and other wines made from varietals she'd never even heard of before. "It must have been quite an experience being a kid in your family."

Maybe talking about the Murphys would prepare her better for this time spent at his childhood home. Besides, she could use a distraction from thinking about how much she wanted to advance to the next level of recharging her mojo—sex with Danny. She'd dreamed about it both nights she'd fallen asleep in his arms after he'd touched her.

"We were fortunate," he admitted, pocketing his phone that he'd just used to text his family that they were airborne. "And trust me, my dad doesn't usually roll out the company plane for his sons to travel home. He runs the business by the book. But Jack's wedding is a special occasion, so I think he pulled some strings to hire out the plane himself this week to transport the family."

"I don't have any siblings." She left the wet bar to investigate a wall full of television screens and a low bookshelf beneath them. "I can't imagine how helpful it would be having a brother or sister to occupy at least half of my parents' compulsive attention."

"You've never said much about them." He slid his shoes off for the flight, making himself comfortable in the leather chair that looked like it belonged in a living room instead of a jet.

She debated what to say about her family, not wanting to lose the fun mood of the trip. They'd kept things pretty light so far, Danny regaling her with anecdotes from life aboard the USS *Brady* and Stephanie telling him about various pets she'd photographed.

Maybe the time had come to share a little more if she ever expected things between them to…escalate.

"My mom will freely admit she wasn't cut out to be a mother." Stephanie would spare him how much that had hurt over the years, especially when she was in grade school and her parents had never shown up for ornament-making day at Christmas, or the dance performances she'd worked hard on all year. "She didn't really recognize the value of treating children like children and was more interested in seeing me excel at math or playing the violin, both of which I despised."

Whereas she'd made kick-ass ornaments and represented herself well at those dance recitals. But she wasn't the only kid to feel that she'd disappointed her parents.

"Sounds like a high-pressure environment. Your mom is an author, right?" He leaned forward in his chair to listen, elbows on his knees. He wore khaki cargo shorts and a T-shirt over his sculpted chest.

"She's a literary novelist with two critically acclaimed books to her name. My mom is an overachiever. She was class valedictorian in high school and has conducted the rest of her life as if she's still competing for the honor. She needs to be the best in everything and I think it bums her out to have a daughter who…isn't."

"She's blind," Danny said matter-of-factly. "It's unfortunate she can't see how incredible you are."

Leaving the wall of TV screens, Stephanie lowered herself to the leather chair beside him, smoothing out her blue-and-yellow print skirt so it didn't wrinkle. Bright afternoon sun filtered through the round windows beside them, the sky clear and cloudless.

"Thank you." She warmed inside at his assessment, still surprised at his easy acceptance of her sudden presence in his life and her unorthodox request of him. "I've grown used to her desperate pleas for me to turn my life to something more worthwhile than photographing pets. It was her idea that I write that book about my experiences, by the way. A book she became highly embarrassed about after critics slammed it."

Stephanie may have recovered from her mom missing the dance recitals, but that slight still bothered her. Especially when her mother insisted on telling her all the ways that she needed to improve her job prospects, her social circle, her dating life. Why couldn't her mother appreciate the things she did well instead of focusing on all the ways she thought Stephanie fell short? She'd been dodging calls from her mom ever since heading to meet the USS *Brady,* knowing her mother would want to know she'd made the trip safely. She'd have to call home when she touched down in Cape Cod, though, as she didn't want her mother to worry herself sick.

Danny took her hand between his and held it quietly until she looked his way.

"At least she admits she wasn't cut out to be a mother," he reminded her. "I hope you remember that when she's knocking your work. Maybe she just doesn't know how to offer maternal support."

"I know." She smiled, liking Danny far too much. He was a whole lot more than the defiant, bohemian rocker she remembered. In fact, he wasn't really much like she'd recalled at all. But there was still an intense attraction between them, along with their mutual need to put their mark on the world outside of familial expectations.

But then, they'd gotten to know each other better the last two days than they had in that sex-crazed fling they'd had in New York five years ago. She now understood his inherent sense of honor, his fierce work ethic—no matter how laid-back he sometimes seemed—and the gentle soul underneath it all who still played guitar like nobody's business. She'd sat beside him on the deck again the night before—he'd played for at least an hour and they'd both been completely lost in the music.

"What about *your* mom? I read a little bit about your family online, but there isn't as much about her." She was curious about the Murphys and wondered if she would fit into the group this week. "You've talked about how competitive your brothers are… Is she as driven as the rest of your family?"

What if his family didn't like the idea of her seeking him out after all this time, especially after she'd accidentally ignored his attempts to contact her? Guilt pinched. Sure, Danny's mother had seemed pleased that he'd have someone to meet him at the dock, but what would she think about them continuing a relationship? She squeezed Danny's hand tighter as the plane wobbled on a patch of turbulence and new doubts set in.

"I wouldn't call my mom driven." Danny leaned over to fasten her seat belt for her, reminding her that the luxurious leather chairs weren't just for looks and that she and Danny were still suspended over the Atlantic for this trip. "She's the real rock beneath dad's ambition, the glue that holds the whole thing together. My father is a scrapper who came from a poor family, and he was sort of blown away when he met my mom as a teenager. They eloped when her parents didn't approve of him. I'm pretty sure he's been trying to impress her for the last thirty-some years by growing a global business out of nothing more than ingenuity and hard work."

"Oh, my God. That's so romantic." She hugged her arms around herself and turned to face him, tucking her legs beneath her so that her skirt fell over the edge of the chair. "I can't imagine being so swept away by love that you just turn your back on everything else to pursue it."

"No?" Danny frowned, his expression turning pensive. "I guess I never thought about how well that worked out for them. They didn't hesitate. Didn't wait around for the perfect opportunity."

She thought he might explain what he was thinking, but he settled back and seemed lost in his own world until the pilot announced they should be past the turbulence in another few minutes.

Closing her eyes while she waited for the wobbling airplane to still, Stephanie hoped that this would be the only bumpy ride they took while Danny was home for the next few weeks. Their time together was too short to waste a single moment.

DANNY FORGOT ALL ABOUT the turbulence, thinking about the way his dad had acted without delay to be with the woman he loved. For some reason, Danny had always assumed that times were simpler back then and that the path to eloping had been more clear-cut because it was the 1970s. But that was the era of the sexual revolution. Women's rights. Maybe it hadn't been easy at all and Dad had pulled it off because Mom was just that damn important to him.

Weird to think about that now, as an adult, with a different perspective from when he'd heard the story as a kid. The elopement had always been just another scrap of Murphy family lore. Now? Danny admired the hell out of his dad for knowing what he wanted and going after it.

Danny had known Stephanie was special five years ago. So why had he been content to let her go with a wave and a grin after the incredible five days they'd spent together? Sure, he'd figured he'd call her when she came back home, but he'd let her slip through his fingers, leaving her vulnerable to...

Crap. The old guilt resurfaced with a vengeance. Especially considering how they'd left things at the time....

STEPHANIE LAY BESIDE him after they'd hit the high note for the fourth time that day. Or was it the fifth?

Depended on if you counted what they'd done in the shower near her condo's pool. They'd been so close to finishing when they'd heard voices outside.

"I can't believe I have to leave in two days." She sighed as she pulled the female superhero sheets up to her chin.

Her furnishings were the eclectic mix of a graduate student. A glitzy, mirrored chest of drawers was covered in old-fashioned crystal perfume bottles, and framed prints of old movie posters were surrounded by ticket stubs from local shows. Of course, Stephanie was a dichotomy, too. Sexy and sensual, but down-to-earth and completely unpretentious. He couldn't believe he hadn't left her place since he'd arrived three days ago.

He was ignoring all his calls and had missed a practice with the band. But who wouldn't if they had a chance with her?

"I wish it was me who was going," he admitted, sharing a wish he'd never told anyone else.

"Seriously?" She propped her head on her hand, balanced on one elbow. The red piece of licorice he'd tied around her wrist like a bracelet earlier slid down her arm and he looked forward to eating it off her soon. "You wouldn't mind heading into a war zone?"

His gut tightened when he thought of her over there. "I've always figured it would be cool to serve. You know that old parable about to him much is given, much is expected?" He shrugged, not sure how to explain it any better than that. "I've been given a hell of a lot."

Her blue eyes turned thoughtful. More serious than usual. "I just want to get away. Christina was looking for volunteers and I jumped. I thought I'd never win the slot to film her interviews, but it turns out that most people at the news magazine where I intern have families. None of them wanted to go overseas. So the next thing I knew, the job was mine."

He realized they'd have an interpreter. Understood that Christina was well-schooled in politics and journalism even if Stephanie was a young film student without a lot of experience. Still…the idea of her over there bothered him. Tough to say why, when they'd only known each other briefly. All along she'd been open about the fact that she just wanted to have fun right up until she left on Friday.

"At least you'll be conducting interviews from a well-secured base, right?" He couldn't ignore the creepy feeling crawling up his back, a spidery chill despite the warmth of his body from their sensual exertions.

"So I hear." She smiled that wry half grin of hers that always made him feel like he was part of an inside joke. "But if you'd rather move in and be my sex toy for the year, maybe I can sell my plane ticket to someone else."

She palmed his thigh and started a slow stroke upward, her gaze never leaving his. His body stirred automatically, no matter the dark thoughts stirring around his brain.

"Sex toy?" He traced her mouth with one finger, dipping between her lips until she closed her eyes and drew on the digit. "I wouldn't give it up for a whole year without a commitment. I think you'd have to elope with me."

Her eyes popped wide and she let go of his thigh to grip his wrist and squeeze the finger he'd been teasing her with.

"Oh, really?" She nodded slowly. "A Vegas wedding. I can see it now—you in a tacky Hawaiian shirt and the free high-roller Ray-Bans from our motel. Me in a feathered showgirl outfit with the big headdress instead of a veil."

"We'd need an Elvis impersonator," he added.

"That'd be the chaplain, of course." She shimmied seductively beneath the sheet that covered her. "And afterward, I'd give you a VIP lap dance worthy of the showgirl outfit."

He clamped a hand on her hip and pinned her to the bed with his thigh over hers.

"We are going to seriously consider this plan...."

BLINKING HIS WAY OUT of the memory and back to the private plane bound for Cape Cod, Danny wished they truly had considered the long-ago plan. What might their lives have been like if they'd talked each other into one more crazy day together, capped by a trip to Vegas?

Instead, she'd risked her life and come home with scars she kept hidden—the kind on the inside that she hadn't really shared with him yet. And he'd altered his path for good so that now he didn't have the freedom that he used to, his future committed to the navy. Should he even try to tell her how he felt about her? Make a bid for her even though he'd be on a ship for three quarters of every year until he moved up in rank?

Or just enjoy the moment as he had the first time they'd met, leaving her free to find a guy who wouldn't be gone all the time?

The answers weren't as obvious to him as they had been even two days ago. He just knew he couldn't allow her to be hurt again, even if that meant letting her go at the end of his three-week stint at home.

While his head throbbed with the need for answers, the turbulence settled. Unfastening her seat belt, Stephanie got up to explore the plane and his iPhone chimed with the tone reserved for an incoming video call.

He checked the ID and saw it was his younger brother, Kyle. He answered, watching as Kyle's face filled the screen, a blur of blue, black and white behind him. Danny recognized the Phantoms' locker room from the din of guys shouting as much as the oversize logo on a wall in the background.

"Hey, bro!" Kyle shouted into the phone in an attempt to be heard over the noise around him.

An NHL hockey star, Kyle had just started training camp with the Philadelphia Phantoms after leading them to the Stanley Cup the year before.

"Hey, yourself." Danny smiled over at Stephanie to let her know the call wasn't private. "It's just my kid brother," he told her. "Want to say hi?"

She nodded, but she lowered her voice. "You're allowed to use a cell phone on the plane?"

"One of many joys of a private plane." He flipped his phone around to let her greet the family runt. Okay, the beast who was bigger than all of them except for Axel.

"Hi, Danny's brother," she greeted him, waving at the device. "Nice to meet you."

Danny gave his brother a second to say hello, then turned the screen around to continue the call.

Kyle pantomimed a silent "wow," no doubt recognizing Stephanie as the woman Danny had nearly lost his mind over five years ago. At least the rest of the family should have been warned since Danny had given his mother the green light to tell people that he'd be coming home with Stephanie.

"So what's up? Still practicing this late in the day?" He knew the Phantoms usually did their team skate in the mornings during the preseason, but the guys he glimpsed around Kyle appeared to be in practice uniforms.

"Double practice today since coach says we got all soft over the summer." Kyle shoved another player who was joking around, pretending to take his phone away. "Ax and I just finished up."

"Hey, Danny." Axel Rankin, their Finnish foster brother, stuck his head in front of the camera for a second. Big and dark-haired, he blended right in with the rest of the brothers except for the Nordic blue eyes. "Welcome home, dude."

"Thanks, man. Good to be here." In fact, he was looking forward to returning to the family's home in Chatham, Massachusetts, more than he had in a long time, no doubt because he had Stephanie by his side this time. "Are you guys going to make it home for the party?"

Kyle's face returned to the screen, his helmet off and his hair sweaty. "Assuming you send the jet to Philadelphia next, definitely. You're not the only one with a hot chick to introduce to the clan."

"So I hear. I'm looking forward to meeting Marissa and Jennifer." Kyle's live-in girlfriend, Marissa, was a matchmaker and the daughter of former pop diva Brandy Collins. Selfishly, he was hoping to meet the singer sometime, since her music was the real deal— gutsy and personal.

Axel, in the meantime, had started seeing a filmmaker from New York who'd relocated to Philly over the summer to be with him. Jennifer Hunter had made a lot of indie films, but she'd met his brother when she filmed a documentary series on the Phantoms that was a lock for a few awards. Danny had seen the series on TV while he was deployed and had been impressed. Plus, it'd been like hanging out with the hockey team for those few months while they made their run for the Stanley Cup.

"And we can't wait to meet Stephanie," Axel said

from behind Kyle, giving Danny the thumbs-up sign. "You'll be happy to know the nose job you gave Kyle five years ago has been redone." He pointed to Kyle's schnoz. "That fight he got in on the ice last spring straightened it right out."

"Uh, yeah." Danny had no desire to discuss the nose incident in front of Stephanie. Why the hell had they brought that up when she was around? "Looks good."

Kyle must have felt the same way because he elbowed Axel in the gut hard enough to make the Finn back up a step.

"Not a big deal, either way," Kyle assured him. "We just wanted to let you know we'll be there tomorrow, but we might be a little late, okay? Welcome home, my brother."

The simple words damn near choked him up. Kyle had never said much about the time Danny broke his nose after a fairly innocuous comment about Stephanie, but the fact that he'd left his nose cockeyed for years afterward had made Danny feel like crap. The guy had played professional hockey for years without half the damage his own brother had inflicted. And wasn't that a testament to how whacked out he'd been after Stephanie was taken?

"Thanks. We'll be looking for you tomorrow, and make sure Axel knows I'm going to be thinking up embarrassing stories about him to let slip in front of his new woman, okay?"

Kyle grinned and said, "You owe him" at the same

time Axel shouted from somewhere behind him, "Hey! What did I do?"

But Kyle disconnected, leaving Danny with a darkened screen and the certainty that Stephanie's gaze lingered on him.

She cleared her throat while he was thinking about what to say.

"I could pretend I didn't overhear a thing," she said finally. "If that makes it easier for you. I don't have any siblings to tell embarrassing stories about me, so I have kind of an unfair advantage."

"No kidding," he shot back drily. "I wish I could say that Axel was the only one of us who is ridiculously blunt and lacking subtlety, but it runs in the family."

"They seemed glad to have you home." Her voice took on a wistful note, and he remembered that no matter how many times his brothers threw him under the bus for dumb stuff about his past, he wouldn't trade them for anything.

"I miss hanging out with them. An-n-n-nd, just to get it out of the way, I broke Kyle's nose when I threw a punch at him." He'd regretted it almost instantly, and the remorse had stretched out over the years. "It wasn't that long after you were released. I came home between training stints, and he helped me pack up my stuff. I was still mad at the world for what happened to you—the news reports were vague and I couldn't figure out what anyone was doing to go after the people who took you."

He'd been climbing the walls and being at home

didn't help. At least on duty, he was busy every second of the day.

"The State Department asked me not to give interviews at first. They really wanted to control the flow of information until they investigated some leads." Taking her seat beside him again, she reached for the bottled water kept in a minirefrigerator beneath the coffee table. "Would you like one?"

Nodding, he accepted a drink now that the turbulence seemed to have passed. They would be starting their descent into a private airfield outside Chatham soon.

"It makes sense, but at the time…" He shook his head. "I was edgy. Tense. Pissed off in general. Anyway, Kyle was on a mission to make me look on the bright side, which was a truly bad plan. At one point when I snapped at him, he said something about me wearing my heart on my sleeve—"

The precise words escaped him now. Basically, he was mad at himself and he took it out on Kyle for pointing out the obvious.

"It sounded to me like he forgave you a long time ago," Stephanie said between sips. "I mean, the way he talked about it on the phone made it sound like the broken nose was a nonissue for him."

Danny shrugged. "Maybe. God knows, hockey players break their beaks all the time. But it's one thing to get blindsided by a puck. Another to field a blow from your own blood."

If it unsettled her to learn that he'd been a walking

time bomb when she'd been abducted, she didn't show it. Instead, she narrowed her gaze, a wicked gleam in her eyes.

"So what kind of dirt do you have on Axel in exchange?" She smiled and he hoped maybe he was in the clear.

He planned to focus on helping put her past behind her this week, not dredging up his.

"Are you kidding? The Finn is a gold mine for stories. When he was learning English, we taught him all the curse words first. Nearly got him kicked out of school."

"Hmm. That story might make the rest of you look worse than him."

"Hey, I wasn't the one who told the math teacher that his trig lecture was the biggest bullshit ever." He flipped on one of the TV screens broadcasting the plane's progress with an updated arrival time and saw they'd be landing in fifteen minutes.

He wasn't sure if he would be grateful to touch down for the sake of ending an awkward conversation, or very worried that returning home would only initiate a whole bunch of other ones. No doubt his family would all want to know what was up with his renewed relationship with Stephanie.

"Sounds like you'll have plenty to talk about." She recapped her water bottle and set it on the table as the plane continued its descent. She hesitated for a moment, then blurted, "And for what it's worth, I'm sorry that I didn't make an effort to get in touch with you after I came home. I really regret missing out on your calls."

"It's not like we made plans to see each other again," he said. He'd been a dumb ass. Why the hell hadn't he locked down some kind of commitment from her before she left? "I'm sure you were overwhelmed. There were probably a lot of other people who wanted to hear from you besides me."

She shook her head. "Not really. My mother was so ill, I spent all my time at the hospital."

That's right. She'd been with the compulsive mom who'd gotten so involved with the drama of the kidnapping, she'd made herself sick.

"I hate it that you escaped one nightmare and came home to another." Danny knew he shouldn't pass judgment on that whole debacle, but damn. Someone should have been comforting Stephanie instead of the other way around.

"Yeah." Slowly, she nodded. Something about her expression struck him as more serious than he'd ever seen her. "Me, too. But you know what?" She slid her feet back into a pair of blue flip-flops with big yellow plastic flowers on the strap. "I feel better knowing you were mad on my behalf."

He raised an eyebrow, unsure where she was going with that.

"I mean," she added quickly, "don't get me wrong, I'm sorry for your brother that he got hurt. But I had to keep the story quiet for so long that I missed seeing anyone be outraged about what happened to me.

My father was scared for my mom. Mom was ill. And when my book came out to finally share what happened, the media focused on such a small facet of the experience that the rest of the ordeal got lost. So, to hear you say that you were upset about what happened to me... In a weird way it makes me feel like I wasn't alone back then."

She spoke quickly, as if she was used to not dwelling on that time in her life. Yet maybe shoving the past behind her so fast hadn't been such a good idea after all. He hadn't planned to let her see how much her captivity had made him crazy, hoping they'd be able to move forward. But what if her mother's ordeal when Stephanie came home had robbed her of the chance to come to terms with what had happened to her? Maybe she deserved to know how freaked out he'd been.

Danny took her hand, shifting his focus for these next few weeks together. He was no shrink, but he knew enough about human nature to know that bottling up the dark stuff inside probably wasn't helpful. Perhaps he wasn't doing her any favors by trying to move past the event that redirected both their lives so dramatically.

"Outrage only scratches the surface of what I felt." For the first time he didn't try to hide the fury that ruled his life that whole year of her abduction. "When I heard you were taken, I was ready to swim the Atlantic with a knife between my teeth to get you back myself. I didn't sleep for weeks."

She looked ready to interrupt, to thank him for his

concern and be done with it, but he didn't think about that time too often himself, and this wasn't a topic he was willing to revisit.

Now or never.

"I was a walking powder keg when I didn't know what was happening to you," he continued, remembering vague arguments he got into with everyone around him. "My father and brothers traveled a lot, meeting with powerful people we knew in the Middle East through the resort business to see if a ransom would help you and Christina."

"She was family," Stephanie said haltingly. "That only makes sense."

"For me, it was about *you*." Sure, he loved Christina like a sister, but he'd been focused on Stephanie, knowing Christina had the whole rest of his family looking out for her. He'd only suffered through the "diplomatic channels" crap because he thought it might help them. "I was less than diplomatic in those meetings—" Calling a sheikh a lying bastard hadn't been his wisest move. "I just really needed to find out if you were okay."

Looking back, he was lucky it hadn't caused an international incident. The Murphys were damn fortunate to get that meeting in the first place. It had been their last hope for trying to arrange a private negotiation with the insurgents who held Christina and Stephanie.

Now, Stephanie studied Danny as if she'd never seen

him before, as if trying to make this glimpse of his dark side fit with her understanding of him.

"My brothers had to take over the negotiations." Actually, both Ryan and Jack had wrestled him out of there, and even then, they nearly hadn't been able to hold him back. The fact that Danny hadn't slept and had hardly eaten for three weeks had ultimately made him easier to subdue despite his fury. He'd been completely depleted and living on adrenaline by then. "At the end of the day, I decided negotiation was a lost cause and that I'd rather fight for you."

He'd still wanted to put his knife between his teeth and sneak into Baghdad himself. But his brothers had convinced him he might be in the way of well-trained specialists who actually knew what they were doing.

So he'd done the next best thing.

"I flew home and signed a navy contract." He figured he'd at least be able to support the war effort somewhere. His brother Jack was so concerned for his mental health that he'd joined the service, too.

"My God," she said softly, breathing the words more than saying them out loud.

His laid-back image was shot. And he'd probably lost whatever chance he had with her now that she understood what a basket case he'd become back then. "Don't ever think for a second that no one was outraged on your behalf. If I'd had my way, I would have scoured Baghdad until I found you or died trying."

8

"IF YOU HAVE SECOND thoughts about being here, I understand." Danny sat next to her in the luxurious BMW sedan that had been waiting for them, his voice sounding stilted. "You've been quiet since we landed."

She hadn't said much since he'd revealed his real reaction to her kidnapping. She was too busy trying to figure out what it meant that he'd cared about her a great deal more than she'd ever realized. Why hadn't the PR agency she'd hired to handle her reader letters forwarded the note from Danny? It bothered her to think she'd missed something personal from him.

More than that, it unsettled her to realize how much her kidnapping had affected him. He'd tried to help her behind the scenes and she'd never known it, making her regret all the more that she hadn't looked him up sooner. It also made the fling she wanted a heck of a lot more complicated since there were deeper feelings at stake.

"I'm right where I want to be." She couldn't walk away from Danny now, not when she was on the verge of healing a wound she'd had for years.

Danny's grip on the steering wheel tightened as he took a hard turn to the right, bringing them closer to Nantucket Sound, according to the signs.

"But you…seem anxious. Worried."

She peered over at him as he drove, his sculpted muscles a feast for the eyes, his green gaze fixed on the road.

He was so much more intense than she'd realized five years ago. So much…more. She'd been crazy about him back then, enjoying every second of their time together. But the wild, no-strings sex and doing things like licking raspberry dessert sauce off each other's bodies had only been a playful prelude to the deeper connection brewing between them now.

"Not worried. Just thinking," she said, trying to keep her voice light. "I realized that it's sort of unrealistic of me to think we can re-create the kind of affair we had before."

He was silent for a long minute. She cracked her window to breathe in the scent of the salty air as they neared the water.

"Stephanie, nothing you want is unrealistic." He took his eyes off the road as they stopped at a street sign. Leveling a look at her across the console, he took her breath away with the heat in his gaze. "If you're really ready for that kind of no-holds-barred, can't-get-enough physical encounter, I will put the pedal to the floor right now and have us both naked in a matter of minutes."

Her heart rate kicked into high gear even if the car didn't. Heat rushed…everywhere.

"But what about seeing your family?" she finally managed to ask, the words catching awkwardly in her dry throat.

"They will give us some privacy to get settled today if we don't head to the main house. We'll lock the door to the gatehouse and won't leave until it's time for the party tomorrow."

He didn't move the car, probably because there was no one behind them anyhow. They seemed to have reached a quiet access road with just a few houses up ahead.

And yes, she was probably stalling, taking a sudden interest in the view while the temperature ratcheted up in the vehicle.

"Oh. Really?" She forced herself to turn toward him again, to confront her feelings and figure out what she truly wanted.

Against all better judgment, her eyes zeroed in on his mouth and she thought about the many ways he'd pleasured her the last two days without ever finding completion himself. Maybe he needed this physical release as badly as she did. Why overthink the situation when they were both ready to come out of their skin?

"Really. But don't think about that. Just tell me what you'd like. Leave. Stay. Lock yourself in a house with me for twenty-four hours. Anything you want—it's yours." He didn't touch her, didn't sway her with a brush of his fingertips or a graze of his knee.

He just waited. Watched.

If she sat here much longer the windows would start steaming from the heat rolling off her skin.

"I don't think I need twenty-four whole hours," she began, her words halting as she tried to force them out. "Maybe just a little time alone to—" she paused meaningfully, unable to put exactly what she wanted in words "—be together. For real. To see this connection through to its natural completion."

The car was in motion before she finished speaking.

"Then I'm right there with you." There was a new conviction in his voice, a certainty and a commitment to the plan. "We'll take as much time as you want. But I've got to warn you, I'm wired tight. I don't know how long I can make this last the first time."

His frank admission—while they were still in a moving vehicle and hadn't even started taking off their clothes—told her a lot. This was really happening.

She didn't even see the scenery outside, couldn't think about anything except what was going to happen when they arrived at their destination.

"That's okay. I'm pretty wired, too. It seems like every time we've messed around the last two days, I peak faster."

He took a hard right turn and shut off the ignition. His eyes slid to hers, a sly grin on his face.

"I thought that was because my technique was improving."

"I think it's because I can't stop fantasizing about going all the way." Her dreams of him had been full-blown sensual scenarios that felt deliciously real. "It's like being a teenage virgin all over again."

Vaguely, she realized they must have arrived at their destination. She couldn't pull her attention away from him long enough to look.

"Only now, you're going to be satisfied by a man who knows what he's doing and not some clueless twit."

"Who says my first time was with a clueless twit?" she teased.

"You have your fantasies. I have mine." He withdrew the keys from the ignition and handed them to her. "The house key is the red one. If you get the door, I'll get the bags and we'll have what we both want all the faster."

He pressed the keys into her palm without touching her and she was pretty sure he'd kept his hands to himself on purpose. He hadn't been kidding about being wired.

Her pulse pounded. She could feel it thrum everywhere, an insistent internal beat that urged her on. Soon, they were going to be together.

"Okay." Her fingers closed around the cool metal. "Deal."

Levering herself out of the car before he could even think about getting her door for her, Stephanie practically sprinted up the cobblestone walkway. The weathered cedar-and-stone structure had been built in a bungalow style with multiple roof peaks and dormers, plus a cute second-level deck. She reached the entryway door and slid open the lock, letting herself inside while Danny retrieved the small suitcases they'd brought.

She'd tried having sex two years ago during her failed relationship with Josh, but it had been awful. It wasn't necessarily his fault, but she'd thought about Danny nonstop and ultimately known she was with the wrong guy. Of course, she'd been so slow to admit that to herself that she'd missed the opportunity to be with Danny on his last visit home. Her timing had been all wrong. Or, more likely, she was just slow getting herself together after her abduction. There'd been the year of nightmares, the fear of the dark, the counseling, the debacle of the book...

Now, she was where she needed to be.

She'd found the light switch and flipped it on when he came into the foyer behind her. Her longtime fantasy, come to life.

He bolted the door and took the keys from her, setting them on a window ledge in the living room, which was decorated in white and neutrals with a few dark wood pieces. A pair of old oars hung above a small stone fireplace. Antique snowshoes stood in the corner near the kitchen.

"You'll warn me if you want to stop," he told her, his voice low in her ear as one hand slid beneath the white cotton peasant blouse she wore. His palm was warm on her skin, his touch possessive.

"I won't want to stop." She swayed slightly, mesmerized by the thought of being with him.

Of ending a five-year dry spell that had made her fear she'd never feel this way again.

He turned her in his arms to face him. His green eyes burned right through her until she thought she'd go up in flames before they ever got to enjoy this time together.

"But if you need to, or if you have any worries—"

"I will warn you. I promise." Her heart squeezed tight at his need to make that point very clear.

His nod was so quick she almost didn't see it before he leaned down to take her mouth. She swooned like an old-time Southern belle, her knees going out from under her as she sank into him. Slipping her arms around his neck, she tried to anchor herself against the hard, muscular length of him.

He groaned and the sound echoed everything she was feeling. She knew she could lose herself in the moment. He'd proven it multiple times to her over the past two days. Now, she could simply enjoy sex like a normal, red-blooded woman.

There was no better gift he could have given her.

"Upstairs," he managed to say between kisses. "Come with me."

"I plan on it." She released him and took his hand, following his steps as he turned a corner and climbed a staircase to the second level.

Dark hardwood floors were covered with a few woven rugs, while overhead the exposed ceiling beams were painted white. A few windows were open to let fresh sea breezes inside, as if someone had readied the place for Danny's return. She hoped that whoever had prepped it didn't mind waiting a little longer to see him. After five years, she refused to feel guilty about claiming dibs on him first.

They reached a large bedroom that overlooked the water in the distance. Big elms brushed up against the deck outside, the close branches making her feel as if they were in a tree house.

He took his shirt off and any fanciful tree house thoughts vanished. He was hard everywhere, his abs chiseled into rows that led her eye downward to more rock-solid body. His need for her could not have been more obvious. Or more gratifying.

She walked toward him, flicking open the top button on her skirt along the way. His gaze followed the movement, zeroing in on the small patch of bare skin she exposed.

"Let me," he coaxed, his hands reaching for the next button. "I want to undress you."

A shiver went through her at the scratchy roughness of his voice, the throaty rasp that made her feel as if he was dying of thirst and she was the drink.

"I'd like that." She rocked her hips from side to side, edging the garment down a little more without ever touching it.

Her thighs brushed together, adding to the ache between her legs that had been growing since they'd been in the car. He hooked a finger in the *V* of the open placket and tugged her closer by the material. She stepped out of her flip-flops on the way. His shoes were already gone. She knew because they brushed toes on the carpet.

And then his fingers were spearing through her hair, cupping the back of her neck so he could cradle her head. He held her steady while he kissed the ever-loving daylights out of her. She was pretty sure she saw stars.

By the time he eased back, her skirt was on the ground and her blouse was falling off her shoulders. She shifted her body to nudge it the rest of the way down until she wore nothing more than a matching yellow lace bra and panties. Sunlight spilled over her, making patterns of shadowed leaves against her skin while Danny bent to trace the edges of the moving outlines with his tongue.

A fierce longing pierced her and she tightened her grip on his shoulders, running her fingers around his back.

"I can't get enough of you," he murmured against the swell of her breast.

"No. It's me who can't get enough of you, and I've waited so long." Already, the coiled heat in her core tightened, her body more than ready for the kind of pleasure he could give her. "Please say you brought protection?"

"Taken care of." He lifted his head and gripped her shoulders, steering her backward toward a queen-size bed with a thick white duvet. "Right front pocket."

She grinned as she dipped her fingers into the place he indicated.

"I've been wanting to get into your shorts." She withdrew two condoms and tossed them on the bed. "Now I'm finally enjoying my chance."

She reached for the fly to unfasten it, but he held her hand in place before she could.

"Actually, this can't be your chance or I'm going to lose it before we get started." He withdrew his grip from her wrist before she even began to worry about being restrained.

But then, he was so thoughtful of her, he'd probably already taken that into account.

"Tell me what I can do," she urged. "I just want to touch you somewhere. Anywhere."

He lifted her palms to his shoulders and left them there. She flexed her fingers, digging into his skin just a little. He reached around her back to unfasten her bra and she let go of him just long enough for him to pull the straps down her arms. Then, her hands were right back where he'd wanted them.

His attention shifted lower, and he dragged her panties down her legs until they fell to the floor. He tucked his hands under her butt to lift her onto the bed, parting her thighs to make room for himself between them. By now, she was so ready for him she tugged him closer to her. He made quick work of his shorts, only pausing for a second to be sure the zipper cleared his erection before they were off.

Her fingers danced down his arms, unable to stay

still, wanting to wrap around the thick length of what he'd revealed. Instead, she waited, seeing the expression on his face as he reached for a condom and rolled it on.

The waiting was costing him. He handled himself very carefully, as if too much friction could send him hurtling toward a finish. She wanted to be the cause of that finish. And she wanted to feel him inside her when they both reached that moment.

DANNY WATCHED Stephanie, her blue eyes taking in all of him as he tried his damnedest to get the condom in place without losing it. But it felt as if he'd been waiting for this moment for five years, not two days. That, on top of being out at sea for six months, meant his control was nonexistent.

Gritting his teeth, he finished the task and allowed himself a look at her naked body spread out before him. She was so gorgeous. So immersed in the moment and the pleasure she didn't have any reservations.

That alone made him want to roar in victory and bury himself deep inside her.

He gripped her waist, moving her hips closer to his where he stood at the edge of the bed. Her breathing was so fast her breasts lifted with each inhalation. Her thighs hugged his as if to draw him near.

Then, he couldn't hold back another second. He nudged the slick heat of her core, her body yielding sweetly to his. He gripped her legs, steering her right where he wanted her as a fierce urgency took hold.

Lights flashed behind his eyes. Her body gripped his, squeezing gently. He bit his lip until he tasted blood, wanting to wait another minute.

Or at least wanting to wait for her…

Remembering the way she liked to be touched best, he reached between their bodies and stroked her lightly, circling her taut sex with the pad of his thumb. She must have been wound almost as tight as him because her body convulsed almost immediately, the spasms wracking her even as they melted into him.

He came hard, moments after, their shouts lost in a sea of pillows as he collapsed on top of her, careful to keep his weight on his arms so she didn't feel restrained. He shuddered again and again, his body barely under his control anymore. She felt so damn good. So perfect.

So *his*.

The spasms went on for a long time, his and hers. Just when he thought the after-tremors were done, some small inner squeeze of her body triggered another response from his.

Sometime afterward, he fell onto his side next to her, turning her in his arms so they faced each other. He wanted her again with the same insatiable need he'd felt for her so long ago, only this was even more insistent.

This new need had been compounded with a possessiveness born the day he'd learned she was taken. It was almost as if those hellish weeks of thinking about her obsessively, praying for her return and basically losing his mind had created a cavernous hole in his chest that only she could fill. Now, she was here, filling that gap for the first time.

He was happy as hell.

As long as he didn't think about the fact that the very same spot would be ripped open all over again in three weeks. He didn't have a clue how he'd let her go. So right now, he planned to hold on tight and enjoy the ride.

"DANNY?"

The urgent whisper woke him. Stephanie was still in his arms and quiet for long moments afterward, so he thought he'd just dreamed her saying his name.

Muted light from a wall sconce in the hallway filtered through the open door across the bed. He guessed it was around midnight. They'd ordered a pizza a few hours ago and he'd played his guitar until she fell asleep listening to him. It had been the perfect night. He'd told her about his work aboard the USS *Brady* and she'd told him more about her time overseas. Not the kidnapping, but the better memories that came before it—meeting locals in the rural parts of southern Iraq before she'd traveled into the city of Baghdad.

Now, her hair fanned out along the pillowcase like an inky tattoo. Sleeping in one of his old T-shirts, she lay with one hand tucked under her cheek and the other resting lightly on his bicep. He still couldn't believe she was here with him after all this time.

"Danny!" Suddenly, she squeezed his arm hard, her

eyes flying open to stare at him in the scant light, her body tense.

"I'm right here." He smoothed a touch along her shoulder and down her back. "You're safe."

She blinked a few times, coming more fully awake. Slowly, the tension in her eased. He tucked the blankets around her on one side and tucked her against him on the other.

"Sorry." She rested her head on the pillow again, a pink daisy earring glinting as she shifted. "Did I wake you?"

"Not really. I'd just closed my eyes." He tipped his forehead to hers, already imagining what it would be like to wake up to her on a permanent basis. "Did you have a nightmare?"

"No." Her soft, sleep-husky voice wrapped around him. "Sometimes I startle easily or have little moments of panic. They're not bad anymore. It probably only happened because I'm sleeping somewhere different."

Yet she'd called out for him, even in her sleep. New possessiveness surged through him, making him more determined than ever to show her how good they could be together.

"You want to…talk about it?" He was rough in the sensitive-conversation department, but for her, he made an effort. He'd seen enough guys screwed up by combat in the navy to know that talking about past traumas was better than stuffing it all down inside and pretending it never happened.

"No. I've discussed the kidnapping with a therapist

and I'm...solid as I can be with what happened." Her hand settled on his chest, her fingers skimming light patterns over his skin. "But thank you."

He searched for something to say, something to take her mind off whatever it was that sent her into panic mode.

"Can I ask you something else then?" He liked the way she touched him, the light caresses straying over his shoulder and down the inside of his arm before jumping back to his chest.

"Mmm?"

"What made you start photographing pets?"

Her touch paused for a moment. Then started again, slower.

"My mother is still upset that I haven't gotten back to my so-called real job, filming news video," she began, her frustration evident.

"Hey." He captured her fingers and brought them to his lips to kiss. "I'm not judging. I think it's a great career. I'm just curious how you made the switch."

"You know I got into the news media because I wanted to travel. See the world. Make a difference." They'd talked about her dreams when they'd met the first time. "But there isn't much call for objective reporting anymore. The media is so entertainment-driven that I didn't enjoy it."

"So you left the old job after you wrote your book." He knew the timeline of that first year after she came home since he'd been keeping tabs on her from a distance. "I remember hearing you volunteered at a counseling center, too."

"My therapist thought it might help. I guess a lot of people are healed by helping others after the kind of ordeal I had, but it had the opposite effect on me. It really brought me down."

"You're a sensitive person."

She shrugged and her fingers resumed their light motion across his chest.

"Maybe that was part of it. But I met a volunteer at the counseling center who brought in therapy animals—cats, dogs, goats, you name it."

"Cool."

"One day she brought a therapy donkey—I kid you not, a donkey." The happiness of the memory was evident in her voice. "Her name was Buttercup and the therapist had an old straw hat that she put on the donkey's head. It was so cute I had to take a photo."

"And your talent became evident." He liked hearing about good things that had happened to her since her return. He'd spent so long feeling a burning in his chest every time he thought of her that this new insight soothed some of his old fears where she was concerned.

"Kind of. I liked the photos and when I showed them to the therapist, she asked if she could use them in an advertisement. Soon, I had developed a word-of-mouth business on the side. The more I photographed pets, the more I enjoyed it." She pressed a kiss against his shoulder. "There is a warmth and acceptance from animals that relaxed me in a way no other form of therapy had. Besides, I was good at it."

"So you started your own business." He couldn't ignore the feel of her lips on his skin, her kiss igniting fresh heat even though he'd planned to let her go back to sleep.

"Exactly." Another kiss followed, her mouth hot and moist.

His heart rate jacked up. And that wasn't the only thing elevating.

"Steph." He gripped her shoulder, holding her at arm's length. Meeting her gaze in the dimness.

"Yes?" A mischievous light danced in her eyes.

"You know you're winding me up over here."

"Thank goodness." She grinned. "I thought I was losing my touch."

With a growl in his throat, he reeled her closer, fitting her body to his. He cupped the base of her neck, tilting her toward him for a kiss and much, much more.

9

STEPHANIE AWOKE TO banging from outside. Still half asleep, she wondered if the siding was getting ripped off the house or if someone had decided to bulldoze the place down.

"Danny!" She clasped his arm, bolting upright in bed. "What is that?"

He moved slower, his eyes still not open.

"Brothers," he muttered.

What the hell?

Shrugging off the last vestiges of sleep, she listened more carefully. The *bang, bang, banging* became clearer. Almost as if a small army had descended on the gatehouse and decided to pound on every side.

"Football in five!" a deep male voice shouted. The sound seemed to emanate from just below the second-floor deck off the bedroom. "Don't make us come in there, bro."

"Are they serious?" Stephanie realized she and

Danny were both naked and definitely not in any position for company. The bedroom was a whirlwind of discarded clothes and tangled sheets.

Downstairs was no better, she recalled, since they'd made a late-night snack, then ended up feasting on each other on the dining room table.

"As a heart attack." Danny yanked back the covers and stood. "Sorry about this, Steph. I'll go knock their heads together so you can go back to sleep."

She glanced at the clock, shocked to discover it was ten in the morning. There was a brief respite from the pounding outside and the quiet seemed to vibrate.

"Actually, that's okay. I can't believe how late I slept." She'd meant to awaken early to walk along the beach and get her head on straight before she met his family. She was nervous and unsure how they'd feel about her coming into his life again—especially now that she'd discovered he had gone a little crazy when she'd been kidnapped. What must his mom think of her not returning his calls afterward?

A chant started outside. Deep male voices shouted in unison. "Murph, Murph, Murph."

Danny swore at their persistence, barreling into a pair of shorts so he could pry open the French doors and holler at them from the deck. "What the hell kind of welcome home is that?"

"Danny lives!" someone shouted and Stephanie recognized the Finnish foster brother's accent. There were some catcalls and wolf whistles over his half-dressed state, but all the voices sounded good-natured, and she was certain the guys were happy to see their brother.

Hugging the covers tighter to herself, she admired the muscles in Danny's back as he braced his arms on the deck railing to lean over and shout down to them.

"No thanks to you all. You nearly gave me a heart attack shaking the damn gatehouse. Go away until I get dressed."

When he turned around to come back inside, he was grinning.

"If you'd like to play football, it would give me time to clean up before I meet everyone." While she didn't think the rowdy Murphy males would really raid the gatehouse to retrieve their brother, she'd also rather not take any chances.

"You sure?" He frowned. "I brought you here to spend time with you."

A smile warmed her on the inside. "Thank you, but I'll be fine. Your family hasn't seen you in six months. I know they're eager to hang out with you, too."

He leaned close to drop a kiss on her cheek. "After tonight's party, it's all about you."

Butterflies stirred in her belly at the thought, part anticipation and part nerves. While she wanted to be with him again and experience more of the mind-numbing, gorgeous release he could give her, she wasn't sure how she felt about the new intensity that lurked in their relationship.

"I'll be fine," she repeated, as much for her sake as for his. Her personal space and autonomy had been hard won from her family the first time, and even more so after she'd come home from Iraq and they'd been twice as protective of her. She would be careful not to give Danny the idea that she needed a protector. "I'm looking forward to exploring the Cape while I'm here. I don't want to steal too much time away from your family."

He studied her thoughtfully, and in the brief silence, she could hear male voices calling to one another and laughing outside. She had the feeling they'd already started their game, never making good on their threat to drag Danny out of the gatehouse he'd said was less than a tenth of a mile away from his parents' main property.

"Okay." He gave a brief nod and pulled on an old concert T-shirt. If her effort to keep things light bothered him, he didn't show it. "The game should be done by noon."

She watched in silence as he grabbed a pair of sneakers out of his suitcase and went to join his brothers. Guilt pinched when she realized she'd put more distance between them. He'd been so very good to her when she'd needed him.

Had it been wrong of her to ask something so superficial of him as sex? Of course, at the time she'd initiated her request, she hadn't known that their past meant so much to him. By staying with him now, was she only making their separation in a few weeks that much harder?

Her chest ached at the thought of hurting him.

Maybe the time with his family would be a good thing, giving them some natural space from each other before the tender feelings inside her had a chance to take root. Her independence was a precious thing after the kidnapping, and she wasn't ready to give it up for any man. Not even the most tempting guy she'd ever met.

DANNY DID HIS DAMNEDEST to walk the fine line between being a good host to Stephanie and still giving her some space. He hadn't protested when the backyard football game went into overtime, dutifully marching his team back out onto the field after his brother Keith insisted on a coin toss to decide possession in the extra period.

He also didn't protest when his brothers decided to throw him—their team captain—into the swimming pool after he'd led them to victory. They'd insisted a dunk in the water was the only way to celebrate since they lacked a Gatorade container to dump over his head.

Sopping wet and fully clothed, he climbed out of the heated infinity-edge pool his father had installed a few years ago, only to come face-to-face with soon-to-be-groom Jack.

His second-oldest brother tossed him a towel. Square-jawed and serious, Jack had the same brown hair and green eyes as all the biological Murphys. In temperament, Jack and he were the closest of the brothers, both tending to be quieter and more intense. Whereas Keith and Ryan had inherited their father's business-mogul tendencies, and Kyle and Axel were content to dominate sports, Jack and Danny shared a rebellious streak that made it tough to find one clear career path. These days, Jack was debating getting into politics in the Maine community where he and his fiancée, Alicia, ran a bed-and-breakfast.

"I expected you to be a whole lot happier when I heard you were coming home with her," Jack said without preamble.

No need to identify "her." Stephanie had been an unspoken constant in Danny's life for five years and Jack was probably the one who understood that best. He'd seen how hard Danny fell for her the night they met. Hell, Jack had ended up as Uncle Sam's property for four years, as much because of Danny's feelings for Stephanie as any personal call to duty.

Drying off his face and arms, Danny squinted against the afternoon sunlight. "It's complicated."

"Isn't it always?" Jack dropped into a wrought-iron deck lounger with fat ivory-colored cushions.

Clearly, Danny wasn't getting out of this conversation too easily. The lawn buzzed with catering staff and people assembling an outdoor tent, tables and chairs, but they seemed to have finished prepping the pool area, so this part of the property was quieter.

"She sought me out for the first time in five years, and she wants to keep things…uncomplicated."

"Ouch."

"Tell me about it." Danny shoved aside the cushion on another lounger so he wouldn't soak the thing through. Sitting directly on the wrought iron, he laid the towel over his knees.

"But she's here, right? You've got an opportunity to change her mind." Jack lifted the lid on a cooler built into a wooden cart between them and revealed an assortment of imported beers on ice that must be for the party due to start in a couple of hours.

Danny scooped up a longneck microbrew bottled locally. He used the bottle opener built into the drink cart and took a long swallow.

"And risk pushing too hard? She could be out of here before you even say your vows if she starts feeling pressured." He'd gotten the message loud and clear from her this morning when she'd said "I'll be fine" not once, but twice. Obviously, she was already warning him not to get too close.

"So don't push. Don't pressure. Duh." Jack opened his bottle and took a swig. "Can't you be…fun? Low-key?"

"Laid-back," he muttered, remembering what she'd said when he'd gotten off the ship earlier that week. *You look kind of dashing in white…and not at all like the laid-back rock 'n' roll dude I met five years ago.*

"Exactly." Jack lifted his beer in mock salute. "Take her out for a sail. Hit up some open microphone nights at the local clubs so you can jam with your guitar and just have fun. I remember she really liked hearing you play."

"That's not a bad idea," Danny mused, wondering if he even knew how to be low-key anymore.

"Hey, I'm getting married to an incredible woman next week, dude. I must be doing something right." He grinned like he'd won the freaking lottery and Danny was glad for the guy.

Jack had gone without Alicia for almost as long as Danny had missed Stephanie.

"I'm happy for you." Leaning across the space between them, he clinked his bottle against Jack's in a makeshift toast. "Seriously. You deserve this."

"Thanks." Jack's expression grew serious again. "But you know, I might not be here now if not for some very savvy advice you gave me a year ago, sitting on the back porch of the house. You remember?"

Danny nodded. Jack had been flipping out after giving Alicia the deed to the bed-and-breakfast. He'd returned to Chatham without making a commitment to her, unsure where he stood with her since she'd been hurt that he bought the inn without telling her.

"I told you not to let her slip away." Hell, Danny even remembered what he'd been thinking at the time he doled out that brilliant piece of wisdom. He'd figured if he ever had a second chance with Stephanie, he sure as hell would hold tight with both hands.

"Exactly. It was good advice then. It's good advice now." Jack turned in his chair as a small band of musicians started tuning up their instruments for the party. "Crap. We'd better go get dressed for this thing. Especially you. You're the man of the hour."

"I suppose I am." Shoving to his feet, Danny knew he didn't dare be late after his parents went to this much trouble to welcome him home. He would find his suit and try to enjoy the party.

Maybe tonight would help show Stephanie he could still lighten up and just have fun. He could introduce her to the family. Surprise her with a few moves on the dance floor. Play a tune with the band if the chamber orchestra was willing to share a stage.

Everything would be fine just as long as he could forget the clock ticking in his head. And the fear that if he didn't make every second count with her now, he might never have a second chance.

10

"I'M SO NERVOUS," Stephanie whispered in his ear as they walked across the lawn toward the homecoming party.

"You belong here," he told her firmly. "My family has all been eager to meet you for years. I guarantee you're going to get more of a hero's welcome than me."

"That's what makes me nervous." She stopped in midstride on a cobblestone path winding down from the main house to the lawn that led to the beach. "What if I don't live up to their expectations? Or what if they resent the fact that I've been MIA from your life for years?"

"They would never judge you like that." He had realized over the past few days that her mother's sky-high expectations had done a number on her, something he hadn't really seen when they'd first met. "They're going to be glad to have you here because I'm so freaking glad to have you here. Okay?"

She looked incredibly beautiful in a hot-pink dress she'd shopped for the day before back in Norfolk. Strapless and embroidered with tiny glittery bits, the dress glowed just like she did in the light spilling from the house onto the lawn. She wore a ring in the shape of a kitten on one finger, a nod to her whimsical side. But her dark hair was pulled back in a glittery clip, a picture of sexy elegance. As much as he'd rather pull her back to the gatehouse and take her hair down, he knew this night was as important for her as it was for him. Her chance to get to know his family.

"Okay." Nodding, she allowed him to lead her down the steps near the rock garden where he used to play hide-and-seek as a kid. "Sorry to be so anxious when this night is a chance for your family to welcome you home."

"About that." He'd seen all his family members privately this afternoon at one time or another. "They're welcoming out-of-town wedding guests who are spending the week here as much as me, so don't think I'm going to ditch you to hang out with my Aunt Gladys or anything. I'm your date and I'm not going anywhere."

Not unless she chased him off anyhow. He still couldn't believe she was here with him, that she'd looked him up after all these years. God, he'd dreamed about her so often. Blown off so many opportunities to date other people—and when he had dated, it had been halfhearted at best. He lifted her hand and kissed the backs of her fingers while the chamber musicians switched to something a little more lively. The tune was a soft counterpoint to the laughter gaining volume as folks gathered around the scattered canopies that sheltered the food and the bars.

"There's my brother Kyle. We'll start with him so you know someone before we make a big entrance."

"We sort of met on the plane, right?" Her blue eyes went to Kyle, the tallest of his brothers except for their foster brother, Axel, who was huge.

"Right." Danny flagged down Kyle and his girlfriend, Marissa. "Stephanie, this is Kyle, your friendly neighborhood power forward for the Philadelphia Phantoms. Kyle, this is Stephanie."

Heaven knew she needed no introduction. Kyle especially had reason to recall exactly who she was from that old argument they'd had. His eyes flicked over his brother's nose and damned if it wasn't straight again.

"Nice to meet you." Kyle was Mr. Debonair in his tuxedo and real haircut, an obvious upgrade since he'd met his girlfriend. "This is my girlfriend, Marissa Collins. She's a matchmaking guru back in Philly, so if you guys want any relationship advice…"

Marissa stepped forward to shake Stephanie's hand, a pair of cat's-eye-shaped glasses perched on her nose. "Despite what Kyle says, I'm not here in an official capacity. How lovely to meet you."

"I love your outfit," Stephanie said in reference to the silver lace dress the other woman wore. "It looks like something from a red carpet premiere in the fifties."

Marissa smiled. "I like shopping for vintage pieces. I usually find great things, and it fits the budget."

"What budget?" Kyle teased.

"Not all of us rake in money for advertising endorsements," she reminded him drily, although she winked while she did so.

Danny was interested in the dynamic there. Kyle seemed utterly taken with his new girlfriend and he'd heard they'd moved in together shortly after meeting. How had the guy managed it so fast? If Danny didn't start making progress with Stephanie soon, he would have to ask. He'd waited for her for too long not to make major strides forward in his limited time home.

He was about to introduce Stephanie to Axel when the chamber music suddenly came to a halt. A hiss of microphone feedback filled the air and Danny had the feeling his time to escort Stephanie around was about to get interrupted.

"Ladies and gentlemen, if I may have your attention please?" An unknown speaker took the mic, probably one of the dudes in the orchestra.

"I might have to go shake a few hands," Danny whispered in Stephanie's ear, hating to leave her side.

"I'll be fine," she assured him, although he knew that she was nervous about being there.

Damn it. He should have brought her to the house earlier to introduce her around and make sure she felt comfortable but he'd hadn't been able to keep his hands off her.

"Mr. and Mrs. Robert Murphy ask you to join them

in welcoming home their son, Lieutenant Daniel Murphy." On cue, a spotlight searched the crowd for him.

Kyle slapped him on the back. "You're wanted at the podium, dude." He waved his arms to be sure the spotlight found Danny.

"I'll be back," he promised Stephanie, meeting her gaze and holding it.

The spotlight spilled onto her as much as it did on him and then he got a better idea.

"Come with me," he urged her, taking her hand. He wanted everyone to know she was a part of his life anyhow. Or at least, he hoped she would be.

She froze, but he didn't give her time to protest. He walked into the bright white light with her at his side.

A FEW HOURS INTO Danny's welcome-home party, Stephanie needed to run for cover.

The Murphys had been gracious and kind. Each brother was handsome and charming in his own way. Every significant other was stunning and successful. But the crush of well-to-do people in their party finery, their expensive heels sinking into the manicured sod as if the shoes were disposable, made her feel out of place. Especially when her cell phone kept chiming with texts and calls from her mother back in Long Island. Ever since Whitney Rosen had learned that Stephanie was seeing a Murphy of Murphy Resorts, Inc., she'd been neurotically sending messages to give advice. Or at least, that's what the content had been when Stephanie had checked two days ago. Heaven knew what

Mom's messages amounted to now, since Stephanie hadn't been responding. She'd planned to call home when she got to Cape Cod, but those good intentions had vanished when things had heated up with Danny and they'd taken their relationship to the next level.

As soon as Stephanie made her excuses to Danny, she headed toward the house and turned her phone to vibrate.

Stephanie slipped into the multimillion-dollar home overlooking the Atlantic, pretending a need to use the bathroom. The sun had started to set, and she could see the ocean twinkling in the muted light through the floor-to-ceiling windows in the living room. *One* of the living rooms. She'd overheard someone say the Murphys' home was ten thousand square feet.

It was her mother's kind of wealthy world. The sort of place that her mom had always hoped to live in or—at the very least—that Stephanie would live in some day. That's why Whitney had been so excited to hear about Stephanie's whereabouts after a series of panicked phone calls to her empty house in D.C. Stephanie had told her the truth, hoping it would buy her a few days' peace from the all too frequent mother-knows-best routine. Instead, her mom's thrilled reaction to Stephanie being with Danny just reminded her that she didn't want this kind of life. After being overseas and witnessing the abject poverty in some places, glitz and glamour made her feel like a big fat fraud.

"Are you okay?" A feminine voice surprised her.

Stepping deeper into the living area, Stephanie spied

a pretty redhead in a wingback chair in one corner, her feet tucked under a huge bear of a dog. The animal cradled its massive head on its paws and gave Stephanie a mournful look. Obviously, there would be no privacy for a phone call here.

"Is that a mastiff?" Stephanie asked, forgetting whatever it was that the other woman had said.

"A Tibetan mastiff. This is Bobby Orr, named after one of the best hockey players of all time according to Axel." The redhead smiled and tucked aside an iPad she'd been working on. "I'm Jennifer Hunter, by the way."

"The filmmaker. I remember Danny mentioning you. I'm Stephanie." She kept her eye on the dog. "Is he friendly? May I pet him?"

She missed the pets she photographed back home, missed the warmth and affection animals gave so easily.

"Of course." Jennifer slid her feet out from under the animal, her yellow-and-blue party dress a little rumpled. "He's sweet as can be. Axel found him rooting through a trash can one day when he was out running. We contacted the local vets and the pound to see if anyone had been looking for him, but after two months, we figured he was a stray and we kept him. Bobby seems grateful just to have enough food every day. And he loves running with Ax."

"He's gorgeous." Stephanie kneeled on the carpet by the animal and held her hand out for Bobby to sniff. When he seemed unconcerned, she stroked his big head, full of dark fur, and tried to forget she sat in a ten-thousand-square-foot mansion.

The childhood home of a man who'd faced down some Middle Eastern sheikh when she'd been taken hostage. God, she couldn't deny that her feelings for him were growing every moment they spent together.

"How are you doing?" Jennifer smoothed out the full skirt of her dress and slipped her feet back into her turquoise-colored shoes. "I hear this is your first time meeting the clan."

"They're great." Stephanie couldn't deny that she'd been treated with complete hospitality. "I'm just having a hard time figuring out where a pet photographer fits in with the glittering world of the heirs to Murphy Resorts."

She didn't know what made her confide in Jennifer, a woman who was as successful as any of them with a burgeoning film career and growing critical acclaim. Over dinner, Stephanie had received a brief tutorial from Danny on the women who'd claimed the hearts of the Murphy males. There was Ryan's wife, Keira, the traveling teacher who worked at a variety of underprivileged schools around the world during the year, then made recommendations to the Murphy Resorts charitable foundation about which groups would make the best candidates as beneficiaries. Jack's fiancée, Alicia, owned a bed-and-breakfast in Bar Harbor, Maine. Keith's fiancée, Josie, was an interior decorator with a design show on Boston television that had been picked up for syndication. Kyle's girlfriend, Marissa, was a celebrated Philadelphia matchmaker and the daughter of a famous pop star.

Then there was her—pet photographer and author of one colossally unsuccessful book that still generated heated reader responses.

"You fit in perfectly. I see the common denominator being that all the brothers chose highly interesting women, right?" Jennifer grinned as she passed over her iPad. "Are your photos online? I'd love to see some of your work."

"Really?" Stephanie took the device. "That's flattering. Thank you." She clicked through a few screens to the master website page where she stored proofs and samples to show her clients and prospective customers. "It's not...you know...world-class photography or anything. But I try to capture the personality of each subject."

She knew that some of her old friends in the film-and-video world looked down on her new career as a fluff job. But after her experience in Baghdad, she'd lost some of her sense of adventure. She kept hoping one day she'd be "recovered" enough to return to her old line of work. But as the years slipped by, she still didn't feel drawn to the gritty field that used to fascinate her.

She turned the tablet around so Jennifer could see her online album of sample photographs.

"Oh!" Jennifer squealed in delight at the album cover, her cinnamon-colored curls falling forward as she bent over the photo. "How adorable."

Stephanie moved closer to peek over her shoulder.

"That's Tennessee." She had a blast photographing the black-and-white cat with the easygoing disposition. "His owner named him for the cartoon penguin, Tennessee Tuxedo, so I figured I would run with that."

She'd taken a series of pictures of the cat on location at a local menswear store—thanks to the highly accommodating boutique owners who happened to be animal lovers. Tennessee sat on one of the mahogany shelves for the shirt displays, a full-length mirror in the background. The cat wore a mini red-and-white bow tie, looking like a dapper gentleman amid the finery.

"I love it." Jennifer ran a finger over the cat's face on the screen, which turned the digital page. "Whoops. Oh! Look at this one."

Stephanie warmed with the knowledge that she'd found a compassionate audience. From Jennifer's reaction, she didn't think she'd receive a judgmental response to her occupation, no matter that Jennifer was an acclaimed filmmaker.

"That's Cody, a red Australian shepherd," Stephanie explained as they looked at the photo of the Aussie in midjump for a Frisbee. "He was so agile and energetic. Seeing his abilities made me want to close my photography business and start raising sheep, just so I could see an Aussie shepherd in action with the work they were bred for. Honestly, what great dogs."

"The light is beautiful for this shot," Jennifer observed, pointing toward the soft golden haze around the top of Cody's head. "Is this dawn or sunset?"

"Sunset. We took Cody to a local dog park so I could photograph him having fun in the outdoors, where he's happiest."

"It shows." Jennifer tucked some of her curls behind one ear as she turned to look at her. "You have a real knack for this."

In the foyer, male voices rumbled. Stephanie thought she detected Danny's along with a couple of others. Music filtered in behind them, the door to the house left open so that the sounds of the party came in.

"Thank you." She felt better for easy acceptance from an unexpected source. "I have some people in my life who aren't terribly supportive of my work, so that's…really nice to hear."

Her mother, for instance, hadn't looked at her photos once even though Stephanie had been working in the business for three years. Her father, never a strong personality, simply followed suit. His main concern was always for his wife.

"Are you hiding from me again?" Danny's hulking brother Axel strode into the living room and flipped on a lamp, his blue eyes locked on Jennifer as they seemed to share a private joke.

"Not this time," she answered with a wink. "I was just looking at Stephanie's photographs and thinking we should ask her to do a picture of us with Bobby Orr." She handed the tablet to Axel to share the photo of Cody.

"Sweet," Axel declared, just as Danny entered the room.

"What's sweet?" Danny held a hand out to Stephanie to help her to her feet.

She hadn't seen him since one of his aunts had claimed a dance from him, but he'd been a truly attentive date considering this shindig was for him. While that was thoughtful of him, it also made it tougher for her to stick to her plan of keeping this light between them.

"Stephanie's work," Jennifer explained while Axel flashed the tablet screen toward his brother. "She's incredibly talented."

Beside her, she felt Danny tense and wasn't sure why.

"She's an incredible woman," he agreed. "Steph, can I see you for a minute?"

"Sure." She gave Bobby a quick pat on the head before she turned her attention to Jennifer. "We could shoot some pictures out on the ice once it gets colder. I'd love to work with you."

Following Danny out of the room, she was surprised when they didn't go back to the party. Instead, he led her up a staircase to an empty office decorated with tapestries, romantic paintings and notable quotes spelled out in calligraphy and scrawling all around the walls. It had to be his mother's office, the feminine touches obvious.

She was about to comment on how beautiful it was. Then she glimpsed the serious expression on Danny's face and remembered the way he'd tensed back in the living room.

He pulled her toward a window seat tucked into one corner. "How come I've never seen your photography?"

DANNY KNEW HE WAS doing a crap job of keeping things light, and that had been his one freaking goal for the day.

But seeing Stephanie share something personal about herself, something she'd never shown him in all the hours they'd spent together, told him a little about his standing with her.

"I don't know." She sat on the edge of the window seat, her dress settling around her with a flounce. "I guess we've never talked about our jobs that much, have we?"

"That first night at my house, while we stood in the surf, I asked you about it. Told you I'd like to see your work sometime." He didn't take the seat beside her, trying like hell to give her the space she seemed to crave. Instead, he leaned a shoulder into the window casing nearby. "Actually, never mind. I don't mean to make a big deal about it. Do you want to go back outside or would you rather hang out up here for a while?"

Proud of himself for dropping it, he still found it tough not to get any answers. He drew the curtains across the bank of windows looking out over the back lawn where white lights were hung in all the trees and strung around the party canopies.

"It's not that I'm not proud of my work." She surprised him by answering his question. She picked up a desktop stone labyrinth his mother kept on a shelf above the window seat and traced the ridges with a pink-painted fingernail. "It's just that a lot of people find it tough to reconcile my current job with my roots in journalism. At least the book I wrote—while a critical flop—was 'serious.' Pet photography, on the other hand…"

"Would you think for a minute that I'd find fault with any job you enjoyed? Steph, if I was ever going to chime in about your work, I damn well should have opened my mouth five years ago and begged you not to go to Iraq." In those days, he'd been a whole hell of a lot better at keeping things light. Laid-back.

And look how that had worked out.

"Well, my parents think my business is a joke." She reached the end of the twisting stone maze and then worked backward from the center. "So do a lot of my old colleagues. But it's been really therapeutic for me. And I've helped a few animals in the process, too."

"In what way?" He liked seeing this new side to her. For years, he'd been remembering her the way she'd been, never knowing the woman she'd become after her ordeal.

She set the miniature labyrinth on her lap, her blue eyes meeting his. With her hair off her face, there was a natural youthfulness about her. Maybe that's why he had a hard time recognizing the ways she'd changed since they'd first met. On the outside, she was just the same.

"I have a lot of wealthy clients who love extravagant photo shoots for their pets." She pulled out her phone and, tapping into a wireless connection, opened a screen full of thumbprint images and handed the device to him. "They like huge, stately portraits for their libraries and more fun, action shots to post on their Facebook pages. That's good work, but it also helps fund the pro bono stuff I do for animal shelters and adoption agencies."

Danny slid through the pictures showing a dog in a green bandana leaping into a backyard pool, a feline curled on computer keys and a pony nuzzling the jacket pocket of a giggling little girl. There were dozens in color and a few in black and white. One showed a parrot perched on an elderly lady's shoulder and another with a lizard draped across the back of a heavily tattooed dude.

"No wonder Jennifer was impressed." He studied photo after photo and, amazingly, no two were even close to the same. "So what do you do for the shelters? Photograph animals to adopt?"

He ignored the band playing outside and the sound of a couple of his brothers' voices downstairs, probably on a mission to find him. Right now, he just wanted to get a handle on this woman who'd been so elusive. No way would he walk away from this chance to get to know her better.

"Yes." She stood to peer over his shoulder and pointed to a fluffy cat wearing a small baseball cap tilted to the side like an eighties rapper. "See that one? That's Missy. She's so fun-loving and good with kids. Getting that across in the picture helps a prospective

owner connect with a pet and brings them in to adopt.
I snap photos of the animals for the shelters' websites."

"It must take a lot of time. You'd have to build some
rapport with each animal before you could photograph
it." Danny could see her irreverence in the photos and
her warmth, too.

"Definitely." She turned the phone so she could see
the screen better, then she tapped down to a picture of a
cute but scrawny mutt with tufted ears and a nose that
must have been pressed right up to her camera lens.
"See this guy? That's Buster, and it took me forever to
get him to trust me because he's super skittish. I went
through a lot of dog treats and time to coax him that
close, but it was so rewarding to snap a good series. I
think he went through some rough times with his previous owner, but the photos helped him find a really
good home with a sweet older couple."

Danny tried to focus on Buster and what she was
saying, but by now she brushed up against him, her
skirt skimming his leg and the side of her breast grazing his arm.

"I'm glad to know that about you." He could see how
she would gravitate toward that work, helping animals
escape the captivity of a shelter after she'd experienced
the fear of being held against her will. "I don't know
how your mother could fail to see how happy the work
makes you."

Shrugging, she took her phone back and clicked off
the screen before slipping it into her purse.

"I'm not sure my happiness is a high priority for her, but yes, I like what I'm doing."

"I promised myself I was going to keep things light and fun for you tonight," he confided, folding her hand into his and savoring this moment alone a little longer. "I didn't mean to turn all serious about your work, but I just… It bothered me that I couldn't even tell Ax's girlfriend that I liked your photos since I'd never seen them."

"I understand." Her lips quirked in a half smile. "When I'm around you, I have a habit of getting distracted."

He recognized the way she navigated the conversation out of deeper waters and back to safer terrain, but he wasn't going to complain. They were together and that meant he still had time to build on the attraction.

For now, that had to be enough.

"What do you say we head outside to dance under the stars, and we'll see how much I can distract you there?" He bent to nip her bare shoulder, then drag a kiss toward her neck.

She shivered against him, her head falling back while he sought out the sensitive place in the hollow of her throat.

"Sounds like a daring move in front of three hundred party guests," she murmured.

Lifting his head, he tugged her toward the door.

"That's why I know you'll love it."

11

As Stephanie followed Danny across the lawn and down to the dock that held a temporary dance floor, she felt her phone vibrate in her handbag.

She should have turned it off when she'd seen all the messages from her mother—no doubt an endless barrage of questions about the Murphy family. Stephanie nodded and smiled at Danny's brother Keith and his fiancée, Josie, who were already locked in a slow dance. But it was hard to focus on the present—despite the twinkling white lights strung around the dock and the crescent moon and stars overhead—when the vibrating phone reminded her of her mother. Why did Mom have such a compulsive need to steer her toward more prominent social circles? Or a more academic line of work? Most days, it was both. She had a hard time finding a sense of balance between having effective boundaries with her mom and still maintaining their relationship.

Before she could reach into her purse to turn the phone off, Danny spun her into his arms, reminding her of his promise to distract her.

"May I have this dance?" He waited for her reply, the tiny white paper lanterns reflected in his eyes.

Her mouth went dry at the invitation, knowing what it felt like to be the center of this man's undivided attention. Sure, on an emotional level, it could be intimidating. On a sensual level, there was nothing better.

"Yes. You may have that and more." She clutched a handful of her skirt in one hand to dip into an old-fashioned curtsy and his hot gaze followed the neckline of her strapless dress.

A heat wave curled through her, starting in the pit of her belly and fanning out to her limbs.

"Then follow me." He slid one hand around her waist to palm the small of her back. With the other, he clasped her fingers and took the first step of the dance. He didn't just turn her around in a circle, shuffling the aimless steps of most modern couples on the floor. Danny led with authority, guiding her body to the music.

"What are we doing?" she squeaked, breathless to keep up with him. She squeezed his waist tighter, her evening bag caught between them.

"I'm pretty sure they call this one a waltz."

He spun her from one side to the other, her hair and her dress swirling in a half circle.

A laugh bubbled up from inside. She had no idea how to dance—the waltz or anything else—but he was

such a strong partner, he seemed to send her in whatever direction she needed to go.

"You're fantastic." And utterly surprising. "You
weren't kidding when you said you wanted to keep
things light. I feel like I'm flying."

Or riding an amusement-park ride where you never
knew which way you'd go next.

"Good. Next, I hope you feel seduced." He brought
them close to the edge of the dock so that the water
was at their feet for a moment. "Have you heard what
they say about men who can dance?"

"Hmm. You'll have to refresh my memory." She
could have stared at him all night in his crisp white
dress shirt and his dark navy suit. A light blue plaid
tie had hints of silver and fuchsia to coordinate with
her dress—although how he'd found something to go
with an outfit she'd only picked out the day before,
she'd never know.

Danny leaned closer to whisper in her ear.

"They're good in bed," he confided, the words a
warm stroke along her hair that made her shiver.

"I already knew that about you." Her skin tingled
with awareness and the desire to be alone with him.

How could she have dreaded intimacy for so long,
only to have all her latent sensuality restored with a
vengeance by this one man? It made no sense that any
man would be a magic cure, right? Still, she couldn't
deny how he made her feel and she closed her eyes to
savor the heat simmering inside.

"I figured a reminder wouldn't hurt." His fingers

flexed ever so slightly against her back, a delicious pressure that made a tantalizing promise about what awaited her later.

She missed a step, forgetting to follow his lead when she was so wrapped up in the moment.

"Oh!" She would have stumbled except that he lifted her gently, saving her feet from having to do any work at all.

It was only one moment, a tiny instant of being airborne with him before he set her on her feet and the music came to an end.

All around them guests applauded the music and, she realized, them. The other dancers paused to look toward her and Danny, lifting their clapping hands to show their approval. Someone whistled. Danny gave a discreet bow and then drew her aside, away from the others, onto a long pier that led out into the water off the main dock. There was a pair of vacant wooden chairs out on the end, bracketed by two wrought-iron candelabra. She guessed that was their destination, but he took his time on the stroll while the chamber musicians transitioned into another song.

"Should you be mingling more?" She peered back over her shoulder, fearful she might find his parents or his brothers glaring after them. "I feel like I've been taking up all your time when your family must want to see you."

"While this party is technically for my homecoming, my parents haven't spent much time with Kyle's or Ax's new girlfriends, so this party is kind of a welcome to the family for them, too." Danny paused to stare down into the water. "I also think they have a lot of plans to make for the wedding. And there are a lot of out-of-towners starting to arrive for the festivities, so my folks have to greet them, as well."

"What about you?" She stayed on the heavy carpet in the center of the pier, which must have been laid down just for the party. "Don't *you* have a lot of out-of-towners to greet, too?"

She'd given him some alone time when she'd ducked into the house to talk to Jennifer, but other than that, he'd only really visited with his brothers over dinner.

"Keith and Ryan are the public faces of the family. They enjoy that kind of thing. The rest of us…we pick our moments. I'm sure the dance bit back there will have won me some points with my mom. That counts as entertaining the crowd for a few minutes anyway."

She peered back toward the house, which was all lit up in white lights, the party in full tilt on the lawn. It was all so gracious and beautiful. For a moment, she could almost see herself being able to fit in here. Certainly, Danny's family didn't seem to have the kind of expectations that her mom and dad did, where an offspring was supposed to follow a preordained path.

"I think it's great that your parents have encouraged their kids to follow their strengths and be their own person." Her vibrating evening bag reminded her that she'd never be so fortunate.

"There's still a certain amount of pressure."

"Really?" It seemed hard to imagine. "You've all done such different things."

Danny shrugged off his jacket and laid it over the back of one wooden chair.

"But you'll notice we've all done them fairly well." He draped an arm across her shoulders so that they both faced the glittering bright jewel box that was the Murphy home in the darkness. "My father was adamant about hard work and tangible achievement. We were pitched in competition against one another from the time we were old enough to run across the yard. It was about who ran fastest. Who skated the best, sailed the smoothest, threw a ball the farthest."

"Were there points for who could play the most bitching guitar riff?"

He threw his head back and laughed. "Definitely not."

"Was that one of the reasons you walked away from the band?" She wasn't sure what answer she hoped for. Part of her feared he'd stopped playing with his group to enter the military, something that her kidnapping had helped spur. Then again, she hated to think he would have given up his shot at a future in music just because his family didn't recognize the value in rock and roll.

"Not really." He turned her toward him in the moonlight, the water lapping up against the dock at their feet. "My priorities simply changed. But the thing about music is that your love of it doesn't go away just because you don't become famous. Sometimes it's enough just to enjoy something you're good at."

She wished her mom shared that point of view—that Stephanie didn't need some highbrow job to be happy and successful. Then again, maybe she hadn't done enough to show her parents that her photography fulfilled her.

"It doesn't?" Her voice caught as he stared down at her and it felt like they were all alone in the world. She'd thought she wanted to keep things light, but she wouldn't trade the intense way he looked at her for anything.

"Nope. You can always find the music again. Pick up right where you left off and savor it." He skimmed his hands up her arms and along her shoulders. Then, he lifted a palm to cup her chin.

When he kissed her, she could have sworn something melted inside her. Her last reserve, maybe. She wasn't sure, but it seemed as if she could take a deep breath and let it out again in a way she hadn't been able to in a very, very long time. She didn't know where this thing between them was going, but she refused to try to force it into some artificial parameters anymore.

"Danny." She breathed his name over his lips between kisses, the man becoming her whole world. "I can't wait to go back to the gatehouse with you."

The air near the water was cooler now, making her seek the heat that rolled off his body. She gripped his biceps, mindful that their silhouettes would be visible from the house with the candelabra lights behind them. Otherwise, she would have been plastered to him.

"Good, because I'm so ready to have you all to myself."

"Is it too early?" She looked back at the party and the full dance floor.

"God, no. This is the most socializing I've done in years." He picked up his jacket and set it around her shoulders, carefully extracting her hair and laying it over the lightweight wool. "When I get home from a deployment, it's usually all I can do to string a sentence together."

He was already leading her back toward the main dock and the rest of the party, so she couldn't gauge his expression, but it unsettled her to think his work would be that draining.

"Oh." She hastened her steps to walk at his side, careful to remain on the carpet runner so her heels didn't fall into the cracks between the planks. "I didn't think about that when I surprised you in Norfolk the other day."

He ducked closer to speak into her ear. "The last thing I feel is tired around you."

Her skin hummed with awareness, his strong arm keeping her tucked to his side. Her breath came faster and she wished they were already back at the gatehouse. Now that she'd recovered her sensual self, she couldn't indulge it enough.

"I'll just say my thank-yous to your family and then you can remind me why men who can dance are so good in bed." Her heart beat faster, anticipation flowing through her veins like high-proof alcohol even though she hadn't visited the bar once tonight.

"Should you check your phone first?" he asked, nodding toward her purse. "It seems like someone really wants to get in touch with you."

Belatedly, she realized he referred to the active vibrating coming from her satiny evening bag. Her phone buzzed so often she hardly noticed it.

Some of the heat in her veins cooled at the realization she needed to deal with her mother before Whitney Rosen worked herself into a frenzy of worry.

"It's my mom," she explained, embarrassed to admit her mom's semineurotic need to check up on her. Stephanie had tried to be patient, knowing that the abduction had been terrifying for an already nervous mother. "I'll catch up in a few minutes after I reassure her I'm still in one piece."

"Of course." Danny's hands vanished from her body, giving her space to handle the situation. "I've got a few people to thank for coming. I'll keep an eye out for you."

Watching him walk away, her chest tightened. Already, she was coming to care about him too much. What would it be like when he sailed off into the sunset on the USS *Brady* until well into next year?

She tugged her phone out of her purse and stepped around the dance floor back onto the lawn of the Murphy home. Seeking out a quiet corner by the boathouse, she ducked away from the ring of white lights that outlined the party space. It was dark over here, which gave her a little case of the heebie-jeebies, but she kept her eyes trained on the party as she punched in her mother's number.

"Stephanie!" Her mother answered the phone in a panicked squawk. "Where are you?"

"Hello, Mom." She kept her voice calm. Reasonable. She always hoped to transfer that tranquility to her mother, but it had yet to work in twenty-some years of trying. "I'm with my friend Danny, remember? I'm fine."

"I'm so glad you're not alone," she blustered. "Our publisher forwarded me some of your fan emails by mistake."

"Excuse me?" Stephanie's gut churned.

She backed up so that her spine was against the boathouse, bracing herself. Her mother's publisher had been the same company to buy Stephanie's memoir of her captivity and time in Iraq, but Stephanie had had little to do with the firm after her book had been so controversial. Besides, she had no intention of ever writing another.

"It must be a glitch in the system that they forwarded the files to my account instead of yours." Whitney Rosen paused and Stephanie could picture her pacing the floor of her bedroom overlooking Park Avenue in New York City. "Honestly, I wouldn't have even read the emails if you'd answered my calls, but I started to worry something had happened to you and I thought I would check the fan mail in case there was anything threatening, and…little did I know *how* threatening it would be. I had no idea you attracted so many crazy people."

Oh, God. Stephanie didn't waste time wishing she'd just returned her mother's calls because her mom would have opened that file from the publisher either way.

Still, the churning in her gut she felt turned to chilly fear even as she reminded herself that her mother frequently overdramatized things. She knew that her book had been controversial for coming down on the side of peace and understanding between cultures during wartime. She hadn't been advocating antiwar sentiments. She'd just thought some more dialogue would help the war efforts come to an end sooner. "I have an agency that vets the letters and email I receive, remember?"

"I know, but you never said that you've been *threatened*." Her mother's voice went up an octave. "One of these emails includes your photograph with a target superimposed on it. We need to contact the police."

Stephanie drew Danny's jacket tighter around her shoulders as she realized she was shaking. Hard.

"Mom, please calm down." *If only for my sake.* "Forward the letters to me and I'll pass them along to the agency that reviews them."

"These could be your kidnappers hunting you down," her mother reminded her, her words edged with dread. "Do you know how easy it is to find an address for anyone in this country?"

"My kidnappers are not looking for me." Stephanie took deep breaths. She'd been in counseling—both for dealing with her mom and for dealing with her captivity. So she knew that getting wound up before she knew the facts was counterproductive.

Still, she'd never fully recovered from that fear of the dark after having a bag over her head for hours. Standing on the edges of the party right now didn't help the rising anxiety, either. But she sure hadn't expected this from her mother's frantic need to get in touch with her.

"You don't know that," her mom snapped. "You need to talk to the Murphy family about this. They have the kind of resources that could protect you—"

"No." Frustration nudged away some of the fear. "I have been dealing with the letters for years. I'm not suddenly helpless just because I'm seeing Danny."

She heard the bite to her words, knowing she only reacted strongly because it would be far too tempting to run to the shelter of Danny's arms. But that wasn't happening. She didn't need to be rescued anymore.

Strained silence lingered and Stephanie took the moment to walk back toward the lights of Danny's parents' home. Back toward the sound of laughter and music. A bonfire on the edge of the festivities lit up more of the night, drawing Stephanie like a beacon.

"Will you at least pick up your phone when I ring through next time?" her mother asked, the words stilted with wounded feelings.

Guilt niggled even as Stephanie knew she needed to stand strong.

"I'm at a party for Danny's homecoming, but I will

call you in the morning, okay?" She tried a gentler tone, her gaze sweeping the grounds for any sign of Danny.

Stephanie told herself she would not collapse into his arms or pour out a bunch of unjustified worries to him when she saw him. She just wanted to feel that heat between them, certain it would burn away the icy cold in her belly.

"Very well." The clipped words barely hid Mom's anger. "But if you don't contact the police by morning, I will."

The call disconnected, adding more guilt to the mixed cocktail of emotions swirling through her.

"There you are." Danny emerged from the shadows, making her jump. "Are you okay?"

I'm fine. She wanted to say it. Wanted to issue a sexy invitation that would make them forget everything but sizzling attraction.

But what if someone truly wanted to find her? Hurt her? Worse, what if someone hurt Danny in the process?

She was shaking her head before she made a conscious decision to confide in him. Damn it. Damn it.

"What is it?" His arm was around her, steering her away from the party toward the house. "Is everything all right at home?"

"No." Swallowing hard, she squeezed her eyes shut for a long moment, hating the past for coming back to haunt her over and over and over. "Everything is not okay."

12

AN HOUR LATER, back in the privacy of the gatehouse, Danny thought he had most of the story straight. Some color had returned to Stephanie's cheeks as she sat on a high stool pulled up to the breakfast bar in the kitchen. He'd made her hot tea to warm her up since she'd been icy cold when he'd found her on the outskirts of the party.

And it was no wonder she'd been chilled.

She received hate mail with regularity, her book apparently targeted by some fringe radical group in the States that suggested her plea for peace was anti-American. She'd pulled up her email on his laptop and shown him a sample of the letters her publishing company had received in the past three months, along with the file forwarded from her mother. What he didn't understand was this group that supposedly vetted her "fan" mail.

He would tread carefully, though, knowing she was

upset with her mother's interference. It was all he could do not to call a private protection agency right now to ensure no one came near her. Sure, he could fill that role for her for a couple of weeks. But what about when he left?

"I'm surprised the publishing company doesn't send the mail straight to the agency you hired to screen the reader responses." He'd love to know what qualified this group to look out for her safety. The agency sounded more like a PR firm than anything.

"They're supposed to," she said wearily, unfastening the clip from her hair so the silken mass fell forward over her shoulders. "It's a low-priority task, though, and they've routinely sent the emails directly to me. Who knows why they ended up in my mother's in-box this time? Someone probably saw the same last name and just attached my mail to hers since we write for the same publisher."

"In the past, what has the vetting agency done about threatening notes you've received?" He added more hot water to her tea and then joined her at the breakfast bar.

"They send anything overt to the local authorities." She took off a heavy ring and set it on the counter near the salt and pepper shakers.

"Have the police ever contacted you about it?"

"No. But I have a friend who works at the agency, a guy I tried dating for a while before that particular experiment failed. Anyway, he explained that the police log the threats so they know where to look if any action is taken toward me, but as long as there is no reason to suspect the sender knows my whereabouts or anything personal about me, the threat is considered less credible."

"That's bullshit." And not just because she'd dated the guy. Although he didn't like to think about that, either. "The post office needs to know about threats received through the mail and there are internet-crime divisions that will investigate threats by email."

He stopped short of telling her to switch vetting agencies, but he hoped it would be obvious this organization was filled with people who sucked at their jobs.

She gripped her tea mug with both hands and hovered over it while the steam rose.

"Okay." She nodded slowly, calmer now that she'd shared the story.

He, in the meantime, wanted to find whoever was scaring her and tear them apart.

"Maybe we can make a trip back to your place in D.C. this week to check on things." He couldn't wait to read the riot act to her local cop shop, assuming they'd actually ever gotten copies of the letters from this joke of an agency she used. "I could help bump up your security system.... You do have a security system?"

"My apartment building has a buzzer on the front door. Everyone has to be admitted who doesn't live there."

"I mean a dedicated system just for your apartment." He tried biting back his frustration but couldn't. "Steph, I can understand that you want to put the past behind you, but as long as these jokers are out there, you've got to protect yourself."

Lifting the cup to her lips, she took a sip and nodded.

"But there will always be 'jokers' like this out there. The fringe lunatics on both sides of the argument have always existed and always will. This is simply the fallout for anyone brave enough to take a reasoned stand either way."

"I'm worried about today and what we can do to protect you here and now."

"That's a good idea." She smiled, but it wasn't that wry half grin he'd never forgotten in the five years he'd gone without seeing her. No, this was an obvious fake. "I'll look into that when I get home. But I don't think we need to visit D.C. during this time we have together. In fact…"

She put her cup back on the counter and slid off the chair to stand next to him.

"I feel better now," she continued. "It's not that I want to forget about the past and I promise I'll investigate all the avenues you mentioned to ensure I'm protected. However, tonight—since no one is going to find me here with you—couldn't we get back to what we were feeling out on the dock after we danced?"

She looped her arms around his neck and he wanted like hell to forget about everything else. Yet hadn't he done that five years ago and lived to regret it? He didn't tell her not to go to Iraq. He hadn't wrapped her up tight and admitted he was crazy about her.

Was he honestly going to let her distract him again now, when her safety was in question?

"Depends." He thought fast, knowing he'd only scare her away if he started outlining plans to keep her safe. He'd begin small. Build from there over the time they had left. "Will you give that vetting agency their walking papers and find a group better suited to protect your best interests?"

He'd tackle the security alarm tomorrow. Right now, he wanted someone besides her incompetent ex-boyfriend handling her reader mail.

"Are you withholding sexual favors until I comply?" Her smile returned, and this time it was the real deal.

Some of the ache in his chest eased as he hoped he'd chosen his strategy well.

"I might." He turned in his chair and clenched her waist with his hands, smoothing over the hot-pink satin. "I'm doing it for altruistic reasons, though, so you can't hold it against me."

She leaned forward to plant a kiss on his cheek. Then, she dragged her lower lip up to his temple, her breath warm and chamomile-scented.

"You have no reason to be jealous of the guy I dated," she whispered against his skin. "If not for him, I might not have realized how much I needed you. Only you."

Possessiveness stirred inside, the need to be with her so strong he didn't stand a chance of fighting it. Tomorrow, he'd move into full-on protector mode. Tonight, safe in a place no enemy would find her, he could afford to touch her. Take her. Make her his.

"I need you, too." He skimmed a touch up her side and found the zipper to her dress hidden under one arm. Knowing that the shades were drawn and the doors were locked, he tugged the tab down until the dress fell in a pool of satin at her feet.

Her eyes found his in the dim light from the pendant lamps over the counter. He wanted to kiss her until she was weak-kneed and pliant against him, but her newly unveiled body called to him like a siren's song. Pearl-gray lace cupped her breasts and spanned her hips, tantalizing him with glimpses through the delicate fabric. She stepped out of her high heels and arched up on her toes as if she would make herself at home in his lap.

But he was past the point of measured touches designed to bring her pleasure. He needed more. Sliding off the bar chair, he stepped over her discarded dress. Next, he lifted her the same way he had when they'd been dancing. He plucked her off her feet and set her back down where he wanted her—against a bare wall in the hallway that led to the den.

"Tell me if anything makes you uncomfortable," he said to her even though he was already licking his way down her collarbone to the swell of her breast.

Her fingers threaded through his hair, guiding him where he wanted to go.

"I don't want to be comfortable." She arched her back, lifting her right breast so that his mouth hovered just above the lace over her nipple. "I want to be wildly aroused. And I want you to take me there."

When he drew on the mound through the fabric, she clawed down the lace cup, exposing herself to his kiss. There was a new edge to her response, a sexual confidence that hadn't been there before.

He increased the pressure, licking and sucking until she lifted her other breast in a demand for equal attention. Gladly, he accommodated her, peeling away the last fastening on her bra until it fell to the floor. He massaged the soft weight of the pale globes, circling the tips with his thumbs until she pulled his hips to hers and swayed against the erection she found there.

Then, things got out of control in a hurry. She tugged his tie loose and then yanked it off. He worked the buttons of his shirt. Her fingers struggled with the belt buckle while he undid his fly. He remembered a condom from his pocket before his pants fell to the floor. Somehow, they got enough off to free him, until only her panties stood in the way.

He reached for the lacy garment, more than ready to sink inside her. But she surprised him by pulling the foil packet from his hand and sinking to her knees in front of him. He couldn't have looked away if he tried. The sight of her soft hands and pink fingernails tentatively sliding down the length of his shaft almost cost him the last shred of his control. Gripping the wall with both hands, he steeled himself for the feel of her lips around him. Her tongue darted out to circle the head and slalom a path down the length of him....

With his release poised and ready, he reached for her and hauled her to her feet, stealing the prophylactic back.

"I've got this," he muttered. "Can't wait. Can't…" He rolled the condom on, his speech disconnected from his thoughts so he made no sense. He just needed to be inside her.

He captured her mouth in a hard kiss at the same moment he lifted her thigh over one arm and buried himself deep. She was so hot and wet, her body so slick and ready for him that it made his pulse throb in his temple, his erection throb with the need to give her everything.

Delaying the inevitable, he focused on the kiss and her hungry response. He thought about her soft skin under his fingers, the taut muscle beneath. He tried thinking about her breasts and the soft weight crushed between them as he found a rhythm between her legs.

But then, the sweet sensation was too much. His release surged through him so hard his thighs strained with it.

For an instant, he worried he might be restraining her, his weight too heavy against her as he pressed her into the wall. He pried his eyes open to watch her, make sure she was okay, just in time to see her expression still and her eyes flutter close. Seeing her orgasm only made his last longer.

She was so damn beautiful. So important to him.

He just hoped the intensity of what he felt for her didn't scare her off. Because this time, he was gambling everything and telling her how he felt and what he wanted—her, always. He just needed to figure out what kind of life he could offer her besides a few weeks out of the year when he wasn't aboard a ship. But before that? He would make damn sure no one else could ever hurt her again.

IN THE LIGHT OF MORNING, staring at the dent in the pillow where Danny had slept beside her up until an hour ago, Stephanie could see that she'd been lying to herself to think she'd ever wanted something light and temporary with him. The frantic need for him that had overtaken her last night like a wild beast should have proven that her feelings were far more complicated than she could articulate. Hell, it had been easier to tear his clothes off and let her body do the talking than admit she might feel…

Love.

It was the ultimate vulnerability. For a woman terrified of ever being defenseless again…the knot of complex feelings inside was scary. Obviously it was a different kind of scary, but it had taken her so long to get her head on straight after the abduction, she wasn't sure if she was ready to risk another kind of hurt. Maybe that's why it had taken forever to work up the courage to see him again. Perhaps she'd known all these years that their relationship had the potential to explode into something this powerful. She remembered she'd shut down those feelings five years ago when she'd had to say goodbye to Danny the first time….

"I WISH WE HAD another day," he told her as they stood in the living room of the crappy Long Island apartment she'd rented to give herself some space from her New York–based parents.

Her bags were packed and her coworkers at the news magazine were having a little going-away party for her and Christina before they left for Iraq. She had been excited for a new adventure and a chance to prove to her mother that she could handle the pressure of a gritty assignment overseas. But as the days ticked down, she found herself wondering what life would be like if she stayed in Long Island and saw what happened with Danny.

He was based in Massachusetts, but that wasn't all that far away. Besides, he might be making more frequent trips into the city after the success of his gig in Manhattan earlier that week. His band had a single that was starting to get some independent radio play. Mostly, she just enjoyed being with him. He never made her feel that she didn't live up to his expectations.

"What would we do if we had another day?" she asked him, tormenting herself with one last look at what might have been. Her taxi would be here any moment and he'd insisted on staying to help her load her bags to take into work, where a company car would then drive her and Christina to the airfield.

"Hmm." He seemed to take the question seriously, peering at the ceiling as if there were answers up above. "We've already entertained ourselves thoroughly in this apartment. I would say that if we had another day, we'd have to venture out into the world and see if we had as much fun together away from home."

"Away from a bed, you mean?" she teased, recalling how many places and ways they'd made love...er, had sex...in the past few days.

But the attraction was fierce and it didn't take much to ignite.

For a moment, she wondered if he was going to say something serious, because his expression turned intense. Darkly brooding. Sexy in its own way and yet... She swallowed hard. She couldn't afford to care about him any more than she already did. Not when she was going away for at least three months—six if the reports she and Christina did were popular with viewers.

Then, he smiled and she could tell he was making an effort to keep things light.

"Exactly. Today, we'd see if we could make it to the corner market without needing to run back here and get naked." He kissed her cheek, the whiskers from the soul patch on his chin teasing her skin. "Then, we'd see if we could get as far as the theater a mile down the road."

"We'd never make it," she said, the words sounding more plaintive than she'd intended. She cleared her throat and tried again. "I mean, one look at the chocolate syrup in the corner market and I would be so overwhelmed with memories, I'd have to sprint all the way home."

A cab honked downstairs, the sound drifting up to her second-floor apartment.

"That's my ride." She couldn't bring herself to say goodbye. Couldn't bring herself to say half the things she was feeling.

Part of her didn't want to go, but that was natural, right? Even tough-guy military men must feel some trepidation at heading into a war zone. No wonder she was keyed up.

"Steph." Danny's voice, calm and grounding, cut through her frantic thoughts. "I will be thinking about you and I'm going to pray you're safe."

The sentiment, so serious after all the ways they'd laughed and played this week, threatened to topple her shaky control. She gave a fast nod, unable to speak without showing her emotions.

"Be careful, okay?" He kissed her hard and fast.

It was all she could do not to cling to him. If only they'd met after she came home instead of now when they were both on the brink of major changes in their lives. Him with his music. Her with her photography.

"I will." She eased back enough to look up into those forest-green eyes. "Maybe next time we see each other, I'll be screaming my head off in the front row at one of your shows."

He was so talented. She had no doubt that he'd make it big in the music business while she was gone. She'd be lucky if he even remembered her.

"I'm going to keep my eye out for you. Trust me." He grinned and reached for her bags as the cab honked again.

Then, the moment of connection was gone. He

kissed her once more before her taxi took off, but by that time, she'd shut down the urge to throw herself at him and beg him to wait for her....

CHICKEN THEN, chicken now?

She didn't want to think so. But even if she dared to take that risk and tell him she was falling for him, what were their options for testing a relationship when he remained at sea most of the year?

Hauling herself out of bed while she mulled it over, she could already smell coffee brewing in the kitchen. She'd showered an hour ago when Danny had first awoken her with, he'd said, a burning desire to wash her hair. Turned out his burning desire had been about a whole lot more than that and her body still glowed with all the ways he'd satisfied her.

As she dressed, her cell phone chimed with a message.

Mom.

She checked the text, hoping there was no new ugliness to report regarding the emails from readers. But her note only said: I thought u would call me?

Tugging on a simple knit dress from her suitcase, Stephanie dialed her mother's phone, remembering all the reasons she liked to have boundaries in her relationships. Was it any wonder she hadn't gotten closer to Danny way back when? Then, she'd been desperate to make her mark on the world as an adult outside her parents' sphere of influence. Now, she was desperate to free herself from her mother's unspoken accusations.

She knew her mother blamed Stephanie for making her ill, for not conforming to her expectations and being an all-around disappointment.

"Stephanie, thank God you're all right." Her mom answered with typical drama.

"Good morning, Mom. I only just woke up or I would have phoned sooner." She slid into the warm and soothing tones of a late-night radio host, detached but comforting. "You'll be happy to know I spoke to Danny about the threats and sent him a copy of the digital file. We're going to work on increased security today."

It was mostly true. She had shared the incident with Danny even though she hadn't wanted to make a big deal out of the notes. And during her conversation with Danny the night before, she had promised to axe Josh's PR firm today. She'd only kept them on to deal with the reader mail, but now that she'd started over and recovered in so many ways, she was ready to supervise the task herself. Maybe reading her own mail and reporting the weirdos herself would give her a greater sense of control and closure.

"Truly? What is he going to do to keep you safe? With the Murphy resources—"

"Mom." She cut her off, her soothing voice long gone. "It's not about what *he's* going to do. And we're not using 'Murphy resources.' He's helping me figure out how to handle this and that's it. I'm fine and that's what I agreed to call about today, remember?"

Just once, she wished her mother would have some

faith in her. Some trust in her judgment or some respect for her independence. But after waiting for years, she would have to concede it wasn't going to happen.

Frustrated and disappointed, she finished up the call and headed into the kitchen, where her day was bound to improve. The coffee was made and the eggs were on the stove. A shirtless, sexy man stood at the counter prepping plates and juice glasses.

"Good morning," she called over the clink of silverware and the hard rock music filtering through hidden speakers in the dining area next to the kitchen.

He stopped what he was doing to turn and look at her, his bold green gaze raking over her as intimately as if they still stood together under that hot shower spray.

"A good morning, indeed." He gripped her waist and pulled her in for a kiss. "I made you some breakfast in case you worked up an appetite in the shower."

"If you keep this up, I'm going to have a more important appetite to feed." She nipped his jaw, liking the feel of his hard body all too well.

He stepped back. "A gentleman wouldn't let that happen. I need to keep your strength up for the next round, after all."

Pleasure hummed through her at the thought. She wanted more days like this whenever they could have them. He was a man worth waiting for, even if he was gone so much of each year.

"Danny—"

"But first—"

They started at the same time.

She carried the napkins and silverware over to the table. "Go ahead," she insisted, savoring the happy warmth between them.

"I just wanted to hold you to your end of the bargain today." He flipped the eggs and salted them. "You're going to fire the PR firm that's handling your mail, right? Because I called the D.C. police to find out about their records of any threats—"

"You what?" The silverware clanked to the table.

"I double-checked with the local cops to be sure they had logged the threats against you." He plated the eggs and brought them to the small bistro table.

"You didn't need to do that." A chill descended over her happy mood as she realized that he hadn't trusted her to take care of the threatening letters.

That he'd stepped right into the situation and taken control.

"I wanted to," he clarified, returning the skillet to the stove top and pulling on a T-shirt that had been flung over the back of a chair. "I couldn't sleep last night and woke up to read through the file you forwarded me. The emails were damn well disturbing enough to warrant some follow-through, so I checked in with your local police station."

"How did you even know which one was local?" She didn't realize she held the napkins in a death grip until he stepped closer and pried them from her fingers. "You don't even know where I live."

He tensed, no doubt picking up on her mood.

"I looked up your photography business online.

Your address is public record since you work out of your apartment—which, by the way, is a bad security risk." He held out her chair for her, but she'd lost her appetite and remained on her feet.

"And you did all this while I slept." She couldn't stop thinking about the fact that he'd woken her with kisses and carried her into the shower this morning, all the while having looked into her personal business and made calls on her behalf.

"I was worried about you, Steph." He tossed the napkins on the table and faced her again. "Doesn't it concern you to know that PR firm hasn't reported anything to the cops in all the time they've been working for you?"

Had Josh lied? That did bother her. But damn it, that didn't take away the fact that Danny had taken charge of her affairs without consulting her.

"Yes," she said tightly, realizing now she didn't know him half as well as she'd thought. "But I don't care to be muscled out of my own life so someone else can figure out what's best for me."

"I'm not telling you what's best for you." His voice took on a remote aloofness that she'd never heard before and she wondered if she'd offended him half as much as he'd insulted her by handling her private concerns without asking. "I did some legwork to help you make an informed decision."

"But I told you I would take care of that today." She felt weary from this battle even though she hadn't waged it with him before. She'd fought it enough times with her mom to know she didn't need it from anyone else in her life. "You didn't give me a chance to even look into it."

Kind of like her mom hadn't waited for her to call this morning even though Stephanie promised she would.

He took a deep breath and frowned, almost as if he'd stopped himself from saying something. Then, he crossed his arms and started again.

"You've had three years to look into it since these threats have been an ongoing problem. I assumed you would welcome some help since this situation has turned serious."

Three years? Obviously, he thought she'd been remiss in taking care of herself for quite some time. The hopefulness that had been taking root inside her withered.

It was a good thing she'd had a lifetime to perfect the calm, rational tone she used with her mother when she was upset because she sure needed it to cover her heartache now.

"I prefer to handle my own business," she articulated clearly even though her heart raced with regret at how quickly things were falling apart. "I worked too hard to recover some independence after what happened to me overseas. I can't allow anyone else to march into my life and say what's best for me."

"You're mad at me for helping you." It was a statement, not a question, though his tone suggested he couldn't quite believe it.

"I don't barrel into your life and take the reins. I don't try to solve your problems without being asked. In turn, I wouldn't expect you to do those things with me."

His eyebrows shot high.

"Well, let me be more clear. You can expect that I will protect you if I feel that it is warranted."

"Why? Because I'm weak? Because you think I can't take care of myself?" Old frustrations bubbled. He had made this a line-in-the-sand moment when he'd gone behind her back in the middle of the night. "I'm a survivor for a reason, you know, and I've confronted worse than a bunch of letter-writing hotheads. So I would appreciate it if you'd let me decide how to address this."

His jaw tightened. Flexed.

"While you're deciding, Steph, these threats are increasing."

"When you sail out of my life again at the end of the month, I'll be right back to handling things alone. If anyone went to the police, it should have been me."

"I won't regret doing whatever I can to keep you safe. *Especially* because I'll be on a ship again in a few weeks."

He didn't regret undermining her? And in the process hurting her, too?

"Danny, I can't be with someone who doesn't respect my independence."

He shook his head, his jaw dropping.

"Do you honestly expect me to believe you want

to be like that chick in the horror flick who goes into the dark with nothing but a baseball bat when there's a psycho in the woods? Come on, Stephanie. We both know you're a whole lot smarter than that. So is all this a smoke screen for what's really going on? Is this your way of keeping me at arm's length?"

Stunned silent, her mouth snapped shut. Did he seriously believe that? What's more…could there be any truth in it?

"I know you wanted to keep things light," he continued, clearly pushed past the point of agitation, "and I've overstepped that in a big way, haven't I?"

Still reeling with the shock of the accusation, she wasn't sure how to respond. But apparently her hesitation spoke volumes to him because he cursed and headed for the door.

"Fine. I'll make it easy for you then. Once your security is in place, I'll give you all the space you need."

The screen door banged behind him and he was out of sight before she even came close to gathering her wits.

It wasn't until she was all alone that she realized her heart had broken somewhere during the argument. It hurt now more than she would have ever thought possible, a gaping wound that caused her to put her hand on her chest where it ached.

Now, more than ever, she recalled that her first impression of Danny as a laid-back guy was all wrong. What a time to realize she loved the intense military man far more than the rocker who had charmed her at first. She'd figured out he meant everything to her just in time to lose him.

13

"DAMN IT." Danny barreled into his parents' house, pissed off and cursing a blue streak.

Thank God his mother wasn't around.

He banged through a back door on the lower floor, directly into the game room, which was mostly a male domain. His mother had her mom-cave upstairs. The game room was dominated by a large-screen TV on the wall, a pool table and a bar. Already Keith and Jack were engaged in a contest at the foosball table. ESPN blared on the big screen.

"Dude. There's a lady present." Keith pointed toward the bar, where Jack's fiancée, Alicia, rose slowly from whatever she'd been doing beneath the counter.

"Just me, Danny. And I've heard that tune a time or two before." She winked at Jack and edged out from behind the bar. "I'll excuse myself, though, so you don't need to censor for my sake."

Danny managed a halfhearted apology, but his

soon-to-be sister-in-law breezed toward him and patted his shoulder on the way past.

"No worries. Maybe I'll go take cover with Stephanie on the female side of the Murphy property." She continued toward the door, her long blond hair swinging. A former champion swimmer, she was a beautiful woman. But she didn't have the quirky smile or the spontaneity that made his eyes seek out Stephanie in any crowd.

Then again, no woman had turned his head the way Stephanie had from the first instant he'd laid eyes on her.

Jack followed Alicia just outside of the room to give her a real kiss that made Danny ache with regret over how thoroughly Stephanie had pushed him away.

Keith turned the sound down on the TV as Jack came back into the room.

"What gives?" Jack asked. "You guys looked pretty damn happy to me last night."

"She thinks I overstepped her boundaries by trying to keep her safe. But I know it's just a B.S. smoke screen for whatever is really going on—trouble committing or something." Would she think he was invading her privacy by sharing as much with his brothers, too?

But he was too confused about his next move not to share. Not to mention, he only had a limited amount of time to figure this out before he shipped out again. He wasn't normally a big family guy, but right now, he needed all the help he could get.

"Is she in danger?" Keith straddled a bar stool, a sleek designer watch flashing on his wrist even though he sported a T-shirt and sweats.

"She wrote a book about her captivity, remember?" His family knew the story well enough. They'd spent plenty of time working to help free her and Christina. "And apparently she's developed a following of hate-mongers who don't like the idea that she suggested peaceful communication might be a good balance to the war efforts."

"A stupid enemy is a dangerous enemy," Jack muttered. "Has anyone made a direct threat?"

Quickly, Danny related the gist of the emails she'd received, the fact that no one had reported the contents, and the news that she had no security system in place.

"I thought I showed a whole lot of restraint not threatening to string up this ex-boyfriend of hers who hasn't been doing his job." Danny had thought about it and held his tongue.

"And that was wise." Keith clapped him on the back. "Good job on that."

"You did the right thing in the wrong way." Jack pulled out a few bottles from under the bar and set them in a row. Whiskey, scotch and something unlabeled, which Danny happened to know was homemade Russian vodka from an eccentric friend of their father's.

"Meaning...?" Danny pointed to the vodka.

Jack poured three glasses of the potent brew.

"Whether it's a smoke screen or not, she has to have a say in how things go down when they concern her."

Jack clinked his glass to the others. "I bought Alicia that bed-and-breakfast she wanted, but was she happy? No way. She was hurt that I'd robbed her of a chance to fulfill her dream of buying it herself. Even though I get that now, I was so freaking sure I was doing the right thing at the time, it never crossed my radar what she would want."

Keith lifted his glass and, like Jack, gently tapped it against the rest. "I sent out a press release that Josie and I were engaged before I asked her. Not only that, but I did it to solve a PR crisis for her that she had told me to stay out of." He shook his head as if to ward off the memory. "I was close to losing her."

But he hadn't. Both these guys were happy as hell and living the dream with their women. Meanwhile, he was pretty sure he'd made Stephanie cry, although she'd beat a hasty retreat out of the kitchen after she told him she'd been wrong to trust him with her heart.

Damn. It.

"This isn't like that. I'm talking about her safety. Her physical well-being. Besides, I think she's just using this as a way to leave because she just doesn't want me in her life full-time." He didn't bother clinking glasses. He shot the vodka in one swallow and got up to leave, too edgy and frustrated to sit still.

Behind him, he heard one of his brothers give a low whistle. As he banged out the door, he couldn't be sure which one of them said, "Some guys learn the hard way, dude."

His brothers meant well, but their advice about letting Stephanie have some say in how he handled things with her security wasn't going to solve the fact that she could be in danger.

Again.

And he wasn't about to let anything happen to her a second time, even if that meant losing her forever.

WHEN A SOFT KNOCK came at the gatehouse door, Stephanie knew it couldn't be Danny. He wouldn't knock, for one thing. And if he did, it wouldn't be softly. Still, her heart foolishly picked up speed.

Just because her brain knew that things were going downhill fast for her and Danny didn't mean that her heart had a clue. She felt as if she had a hole in her chest, the ache there so deep it went right through her.

"Come in," she called, raising her voice as she hurried down the stairs to open the screen door.

An unseasonably warm breeze filtered into the living room as Jack's fiancée, Alicia, let herself into the gatehouse. Fair-haired and beautiful, Alicia Le Blanc carried a small basket under one arm, a bright yellow tea towel covering whatever was inside. She wore jeans and an apricot-colored sweater that added to her healthy glow.

"Hi." She passed the offering to Stephanie just as her eyes went to the bistro table where the plates of untouched eggs still sat. "I brought you some breakfast, but it doesn't look like you need it with the spread you have here."

Stephanie took the warm basket and peeked under the towel to find fresh blueberry muffins.

"Thank you," Stephanie managed to respond, too hurt inside to make small talk with someone she didn't know very well, even though she recognized the thoughtfulness of the gesture. "Danny and I…" She didn't know where to go from there, unsure where they stood or what had happened. "He left and—"

When her voice broke, she didn't bother trying to finish the sentence.

"I'm sorry," Alicia said into the silence, taking the muffin basket and setting it on a kitchen counter. "Maybe I shouldn't have intruded. I just saw Danny moping around the main house and thought you could use a friend."

She reached a tentative hand to clutch Stephanie's arm. It was as if the sympathetic pressure squeezed out the tears she'd been holding back and she had to wipe away the proof of her sadness.

"That's thoughtful of you, but I'll be okay. I was just packing my things." And feeling sorry for herself.

"I don't have any intention of prying, and I don't know what happened," Alicia began hesitantly, but her words picked up speed as she spoke. "But I wanted to share just a couple of insights about the guys in this family—things that might not sway your decision, but then again…"

Stephanie was touched by Alicia's uncertainty. Her mother gave advice without asking all the time. Instead, Alicia offered to shed light on the situation without preaching. A simple but refreshing twist on the way Stephanie was used to being approached.

"I'm listening." She gestured to the chairs at the counter. "Have a seat. I could at least get us some coffee. It's already made."

"Let me." Alicia waved her away from the coffeepot. "I'll be less nervous if I have something to occupy my hands." She smiled sheepishly. "I know it's bold of me to march over here when we only just met yesterday. But I remember so well the way it hurt when Jack and I fought. Seeing Danny torn up this morning just made me want to run down here and give you a hug."

Stephanie reached for a napkin as another tear spilled down her cheek. Could Danny be hurting as much as her? Far from soothing her, the notion only made her sadder since her independence was one area she couldn't cave on.

Unless she really was just pushing him away? She hadn't given much thought to his accusation yet, because she didn't want to believe that about herself.

"It just hurts so much because I was thinking about telling him how I feel this morning. Over breakfast, in fact." She looked toward the uneaten eggs and wished she could wind back the clock on their relationship. "I was ready to be vulnerable to love. Ready to work around his career, which takes him away for so much of the year. But I won't relegate control of my life to strong-arm tactics."

Alicia passed her a mug of coffee along with a dish of sweetener packets and creamer.

"Of all the Murphys, Jack and Danny are most alike. That's not just my observation, that's generally accepted family wisdom." Alicia stirred cream into her coffee as she spoke. "They're less social. Quieter. Stubborn."

"I know they're close." She hadn't seen Danny in many social settings after having dominated his time and attention at the party where they'd met. But he'd intimated last night that his family didn't expect him to socialize much. "Jack joined the navy with Danny, right?"

"Yes." Alicia slid into a seat at the counter beside her, her beaded necklace clacking against the granite. "In fact, Jack and I were dating at the time, and he dumped me unceremoniously to go into the service."

"Really? I didn't know the two of you had known each other that long."

"Well, I was out of the picture for a long time. And I was hurt about what he'd done. I only found out last year that one of the reasons he'd entered the navy was to support Danny, who was totally torn up and out of his mind with worry about you."

Alicia's brown eyes met hers. Stephanie set her mug back on the counter.

"Jack said that?" She should believe it. Danny had hinted at as much. But it was different hearing it from Alicia. From knowing that Danny's concern for her had affected his whole family.

"Yes. I know how reticent Jack is about sharing his feelings with me, so I can only imagine that Danny might be the same. But it's commonly acknowledged among the Murphys that you're 'the one who got away' for Danny. You're the reason he's hardly dated the last few years. You're the reason Kyle had a crooked nose for years after Danny's fist connected with it in an argument over you."

Stephanie knew those things peripherally…well, except for the fact that he hadn't dated much since her. It floored her to think his family all thought she'd played such an important role in his life. Still, was it because she meant so much to him? Or was it merely because she'd had a traumatic experience and he felt… sorry for her?

The thought caused a knot in her gut.

And yeah, it also made her question if she really was just pushing him away because she was still scared. Did she want to be the kind of person who would cut and run when things were tough?

"I don't know." She shook her head, more confused than ever.

"There's one more thing." Alicia blew on the surface of the coffee, causing a light ripple. "Jack broke my heart when he first swooped in and purchased the bed-and-breakfast we own in Maine. He knew I wanted to do it on my own. I'd worked out a plan and I'd been saving for years. But sometimes men—especially guys like the ones we care about—are so focused on an outcome, they fail to see the emotional fallout."

"Kind of like Danny wading right into my personal business even though I said I wanted to take care of it myself." She could see the connection. "How did you move forward from that?"

"I remembered that there was no one else I'd rather be with in the world. Even if we don't see eye-to-eye sometimes, I love him like crazy." Alicia smiled and Stephanie could see her affection for her fiancé shine through her eyes.

"And that was enough?" Stephanie hated to sound like a cranky cynic. But her feelings for Danny were so new and untested. She wasn't sure she could dive in headfirst with him and expect love to carry her through disagreements like this.

Disagreements that would only be worsened by time and distance apart.

"Well, that combined with the fact that Jack means well." She frowned. "Does that sound lame? I just came to understand that he thinks so differently from me and that sometimes the things that frustrate me the most are the things he's trying to do because he cares."

Alicia's cell phone buzzed along the granite, lighting up with a photo of her and Jack hugging in front of a sprawling seaside property. The bed-and-breakfast, no doubt.

Snagging it, Alicia put it in her pocket.

"That's Jack." Standing, she leaned forward to give Stephanie a hug. "I told him to call me when my brother arrived at the main house. He was supposed to drive in from Boston to take me out to lunch and deliver a wedding gift, so I'd better meet him. Do you want to come with us? It'd be better than packing."

She looked so genuinely hopeful that Stephanie had to smile despite the heaviness in her heart. Apparently, she wasn't just losing Danny. She stood to lose a truly wonderful, supportive family that could have been an uplifting counterpoint to the relationship she'd always had with her mom.

"Thank you, but no. Enjoy your visit with your brother and I appreciate you taking the time to talk to me." As much as she would like to have Alicia's sunny outlook and assurance that love could carry her through disagreements like this, she had too much baggage to juggle. Maybe her captivity had made her more deeply wary of a relationship than she'd ever suspected.

With a clipped nod, Alicia was out the door, leaving the blueberry muffins behind. Leaving Stephanie to hope she could find Danny long enough to tell him goodbye without all the drama of their previous parting. She couldn't just let things end on that note—with her tongue-tied and him walking away.

Her little bit of packing almost done, she searched for her phone. She needed to talk to him before she called for the cab, after all. He deserved that even if the thought of facing him and saying another goodbye almost tore her in two. She'd barely survived the first one five years ago.

Besides, Alicia's words had been an important reminder. No matter that Stephanie couldn't relinquish control of her life to Danny's certainty he knew best, she could at least admit that he'd only been looking out for her.

Digging the phone from her purse, she came across the notepad with the details from Danny's homecoming on it. She'd taken those notes while talking to Danny's mom. She'd scribbled the time and date of his ship's arrival in Norfolk in peacock-blue ink, her handwriting neat and deliberate as if she was taking the most important information of her life. The name of his ship was underlined and for some reason that hard line of ink reminded her how hopeful she'd been when she'd written it down.

She'd waited for this moment for over a year after deciding she really needed to see him again. But had she been waiting for the reunion far longer than that? Holding the petal-pink notepaper in her hand, she squeezed it tight. What if she was making a terrible mistake to put her need for autonomy above love?

More importantly, what if she was just using that need as an excuse for a deeper fear of committing?

The scrawled heart inside the *D* in Danny's name sure wasn't the artwork of a woman prepared to give him up.

When the phone in her other hand rang, she nearly jumped, dropping the notepad back into her purse.

Danny.

Her heart did another flip, hopeful and fearful at the same time.

"Hello?"

"We need to talk." His words were brusque, but this time, Stephanie tried to see beyond that.

He was hurting, too.

"I know. I was just going to call you." She paced the floor of the living room, walking in circles with nervous energy.

"Are you still at the gatehouse?"

"Yes."

"Why don't you meet me down by the dock? We can talk there."

"Okay." She slipped her toes into a pair of flip-flops by the front door—the blue ones with the big flowers on the thong. Weren't those the shoes of an optimist? A woman who could see the positive side of things? Oddly, they gave her courage. "Good idea. I think I need some fresh air and a fresh perspective."

Already, she was out the screen door, letting it bang softly behind her.

"The sea is great for that." Was it her imagination, or had his tone lost some of its defensiveness?

"I can be there in five," she assured him, her fears turning to hope. Or at very least, determination.

She wasn't going to give up on her Murphy man easily. Clicking off the phone, she picked up her speed and jogged toward the beach.

14

SETTING ASIDE HIS cell phone on the wooden deck lounger at the end of the pier, Danny breathed in the sea air. It helped him calm down more than the Russian vodka or the support of his brothers. Maybe that was one reason he couldn't give up the navy. He felt a balance out on the water that he never experienced on dry land.

Although, he had to admit, he'd glimpsed moments of possibility with Stephanie over the past few days. When things were going smoothly between them, he felt more grounded with her than he ever had anywhere else. She charmed him. Amused him. Humbled him with her giving spirit when he saw the pictures of the shelter animals she photographed.

He'd accused her of running scared this morning, and while he still believed that was true, he also remembered she was entitled to a few hang-ups. Hell, he'd been so quick to join the navy to help the war effort and keep people like her safe abroad. Over the years, he'd told himself he'd do anything to be with her again. Yet, the first time she'd pulled away, he'd gotten mad instead of trying to understand where she was coming from.

Some hero.

Footsteps on the dock surprised him. Turning, he saw her jog down the dance floor, then slow her pace as she hit the narrow pier closer to the chairs where he sat. He rose to his feet, needing to confront the mess he'd made head-on.

Her turquoise-colored dress swirled around her knees as she stopped a few feet away. She was so beautiful she stole his breath with her vivid blue eyes and hair so dark it was blue-black. Her ponytail drooped to one side after her jog, the hair-tie hanging limply near her shoulder. He could have just stared at her forever, taking in the details that he'd missed or forgotten in the years apart.

"You want to have a seat?" He gestured to the chairs at the end of the pier.

Her lips twisted in indecision and she pointed toward the planked wood beneath their shoes. "Can we just sit here? With our feet in the water?"

"Sure." He toed off a pair of tennis shoes he'd worn over bare feet while she slipped out of her flip-flops. "Thanks for coming."

"I was anxious to see you." Tugging the elastic band from her hair, she let the silky strands fall before she took a seat. Then, edging her skirt to her knees, she tucked the cotton knit under one thigh so the fabric didn't get wet.

"That surprises me after the way I walked out." He'd let his emotions get the best of him. "I'm sorry about that."

"I probably needed time to let what you said sink in anyway." She flexed her legs, bringing her pink-painted toenails to the surface for a minute before sinking them back under water. "When I didn't deny the accusation about using my independence as a smoke screen, it wasn't that I *couldn't* deny it. I was just sort of…shocked."

"It wasn't my place to back you in a corner like that." He'd waited quietly for her for years, always half hoping she'd seek him out one day. But when she had, he'd been quick to let things derail.

For all he knew, he was the one too scared to commit.

"Actually, I keep wondering if there's something to what you said."

"You're kidding." Now he was the one who was shocked. "Steph, I'm no psychologist. I was just spouting off because I hated to think we'd been back together for all of a few days and I'd hurt you already."

She swished her legs in the water, first sending each in the same direction, then twirling them in opposite ways. He watched her, curious where this conversation was going but unwilling to push for answers she might not have yet.

"We always hate the chick in the horror movie that

refuses help, don't we?" she observed lightly, reminding him of yet another accusation.

Yeah, he'd really been on his A-game this morning.

"We don't *hate* her. Think how many movies wouldn't get made without her. But yeah, I guess we wonder why she doesn't call the cops or—"

"—take better care of herself," she interjected. "It makes sense for you to help and I can understand why you would, so thank you. I'm sensitive about that stuff because my mother is super pushy about knowing what's best for me."

"I just couldn't see myself backing off an issue like that." He nudged her foot with his under the water. Gently. Briefly. But damn, it felt good to touch her any way he could. "You're too important to me."

She nudged his foot back. Gently. Briefly.

But just the same, the contact was there and it soothed the raw edges on his mood far more than looking out over the water.

"That's what Alicia said I needed to remember."

"Alicia?"

"She came by this morning to see how I was doing. And she—very tactfully—helped me understand that you had probably only acted out of concern for me."

"That was nice of her." He made a mental note to send his future sister-in-law a kick-ass Christmas present. "I'm sure you appreciated the tact after I went storming away like a bat out of hell."

"It's okay. Really." She turned toward him, fixing

him with those bright blue eyes. "I just want to know, where do we go from here?"

It was a question he'd thought he had the answer to a few days ago. Hell, he'd known since he'd seen her waiting for him at the naval station in Norfolk that he wanted more from her. Much, much more. He'd also known his career might not allow him to offer her the kind of everyday love she deserved.

Of course, given the argument they'd had this morning, he knew he ought to let her weigh in on the question. Something she couldn't do until she had all the facts.

"Remember the letter I sent you a few years ago?" He figured he'd start there since he'd laid it all out neatly in a note he'd put a lot of thought into. "The one your admirer at the PR agency never passed along to you?"

She nodded.

"I renewed my bid for that Vegas wedding we talked about." He'd laid it all on the line back then when she'd never even known about it. Why not give it a shot now? "I had no luck reaching you on the phone, so I declared my undying love in a note I thought might find you through the publishing house."

"My God, Danny. You realize I had no idea…" She paled and he didn't think that was a good sign.

When would he learn not to be Mr. Intense around her?

"I'm sure the guy you dated was already crushing on you and didn't care for the competition. Who knows what happened? Either way, I just figured you ought to know that my feelings for you haven't changed since we met. And I didn't totally fall off the map for five years. I did try. I should have tried harder. I see that now. But I need to make sure you realize, I wanted you then and I want you even more now."

Stephanie guessed she looked like a blowfish, her mouth working even though no words were coming out. But she'd been tongue-tied earlier and regretted not pulling her head together sooner to say what she felt. No way was she going to rob them of this moment, too.

So she blurted the first thing that came to mind.

"I love you." She cupped his face in her hands, her heart full to overflowing. "I suspected it when I didn't really connect with anyone else I dated. I mean, I blamed it on the abduction thing and went to counseling, but I always ended up talking about you."

It had been embarrassing, actually. She'd felt like a teenager with a crush she couldn't forget.

"Why didn't you look me up sooner?" He combed a strand of windblown hair from her face. His green eyes so serious.

Intent.

"Because I was confused about what I felt. I thought maybe I just sort of idealized what we had since it was so fun and it was the last real happy memory I had before I was thrust into a war zone. And since we never made any promises, I pictured you going on to big things and being really successful without me." She swallowed hard and smoothed a hand over his jaw. "I tried to write my way to a happier place with the book, but that sort of pushed me in an even darker direction. I think I just needed to be in a better place emotionally before I tried my luck with you again."

She'd let so much time go by. And even after she'd found him, she'd put up barriers without realizing it. How could she have feared giving him her heart when it had already belonged to him?

He let out a shuddering sigh and pulled her hard against his chest. Squeezed her tight.

Without a single word, she understood how much she meant to him. She felt his love for her in the way he held her, as if he'd never let her go.

He kissed her just above the temple, his lips soft on her sun-warmed hair. Then he kissed her a few more times, his hands stroking over her back.

When he pulled back, he gripped her shoulders and studied her, his expression still serious.

"You don't know how much that means to me. You just have no...idea." His hands roamed up and down her arms. "I'm ready to do whatever it takes to make sure we're rock-solid. I'm just so glad you're talking to me. Confiding in me. It might not be easy being apart, but I'm willing to work at this."

Her chest tightened at the concern in his voice and she vowed silently to bring some laughter and lightness back into his life. He needed her for that and for the first time in a long time, she didn't feel even remotely like damaged goods. She felt like a woman with something very tangible to offer the man who she'd once imagined had everything.

"Not easy, maybe. But compared to pouring our hearts out just now, I think it's going to get easier from here." She couldn't hold back a smile and he traced the corner of her lips with his fingertip. "We can figure this out."

"We only have two and a half more weeks together," he reminded her, his brows lifting.

Did he doubt they could pull it off?

"We fell in love in five days and were ready to hop a plane to Vegas to hit a drive-in chapel," she reminded him. "I can't even imagine what we can accomplish with *weeks* together. Gosh, it feels like a lifetime." She winked and finally teased a smile from him.

"True enough. But six months apart is a long time. After that, I should have a solid chunk of time at home, though. It should balance out. Down the road, who knows? Maybe I could take a job on shore—"

Pressing a finger gently to his lips, she wouldn't even let him continue with talk like that.

"Don't even think about that yet." She slid away her finger and kissed him where she'd touched him. "I know how much you enjoy your work and I'm so proud that you do it."

She watched some of the tension slide from his shoulders, confirmation that he was right where he wanted to be in his job. While it would be hard to be without him while he was away, she did have a career she was passionate about, too. Plus, she'd spouted off so much about her independence. At least that would come in handy when she was on her own.

"Thank you. But I don't want you in D.C." His green eyes went a shade darker and she guessed he was probably expecting some resistance.

However, after glimpsing the payoff of compromise, she didn't have any problem conceding this one. They were edging their way closer to a solution. She could feel it with new certainty.

"You're in luck then, because I wouldn't dream of hanging out there when you make your home in Norfolk." She wound her arms around his neck, savoring the feel of his strong shoulders. "Although it would help if I had an invitation…"

"I can have you moved into my place before Jack's wedding this weekend." He pulled her against him until she was all but in his lap. Her wet feet dripped on the dock, drying quickly in the sunshine.

"Wow." She laughed, delight bubbling up from a new well of happiness that would only deepen in her days with Danny. "That's even better than an invitation. Seriously?"

She'd have to find someone to take over her work for the local shelters, but she'd had her eye on one of the adoption agency workers who liked helping her stage the photographs. The young woman probably knew enough from assisting her to do a good job with it.

"You can set up a new business there. You said it would be great to take pictures by the water, right? Plus, my neighbor across the street is a cop. I can let him know to keep an eye on you. For that matter, the security system is already there and state-of-the-art, so it solves that problem, too."

Her head was spinning, the plans falling into place as easily as their long-ago scheme to get married in Vegas. Only this time, they were following through. Committing to the happiness they'd always been able to give each other.

"I would love that." She could already imagine the homecoming she could give him next time, in a house they shared. "We could get a dog or two of our own now that I'll be around to take care of it while you're away."

"Yeah?" He shuffled her weight and tugged them both to their feet. "We'd better get going then. We can figure out what we want on the plane, although I heard a rumor you like Australian shepherds."

He picked up her shoes and his.

"We're really going to do this?" She looked around at the big, beautiful Murphy home on the hill and thought about how amazing it was that this man had the ability to simply step on a plane and take care of moving her things into his seaside house in Virginia forever.

Most of all, she gazed in wonder at the strong, handsome man beside her who had loved her since they met.

It was a perfect moment she never would have guessed waited for her after the hardship she'd been through in the past years. An ending too magical for

Stephanie Rosen, the daughter who'd never quite measured up.

Danny dropped the shoes back to the deck with a clunk before he wrapped his arms around her waist. His touch gave her a sweet thrill inside.

"We're going to spend every second we have together making our dreams come true. It all starts today." He tipped his forehead to hers, his warmth surrounding her. "I don't know about you, but I think we deserve to be the happiest couple on the planet."

"I can really get behind that plan," she whispered, not trusting her voice enough to speak any louder than that. Happy tears made her throat close right up.

"And for what it's worth, we can do Vegas and keep it secret until after Jack's wedding so we don't steal their thunder. Or we can do it up right in the biggest freaking wedding this town has ever seen when I come home next summer. Your choice."

As the tears started leaking down her cheeks, she realized she was going to inherit a massive family with her marriage to this man. A ready-made group of siblings like she'd always wanted.

"I love all the choices." Laughter swelled inside her, emotions too big to be contained. "It makes me feel very independent."

"We'll figure it out on the plane to D.C. But I don't want to wait another second to start planning our future together. Sound good?"

"It sounds the best." She arched into him, her body responding to his. "But I don't know if I can plan a wedding until I receive a few reminders about how fun marriage to you is going to be."

"There are several benefits of a private jet." He kissed her long and hard until her knees wobbled beneath her. "As soon as we get airborne I'll refresh your memory on why you're going to be a very well-satisfied bride."

Desire tingled through her veins, all the more delicious now that she knew how much love was behind it. She slid on her flip-flops and nudged Danny's shoes toward his feet.

"Then what are you waiting for?" Taking him by the hand, she strode up the dock. "I want you like crazy, Danny Murphy."

Epilogue

"TO THE BRIDE AND GROOM!" The hearty toast reverberated through the outdoor tents dotting a hill overlooking the Atlantic Ocean.

Crystal chandeliers lit every tent as evening fell, and an abundance of bright poppies and dahlias spilled from cast-iron urns and centerpieces. The whole lawn glowed with color and happiness as the guests raised their glasses to Jack and his new wife, Alicia. The reception was in full swing on the Murphy family front lawn in Chatham, Massachusetts, on Cape Cod. But when Stephanie heard the toast to the bride and groom, she couldn't help a sly look over at Danny.

He must have felt her eyes on him, because he turned to her then and whispered in her ear.

"Cheers to *both* brides and grooms." The words were a soft caress on her ear and it was all she could do not to pull out the diamond ring she wore on a chain beneath her wedding-guest finery.

She loved savoring their secret even as they celebrated Jack and Alicia's big day. Like Danny, she hadn't wanted to wait another moment to start sharing their future together. They'd lost five years after they first met and neither of them wanted to miss out on one more day.

"Cheers." She lifted her champagne glass to Danny's, toasting two marriages—the one in progress and the one just the two of them had celebrated privately in Vegas three days ago.

She'd decided she wanted to elope with Danny in secret, just the way his parents had done thirty-five years earlier. Danny had agreed wholeheartedly, liking the idea of firming up their vows before he went back to sea. His practical side had also pointed out that if she chose to take his name, the switch would help her remain safely anonymous at the Chesapeake Bay house for a bit longer. Little did he know how much she looked forward to being a Murphy. His family had won her over in a hurry for the way they'd tried to help steer them back together after their falling-out.

The Vegas drive-in chapel marriage had been their way of honoring the fun, spontaneous time in their lives when they'd fallen in love. Their Filipino Elvis-impersonator chaplain had launched into a gorgeous rendition of "Can't Help Falling in Love" after he'd declared them husband and wife, and it had been so perfect Stephanie had cried more happy tears all over the white lace tank and poodle skirt she'd bought in a vintage clothing store for the occasion.

But they were going to get married in front of the

family next summer—right back in Cape Cod—as a nod to the more grounded people they'd become. Stephanie figured they'd waited long enough to live out their happily-ever-after, so they might as well enjoy every second of it. What could be better than marrying this fantastic man twice?

The band struck up a romantic tune and Jack led Alicia to the dance floor. The official bride and groom of the day had already taken their formal first turn as husband and wife. Now, the party really came to life as more couples joined them and the candelabra lights flickered in the night, the glow reflected on the waves so that it seemed as if the celebration stretched out into the Atlantic.

"Should we go check on Cody?" Danny asked, backing away from their table.

They'd adopted the Aussie shepherd she'd once photographed. The dog had been at the shelter she'd worked with in D.C. after his former owner had died suddenly. Only two years old, Cody was full of energy but smart and well trained, a perfect fit for them.

"Are you kidding?" Stephanie followed him and looked toward the temporary playground set up for the younger guests of the wedding, complete with a bounce house and three caregivers. "He's having the time of his life herding the kids."

The play area was the only spot on the lawn lit with bright spotlights so parents could keep an eye on the activity. Cody was easily visible working the fringes of the playground, keeping all the little ones corralled with the skill that came naturally to his breed.

"Looks like we're going to need a boatload of off-spring to keep the dog happy." He kissed her bare shoulder as they walked the perimeter of the reception hand in hand.

She laughed, happier than she'd ever been. Not just because she felt so fulfilled, but also because she could see a renewed joy in Danny. It had been obvious the day that he oversaw the arrival of her possessions from D.C. to his home on Chesapeake Bay. He'd hired a moving company, but she didn't own much so it hadn't taken the movers long to insert her things among his, blending their worlds. Her photography equipment had gone into the den that she would remake into a dedicated studio. Cody had a kennel in the garage and beds in the living room and bedroom. He'd been really good with other animals, so she didn't anticipate any problems when clients came to the house to have their pets photographed. Her cats had seemed to like the new digs, but they'd made the trip to Cape Cod with Cody.

Truly, combining their lives had been the work of mere days, leaving plenty of time for the Nevada trip and shopping for a dress for Jack and Alicia's wedding.

"We still have plenty of time to plan for kids." She squeezed Danny's hand as they watched a couple of flower girls tumble over one another in the bounce house, their floral crowns askew and their white tights sagging at the knees. "We have over a week left together to figure out our future."

"Or we could just revel in the secret of our marriage. Spend all day in bed."

"How decadent of you." She turned toward him and wound up in his arms just as Danny's mother approached.

Colleen Murphy was a tall, elegant woman to whom Stephanie felt an immediate kinship since she'd facilitated Stephanie's chance to see Danny again at the Norfolk naval station. Mrs. Murphy wore a floor-length champagne-colored gown as the mother of the groom, her blond bob tucked behind her ears in a way that showed off simple diamond earrings.

"The reception is beautiful," Stephanie gushed, eager to make a good impression after the way she and Danny had taken off alone at the end of his homecoming party the week before. "Jack and Alicia couldn't have asked for a better place to have the party."

Colleen held her arms out to both of them in an unexpected hug. Only when she was tucked between them did she speak.

"I hear more congratulations are in order," she said softly before straightening.

"You told?" Stephanie turned to Danny, surprised.

"Admit nothing," Danny advised, never taking his eyes off his mom. "She's bluffing."

Colleen's mouth twitched, clearly amused.

"Daniel Murphy, I know you too well. I had lunch with the company pilot's wife yesterday and she mentioned the jet went to Nevada a few days ago. I didn't say a word to anyone else either way, but I know my sons aren't much for gambling."

Stephanie smiled at the standoff between them, waiting to see if Danny would cave.

"Maybe Stephanie loves roulette," Danny offered.

Colleen simply enveloped her in a hug. "Welcome to the family, sweetheart. I hope to hear official news soon and please know that if you need anything at all while Danny's gone, we will do whatever we can to be there for you."

"Thank you." She nodded, a lump in her throat. "I love your son so much."

With another squeeze of her hand, Colleen stepped away, joining Danny's father by the dance floor.

"Nothing gets past my mom," Danny muttered, although he watched his mom and dad with just a hint of mist in his eyes.

"You're lucky to have such an amazing family."

"I'm even luckier to have an amazing wife." He bent to give her a lingering kiss that left them both breathless. "We'd better go cut a rug on the dance floor and show them all how it's done before I have to haul you back to the gatehouse and make you my own."

Her heart sped up as she took the arm of her sexy navy lieutenant in his tuxedo.

"I already am yours," she reminded herself as much as him, the knowledge of their love still so special.

Under the glow of white lights, Danny guided her across the floor and spun her into his arms.

"This has been the best homecoming ever," he whispered in her ear, sending a pleasant shiver down her spine.

"They'll only get better with time," she promised, thinking how much she could improve on the reception she'd given him back at the pier.

"Do you think so?" His gaze heated as he looked into her eyes. "Then I'd better debunk the myth that the first thing guys want to do when they step off the ship is eat."

"Did I say that?" She warmed all over at the feel of his hands on the small of her back.

"Yes." His steps slowed as one hand cupped her cheek. "But when I come home next time, my priority will be getting you alone as fast as possible."

"I'll make sure I keep that in mind." Stephanie twined her arms around his neck, unable to keep track of the steps when all she wanted to do was take him home.

Thankfully, as the slow song ended the wedding guests began to clink their silverware against the cut-crystal champagne glasses in a time-honored tradition.

"Sounds like they want the bride and groom to kiss," she observed.

Danny never took his eyes off her.

"Then I wouldn't dream of disappointing them." He lowered his mouth to hers, igniting a flame inside her as they celebrated their own promise of forever.

* * * * *

MILLS & BOON®
By Request

RELIVE THE ROMANCE WITH THE BEST OF THE BEST

A sneak peek at next month's titles...

In stores from 11th February 2016:

- **A Secret Worth Keeping?** – Michelle Conder, Susanna Carr & Robyn Donald

- **The Ultimate Persuasion** – Cathy Williams

In stores from 25th February 2016:

- **His Seductive Proposal** – Janice Maynard, Ann Major & Maureen Child

- **A Groom for the Taking** – Ally Blake, Rebecca Winters & Melissa McClone

MILLS & BOON®
The Sheikhs Collection!

This fabulous 4 book collection features stories from some of our talented writers. The Sheikhs Collection features some of our most tantalising, exotic stories.

Order yours at
www.millsandboon.co.uk/sheikhscollection

MILLS & BOON®

Why shop at millsandboon.co.uk?

Each year, thousands of romance readers find their
perfect read at millsandboon.co.uk. That's because
we're passionate about bringing you the very best
romantic fiction. Here are some of the advantages
of shopping at www.millsandboon.co.uk:

* **Get new books first**—you'll be able to buy your
  favourite books one month before they hit
  the shops

* **Get exclusive discounts**—you'll also be able to buy
  our specially created monthly collections, with up
  to 50% off the RRP

* **Find your favourite authors**—latest news,
  interviews and new releases for all your favourite
  authors and series on our website, plus ideas for
  what to try next

* **Join in**—once you've bought your favourite books,
  don't forget to register with us to rate, review and
  join in the discussions

Visit **www.millsandboon.co.uk**
for all this and more today!